JEANETTE GREAVES

SILVERWOOD RISING

RANSOMED HEARTS, PART FOUR

Published by Bardale
Press

Cover by Ravven
www.ravven.com

First paperback edition 2024

ISBN 978-1-8383267-3-9

Previously

Diana, a young geneticist, chose her profession to research a secret shared with her sister, Joyce. They are werewolves. After Joyce left with other female werewolves to search for others of their kind, Diana stumbled upon three male werewolves, Andy, Mark and John. Along with the drummer, Xan, a normal man, they are the Ransomed Hearts, a rock band. Mark and John are the sons of Anthony and Tomas, whose stories were told in *Fight for the Future*. Andy was infected with the werewolf trait by Mark and John after discovering their secret.

Their relationship with Diana deepens and Mark becomes her lover, learning too late that they have created an irrevocable bond. Mark is torn between Diana and his fiancée, Katie. He marries Katie, despite the birth of his twin sons to Diana days before the wedding. With feelings running high, Diana and Xan make love, angering John, who is in love with Diana. Xan follows John to Ibiza, where Xan is murdered.

In *Hearts Home*, the werewolves create a large family. Diana is contacted by Joyce, but on reaching the rendezvous site she finds her dead, along with several white wolves and blond men. With Andy's help, she escapes from the surviving blonds. She recognises her vulnerability and buys Silverwood, an old hotel with spacious grounds, which she fortifies and remodels to become a suitable home for her large family. Silverwood is attacked by more blond werewolves who are overwhelmed by the unexpected strength of Diana's pack. Prompted by the attack, Diana and her mates confess their secret to the wives of Mark and Andy and start to search for evidence of other werewolves, or Shapeshifters, as Diana prefers to call them. They find a young woman, Zoe, who becomes John's and Diana's lover, and later, Mark's lover. Zoe's children add to the pack. It becomes clear that the existence of Shapeshifters can't be kept a secret much longer, and Diana's pack lays plans for Revelation Day. When the time comes, Zoe, the Hearts and Diana run simultaneous press conferences, publicly revealing their secret and their relationship to each other.

Not long after…

Chapter 1

Silverwood was a far cry from his previous home, and Mark found he had swapped Katie's quiet elegance for Diana's borderline chaos. At Silverwood, everything came together … just. The place buzzed with energy, and for the first time in his life he felt he could achieve his real potential. He didn't have to explain how he could thrive on two hours' sleep, he could Change whenever he wanted to, and he was surrounded by young people who were keen to learn from him. Living with John again was surprisingly easy to get used to, and Diana and Zoe made no social demands on him. When he mentioned it to her, Diana laughed and said so far as she was concerned, he never had to go to a dinner party again.

The absence of his sons Jacob and Matthew was the only dark spot on his heart; Matthew already looked at him warily, and he missed his little boys.

His divorce papers from Katie had arrived, and he'd bundled them into the back of the wardrobe, ashamed of this proof of failure, unwilling to talk about his feelings with any of his pack. John found them, of course. John had no concept of privacy within the pack, and Mark was unsurprised to find his cousin sitting on the bed openly reading the documents.

'She named both Diana and Zoe as co-respondent,' John said, surprised. 'Is she really going to be that much of a bitch?'

'It made her case look better,' Mark said, rolling his eyes. He put his hand out. 'Give, that isn't yours.'

John shrugged and handed the papers over. 'Have you told Diana?'

Mark didn't answer, but folded the documents and hid them in the inside pocket of a suit jacket. 'Let it be, John,' he murmured, and went downstairs.

The house phone was ringing, and nobody was showing much inclination to answer it. Mark snatched it off the hook. 'Mark Preston,' he said crisply.

'Oh, hi. Could I speak to Seth Foster's mother, please?'

'I'm his dad,' Mark said. 'What's it about?'

There was a short silence before the woman spoke again. 'I would really prefer to speak to his mother, if that's possible?'

Mark shrugged and took the phone to Diana. 'It's about Seth Foster,' he said, scowling. Diana looked at him, puzzled, and took the phone.

'Hey, it's Diana Foster. Can I help?'

She spoke for a few minutes, looking pleased, then called for Seth.

'He's eighteen now, I think it's up to him,' she said, and handed the phone over to him.

Mark caught up with her as she left the room. 'What was that about?'

'Oh, that was his old art teacher. She wanted to use a picture of his for a charity project she's got involved with. I said it was up to him, he's supposedly an adult now.' She shook her head, feigning confusion. 'Anyway, what're you sulking about?'

'She didn't believe me when I said I was his dad!'

Diana laughed. 'Well, I told her I was a single parent at all the parents' evenings. She's bound to be suspicious. Don't take it personally.'

'It's not a secret any more,' Mark insisted.

'So put an advert in the paper or something. Hellfire, Mark, it's not a big deal.'

He opened his mouth, but she'd already walked away.

Seth had heard the conversation and shook his head. 'Dad, you are so fucking clueless,' he muttered.

'Well? Would you change your name,' Mark demanded, 'if I asked you to?'

'It's not me you should be asking, is it?' Seth said. 'Look, all I know is that she's said dozens of times it would be nice if we all had the same surname.'

'Well, why doesn't she change it?'

'I think she's waiting to be asked, sort of.' Seth looked at his father, not breaking eye contact, until Mark's eyes widened.

'Oh. Yes. I see,' the older man said before walking quickly after Diana.

Getting Diana alone was never easy. For someone who claimed not to be sociable, she spent an awful lot of time with her mates and children. Mark thought he'd struck gold first try when he found her in the lab, but the presence of six toddlers made him shy. They were making a hell of a mess, but Diana explained that they were 'being creative' with pots of fabric paint and a hundred white T-shirts in every size imaginable. 'Why pay a fortune for designer clothes? These will all be one-offs,' she said blandly, and Mark couldn't decide how serious she was being.

He had a meeting in Manchester that afternoon and had to leave. When he got back he tracked her down to the music room. To his alarm, she was fiddling with a synthesiser: the back was off and she was peering inside.

'Do you know what you're doing?' he asked cautiously.

'I think so,' she said, surfacing and grinning. 'I do have a science degree, you know.'

'OK.' He watched her for a while longer. 'Do you want me to have a look?' he asked, wincing as she jumped and banged her head on the case.

She glared at him. 'Are you trying to be unhelpful?' she demanded.

'I was wondering if you wanted to change your name, actually,' he said.

'Diana's always worked for me,' she mumbled after a short pause. 'Pass me the screwdriver, the one with the green electrical tape wrapped round it.'

'I mean, to Preston?' Mark asked.

'I know what you mean,' she said more clearly, looking at him this time. 'Is this about Seth?'

'Um, it's about us,' Mark said, wondering how hard she was going to make it. 'I think we should make it legal.'

She looked at him thoughtfully, tapping her chin with the screwdriver, then returned to her work. He heard her mumble again, and sat down next to her. 'What did you say?' he asked cautiously.

'We're fine as we are. Plug it in.'

'D'ya want to put the back on first?'

'Nope, plug it in.'

He rolled his eyes and did as he was told.

'Play something,' she said.

'What?'

'I don't know, you're the musician. I'm just the muggins who gets yelled for when things don't work,' she snapped.

He shook his head and sat down, playing a Hearts ballad. He nodded. 'It's working,' he confirmed.

She refitted the back and stood up, massaging her spine. 'Are you ready for some tea?'

'I want an answer,' he said stubbornly.

'You got one,' she pointed out.

'It's not the right one.' He smiled.

'Maybe it was the wrong question,' she snapped back. His face fell, and her expression softened. 'Why do you want to make it legal all of a sudden?'

'Cos it's way overdue. I want to be married to you,' he said. 'Don't you feel the same way?'

'I can't be bothered with all that fuss,' she said. 'It's too much trouble.'

'OK. You, me, two witnesses and the local registry office.' He kept his face straight. 'It'll take an hour of your precious time, and you'll be mine forever.'

'I'm already yours forever, idiot.' She packed up the toolkit and returned it to the cupboard at the back of the music room. 'Anyway, you're married already.'

'I am not. I'm divorced. Divorced, middle-aged…'

'Non-smoker, crap sense of humour, father of umpteen, own car…' Diana supplied mischievously. 'Anyway, since when are you divorced?'

'Um, three weeks ago.'

'Were you going to tell me?'

'I am doing,' he said. 'Look, you won't get a better offer.'

'The guy who services my car said I've got nice boobs for a lady with so many kids,' she said, pulling her sweater tight to make the point. 'He's single.'

'He's gay,' Mark said. 'He told me I had a nice arse for a man my age.'

'Ah, he's overcharging us then,' Diana said, and Mark grinned, moving closer to kiss her.

'Will you think about it?' he asked after a while.

'Mmm.'

'Seriously?'

'With deadly seriousness,' she said.

Later, back at the house, all was quiet, and he made his way upstairs. He found Diana sitting with Meg and Beth, reading a story to them as they dozed off.

'Bethie's having nightmares,' she whispered. 'I got to the bottom of it, though. Zak told her that she'd turn into a wolf when she was older, but he didn't mention it wasn't permanent.'

'Ah. Can we send him back?' Mark asked seriously.

'I think Zoe would object,' his mate replied. 'He also told Nancy that if she ate her crusts, she'd get hairs on her chest.'

He fought a smile, until he realised she was hiding her own behind her fall of red hair. He looked at the sleeping girls. 'Are they really beautiful, or am I just a doting dad?'

'They're like you, of course they're beautiful,' she said quietly. She smiled. 'Come with me, I want to show you something…'

She led him back to their wing, where the youngest children slept, and quietly opened the door to the nursery. Noah dozed in the armchair, Joy asleep in his arms with her head on his shoulder. Diana put her finger to her lips and closed the door again. 'He heard her crying and volunteered to shush her. Aren't they cute together?'

'Aren't you going to rescue him?' his father asked.

'What, and wake up madam? No way. Noah'll ask for help if he needs it. He's really taken to those two. I think it's because they're the first redheads since the Kittens.'

Mark drew her close. 'Hon, they're growing up fast. It would be nice if we got married before they do.'

She looked up at him. 'Mark, why didn't you tell me your divorce had come through?'

'I don't know,' he admitted. 'I know I should have…'

'But?'

'But she brought Zoe into it, and I didn't want you to know that.' He hugged her again. 'I thought you'd be pissed off.'

'Why?' Diana asked quietly.

'She did it on purpose, to put you down. She knows I'm in love with you, and she brought Zoe into the picture to imply you weren't so important. I didn't want you to know.'

'You've gotta tell me everything, or I'll think you're being sneaky,' she pointed out.

'Um, yeah. OK.'

'So, is there anything else I need to know?'

'I love you and want to marry you,' Mark said. 'And I have no pride where you're concerned, so I'm going to keep on asking until you say yes.'

Diana rolled her eyes. 'Well, so far, I've had "I love you and want to marry you", "Have you ever thought of changing your name?" and "Let's make it legal". Do you want to give it one more try?'

He grinned and moved closer, pinning her against the wall, kissing her deeply, one hand cupping her bottom, the other in her hair. He broke free and took a deep breath. 'Diana, hon, will you marry me? Please?'

'Yeah, fifth of August, eleven thirty, registry office. Be there on time or I'll rip your guts out.' She laughed at the expression on his face.

'Wha——?' he said.

'I booked it provisionally this afternoon, as soon as you asked me. Me and Zoe are going shopping for outfits next Saturday. And I knew about the divorce too. Katie told your agent's wife, who told one of John's exes, who told Helen, who told me.' She giggled. 'Gotcha.'

Chapter 2

Sunlight streamed through the unshaded window of the compact, tidy lab. The sole occupant, a small redhead with a nice line in pirouettes, was dancing to rock music while a centrifuge whirred and a printer piled up with sheet after sheet of coded information.

Her phone was only halfway through its first ring as she swung gracefully around a bench and picked it up. She smiled with pleasure. 'Laura, sweetheart, what's up?'

She paled, and sat down. 'How?' She listened. 'You're not alone, we'll get through this. I promise you. Look, I'm on my way, don't argue, love.'

She put the phone down and methodically turned off her equipment, made brief notes and tidied the lab. She took a deep breath and made her way to the house. John stood up from the kitchen table and frowned. 'What's up?'

'Stuart … Laura's Beta. He's dead. A stupid car accident. He was on the way to a football match with his dad. Instant, Laura said. She's very calm, I don't think it's sunk in yet. I'm going over there now.'

'You're very pale, should you be driving?' John frowned.

'I'm fine. Stay here. Let everyone know. Ask Zoe to keep in touch with Duncan and Laura while I get over there. Should take about three hours to drive. I'll go alone. I'll keep in touch. Oh, and please make sure this doesn't ruin Seth and Noah's birthday – Zoe knows where their pressies are. And there's a big cake with "19" iced on it in the back of the pantry.'

As Diana made her way to Duncan Moss's farm near Whitby, she ordered her thoughts about the young pack. Duncan had been the first young Shifter she'd found during her outreach programme, and it hadn't been long before his introduction to two young Shifter women, Laura and Chloe, had led to their mating and the formation of a brand-new pack. Andy had helped them with loans and advice, and the youngsters had bought a neglected farm and turned it into a thriving business within a few short years. Laura and Duncan were the parents of the first three sets of twins, but the discovery of a young Shifter named Stuart Highfield, and his introduction to the Whitby Pack, had led to him and Chloe falling head over heels for each other. Their twins were already a year old. They were a hard-working pack, with eight kids and a farm to look after, but they relished the challenge and had always seemed happy and cheerful when Diana visited them.

Diana fought down her own rising panic, remembering the physical and mental pain of her long separations from Mark, and wondering if Duncan's pack could survive the permanent loss of their Beta. They'd been mated to Stuart for less than two years, but they'd been living and working together for all that time.

Duncan was waiting at the farm gate when she arrived. He held it open while she drove through, then he slid into the passenger seat.

'What happened?' Diana asked, driving up the lane towards the house.

'All I know is Stuart was driving, there was a collision, and his car got crushed with him and his dad in it. Police say it'll be a while before they can tell us more than that. My mum and dad are here. They've offered to take the kids but, honestly, eight of 'em in that little house? I've asked them to stay, we're gonna need the help.' He swallowed. 'Are we gonna die? You know ... the addiction?'

'It's going to be hard. But if this is survivable, I'll do all I can to get the three of you through it. Both of us know there aren't any real answers. This is the first pack bereavement we've encountered, so I can't make promises.'

'If we don't make it, will you take the kids?'

Diana hesitated. An immediate answer would seem like she'd already thought about the question. 'Of course we will, if the worst happens. But let's not get ahead of ourselves. How are Laura and Chloe?'

'Laura's gone into management mode. Chloe's hiding in her room with the littl'uns. Our eldest lads are helping my mum and dad with the farm work right now but I'll get one of 'em to look after you.'

'I'm here to help, not get in the way. You get on with what you need to, I'll talk to Laura.' They'd reached the farmyard. Diana parked near the house and surveyed the property. 'You're doing well here. We'll make sure the business doesn't suffer while you're grieving.'

Duncan nodded. 'Thank you.' He got out of the car, moving uncharacteristically slowly. Diana took a moment before getting out of the car. This young pack would be dealing with grief, and with bonding withdrawal, and they would need to understand how to cope with both. It wasn't going to be easy.

Chapter 3

'Off to Whitby again?' Mark asked. He'd noticed Diana picking up a set of car keys; she was carrying a blood-testing kit. 'Want some company?'

Diana sighed. 'It's getting difficult for them. It's been nearly a month and the withdrawal is kicking in, and I know they all said they were OK with me monitoring the process, but I feel like some kind of mad scientist, drawing blood when they're so obviously sick.'

Mark shrugged. 'Duncan offered, Laura and Chloe agreed to it. It's horrible, but they're right. We need to know what's happening to them, and you're the expert. I'll come with you – the sheep need dipping and I promised to help.'

Diana smiled 'Rock star does sheep-dipping?'

'Gotta be easier than wrangling toddlers. Speaking of… Joy and Faith's birthday party yesterday was fun. They're getting to the cute stage.'

Diana shrugged. 'If you say so. I'd never thought of two as the cute stage before. Oh, they're starting to properly bond with Mandy and Mia – they're teaching them to talk. It's hilarious.'

Mark grinned. 'Let me drive, you relax.' He grabbed the keys that she threw in his direction, and followed her outside. Frank and Bill were standing at the top of the slide, and Mark wandered over to speak to them. 'Aren't you two supposed to be at college?'

'Study day,' Bill said. Frank tried to keep a straight face.

'Come on, you can study sheep-dipping. We're off to Whitby, and you can make yourselves useful.'

'Can I drive?' Frank said.

'Absolutely not.' Mark laughed, heading for the car.

An hour from Whitby, Diana rang Laura. 'We're on our way. Mark's coming and we're bringing Francis and William, so we should be able to get a lot done. Are you all resting?'

Laura sounded exhausted. 'As much as we can. Dunc's parents have just gone home – they need a break, to be honest. They'll be back next week. We're going to try to get the kids back into school – they've been off long enough.' She paused. Diana could hear something … kids screaming. It didn't sound like play. Laura spoke again. 'Did you hear that? I have to go. I'll call you back.'

Diana bit her lip. 'Mark, did you hear that?'

Her mate frowned. 'No, what?'

'Someone was screaming. It didn't sound like play.'

'Kids, being kids?' Mark asked.

'I don't know. I'm going to try Duncan.'

Diana spent five minutes repeatedly trying to get through to Chloe, Laura and Duncan. She glanced at the speedometer; Mark was driving faster, his face a mask.

'Am I over-reacting?' she said quietly.

'Try Duncan. Use my phone, he's never taken more than three rings to reply to me,' Mark said, reaching for his mobile and passing it to her.

Two minutes later, Diana shook her head. 'None of them are responding. I'm going to ring the police.'

'And say what? A farming family isn't answering the phone? No, ring Andy, he's got contacts everywhere. Make sure that whoever goes in there is prepared. You know.'

Diana took a deep breath and turned to her sons, who were sitting very quietly. 'We may be driving into trouble. Do you want to go home?'

'No, get there quick,' Bill said, without hesitation. 'Will they be OK?'

'They've got a panic room. It's very safe, but Chloe mentioned that the phone line in there was on the blink. They've had a lot to deal with – it probably hasn't been fixed.' Diana bit her lip, drawing blood. 'If this is an attack, then it might not be an isolated one. Bill, I'll ring home, you boys start calling everyone else … packs, kids living with carrier parents, everyone you can think of. Use MarkDad's phone, they'll pay more attention to that than to yours. When you've done that, start calling Laura and Chloe in turn. I'll focus on the farm's business line and Duncan's phone.'

'What if it's just an accident. You know, it's a farm…'

'Then we'll stand everyone down as soon as we know.' Diana passed Mark's phone to Frank and closed her eyes for a second, deciding who to call first. She dialled. 'Andy, I need you to pull strings. We're fifty minutes or so from the Moss Pack, and they've gone silent. I heard screams when I was talking to Laura, and I really don't like it. Can we get a police patrol out there? There're no adult Shifters closer than me and Mark, and we can't get there any faster. Oh, and get yourself, Helen and the girls to Silverwood, you'll be safer there.'

Her next call was to Zoe. 'Sweetheart, is everything OK at home?'

Zoe was instantly alert. 'What's happening?'

'I've got goosebumps about the Moss Pack – they've gone silent. Can you recall the kids and go into lockdown, please? Frank and Bill are alerting everyone else but it won't hurt if you do the same.'

'Can you come home? Leave it to the police?' Zoe asked.

Diana hesitated. 'I can't, I'm sorry. I know it's risky, but we might make a difference. And … get word to Katie – she needs to make sure that Jake and Mattie are safe.' She rang off, reached out and squeezed Mark's hand. He was pale, and focussed on the road ahead.

Her phone rang. 'Diana? It's Andy. Don't worry, Helen's getting our girls, and I'm on our way to get the kids now. Give me a quick countdown of who I need to get, will you?'

'Bridget, Beatrice, Caleb and Sammy from the school, and the Kittens from sixth form. All the little kids are at home, thankfully. Miranda had a study day, so she's at home. Seth and Noah…' she paused. 'Seth and Noah are at uni. Will you go for them as soon as the younger kids are safe?'

'I've already rung them. They've got a free afternoon and are halfway home already.' Andy sounded anxious.

'Fine, someone stay on the phone to them at all times. Bill and Frank are with me too – little sods were skiving off. This'll teach 'em.' Diana sounded grimly determined.

Andy drew a deep breath. 'What do you think?'

'I don't know.' Diana twirled a strand of hair around her finger. She looked blankly out of the window, seeing nothing but Laura: tall, dark-haired and blue-eyed, vivacious – the way she was on her mating day with Stuart – drinking red wine and bragging about her children. Diana was brought back to earth by Andy's voice.

'Trust us, we'll make sure Silverwood is protected.'

'Thanks. Stay in touch. Ring me as soon as you know the kids are safe.'

'Of course.' Andy went quiet. Diana could almost see him, that way he had of rubbing his head anxiously. 'Look, hon, don't do anything you don't have to, you know what I mean?'

'You mean be careful?'

Andy laughed shortly. 'No, I mean… I know what you, Frank and Bill are like. If you kill someone, revenge isn't a defence. Just remember that.'

'Fuck that. If that bothers you, get the fucking police there before we arrive. Is that clear?'

Andy was silent for a few moments, and then cleared his throat. 'I guess I've just given up any hope of our daughters growing up to be sweet young ladies. I love you.'

'Love you too. Bye.'

Mark looked across, the first trace of a smile on his lips. 'There's nothing else to do. Andy can handle the police better than you can – he's a posh git, they'll listen to him. Music?'

Diana startled. 'Music? Our friends could be dying.'

'The Doors, then.' Mark's lip twisted a little, and Diana understood. 'Yeah, music, anything to take our minds off what we can't change.'

Before the first verse of 'Riders on the Storm' had ended, the first drops of rain pattered on to the car. 'You drew it down,' half joked Diana. Her mate put his hand on her knee, for his comfort as much as hers. The sky above them was solid grey, darkening to black at the horizon.

Chapter 4

The redhead, her mate and children discussed what they might find at the Whitby farmhouse, running through possible scenarios, Mark drily punching holes through ideas and plans that seemed initially to be sound. The storm grew; rain lashing down noisily, windscreen wipers running at full speed. Mark withdrew from the conversation and concentrated on driving. Few other vehicles were on the road, and they passed many cars pulled over by the verge, waiting out the storm. Diana took several calls from Andy. All the pack kids and Andy's family were safe at Silverwood. The Whitby police were taking some notice, but the storm had brought floods and they were overstretched and unwilling to leave known emergencies for a second-hand report of a screaming child on a farm.

Bare miles from the farmhouse, with rain still sheeting from the sky, they turned off the main road to Whitby and on to a single-track road. Mark was forced to slow down; visibility was low. A police siren blared in the distance, getting louder for a minute or two, then fading. Mark frowned and reversed the car, he got out and gazed into the storm. 'Look, lights, in the field.' He ran towards the lights, followed by Diana and the boys.

The police car was on its side, a long scratch down the side, the officers inside unconscious. Bill and Frank carefully moved the car back onto its wheels, taking care not to move too quickly. Mark was on the phone, calling the emergency services. Diana tried the driver side door. 'It's not locked.' She said, relieved. She checked both of the officers. 'Alive, strong pulse, probably concussion, both of them. It looks like they were run off the road. Bill, stay with them, you know first aid. When they wake up, encourage them to stay still. As soon as you see help arrive, come to join us. OK?' She waited for Bill to nod, then ran back to the car with Frank and Mark.

At the entrance to the farm track, the gates were swinging open. Diana shuddered; the Whitby Pack never left an open gate. Mark drove through, and towards the farmhouse.

'Oh shit, look at that,' Frank whispered.

Out of the window Diana saw rivulets of bloodstained water flowing away from a dirty grey mound of rocks. She looked again, and realised the rocks were sheep.

They arrived at the farmhouse and looked round cautiously. The stink of blood and shit in the air was overwhelming, despite the rain that was lessening every moment. The only movement was the lazy circling of flies around the dead fowl, cats and rats that littered the farmyard. All the animals had been ripped apart and left where they fell.

Mark surveyed the yard. 'Fresh wolf tracks everywhere. Fresh tyre tracks – ours, and two others. It looks like a vehicle came in pretty recently and left sharpish, they were probably spooked by the police siren.'

Frank looked at him, then at the tracks. 'So the attackers arrived on foot, but had backup ready? Their backup had some warning that the police were on the way and came for them? Do you think it's safe here now?'

'Don't assume anything. Stay on guard.' Diana moved towards the farmhouse door, poised and alert. Mark and Frank followed. The smell of blood in the enclosed space hit them straight away. Diana locked her emotions down tightly. She heard one soft protest from Frank, then silence.

The first body, flung against the stone wall of the kitchen, head crushed, was that of an eight-year-old boy. Diana walked over and crouched next to him. 'It's either Phil or Drew.' She spoke, her voice flat. 'Mark, could you and Frank go back outside?

If anyone has escaped we need to track them now. Frank, you go wolf and follow your dad's instructions. Good lad.'

'I'm not leaving you …' Mark said.

'I'll be fine. Go.'

Mark understood, she wouldn't change her mind. He led Frank out of the house, careful not to touch or disturb anything.'

There was something red and bloody on the floor of the hall, just yards past the kitchen door. A thick pool of blood had spread around it. Diana moved closer, not quite close enough to disturb the slowly creeping red flood. She kneeled, a small sob escaping her. 'Duncan …' she whispered. Her protégé hadn't had chance to Change, what was left of his body was still fully human. She rose to her feet and took a deep breath, then walked around the corner to the bottom of the stairs. She muffled a cry and approached the pitiful group of bodies. The urge to touch, to comfort the dead children was overwhelming, but she fought against it. A six year old girl trying to shelter two younger girls, they'd all died quickly, from the look of the bodies. 'Sally or Mareta, with Lily and Rachel.' Diana murmured to herself, before heading upstairs cautiously and quietly.

She went to the parents' bedroom first. She stood in the doorway, fighting to control her fury. Laura's body, a grotesque mixture of wolf and woman, almost blocked the door to the adjoining bathroom. A wide shotgun wound on her chest was the only visible damage, but her claws and face were red with blood that wasn't her own. Diana moved with delicate care until she could see into the bathroom. She cried out, and closed her eyes. The bodies of the Pack's youngest babies, Deborah and Victoria, lay like broken dolls against the wall. There could be no doubt that they were dead. Diana withdrew from the doorway carefully, and looked behind the bed. Two blond men lay dead in a thickly spreading pool of blood, their throats torn out. Diana's lips curled, she resisted the urge to Change. She backed out of the bedroom slowly and checked the other three bedrooms and the bathroom. Nothing but a smear of blood on the open door of the safe room behind the second bedroom. Somebody had nearly made it, then been dragged back. A child, from the height of the smears. Diana moved back to the landing. She could hear sirens, moving closer. A fall of dust on the carpet caught her attention, and she glanced upwards at the loft access hatch. There was no sign of a hook to open the hatch, so she dragged a chair from a child's bedroom. Standing on tiptoe, she could just reach the hatch and push it back. She jumped, grabbing the sides of the hatchway, and pulled herself up, scrambling her body into the loft and rolling to the side. She raised herself into a low crouch. 'It's Diana. Chloe? Are you in here?' She waited, hearing nothing, not a breath. There was a window on the other side of the loft, and she found it open, with a scrap of fabric caught on the latch. She looked out, spotting Bill as he strode towards the house. The siren was louder now, and she made her way downstairs, checking the rooms on the ground floor. They were empty. The bodies of the dead children and their father still rebuked her.

As she left the house, the police arrived.

Mark and Frank stepped out of the kitchen, breathing the outside air. It was tainted, but not as thick with blood as the air indoors. Mark looked around the farmyard. 'We need to see if anyone escaped. We'll start with the obvious – let's check those footprints leading to the blonds' car. If any of them are small enough to be kids', we might as well give up now.'

A minute or two later, he shrugged. 'Right, no sign, so unless they were carried into the car, we need to widen the search. Circle the house with me. Look for fresh prints.'

Near the back of the house, Frank called out. 'Three kids escaped. Look at these prints.' he said.

Mark looked at the ground, then up at the house. 'Scooted down the roof, then dropped from the porch. I don't think it's three kids, I think it's two, and Chloe. Look.' He followed the tracks to the fence, vaulted over and picked up a strand of dun fur from the wire.

'She Changed and jumped the fence. The kids would have wriggled through. This is wolf fur. She's got light brown hair, I'd expect her wolf fur to be this colour. We'll try to track them. I'll stay on two legs, you go to four. OK?'

Frank nodded, stripped and Changed. Mark tied Frank's discarded jeans round his waist, and stuffed his T-shirt into his jacket pocket. They set off, casting around for prints or scent trails, finding and losing traces, abandoning trails that were days old, looking for the freshest scents, the newest footprints, gradually moving further uphill until they reached a small stream. They split up, each of them taking one side of the stream, moving upwards, looking for the point at which the woman and children had left the stream.

After fifteen minutes, Frank whined and pointed his muzzle to his right, indicating he'd picked up a scent again. Mark jumped the stream and followed him into the dying bracken. It was difficult to pick up a scent, but the trail was obvious to the eye. Mark reflected that Chloe must have been desperate to stay in the water so long: the stream had been close to freezing, and the children would have been suffering.

Over the next rise, Mark stopped dead, peering into the darkening sky, seeing a tiny figure skylined atop the fell. He concentrated his strength into his voice and yelled as loudly as he could. There was no response and, for a moment, he reflected that John should have been there. John in full voice could be heard across entire counties, he was almost sure of that. He kneeled next to Frank and mimicked a wolf howl. Frank got the message and let loose a magnificent cry. The figure on the hillside paused, then sped up.

'Fucking great,' muttered Mark, also increasing his pace. Frank was whining and looking at him urgently. 'Go, lad. Catch them up. I'll stay human, save my strength.'

Frank needed no further urging, and sped low and fast across the moor, invisible but for the wake he left in the fading autumn heather. Mark settled into a fast walk; the ground too treacherous for a run. He aimed for the spot where he'd seen the figure disappear. Within ten minutes he was looking down over the ridge, seeing two small motionless human figures standing on a high rock, looking down. He shouted, and they looked towards him. He waved, and they clung to each other. Wasting no more time, he made his way to the rock. As he drew close, he heard a low vicious growling. He approached cautiously.

'Frankie? Francis? Son? Where are you?'

The big black wolf rose from the shelter of the heather, his mouth open. His shape shimmered and he Changed. Frank stood up, shivering already in the damp October chill. 'She's terrified,' he said, gesturing to the dun she-wolf growling as she patrolled the area between him and the rock.

'I don't blame her,' muttered Mark, throwing Frank's jeans and T-shirt to him. 'Chloe? Chloe? We're friends, OK?'

The she-wolf made a blood curdling noise, and whipped around to face him. He sighed and addressed the older of the two children.

'I'm Mark Preston. You know me. I'm not here to hurt you. Can you calm her down?'

'How do we know you aren't with *them*?' the boy asked. He was trembling, cold, scared.

'Are you Drew or Phil?' Mark asked.

The boy blinked. 'I'm Phil. Where's Drew?'

Mark shuddered. There was no easy way to do this. 'Your twin's dead. I suspect the rest of the family are too, I am so sorry. I've come here with Diana, to rescue you.'

Phil blinked. 'You're gonna take us home with you?' he asked.

He looked at the boy, no older than his own Quads, and swallowed. 'We'll take you home – we'll look after you. We'll protect you.'

'Who's the big guy?' Phil blurted out.

'That's my lad Francis. You've heard of him?'

'Ian's big brother?' Phil said. 'Yes, he's tough, isn't he?'

Frank blushed, and Mark found a small smile inside him. He released it, and the child relaxed. Phil climbed down off the rock and embraced the she-wolf, who was still growling. He spoke to her, and gradually she stilled, eventually shuddering and Changing.

A tiny woman, too thin, exhausted, stood before Mark. She reached out, and fell into his arms. 'Save us,' she muttered, and fainted.

Mark lifted her from the wet ground on to the rock. He removed his own jacket and managed to dress her in it, buttoning it to the throat and wishing he'd thought to bring something warmer.

Frank had turned away while Mark was caring for Chloe, but now he held his arms out to the little girl who trembled on the rocks above him. 'What's your name, honey?' he asked, and Mark almost laughed. Frank was using the same casual easy charm that John had used a thousand times.

The child blinked. 'I'm Mareta. Can we stop running away now?'

'Sure you can. Can you walk? Or do you want to be carried?'

The girl winced and showed an ankle, swollen and bruised. 'I fell. I can't walk.'

Mark spoke. 'Can you manage the little girl, Frank? I reckon this young cub can get down the hill on his own feet, can't you, Phil?'

The boy nodded. 'Course I can, I'm a farm boy.'

The five of them made their way downhill in the deepening twilight. Chloe was unconscious for most of the way. When she came to, she started to scream, and Mark stopped and let her down. He'd been carrying her across his shoulder, which he found embarrassingly undignified for both of them. He started to apologise, but she brushed his words away.

'Thank you. I'm sorry I tried to frighten you away. I didn't trust anyone.' She glanced down at the jacket, which reached halfway down her thighs.

'Shame Andy's not here,' Mark commented drily. 'His jacket would be floor-length on you.'

Chloe remained silent. As they neared the farmhouse, she looked up. 'I know. I heard everything. They knew where we were too. They were laughing at me. They were going to get a ladder and get us. If they hadn't heard that police siren…'

'It's done,' said Mark sharply, uncomfortable. 'We'll care for you, from now on. I won't let any more harm come to you.'

Chloe went silent. The last hundred metres were crossed in silence. The yard below them was full of flashing lights and busy people. The murder of Chloe's family had become yet another job to be dealt with.

Diana had seen them picking their way down the fell and was waiting for them with dry clothes. She persuaded Chloe to stay out of the house. 'You can see them later, at the funeral home. But not like this.' She winced. 'It's probably better if you don't see Laura and Duncan at all.'

Chloe nodded. She closed her eyes. 'What do you want me to say?'

Diana took a breath. 'Tell the truth about what happened. It might be best if you didn't mention that we've all been preparing for an attack. The panic room can be explained by worrying about the anti-Shifter movement.' She spoke more gently. 'It was fast … for the kids.' Diana forced down the rage that had been building since she arrived. 'Someone will pay for this, I swear. For now, get yourself into these dry clothes. The police officers kindly got them from the house. I've already spoken to the officer in charge, and he's agreed to come to our place tomorrow to take your statement.' She glanced at her car, and blinked. 'May we borrow your minivan? We need seven seats.'

Chloe nodded. She staggered and almost fell, but Frank was there to catch her, half carrying her to the mud-streaked Toyota minivan that had been Laura's workhorse vehicle. Bill joined them, and the boys took seats on either side of Chloe on the back seat.

Bill spoke to Chloe quietly. 'I don't think those bastards meant to leave survivors. They'll track you down, wherever you are. You're safest with us.'

'Thank you. You don't owe me anything, though. I can look after the kids.' Chloe's voice was firm.

Diana's two teenage, scrappy sons suddenly looked like they'd go to hell and back to protect this bedraggled and terrified woman who was ten years older than them. She said nothing; the woman needed protection and kindness right now.

Mark shook his head. 'Boys, take the middle seats. Let Mareta and Phil sit either side of their mum.' He nodded at Diana. 'Coming?'

She shook her head. 'I'll stay here, talk to the police. I'll bring our car back.' She kissed him briefly, and watched as he left.

Behind her, a woman spoke. 'Mrs Preston? I'm Detective Inspector Ripon. What's happened here?'

Diana explained that she'd been on the phone to Laura when the attack happened, and had been worried enough by the sound of children screaming to take action.

'You knew? Some sort of sixth sense?'

'Yeah, common sense. We've lost friends, eight people are dead in that house. I'm no superhero, and the killers are getting further away every minute.'

The forensics team were looking at Diana, but she kept her attention on the detective in charge, who asked her for the basic layout of the house.

'Mrs Preston, have you been in the house at all?'

She nodded.

'And what did you see?'

Diana went through the events of the afternoon, describing the dead toddlers, Laura's tortured body, and how they'd found the survivors.

'Do you have any idea who did this?'

She hesitated, and then shook her head. 'I don't know.'

The police detective took a breath. 'Do you think this is werewolf business? Some sort of feud?'

Diana stiffened. 'It's murder, pure and simple. Duncan and his family were well respected locally. It's an atrocity. You surely can't be thinking of writing this off as some sort of ethnic trouble that doesn't affect anyone else?'

'I'm sorry, I didn't mean to imply anything of the sort … I'm just trying to find out if you know anyone with a motive for this. And I agree – it *is* an atrocity. I've never dealt with anything so horrible in my entire career.'

Diana nodded, and calmed down a little. With her children on the way home, and the authorities taking over the situation, she could feel the burden of responsibility slipping away. Scenes in the house kept flashing back to her. She could feel the grief welling up inside herself and fought to stay calm. She was remembering her first meeting with Duncan, a young wolf on the streets of a quiet north-eastern town, confused, terrified. He was her first victory, the first one she'd found and saved before the despair of solitude claimed another victim. She'd chased him down and caught him, reassured him that he wasn't alone and given him someone to talk to. He'd often said that he owed his life to her, that he wouldn't have survived for long without that comfort. And now her efforts were nulled, and the hard-working conscientious man was dead.

The police detective had taken out a notebook. 'We need the names and next of kin of those who were killed. Was the surviving woman married to the dead man?'

Diana shook her head sadly. 'No, no marriages in that pack. They were waiting for the new Contract legislation to come in. Duncan Moss, Laura Matlock, Chloe Stephenson. The children are all Moss. The toddlers weren't Duncan's, biologically, but he registered their births and formally adopted them.' She stopped and thought for a minute. 'The eldest boy is called Andrew. His twin, Phil, is safe with my family, on the way back to our home. The six-year-old girl is Sally. Her twin is Mareta, also with my family. The four-year-old twins are Rachel and Lily. The babies are Deborah and Victoria. Chloe may be able to identify each twin.'

Her mind went blank. She could see the babies covered in blood – nightmare dolls. Her voice broke. The detective reached out to take her hand, but Diana pushed her away. 'I'll be fine. Give me a minute.'

She held her anger back. 'Laura's dad is still alive, but I don't remember where he lives. Duncan was adopted. His adoptive parents are alive and live nearby but, again, I don't remember where. I have the details at home, somewhere. Chloe's parents are both dead, as are Stu's – his dad died in the same accident as him. That's the thing with us "throwbacks", our parents die young.'

The detective was gentle, and her tone was reasonable.

'So these two surviving children – they have three living grandparents? And they aren't related to Ms Stephenson at all?'

Diana felt like screaming. 'You see, this is exactly why we're pushing for the Contract legislation to come in. Chloe is a mother to them – she nursed them, watched them, taught them. And by existing law, she's nothing to them.' She fell silent, her head down, wondering how she'd feel if anyone tried to take Isaac, or Leanne, or any of Zoe's other babies away from her.

The woman nodded. 'I just need to know who we have to inform. If the children are safe, that's good news.'

'Do you need me for anything else?' Diana asked.

'You can go now, we have all the information we need from you.'

Diana nodded her thanks, and managed a small smile. 'I don't envy you your job. Please, be gentle with my friends. Let me know when you've moved the bodies and collected your evidence, then I'll arrange for the house to be cleaned.'

Mark and John were waiting for her just inside the gates of Silverwood. John was in wolf form.

'Those trees need cutting back,' Diana observed. 'They're too near the fence for my liking.'

Mark agreed; security had become lax recently. He kneeled before John, hugging him, and then undressed and Changed easily and smoothly. He nuzzled his cousin before taking off to patrol the perimeter. John followed Diana to the bedroom, and Changed back.

'What's happening?' he asked, pulling on a pair of black denims. 'How long have I been like that? It feels like ages.'

'About six hours. You've done more than that before, but not for years, and not under stress. John, I feel drained.'

John went over to her. 'Bad?' he asked, solicitous of her, as always.

'Didn't you talk to Mark?'

He shook his head. 'I saw him arrive with a woman and two kids, but I wasn't going to Change back until you were home.'

Diana shrugged, jumping slightly as the bedroom door was pushed open and Zoe came in. She was pale. 'What happened?' the Beta asked.

Diana described the murders – her mates had every right to know. Zoe ran into the bathroom and vomited. John sat stunned.

'I'm going to kill every last one of the bastards,' he swore.

'No, you're not. When *we* were attacked, we managed to keep the whole thing quiet, but nevertheless our pack killed nine men. We got away with it because those men weren't traced to us, and nobody ever reported them missing. This is different. We can't keep these deaths secret. Duncan's family was part of the local farming community, we have to let the authorities pursue it. John, my love, we have to take a back seat. It would be different if we had legal backing, but that's for the future.'

He was pacing the bedroom, tense and furious. She went to him and held him close.

'That could have been you…' he muttered.

'But it wasn't,' she whispered. She could feel him burning against her and pulled him even closer.

'I want you now. How can I feel like this after that sort of news?' he whispered.

'It's life, we just want to feel alive.' She kissed him, gave him one last hug and went downstairs to check on progress. Andy was busy online and on the phone, sharing the news with other packs and their families. Phones were ringing all over the house. One by one, Mark and the older children trotted into the house and ran upstairs to Change back to human form and get dressed. Eventually the whole family gathered in the main downstairs room. A large split screen on the wall showed security camera views around the property, and the whole pack kept glancing at it.

Mark was silent, watching the pack. Gradually they quietened and looked towards him. Within a minute or two, there was complete silence. He stood up, pushing his hair back with both hands before looking around the room. When he spoke, his voice was clear and even. 'We've got some very bad news for everyone. Chloe and Mareta and Phil are here because their pack has been killed. Even the children.'

There were wide eyes around the room.

'Even the children…' Mark repeated. 'We might be in danger too, but we don't want to change the way we live. The older kids are going to carry on going to school, or college, or university, unless something else happens. We have a very safe place to live here, and all of you know how to look after yourselves. This might be a one-off attack. To be on the safe side, though, I want anyone who leaves our home to carry a charged phone at all times, and if you're asked to do something by a parent, or by someone a parent has left in charge, then you do it without question. Do you understand?'

He looked round. Everyone was quiet. Sam raised his hand. 'We can't keep our phones on at school,' he pointed out.

Diana nodded. 'I'll speak to your teachers. They'll make an exception for family emergencies.'

Helen raised her hand.

'Helen,' Mark acknowledged Andy's wife. 'We're glad you're here. What is it?'

'How much danger are *we* in … me and my daughters, I mean?'

Mark smiled at her. They'd known each other since their teens, much longer than he'd known his mate. Despite the secrets he'd kept from her for almost two decades, she was one of the few people outside the pack who he trusted.

'Honestly? We don't know. It's almost four years now since we were attacked. This is the first attack since then. We don't know if they'll see you as a target.'

'So we're not definitely in danger?' She was frowning.

Diana spoke up. 'You're not definitely out of it either,' she pointed out.

Andy spoke up. 'Helen wants us to go home. On the other hand, she doesn't want to be completely stupid and put herself and the girls at risk. We've got security alarms and a panic room, but do we have a target on our backs or not?'

The adults looked at each other, helpless, unsure; aware that they didn't have the answers they needed. The pack was stirring, the kids getting restless.

Diana held her hand up. 'We've got a lot to talk about tonight, and not all of it is going to be interesting to everyone. Let's get the stuff that the little ones want to know out of the way, then they can all go to bed. Is that OK?'

The other adults assented. Liam, one of their five-year-olds, raised his hand. 'Can Laura and her pack not just Change back to being alive?'

His parents looked at each other, and at Laura's two children, who were sitting with the eight-year-old Quads.

John spoke up. 'No, it doesn't work like that. When you're dead, you stay dead, and you can't do anything else, or Change to anything else, ever again. That's why we're very careful to try not to get killed.'

Liam nodded gravely, then turned to Patrick, his twin. The whispered words, 'Well, that's just *stupid*,' were heard.

Mark took over again. 'Mareta and Phil and Chloe can sleep in one of the spare rooms in the house tonight.'

There was uproar for a few minutes; it was the first time that a non-pack member had been allowed to sleep in the house since Diana's late mother had lived there.

'Please be quiet,' said Mark calmly, and the buzz died down. 'They are our guests. Mareta and Phil have been orphaned, and we will look after them tonight. Tomorrow we'll talk about it again, but, for tonight, I want to know exactly where they are. Helen, you and the girls are welcome in the house too.'

Diana tensed, but stayed silent. Helen shook her head. 'No, we'll take our usual rooms in the annexe with Andy.'

'OK, but we'll have the security cameras on.' Mark held the floor. 'Any more questions from the little ones?'

It was quiet.

'OK, we'll take a short break for supper, then all the little kids go to bed. Helen, your two can stay here with the rest of us – it's probably best if they aren't alone in the annexe.'

Half an hour later the group reassembled.

Diana stood, hands behind her back, addressing her pack and its friends.

'Chloe.' The young woman looked up, eyes dull, exhausted. She listened carefully as Diana spoke. 'For the time being, you can stay here with juvenile status. We'll do all that we can to keep the kids with you. I'm proud to say that every single pack in this country has offered to adopt Mareta and Phil and treat them as their own, and to take you in as a mate if you wish. Also, we're waiting to hear from Laura's and Duncan's parents sometime in the next few days. They've only just learned what has happened, and need to make a decision, but legally they have more rights over their grandchildren than we do.'

Chloe shook her head. 'I can't think about any of this yet.'

Diana nodded. 'I understand, but I want everything out in the open.'

Chloe looked up. 'I'm not looking for another pack – it's too soon for me to make any decisions.' She turned to Helen. 'May I stay with you when you go home?'

There was a dumbstruck silence, then Helen laughed. 'Sure, no problem. I'll feel safer with someone else in the house, and there's plenty of room for the little ones too.'

Diana nodded. 'OK, we'll see how it goes. I think this is an "awaiting further developments" situation, but I just wanted everyone to know where we stand.'

'Okaay,' said Mark, 'I think that's made several things a lot clearer, but we'll have to see how things go. Any more questions? No? Right, bedtime for schoolkids. You older kids, Seth's drawn up a patrol schedule – check it before making plans for sleep or night-time activities.'

Chloe left to join Mareta and Phil in a spare room; the children had cried themselves to sleep. At least they felt safe enough to mourn and rest. She pushed her single bed next to the one that they shared, and collapsed, thinking of Laura's screams. Diana had been kind, and had made sure she didn't see what was in the bedroom, but Chloe had been sitting directly above that room, holding the children tightly to her, her hands over their ears so that they were spared their mother's agony. Chloe had heard everything, then realised in horror that whoever had murdered her family knew exactly where she was. She'd managed, miraculously, to escape over the roofs with the two little ones and flee for the hills, expecting any moment that one of her enemies would find them and kill them. Instead Diana had come, with her beautiful sons and her grave, courageous Alpha, and taken charge, and brought her here to this bewilderingly large pack, where non-Shapeshifters helped to make decisions on pack safety. She shook her head, and stayed resolutely awake, listening to the children breathe. She didn't feel safe yet.

Miranda found Diana in the little sitting room that was her refuge. 'I'm vulnerable, so I make you all more vulnerable. I need to be able to fight,' the blonde girl said quietly.

Diana closed her eyes. 'You've had the same training as the others,' she said, knowing what was coming.

'Can you try? Can you try to turn me, like Mark and John did with Andy?' Miranda's voice was little more than a whisper.

Diana reached out, and took her eldest daughter's hand. 'I've told you, so many times, there's a rare genetic sequence that Andy and Helen both have, but you don't, that your father lacked too. It repeats, and Andy's DNA has more repeats than I've ever seen. I truly believe that it's designed to accept viral W genes – all my tests have confirmed it. You don't have it at all. Your dad didn't have it at all. Most people don't have it at all. Hell, I don't have it! We've already tried in vitro injections, and do you remember those injections? They made you ill for weeks. I'm so sorry, my love.'

'Biting might work…' Miranda said, her voice low.

'It might, but I won't do it,' Diana said.

'I'm eighteen…'

'You're not a Shifter, so my Alpha voice doesn't work on you. You're independently wealthy, thanks to your father, and if I chuck you out, Helen will take you in – not that I ever would.' Diana opened her eyes and sighed. 'I can't stop you from trying, but I can refuse to do it myself. And if I asked any of our pack not to do it, they'd do as I ask.'

'Zoe wouldn't, anyway. Or Andy.'

Diana looked up. 'You've asked him?'

'I asked him what it had been like for him, and he said he'd never inflict that level of pain and terror on another human being.' Miranda's voice was utterly free of inflection.

'You're going to do it, aren't you?' Diana said.

There was silence.

'Don't ask your brothers or sisters. They'd all do it in an instant, for you, unless I forbid it. But the trauma to them would be immense. I have to protect them.'

'Which leaves MarkDad and JohnDad,' Miranda stated.

Diana flinched. 'I can't forbid you, but I won't interfere. You're an adult. But one last thing… Your father's infection failed, utterly. He was a fully adult, strong, fit, healthy man. You're barely adult, and your single W chromosome means that your immune system is barely functional. Whatever you do, don't oppose any medical attention that I arrange for you. Will you accept that?'

'Of course.' Miranda hesitated. 'I'm sorry, Mum, I know this isn't what you want.'

'You've always been enough for me as you are, my brilliant girl. Now, get some sleep – you know you always need it.'

Chapter 5

Diana woke early the next day, with a sense of dread. Mark's hand was on her hip, and as she moved, he groaned and held on tighter. She sighed and moved back again; his lips were on her throat, and he was moving himself so that she was wrapped in him. He squeezed. 'I missed you.'

'I was right here…' she pointed out.

'Yeah, but you were asleep,' he murmured in her ear.

She pushed back against him, joyful in the fact that he was there, he was staying, he didn't have to leave to be with anyone else. She lay there for a moment. He was saying that he loved her – he only ever told her that in bed – but she decided that, for the moment, that didn't matter to her. She twisted around in his arms, facing him. He was still too thin, and was beginning to look older; he wouldn't be able to get away with that long glossy dark hair for much longer. But for the time being she was more than happy to plunge her hands into it and let it run through her fingers. He looked like a man in his mid-thirties, fifteen years younger than his actual age. He shook himself free of her hands, and began to place tiny kisses at the base of her throat.

He was moving further down, wriggling around so that she could feel his erection hard against her thigh. He looked up. 'Do you love me?'

She closed her eyes. She loved him more than life itself; he was the sun that she orbited, and wherever he was, she could feel invisible ties binding herself to him. Yet, still, she found it so hard to tell him. For years, he'd discouraged any show of affection from her, making it all too clear that Katie was his love, Diana merely his mate. That sort of history left scars. It was always so easy with John, her Beta; they exchanged endearments almost every time they saw each other, and meant every word. But here Mark was, waiting for her, watching her, still needing reassurance that his change of heart hadn't come too late, that she was his lover as well as his wife and Alpha.

She looked into his dark, dark eyes, so like his cousin's. But where John's eyes were open and expressive and deeply honest, Mark's were intense and demanding. She was lost in them as thoroughly as the first night she'd met him. She was falling into them, wondering what he was thinking, what was going on in his head.

'I said … do you?' He had moved away a little and was resting his head on one hand, gently tracing letters on her stomach with the index finger of his free hand. She knew he was spelling out words of love, and smiled.

'What was the question again?' she teased. His eyes widened in mock hurt, and she bent to kiss him. 'Of course I do. I love you. Diana loves Mark, there. I'll carve it into a tree and let the kids laugh at us.'

'They already laugh at us,' he said wryly, moving her closer to the middle of the bed and lying on top of her, knowing that she enjoyed the feeling of his full weight on her. She was licking his face, at the hairline, and he laughed again. 'You are such a tart – when have you ever said no?'

'S'why you love me so much,' she whispered, opening her legs just enough to give him the quick and dirty access to her depths that he wanted. He kissed her greedily, the Alpha moment on them with a suddenness that took them both by surprise, sweat pouring off them. The scent they made together confirmed and strengthened the unbreakable bond first forged almost twenty-one years earlier; the Shapeshifter chemistry responding to the stress of yesterday by binding them closer together, feeding their mutual wild addiction.

In the next room Zoe was awake, and fully aware of what was going on next door. The noises and the scent were unmistakeable, and she found herself aroused and restless. John was fast asleep next to her, and she reached down and started to stroke him gently. He was instantly awake, and submitted to her kisses, lying back and enjoying the eager way she worked on him while they both listened to their mates in the next room. Zoe straddled him and looked down wickedly, watching him watching her, enjoying the hugely full feeling that he always gave her. His hands were on her hips, controlling her thrusts for his pleasure, and she wriggled in protest, giggling as he almost lost it, and then letting him lift them both up, against the wall, where she wrapped her legs around his hips. Her nails were buried in his muscular shoulders, and she was screaming his name.

In the next room, sated with each other, Mark and Diana listened wide-eyed. Mark fully understood the look on Diana's face, and slapped her lightly, affectionately. 'So I'm not enough for you?' he asked.

'Hell, no. But you've always known that,' she said, bestowing a queenly kiss on his lips, and heading for the bathroom, leaving him lying on the bed and grinning. He'd heard her moan in her sleep, and been helpless to comfort her, but the reaffirming of the bonds between the pack restored her energy.

He shrugged on a robe, and wandered out to the corridor. Downstairs he could hear kids of all ages engaged in morning routines: food being made, school things desperately sought for, and every voice echoed by its twin. He leaned over the balcony, looking down into the main living room, and drank it all in. He sensed someone standing next to him, and looked around. John could be light on his feet when he wanted to be. They smiled at each other.

John was totally energised, drinking in the sounds of the pack. 'S'great living here, innit?' he offered. He'd moved in with the women less than three years ago, immediately after the first attack. Mark had moved in over a year later, when he'd finally admitted to Katie their marriage was over. They'd both been nervous about making their permanent home there, wondering guiltily what it would be like to have nowhere to escape to when the noise and demands of the kids got too much, but they'd found themselves happier than ever; at last they could be themselves.

'Where's Diana?' John asked, trying not to smirk.

'In the bathroom,' Mark informed him, his face equally deadpan. 'She said she was going to have a nice long bubble bath. And that I could make breakfast for her. Where's Zoe?'

'Er, in the bathroom…' John said.

Mark studiedly looked away. 'Well, looks like Diana's on a roll. You'd better have breakfast to keep your strength up. And one of us will have to get Helen out of the way – you know what Diana's like in this mood. Andy won't be safe either.'

John was distracted by odd splashing noises and low laughter from the bathroom, and went to investigate, hoping he wouldn't find the door locked.

In a bedroom at the far end of the corridor, Chloe was curled into a tiny ball, the ache of bereavement so hard that she wanted to die there and then.

Mark descended the stairs. He ignored the kids and went out on to the lawn, savouring the wet grass under his feet. Dropping his robe to the ground, he Changed smoothly, not needing to think about the process any more than he needed to think about breathing. He padded towards the woods. He heard a growling behind him and turned. Two skinny young red wolves were shadowing him. He paused and waited for Seth and Noah, his eldest sons, to catch up, accepting their submissive licks, then the three of them fanned out across their property, looking for trouble, for alien scents. Halfway to the gate he caught Andy's scent, and found the huge grey wolf staring out at the fence. They sat companionably together for a while before trotting back to the house. The sun was up completely now, and the dew was starting to dry. It was going to be a warm autumn day. The thought of Duncan's house, swimming with blood, flashed into his mind. He prayed that someone had cleaned it up by now.

Human again, he wrapped himself in his damp robe and swept through the kitchen. Seth and Noah had returned, showered and dressed, and were arguing about who was going to drive their tatty old Fiat Punto to uni. Mark grabbed the keys as he passed, and threw them in the air. Noah just beat Seth to it, catching them as they fell, and beamed triumphantly. Mark winked and carried on. Zoe was sitting at the kitchen table trying to persuade her ten-month-old babies to eat. They were fascinated by everything else that was going on. She was amused, and had brought Faith and Joy into the game. The toddlers were just two, and were happy to eat anything that Amanda and Mia refused. Before long, the babies were getting annoyed at the competition, and were eagerly accepting every spoonful that came their way. The older kids were filing past. Miranda charged through the door, blonde hair flying around her as she raced to catch her brothers before they left; she didn't see any point in paying for her own petrol when the lads were driving past Salford Uni anyway. She skidded to a halt as she saw Mark, and bent to kiss him on the forehead. 'Love you, Dad,' she said.

'Be safe, be bloody careful out there...' he tried to shout after her, but she was gone, chasing the boys down the drive, as she did every day. Eventually, as always, they relented and stopped the car, and she scrambled in.

Bill and Frankie were escorting the Kittens through the door. They were all at the same sixth form college, but while Bill and Frankie were struggling with their minimal academic options and heartily wishing that they'd chosen vocational subjects, Darlene and Sara were sweeping all before them in their first year at college, each taking the maximum number of subjects. They were both studying chemistry and biology, but their other choices were spread, deliberately following Diana's and Joyce's strategy to gain as much training as possible to study their own kind.

The schoolkids were piling out too, Diana checking everyone's phones and watching carefully as they all got into the people carrier. Andy was driving, Helen next to him. Their own kids, Eva and Naomi, were with them. Mark watched Diana thoughtfully. Three years earlier she would never have dreamed of trusting Andy's wife with her children; she was slowly mellowing.

Finally the older kids were gone, leaving just the babies and the primary school-aged kids. Diana was sticking to her guns on home education for the little ones, and nobody was arguing. It had worked out just fine so far. Mark made a pot of tea and filled a mug for Zoe. She was wiping the babies' faces gently. She hadn't bothered styling her hair after whatever she'd been up to in the bathroom with his wife, and it was tousled and pretty. He leaned across the table and spontaneously kissed her. She smiled. 'What was that for?' she asked.

'For making John and Diana happy,' he told her.

'I could make you happy too…' she offered.

'Maybe. Let's see what the day brings us.'

As he picked up his tea and left the room, she reached behind her and grabbed his robe, pulling him back towards her. He turned and kissed her gently, before pulling away. Satisfied, she went back to dealing with the children.

They'd switched all the phones off before they started last evening's meeting, leaving only Diana's mobile switched on in case of emergencies. Mark remembered abruptly, and switched on the phone in the main lobby. It started to ring straight away. He sighed and picked it up.

It was his agent, Paul Dixon.

'Mark, what the hell is going on? This Whitby murder thing is all over the TV. Are you involved? Is your family OK?'

'I'll tell you everything later, right now I just want to get dressed and maybe have some breakfast. Look, thanks for ringing, but you'll understand that I've got a lot to deal with today.'

'No! Mark, don't hang up, I'm not ringing to gossip. I've had a call from someone who wants to talk to you. He's called Anthony, and he claims to be your father.'

Mark's bowels spasmed and his brain turned to ice. The mysterious brothers, Anthony and Tomas, had disappeared when he and John were toddlers. All he had of them was a memory of waiting year on year for his father to come back. He'd long ago deduced that the brothers must have been Shapeshifters and must have worked hard to find two women who were likely to be carriers of that all-important chromosome. But why had they left? That had hurt more and more with each year that passed. He knew what it was like to be parted from your children.

'I don't really want to speak to him,' he heard himself say, his voice sounding like it came from far, far away.

'He said you'd say that. He said I have to tell you, "You'll understand how hard it's been to keep away, but now I can't protect you any longer by my absence."'

'Is he there?' Mark's empty stomach felt like lead inside him. He could hear Chloe upstairs, retching in the bathroom. He realised that she hadn't eaten since they'd rescued her, since her pack had been all but wiped out. Further away, he could just hear two strange children crying. He was filing the information away. Something else to deal with, someone else to protect and care for. Someone was talking to him…

'Mark? Hello? Are you still there?'

'Yes,' he replied automatically. The world was grey, and he needed Diana. More than anything in the world, he needed to touch her, to be touched by her.

Paul was speaking again, from a great distance. 'No, he isn't here, but he sounded completely genuine. He's in France, and he's left you a number to call.'

At last, Diana was with him, her head to one side, eyes wide, watching him carefully. She took the phone gently, taking his hand in her free hand, squeezing it reassuringly. She spoke cautiously.

'Who is this?'

'Diana? It's Paul Dixon. Look, is Mark all right?'

She relaxed, knowing that Paul was a loyal friend to Mark. 'No, he's not. What's up? Is it Katie? Is it his boys?' She knew that Paul remained the point of contact between Mark and his other family. Paul was still a good friend to Katie, and had made it clear that he wasn't interested in making friends with 'the other woman'. Diana could deal with that.

Paul spoke again. 'No, no … look, his father has turned up, out of nowhere, and wants to get in contact.'

'How do we know it's his father?'

'We can't, not for sure. But that's not my job. Can I just give you the number and leave it up to you?'

Mark was leaning against the wall; he suddenly looked ten years older. Diana wrote the number down.

The agent was still speaking. 'Diana, he said it was urgent. I get the feeling it's linked to these murders – they're international news, especially with your pack being on the scene…'

'Yes, I understand. Someone will get back to you with a statement later in the day.' She thanked the agent, and hung up.

Then John was there. He took the paper from Diana and looked at the name and number, and Mark's face. 'Your dad?' he asked.

Mark nodded. John looked down, looking curiously young and vulnerable. 'No word from mine?'

Diana wanted to hug both of them. She'd never seen them both like this at once. There'd always been a strong one, usually Mark, but John had always been ready to step in if Mark had weakened. She drew them together in a shaky group hug that gradually became steadier.

Mark drew away first. 'I'm OK, but I'm not ready to deal with this yet. If either of you want to speak to him, that's fine. I'm going to check on our guests.'

John broke away from Diana too, still unsteady, looking lost but also worried. He went downstairs. He'd still not had breakfast, and his stomach was telling him that the matter was becoming one of urgency.

Chapter 6

Mark was escorting Chloe and her kids downstairs. She was in bad shape, worse than when she'd arrived. Diana followed them down. John was already in the kitchen, a hastily written menu in his hand, which he presented to Chloe.

'For the young lady,' he said, holding her chair while she sat down at the kitchen table, and presenting her with a large piece of kitchen roll as a napkin. She smiled weakly, as Zoe fussed around the children, finding out what they wanted to eat and going to look for it.

'I'm not hungry,' Chloe said.

Diana nodded. 'I know. I understand how you feel. Mark left me for a year once. It wasn't the same situation, I knew he was alive, and that's the only thing that kept me going, but it hurt like hell. I know you're not hungry. But you *are* going to eat, because you *will* survive this.'

The younger woman looked down. 'Some fruit then,' she murmured. She looked up, startled, as something flew towards her, but her reactions were fast enough to catch the peach that Diana had thrown to her. The red-haired Alpha smiled; Chloe would recover from this. Zoe was busy making and buttering toast, piling it up in a rich offering that was disappearing almost as quickly as she could make it. John was cooking a huge fried breakfast for all the adults. While Chloe picked at fruit and toast, the pack ate well.

The phone was ringing again. Mark picked it up cautiously. It was Andy.

'Fucking *shit*. We're coming straight home. There were strangers outside the school, and they looked like—'

'Shh,' reminded Mark.

'OK.' Andy was quieter. 'I don't like the look of them anyway. Four men, all of them strangers. They're blond, very blond. Didn't Diana say that the dead guys in the bedroom were blond?'

'Yes. Come straight home, with the kids. Have you phoned the police?'

'That's my next call. We're playing this by the book? Be ready to open the gates for me. And will someone please phone the older kids?'

'I'll get John to sort it out. Don't worry, just get back safely.'

Mark found John in the living room, munching on a bacon sandwich. He'd done his usual trick of finding a room full of relatively quiet young children, and encouraging them to turn into a pack of wild animals. He was revelling in the screaming and shouting, and his favourite sound of laughing children. He turned when Mark came into the room, instantly serious. 'What now? More trouble?'

Mark squeezed his eyes closed, and shook his head. 'John… I don't know what I'd do without you. Have I ever said how much…?'

John briefly put a strong arm around his cousin's shoulder. 'Hey, it's OK, it's mutual. Now, what's happened, and what do we need to do about it?'

Mark nodded and gathered his thoughts.

'We're being targeted by these blond bastards, whoever they are. There were some suspicious-looking characters outside the school, so Andy and Helen are bringing the kids straight back home. Can I leave it to you to ring our eldest?' He waited for John to agree, then went to find a quiet room to think about his father, and how he felt about this sudden attempt at contact.

John rang Frankie, who sounded as if he was somewhere noisy and not conducive to study. John tried to speak calmly. 'Those bastards were outside the high school, you can't assume they don't know where you are.'

Frankie was alert and eager. 'Anyone hurt?'

'No. Andy spotted them and turned straight back.'

'Do you want us to come home?' Frankie asked after a short pause.

'Well, Andy will be impossible if the Kittens don't, and he'll skin you alive if you don't escort them.'

Frankie sounded confident. 'He worries too much. Sara and Darlene are the only people I'd be scared of in a fight … except you Dads and Mum, of course. How many of them?'

'At least four,' Andy said.

'Well, there are four of us. Trust us, Dad. You can't guard us forever, and we need to learn to look after ourselves.'

John was silent; he didn't want to make this decision.

He compromised. 'Stay for now, but if Andy or Mark disagree with me, you come home straight away. I'm sure you can outfight these guys, or even outrun them if you have to, but they might try to run you off the road, or arrange an accident. You know how to check the car? The brakes? The fuel tank? For bombs?'

'Yeah, Zoe taught us a couple of years ago, after she wrote that spy book. Relax. I'll bob over to chemistry now, tell the girls.'

'Where are you now?'

'Er, cafe…'

'No classes, then?'

'Erm, no.' Frankie was trying hard to sound innocent.

John smiled to himself; Frankie was too much like himself at that age. 'You lying little sod. Look after yourselves.'

'Trust us, Dad – we can and we will.'

John took a deep breath. He wasn't sure if he was doing the right thing, but he trusted the boys.

He rang Seth next. 'Those murdering bastards that hit Chloe's pack are still around, son, and they were outside the school. What do you want to do?'

'We're not moving,' Seth said.

'Where are you?'

'I'm sitting in the quad outside Miranda's lecture room at Salford. Noah is sitting right outside her lecture room door. We decided this morning that we didn't want to leave her unguarded. We'll come home with her when she's finished for the day. We can catch up with our stuff anytime, it's only architecture after all.'

'Seth, you're overconfident. Come home before you get caught out.' John was uneasy.

Seth refused. 'What did you tell Bill?'

John was caught off balance. 'I spoke to Frankie…'

'Yes, you spoke to Frankie, and I'll bet you've agreed to let him stay at college. I'm older than him, and I might look skinny but I can look after myself. Dad, the seven of us discussed this last night. We're all going to face this out. We're not stupid, but we're tired of being nurse-maided. You know we can fight, if we have to. Noah and I can protect Miranda, and if the murdering sickos stick to human form, she's no slouch at self-defence herself. In fact, we're probably most at risk on the way home, in the car.'

John broke in. 'That's just what I was going to say. I'm thinking of driving to the college later on and escorting the others home. And if I see those blond creeps, I'm going to, er, call the police.'

Seth was suddenly serious. 'Dad, just keep the little kids safe, OK? We'll be fine.'

John stared at his phone; the call had ended.

Diana was standing behind him. She'd been listening. 'So much for doing as they're told,' she said.

'You'd better speak to them,' John said sheepishly, offering the phone to her. Disciplining the kids had never been his strong point.

Diana reached up affectionately to touch his face. 'No, actually, they're right. We have to start letting go. Andy won't agree, but he'll fall in line if I back you up. Seth's right. It would take a small army to get past them to Miranda. We've just got to wait it out, see how many of these white wolves there are around. Zoe just checked the forums — nobody else has seen them, so maybe there are only four.'

John disagreed. 'Chloe said she saw at least a dozen at the farmhouse, and you said there were lots of tracks.'

'In that case, we need all the allies we can get,' she said, waving the slip of paper at him, reminding him of the other issue at hand.

John sighed, and reached for the phone again, hitting the numbers, waiting for the connection to France. The phone was picked up on the first ring.

'Yes?' The voice at the other end was deep, rich and utterly confident.

'It's John.' He felt suddenly helpless and childlike. That voice released long-buried memories of being comforted by someone infinitely strong and protective. Diana was behind him, breathing in time with him.

'John.' There was a choked silence, then the voice again, that vaguely familiar deep voice, so like his own but with a different accent — some sort of generic southern European accent.

'Am I too late? Has something happened to Mark?' the familiar stranger was saying.

John recovered. 'No, no, of course not. Mark is fine, absolutely fine, but he isn't up to talking to you yet. This has knocked him back. Before I say anything else, I need some proof that you are who you say you are.'

There was silence, and then Anthony quoted a very specific website address. John moved to the nearest computer and tapped it in. He was shaking, and it took a while. It was a webcam. The man was sitting in a dark room, nothing visible but his face, which was brightly lit. Nobody could identify the room, though – it was a nice trick.

Diana stared at the face, leaning over John's shoulder. 'It's like looking into your future,' she whispered

'You don't look much like Mark,' John said to the man, astounded to see himself mirrored through a filter of over twenty years.

The older man smiled wryly. 'No, I know that – he takes after his mother. You take after your father, my twin. It doesn't surprise me that the Whites finally made the connection between my brother and I, and you.'

Diana was fascinated. Anthony was almost identical to John. He must be in his seventies, at least, but looked to be in his early fifties. His hair was black and silver, cut short, but still identifiably curly.

His eyes fixed on hers. 'Ah, Diana, I'm so pleased to meet you at last.'

She found herself charmed. There was no doubt where John's manners had come from.

'So you and John's father are identical twins?' she asked, wanting to clear up something she'd wondered about for a long time.

Anthony's face clouded. 'We were… John, I'm sorry. Tomas died, years ago.'

John nodded, his face frozen, refusing to admit to the hope he'd started to feel. When he spoke again his voice was stilted. 'So why have you waited until now to tell me?'

'It's a lot to explain.' Anthony was measuring the situation; John was obviously distressed, but not aggressive. Diana was silent and looked very wary, and her whole stance towards John was protective.

The older man held out his hand towards them in supplication. 'I'm coming back to England – I should have done it a long time ago. The most important thing for all of us is for me to tell you what I know.'

Diana blinked. 'Email's been around for a long time, old man.'

He smothered a smile. 'I know, I'm not stupid. But I don't know when I'm being followed or monitored, and I didn't want to lead our enemies to you. It looks like that ship has sailed.'

She looked at him. He was charming, and in appearance, so much like her mates she was half-convinced. She nodded.

'If you *are* Mark's dad, that would be very understandable. But I'm still not convinced that you are. Some bastard Shapeshifters have just killed close friends of mine, and I'm not letting any strangers into this house.'

Anthony's face was impassive. He nodded once. 'I respect that. I didn't really expect anything else of you. In that case, it's been good to speak to you. Can we keep in touch, even if you won't allow me to come to you?'

John stirred. 'No, don't go. My mate is right, you can't come here, but I can come to you.'

Diana started to speak, but he turned and placed a finger on her lips. 'Shh.'

Anthony nodded. 'It's dangerous – the White Pack have been looking for me for decades.'

John understood. 'You look pretty dangerous yourself. I still want … need … to see you.'

Anthony looked thoughtful before suggesting a time and a place to meet John, then broke the connection.

'I can understand you wanting to meet your father's twin, but this isn't the best time to leave us,' Diana objected.

'Mark won't be any use at all until this is sorted out. Have you seen him? He's hiding. He's shaken up. It's not the murders that got to him, it was that phone call. Since when does Mark hide? Sweetheart, I'm going to meet this man, and I'm doing it for my peace of mind, and for Mark's.'

Diana didn't agree, but was unsettled by John's determination. 'John, this is exactly the wrong time to split up our pack, to make us more vulnerable. I don't like it. And I don't want you going off alone. It's too dangerous.'

Her mate put his hand on her shoulder and met her gaze. 'Go and find Mark. Take a good look at him, then come back here and tell me you really don't want me to go and check out this man.'

Diana shook her head. 'John, it's dangerous. I'm scared for you.'

'You'll have to trust me. I'll be very careful.' He bent and kissed her forehead. 'Do you think I have some sort of death wish? I'm happier than a pig in muck here, and nothing will stop me coming back home to you all. Trust me.'

'You'd better tell Zoe…' Diana said. It was her way of giving in.

John's eyes clouded. 'She'll be furious,' he said. 'Will you tell her?' he begged hopefully.

'No way!' She looked at him again; he was trying his hardest to look irresistible, and, as usual, it made her smile. 'Look, you'll have to tell her. She won't like it, but I'll support you if this is really what you want. That's the best I can do. But she deserves to hear it from you, don't you think?'

John agreed, reluctantly. 'OK, I'll tell her. I *am* going to do this. For me, and for Mark. I need to make sure that this guy *is* Anthony, and if he is, I'm bringing him back here. Is that OK?'

He was smiling at her. He loved that he had to seek her permission, as his Alpha. And he loved that she could rarely refuse him anything.

'OK, if you think he can be trusted. But *you're* still telling Zoe.'

He was almost laughing now, looking at her. She was already making plans, wondering where Anthony would fit into their lives, how they would deal with John being away when the pack was under threat. She'd been described as selfish by those who didn't know her, but her focus was her pack, her children, her mates, and she rarely thought about her own needs. Ruthless was a more accurate description. He wanted her, then and there. He'd found the bathroom door locked against him that morning, and was becoming aroused thinking about it.

She caught his look, and shook her head. 'Too much to do, honey, but don't leave without saying goodbye properly. OK?'

Reluctantly, he let her go.

Chapter 7

Andy screwed up his eyes at the afternoon sunlight as he came out of the music room. He'd been teaching all day, and was glad for the chance to get out for some fresh air and relative peace. He watched the kids tumble out of the music room and chase each other into the house. He'd always had the theory that music was a subject best taught informally, but he was beginning to change his mind after experiencing the chaos back there. He combed back his still thick blond hair, and scanned the grounds automatically for strays. Not a kid to be seen; they were all occupied somewhere. His eyes rested on John, who was sitting at the top of the big slide in the kids' playground. He wandered over and joined him on the platform. It was about twelve feet off the ground and a great place to keep watch from.

'There were twenty kids in there, every one of them barmy,' he commented.

John looked up, pride mixed with wary amusement.

Andy shook his head. 'I drew the short straw! I spent the day with twenty rampaging kids and associated noisemaking equipment, while you got to drive around rescuing our teenagers from murdering maniacs. Where are the Kittens anyway?'

John shook his head. 'I didn't go for them.' He tried to meet Andy's eyes.

'Who did, then? Diana? Mark?'

'Nobody.' John finally looked up, troubled.

'Where are they? Did they come home alone before you could get to them?'

'I guess they're on their way now.' John was holding Andy's increasingly bewildered gaze, watching his expression change from puzzlement to worry, and then to anger.

'They're out there alone? My girls?' Andy was stock-still.

John frowned. Andy was impossible on that subject. 'They're *our* girls, Andy. They're my daughters too. And they're not alone, they're with Bill and Frankie.'

Andy was silent. His brilliant blue eyes were filling with storm clouds, and John braced himself.

'Why the *fuck* didn't you go for them? Mark *told* you to ring them.'

'He didn't tell me to get them. He told me to ring them. I did. I spoke to Frankie. He said they could cope. I decided to trust them.'

'*You* decided to trust them? It's not your daughters out there! Do you *know* what happened to Laura? Do Diana and Mark know about this?' Andy was spitting with rage.

John felt a moment of fury: the Kittens *were* his daughters, as much as any of the other girls. He drew a deep breath. 'Andy—'

'Don't *Andy* me. You've surpassed yourself this time. You seriously think those cocky lads of yours can protect my girls?'

John shook his head impatiently. 'Andy, *our* girls can protect *our* boys, and vice versa. And I'm no less worried about them then you are.'

'You don't bloody show it. I'm going for them. And I suppose those skinny ginger intellectuals are "protecting" Miranda?' he said, turning and climbing down the steps.

'I hope so, they promised to,' murmured John.

Andy stopped abruptly, turning his head. 'You didn't go for Miranda? Now you're taking the piss. You can't leave her out there.'

John looked bleak. 'They have to learn to survive, Andy. We can't protect them forever.'

'Miranda? She's got nothing to protect herself with. You think I'd leave Eva or Naomi out there alone?'

'They're children, but Miranda's eighteen years old. We have to start trusting her.'

Andy drew himself up to his full, impressive height. 'I'm going for them now. If *anything* has happened to Sara and Darlene, I swear I'll kill you.'

John's eyes flickered yellow, just for a moment. 'Andy…' he warned, and the taller man glanced down submissively. It was instinctive after almost twenty years as Third. Then other instincts came to the fore, and Andy glared back before running down the slide and going to search for Mark.

In the main bedroom, Zoe had just finished feeding her youngest daughters. She was silent, furious, and they'd fed quickly and quietly, picking up on her dangerous mood. She strode through the door and looked around. Bridget was passing.

'Put the babies to bed somewhere,' Zoe snapped.

Bridget stared at her. Zoe was almost always sunny-natured, and never wanted to be apart from her youngest if she could help it. Zoe almost snarled at the girl's hesitation. 'Now, please, Bridget.'

The sixteen-year-old nodded, taking a baby girl in each arm, and carrying them to her room. Amanda started to squawk a protest, but quieted in her sister's expert arms.

Zoe went back into the bedroom and lay down. She was shaking with anger, and had no idea what to do, where to turn. She closed her eyes and tried to calm down. She hoped and prayed that she would just go to sleep, but the sound of the door opening put paid to that. Her eyes snapped open, and she glared at Diana.

The petite redhead smiled, trying to put off the worst. Zoe was rarely upset, but when she was she usually took it out on

John, who was an expert at weathering her sudden storms. 'Shall I look for John?' she offered.

'Yeah, you might as well, before you send him off to die,' snapped Zoe.

'Whoa…' murmured her packmate. 'Shall we talk about this?' She sat on the bed next to Zoe, reaching out to play with her hair.

Zoe rolled so that her face was turned away. 'I've been talking to Chloe…' she said, trying to make her voice level and reasonable.

Diana got up, and walked around the bed to be close to her. She sat on the floor, leaning against the bed, her head almost next to Zoe's but turned away, listening without confronting. 'She's not staying here, if that's what's worrying you. She's grieving, and the bonding withdrawal will hit soon. A pack home is the last place she needs to be.'

Zoe spat out her reply. 'I know that. I'm not stupid.'

Diana closed her eyes and regrouped her thoughts. She wanted to make everything OK, but the day was going badly with everyone. 'What's bothering you about Chloe then?'

'Apart from her babies having their throats ripped out? Her children being torn apart? Her mates being murdered and mutilated? What's fucking bothering me? She's alone, that's what's bothering me. And everyone is treating her like an orphan, not a widow. Why? Would you be treating her differently if she was the Alpha?'

Diana scowled. The thought of being without Mark caused her guts to twist. 'If it was Laura who'd survived, she'd be begging me to kill her by now, and I'd probably find myself agreeing to do it. You have *no* idea what the Alpha bond is like. And as for Chloe, we're treating her as an orphan because, as long as she's being cared for by the pack, she *has* to be seen as a child. You need to learn that quickly, because whatever our *plans* are, and whatever we *want*, if John or Mark suddenly start thinking of her as a potential mate, we've got problems. She is way too young to be joining us as a mate – it wouldn't be fair to her. But you know John, if he takes a fancy to Chloe, Mark won't stand in his way. You and I would have to veto it, and he wouldn't like that one bit. It's best to just keep temptation away from him.'

Zoe thought about it, and then spoke again quietly. 'She loved her mates. Is nobody going to even talk to her about what happened?'

'She'll talk when she's ready. And she's with Helen at the moment. Helen will keep her well away from Andy, and she's a good listener too.'

'You don't care…'

Diana stood up and looked at her appraisingly. 'Where are you going with this?'

'I don't want to be alone,' whispered Zoe, closing her eyes, refusing to meet Diana's stare.

'What?' Diana was losing patience.

'You're sending John away on some crazy mission. If he doesn't come back, I'll be alone, and I *love* him, Diana, you have no idea how much.'

'Zoe, we're one pack. If anything ever happens to John, we'll *all* suffer. We all love him. Don't you understand that yet? After all these years?'

'Diana, we're not communicating. I'm saying that I love John. I don't want to lose him. Don't send him away.' She still had her eyes shut.

'It sounds like you're telling me, not asking me.' Diana tried to sound amused. 'And it's not my choice, it's his. It's his idea.' She was trying to be patient, but her Beta was acting like a teenager.

'Yeah, but you're not doing anything to stop him, are you? Because he's doing it for Mark, and you'll go along with anything for Mark. You'll pay for Mark's happiness with John's life, and then I'll be alone.'

'Oh for fuck's sake, Zoe! Grow up.'

Zoe refused to answer, just lay on the bed, quiet, until the silent tears started to come.

Diana rolled her eyes and walked out, exasperated.

Mark was sitting in the kitchen, alone except for Caleb, who was cautiously making a pot of tea. He looked up and smiled weakly at Diana.

'Hi, hon.'

'What's up?' she asked cautiously. She could read his moods, and could tell he was close to tears.

'Oh, John's just decided on a whim to let our enemies wipe half the family out, and I'm trying to decide what to do about it. I thought I could trust him. Do I have to do everything myself?' His voice was almost breaking, and Diana sat opposite him.

She glanced up at her fourteen-year-old son, who was trying not to be noticed. 'Be somewhere else, eh?' she suggested gently. Caleb blushed and left. She took Mark's hand. 'What's happened?'

'Andy just came in, all guns blazing. It seems that when we asked John to ring the kids to tell them about those murdering blonds, we neglected to make it clear that we wanted them to come home. He considers it enough that he's warned them, and he thinks that *this* is the ideal time for them to learn some independence.'

'And what do you think?' she asked, cautiously, blaming herself for not finding him and letting him know what was happening, and for leaving it to Andy to tell him.

'All I can think of is Miranda,' Mark said. At this point, he broke down. 'I won't lose her – it's too much that I lost Xan,' he managed to say.

She said nothing. Mark would never stop blaming himself for Xan's death, and it was pointless to take the subject up again.

'Has someone gone for them?' she said.

'Andy and John are getting ready now.'

'No, that will leave us too vulnerable. Only one of them goes,' she said decisively.

Mark nodded. 'So you choose, because I couldn't. Who do they go for first, the Kittens or Miranda?'

She smiled and shook her head. 'Or your boys, or John's? When will you learn? The Kittens can fight their own corner. John can go, his head is obviously clearer than Andy's. And for the record, I agreed with him on this. I should have spoken to you earlier. And he's going to get Miranda.'

She reached for her mobile.

'I've done that. None of them are answering,' said Mark.

Diana shook her head. 'They're my kids. I'd know if anything had happened. Don't worry.'

Her guts churned nevertheless. Her eldest children were out there, unguarded; they had been for hours, and Mark and Andy's distress was bothering her. Had she made a huge mistake in trusting the teenagers? Her only comfort was that none of them was alone. She decided that if they wouldn't, or couldn't, answer Mark's calls, there was no point in ringing them, and went outside to get some fresh air.

To her amazement, John and Andy were still arguing. She raised her hands and glared at them. 'Shush, both of you. Please, this isn't helping anyone.'

'Can you believe him?' Andy said, appealing to her.

'Yes, and I think he has a point,' she said.

Andy frowned. She was a foot shorter than him, but when she spoke, he listened. He subsided. She took his hand, and John's, and continued.

'He has a point, but he's also an idiot for not talking to you and Mark about it. John, we think you should go for Miranda now. If Noah and Seth aren't with her, don't wait for them, you get her and come straight home.'

Without argument, John turned and left.

'And I'll go for Sara and Darlene and the boys…' added Andy.

'No, you won't. Andy, I need you here. We've got thirty kids on the grounds, including Eva and Naomi and Chloe's pair, all under sixteen. Only three of them can fight. Mark is running on empty after dealing with the massacre yesterday, and learning about his father today. Chloe is a basket case, and Zoe is freaking out on me. I hate to say it, but I'm going to need you and Helen to stay here. Can you do that for me?'

He nodded, visibly calmer. His blood was up and his temper high, but he was willing to listen to her.

She sighed, moving closer to him and accepting the comfort of the embrace he offered. Not for the first time, she was thankful that the kids mostly took care of each other these days. Having the high-school kids home for the day was a blessing; they'd automatically assigned themselves to look after the younger children and make sure the house was organised. Beatrice and Bridget had everyone under control, and it sometimes felt like they always had.

'Andy, I really think that John's right. I think—' Her phone was ringing. John's name flashed up.

'Where are you?' she asked; he'd walked away less than two minutes earlier.

'At the gate. You can stop worrying about Miranda and the boys – they're home.'

'The others?' Diana was tight-lipped.

'I'll go for them,' he said.

'No,' she snapped.

'No?' John waited.

'You're not going out alone to "rescue" four strapping teenagers,' she said.

Andy grabbed the phone off her. 'John, bring the car back here. You bloody stay here, I'm going for them.'

Diana took the phone back from him and made sure John could hear. 'No, Andy, you are staying here. Where the children are,' she told him 'Trust the older kids,' she growled. Now that Miranda was home, she was more relaxed.

Andy stalked off, moving towards the annexe, furious with her, furious with John.

Diana watched the Punto roll down the drive, and waited while Noah parked fussily. Her three eldest children got out and walked cautiously towards her.

'Are we in trouble?' Miranda asked.

'Did you do anything you were told not to?' her mother asked.

'No.' Miranda was flushed and happy. 'Does that mean we're not grounded?'

Diana allowed them a trace of a smile, and was rewarded with grins from all of them.

Seth was beaming. 'We tricked them. They didn't stand a chance.'

Diana's gaze fell on him, alert. 'They were there? At the uni? You saw them?'

Seth nodded eagerly. 'Yes, but we got away OK.'

For the time being, that was enough for Diana; she could wait until later for the full story. For now, she wanted Mark to know that the eldest kids were safe. 'You got away this time. Don't get cocky. Mark's in the kitchen, it will do him the world of good to see you. And don't bother Zoe, she doesn't even know you've been in danger. For now, I want to keep it that way.'

She was stiff-backed, and refused to accept Seth's hug. 'Tomorrow, you all stay at home. Forget uni for now. You might not be this lucky again.'

Her firstborn didn't move from her side, and signalled at his brother and sister to leave him.

'What's wrong? I thought you'd be glad to see us.' Seth was concerned, suddenly realising how worried his mother was.

'I am. Of course I am. Three home, four to go,' she told him, refusing to unbend even a little.

Seth nodded. 'Mum, please relax. They'll be safe. Did you think we didn't expect danger? Do you really think we're still children?'

She shook her head. 'Just go, Seth. Please.'

'No, no. You're upset, I can't leave you like this.'

'Yes, I am, but you can go.' She looked up, smiling. Seth had always taken far too much responsibility for her welfare.

He hugged her again, and tried to imitate the way that Mark spoke to her. 'Look, they're not due home until half four, it's only four now. We came home early because of Miranda. I'll go to look for them, if you want?'

Diana covered her eyes with her hand before brushing her fine red hair aside and sighing. 'Have we brought you up stupid, or what? I've just told Andy *and* John that they're not going out alone. Why would I let *you* go? Go and see Mark, get something to eat, and take over from the Bees – they've had a hell of a day. Tell them I love them, and that they've got the rest of the day to themselves.'

'Anything else?' He was respectful. He clearly wanted to tell her about his day, but decided it could wait.

'Yes. How long was Miranda alone?'

'Not for a second,' he told her.

She relaxed then, and Seth left. She watched him walk into the kitchen, then she wandered over to the slide, climbing up to the platform and leaning on the barrier, watchful. John approached cautiously, looking up.

'Are we OK? Me and you?' he asked.

'Always,' she said, but he heard the anxiety in her voice. He joined her on the platform, and took her hand.

'They'll be fine. *I* wouldn't like to tangle with them, anyway,' he tried to reassure her.

She turned to him and put her head on his broad chest. He pulled her close and hugged her. At the bedroom window, Zoe watched them for a moment, and then threw herself back on the bed.

Diana took in his familiar scent, making herself feel safe and wanted and loved.

He could hear her mumbling something into the fabric of his shirt. 'What did you say?'

She mumbled again, and he ran his hands through her dead-straight red hair; it was still bright fire, no trace of the smoke to come. 'You'll have to speak up, hon, because last time I checked, those were my nipples, not my ears.'

She looked up, smiling through tears. 'I *said* … Zoe is pissing me off. She keeps saying that I don't care about you.'

John raised his eyes to the skies. 'How old are you two?'

'Younger than you and Andy, but I caught the two of you in a pissing contest less than half an hour ago,' she pointed out, sweetly reasonable, regaining her calm.

John was quiet, distracted. She looked at him enquiringly.

'I can hear the Mini…' he muttered.

She went down the slide on her bottom, John ran down after her. It was four twenty-five.

Sara was the first out of the car, standing stock-still, trying desperately not to look too pleased with herself. Darlene was swinging her long legs out from the driver's side of the car, and pulling the seat forward to let her brothers spill out noisily and excitedly, crowding around their father like eager puppies. John was trying to hug them all at once, and he started to yell. '*Andy!* They're OK.'

John could put some volume into his voice when he wanted to, and Andy soon joined them, hugging the girls tightly, not speaking.

Darlene pulled away eventually, and went to Diana, who stood to one side, quiet, watching them. 'Spokeswoman, I presume?' Diana said.

'Yes. Well, I'll tell you the whole story later, but basically we were fine so long as we stayed in college. Security has always been a bit OTT there – strangers would be noticed, and asked to leave.'

'And when you left the college?'

Darlene was laughing. 'Mum, watch!' Her eyes took on the inward expression that signalled a Change, and Diana almost started to nag about ruined clothes, until she realised that Darlene's hair had taken on a darker brown tint and developed a definite wave. Her daughter was shrinking in height, but the body mass was being moved around. Darlene was adept at Changing, finding it painless and natural, but this was amazing. Diana and the other adults had always found it almost impossible to change their human form to anything other than younger versions of themselves. Zoe had termed it 'The Body Image Problem'.

'Darlene?' Her mother's voice trembled; she was awestruck.

The girl's voice was the same, at least. 'Yeah, it's me. We've been practising for ages. Sara figured it should be possible. The six of us have been working on it for about a year now. I'm the best, but the others can all change hair and eye colour, and change their faces. We fooled those idiots outside the college anyway. Luckily they didn't seem to have the car staked out, but next time we won't be able to use it, I suspect.'

'And that's how you got away? And Seth and Noah did the same, while they watched over Miranda? No fighting, no running, you just changed the way you look and walked straight past them? You little genius. I'm so proud of you. Oh, change back, please. I want my Darlene back!' It was unsettling to be talking to someone who looked like a stranger. Diana was unnerved but happy. 'Is it difficult? Do you have to concentrate all the time?'

'It's getting easier, but it's still harder than taking an animal form. There's so much you assume when you're human. Zoe is right that you automatically try to match your body image. I'm sorry, we shouldn't have kept it from you, but we wanted to wait until we were all adept.'

Diana was staring at her in delight. 'What about Miranda?'

'Ah, there's nothing new under the sun, is there? She just put a black wig on before she left the lecture room, and changed her walk. She's not daft,' Darlene giggled. 'You know what's the hardest thing to do? Trying *not* to look like your twin! I'm great at this, but if I'm with Sara, we want to look alike! Stupid isn't it? Anyway, we all avoided that problem when we got out of college.'

'Darlene, you're a scheming little witch, but don't keep anything from me again, eh? And in the meantime, you guys are going to start evening classes in this for Sam, Caleb and the Bees. OK?'

'Caleb too?' Darlene was puzzled.

'Yes, he might as well know the theory, even if he's having trouble putting it into practice. And this may be the way to get over this block he has about Changing.'

'What about you? Don't you want to try?'

'You can't teach an old dog…' laughed Diana, then saw the serious expression in her daughter's eyes. 'You're worried about me!' she said.

'Of course I am,' Darlene said indignantly 'This could save your life one day. You should all try to pick it up.'

'OK, I'll come to class whenever I can, but I've tried it before and the best I can do is make myself look a little older or younger than I really am.'

'Belief, that's what you need,' said Darlene with a mischievous wink. 'Right, I've got a ton of homework to do. Can I get on with it?'

'Yes, of course. Spend some time with Andy tonight, though – he's been worried sick. All your dads have been.'

'OK.' Back to normal, the teenager ran across the garden and into the house.

The big kitchen was getting full, lights going on all over the main building and in the annexe. Older kids kept prowling out in wolf form and stalking the perimeter and the woods. Diana sat under a tree, frequently interrupted by the younger children running out to her for cuddles and attention. For two hours she watched her family moving behind lighted windows as evening came.

The main bedroom light went on, and Diana glanced up. Zoe was alone, staring out of the window. Apparently she'd not moved out of the room since John told her he was going away. Diana braced herself and went back into the house, ignoring the kids and making her way to the biggest bedroom.

Zoe was still standing at the window when Diana slipped through the door. 'Are you still angry?'

'Yes. I'm still angry,' Zoe whispered.

'I need your help with the children,' the Alpha said quietly.

'You need? *You* need? What about what *I* need?' Zoe raised her voice. 'I don't give a shit what you need right now.'

'OK, then, the family needs you downstairs. Does that work for you?' Diana was getting impatient.

'No, it doesn't,' Zoe said flatly. 'We're going to talk about this. I would never, ever send John away on such a stupid errand. You've made a mistake.'

'John wants to go. Mark and I have agreed. Andy has no objections. You've had the chance to speak to him and try to change his mind, haven't you? There's nothing more to talk about.'

'Oh yes, and you've had chance to speak to him too. I saw you with him, up on the slide.' Zoe was bitter.

Diana tried to be gentle. 'Zoe, you will never be alone … even if the worst happens, you will not be alone, I promise.' She moved towards her, then stopped short, surprised by the flash of yellow from Zoe's eyes.

'If I were the Alpha…' Zoe whispered.

It was too much. Diana closed her eyes for a count of three. When she opened them, she was still angry, her fury building fast. She walked away, slamming the door behind her.

Mark found her, an hour later, in the old cottage. The back door was wide open. 'Did you want to be found?' he asked gently. 'I spoke to Zoe, she asked me to mediate. She's sorry, she knows you wouldn't do anything to hurt John.'

'I'm going,' Diana said.

'Going where?'

'To meet your father. John's too well known, too obvious. He's a target. Nobody really knows what I look like, other than short, scruffy and redheaded. If I cover my hair, or dye it, I stand a better chance of getting back home safely and unrecognised than John does.'

'No, I'll go myself,' Mark said quickly.

'Nope. We both know why – you're not objective, too emotional. I'll go. Your dad is nothing to me. I can assess the situation without getting upset. I've made my mind up. I need to talk to Andy first, about getting some help from his father. Ask Andy to come over here for a chat. Helen too. She can drop her girls off in the big house. Don't say anything to this guy who says he's your dad – let him still think he's meeting John. And give me a couple of hours more to calm down, because Zoe has no idea how much she pissed me off. Tell her we're fine, I don't want to scare her. What's she doing?'

'She's in the basement, doing that massive pile of ironing. She was crying and ironing. John's gone to help her. I thought it best to keep the kids away from her right now, no point upsetting them.' He kissed the top of Diana's head. 'Thank you. I don't want you to go, but I know when I can't talk you out of something. I'll send Andy and Helen.'

Diana watched him leave, and made her plans.

Andy and Helen arrived at the cottage soon after, and she explained what she needed. They listened, and argued, and listened again.

Eventually Helen sighed. 'OK, we're with you. Look, I'm going to get an early night. Whatever happens tonight, I'll be fast asleep. Andy, if you want to hang around the house, I'm fine with that.'

Diana flashed her a grateful look. 'Sleep well, there's a lot to do tomorrow. Andy, I'll see you later.'

Her next stop was the bedroom where the bereaved Chloe lay still, staring at the ceiling. Diana sat on the edge of the bed. 'I've not had chance yet to tell you how much I feel for you – to tell you that I understand your pain, but most of all, to tell you that you have my support, day and night, to get you through this. Whatever you need, you will have. But first of all, you've not eaten a thing since breakfast, and you won't get through anything if you don't eat and drink. I'm going to bring some food to you and wait here until you've eaten every bit.'

'It's not fair,' Chloe whispered.

'Oh, it most definitely isn't. But it's done, and you and Phil and Mareta have to survive it now. You're still a family, and if you want to stay a family, I need you to show that you still want to be their mother. Social services are already circling, and Duncan's parents are willing to take them both in. They are their grandparents, and I'm not completely opposed to the idea if you can't cope.'

Chloe sat up. 'Nobody is taking my kids away from me.'

'Well, I know and you know that they're your kids but, so far as most people are concerned, they're your boyfriend's kids with his other girlfriend.'

'They made a will – we all made a will. It's very clear. I keep the kids, and they only go to Duncan's parents if I die too.'

Diana breathed a long sigh. 'That's good. That's the best news I've had all day. I'll let Phil and Mareta know where things stand – they've been worried that nobody would want them. So now, we need to make sure you don't die, don't we?'

'They were your friends,' Chloe whispered.

'They were. I was very fond of Duncan, and Laura was funny and charismatic and good company. I know that I focussed on them and sometimes I neglected you.'

'You're not my mother,' Chloe muttered.

'No, but I am your mentor. I took on that job, and then I paid so much attention to Laura and Duncan that sometimes I forgot about you. I'm sorry about that. It's a lesson I need to learn because there'll be more young packs and I can't just focus on the Alphas. Also, I'm old enough to be your mother, and I'm happy to stand in as another grandparent to the kids if you want me to.'

'You're taking over.' Chloe's eyes flashed yellow.

'Ah, there it is – resistance. You're going to survive, Ms Stephenson. I'll go and get that food for you. I've always found that keeping busy is good for the soul, and there's a pile of ironing that's built up lately. When you've eaten, would you mind taking over from John and Zoe?' Chloe nodded and Diana left.

An hour later, with Chloe busy with the ironing, Diana led Zoe to their bedroom.

'Mark says that you're going, instead of John. That doesn't help, you know?' Zoe grumbled.

'Shh, don't argue with me again, just kiss me,' Diana whispered. 'We need to be strong, and I need you to know how much I love you.'

'What if…?' Zoe said, then moaned as Diana pushed her on to the bed, kneeling beside her and bending to kiss her.

Diana's blood was high, and the bonding hormones hit Zoe like a steam train. The Beta closed her eyes and urgently returned the kiss, wriggling to help Diana undress her, making tiny noises of pleasure as her Alpha's clever tongue and hands brought her to a swift climax, smiling because she knew that this was not the end – this was never the end for her and Diana. The second orgasm came immediately. Zoe felt the hit as Diana kept up the stimulation. There was an agonising pause as Zoe heard Diana undress, feeling the weight of her body moving on the bed, pulling Zoe forward. Zoe was weakened by the hit, but responded to Diana's demands as the Alpha encouraged her to lie down and move closer. Diana's legs were wide apart and Zoe responded, letting Diana take control, rubbing against her, mingling their fluids. Zoe screamed as the bonding hit, and moved away. Diana was laughing, lying back.

'My turn,' growled Zoe, getting to her knees and grinning at Diana. 'You're gonna get the fucking of a lifetime, my girl.'

Ten minutes later they were interrupted by Mark. 'Keep the noise down, girls. The kids are trying to sleep.' He grinned. 'Need any help?'

Diana rolled out of bed and started to get dressed. 'Sorry, Zo, there's a lot to do. Stay here with Mark, if you like, or have the evening to yourself. It's been a while since you had a proper break.'

She found Andy immediately, and led him, wordlessly, to a quiet spot in the woods, out of sight of the annexe. She Changed. He followed suit, and they lay in the fallen autumn leaves, relaxing and taking in the sounds and smells of the evening. Eventually Andy Changed back and she did the same, falling into his arms and moving closer, shocked by the intensity of his kiss and her response to him.

Afterwards, as he kissed her throat and tangled his fingers in her hair, he whispered, 'Will she die?'

'Not if I have anything to do with it. She's going to go into deep withdrawal. She'd already started with symptoms from losing Stu – that's why the three of them were such an easy target yesterday. I should have seen it coming. But, hell, we were all grieving for Stu, weren't we? It's going to get harder for her. She might go into a coma even, but if she can be kept nourished and hydrated, she'll get through it. She's been mated for, what, nine years or so? That's a long time. But she was Beta, and those blood samples I took showed a weaker bond than I'd expect to Dunc, and none to Laura. I think Laura monopolised Duncan way too much.'

Andy nodded. 'Helen's really taken to her, you know? She's gone into mother hen mode.' He stood, and started to get dressed. 'I'm taking them all back to my place tomorrow. I saw the way Frank was looking at Chloe, and we don't need that kind of complication.'

'Agreed.' Diana blinked slowly, and Changed again, rising to her feet and starting a patrol of her realm.

John found her at the site where they'd buried the white wolves. He approached her cautiously and nuzzled her. They ran into the woods, not hunting, not guarding their family, just running for the pleasure of it, for the thrill of being alive. Every tree, every stump, bore a trace of their ownership of the land. The familiar scents of their children and mates, wolf and human, reassured them and strengthened their bond. At the fence line, the low hum of electricity made them pause for a moment, distracted, until they remembered, once more, that it was OK – it was under their control. At last, they fell to their knees in a familiar clearing, Changing back to human form in the earthy smell of autumn leaves, and came together in love, in passion, and in perfect understanding with each other.

Afterwards, lying together on the forest floor, watching the stars disappear, John stirred in his lover's arms. 'Diana, if anything happens to you, what will happen?'

'Nothing's going to happen to me. We're going to live forever,' she said with absolute conviction.

'And if we don't?' He suddenly realised she had tears in her eyes.

'John, I've only just realised… They must all be dead. All of them.' Fear darkened her eyes.

He didn't understand. 'Who?'

'My old friends. The women who left with Joyce. They were all older than me. If any of them were alive, they'd have contacted me by now, surely? If I was out there alone and I knew a pack like ours existed, I'd at least make contact, to ask if I was wanted. John, they were all intelligent, healthy women. I'm only just beginning to realise how dangerous it is out there.'

He replied with a kiss, then helped her to her feet. They walked back to the house silently. They didn't go back to bed, but sat up talking quietly until a hungry cry from Mia signalled that morning had arrived.

Chapter 8

The cafe was bigger than it looked, with tables fading into the shadows beyond the reach of the autumn sunlight. Diana was early, and took a table facing the door, with her back to the wall. She was the only customer so far, apart from an elderly man sitting at the counter, chatting to the waitress. She took off her sunglasses and ordered hot chocolate, then settled back to wait. The old guy stood up, straightened his back and turned to her.

'So John sent you?' he asked.

Diana fought back a scowl, and tried her most charming smile. It felt fake. 'Nobody sent me. And well played, I didn't spot you … whoever you are.'

'Anthony Aubin. Your husband knows me as Anthony Preston – I'm his father. I have a confession… I married his mother under false papers and a false name. As she's dead now, I can let that particular secret go.'

Diana blinked. 'Are you saying that Mark's a bastard? Ah well, that's not news to me, or his ex-wife.' She was studying Anthony carefully. 'And keep your distance, eh? I'm a bit on edge at the moment.'

'I'm not surprised. Were you followed, do you think?'

'I left home in the back of a delivery van, travelled south in a car with tinted windows, and came to Paris on the Eurostar with my hair covered. I didn't see anyone who looked dodgy. You?'

'Oh, they know I'm in Paris, but not exactly where.' Anthony fell silent. 'Why don't you believe I am who I say I am? I know I look like John.'

Diana glanced at the waitress, and gestured to Anthony to move closer. She lowered her voice. 'In theory, we can change our faces.'

'In theory? Has it been done?' Anthony sounded genuinely curious.

Diana shrugged. 'I have no idea. But if those blond bastards can do it, we should both be careful, you know?'

'Oh, you're definitely Diana. Nobody could fake your sorrow for your friends, or your love for my son. You're an open book, you know that?' He swallowed. 'We lived in Bardale, in North Lancashire. Mark's mum, Frances, was the daughter of a farmer named Eddie Shepherd. She had six younger sisters. John's mother's maiden name was Miriam Hartnell and her father was a local magistrate, she had an adopted brother. If Frances and Miriam kept quiet, then Mark and John won't know that, but if Eddie is still alive, he'll know things about me that the White Pack couldn't possibly know. Eddie would be in his early nineties now. His second daughter, Maisie, would probably remember me too, she'll be in her late sixties. They have no reason to lie. There's your test. If Frances was alive, she'd know me. She'd know me in an instant.'

'What was the last thing you remember about Mark, before you left?' Diana asked.

'A football game, with Tomas and John. At the farm.' Anthony shrugged. 'Mark was very young, he won't remember that.'

'But John does. It came to him when he was having a kickabout at home with some of the kids. He said there were two men, and Mark.' She took a sip of the hot chocolate. 'Why did you want to meet us?'

'Because the White Pack are going to kill every last one of you if they possibly can. Your family, your werewolf friends and their children. Whitby was just the beginning. They have an army of killers, and they won't stop until they've wiped out British werewolves just as they did over a hundred years ago. I don't want that to happen, and I think I can help you.' He smiled ruefully. 'And I hope you can help me.'

'You mentioned them before when we spoke – the White Pack?'

'Our ancestors. Well, the inbred descendants of our ancestors. Have you seen them?'

'A few. They look alike.'

'More inbred every generation. They used to be relatively sane, but their last three Alphas have been progressively more crazy. Harald is the current Alpha. He's fathered pretty much every child in the pack since the early 1970s, which, considering all the mothers were his aunts, sisters, daughters or granddaughters, is not good news for them. Harald's father was Gunther. He let some of his brothers breed, but not his cousins. Gunther's father was the first of a short and vicious line of lunatics, the first to establish control over the pack's women and try to keep them to himself. He wasn't always successful. Oral history says that we all come from the White Pack, even if the nearest ancestor was hundreds of years ago. That's where the gift comes from.'

Diana sat up straight. She studied Anthony's face, so familiar to her in everything but age. 'OK, I'm convinced. I've never had a conversation with any of them, but I can't imagine them dissing their dad like that.' She smiled. 'Let's get you home. Do you have ID? A passport?'

'Always. I lost them once, when my twin was murdered, so I always carry them on me now.'

'Do you need to collect anything?'

'I have a cottage. It's fairly remote – you couldn't get a removal van there – but there are things I'd like to keep. I've been nomadic, and losing everything gets tiring after a while – maybe it's my age. I have to warn you, the White Pack keeps an eye on the ports and airports, even the trains. If I tried to leave the country, they'd know.'

Diana grinned. 'Old man, they have no idea what they're dealing with.' She unlocked her phone and sent a text. 'We just have time for another of these excellent hot chocolates.'

An hour later Diana was enjoying Anthony's obvious approval of the comfortable car that had collected them from outside the cafe. 'You've got money, obviously,' he noted.

'We do, but this little jaunt isn't our treat.' The car pulled off the road on to a medium-sized science park and parked next to an unobtrusive office building. Diana was out of the car before the driver had chance to open the door. 'Now, are you coming straight to Silverwood or will you go home?'

'I'd like to grab some stuff from my cottage, but it's not accessible by car,' Anthony said. 'It's just about accessible with a trail bike, but—'

'Show me where it is,' Diana said. She escorted Anthony into the building and took over the laptop on the reception desk. She studied the terrain around Anthony's cottage, and then showed it to the driver, who nodded and left.

'They'll collect everything for you,' Diana said.

'Feels military,' Anthony murmured.

Diana turned to him and nodded. 'He's security, ex-SAS. This building is Ransome Industries mainland Europe HQ. Ransome as in Andy's dad, who is granddad to four of my kids and more than happy to do anything he can to make sure they live. Andy convinced him that having you around would help a lot. There's a chance we were followed here by the … White Pack, you call 'em? So, we're leaving by helicopter – I doubt they have the resources to deal with that. Will they retaliate against this organisation?'

'No, they have a code. They can murder Shifter babies, but normals and even half bloods – carriers – are safe. Helicopter to your home?'

'Just to the airport, then a scheduled flight to Glasgow. We'll clear customs VIP track. Manchester would be the obvious destination, so we won't do that. Unmarked car with tinted windows as far as Preston, then we're doing the last leg in the back of a supermarket delivery van. If we've been lucky, they won't know I left, and won't have recognised me in Paris. If they recognised me in Paris they'll guess that I'm taking you back to Silverwood and might already be waiting there. Luckily, using the word at its loosest, UK police are looking for anyone answering the description of the Whitby Pack murderers, so the bastards are lying low. Is your cottage known to them?'

'I'm still alive, aren't I?' Anthony replied.

'Fair point.'

The driver approached them. 'Chopper's ready for us, Mrs P.'

Diana grinned. 'Anthony, I can't wait for you to meet your grandchildren.'

At the house, Anthony was met by his son. Mark had dressed carefully in a dark blue suit and shirt and his long hair was freshly washed, cut and brushed. Zoe'd playfully told him that he looked like the hippy mafia, and he'd tried to smile. He left the house, alone, when the van arrived, striding up the drive to where Diana and Anthony were watching the gates close. They turned at the same time, and Diana ran to Mark.

Anthony walked up to him and nodded. 'Mark, my son. Thank you for your offer of protection and shelter. I am grateful.' He stood, poised, looking at the man who'd been just a toddler when they'd parted. 'Mark … I had to leave you,' he said, trying to explain. Mark didn't speak, but simply looked at the older man, taking in his incredible physical similarity to his cousin and trying to find some common ground with him, searching for the words he needed. Anthony broke the silence again. 'I did what I had to – to protect you, not to hurt you.'

Mark looked up, recognition in his eyes. 'I can understand that,' he acknowledged. 'I hope I can forgive you as freely and generously as Diana's children forgave me. We've started to tidy up the old cottage for you. It's a little primitive, but it has the basics. Would you like to see it?'

Anthony assented. He hadn't expected to share pack quarters, and had been prepared to build his own home elsewhere. The cottage stood a few hundred yards from the main house. He followed his son across the lawn, taking in the size of the hotel, an unpretty three-storey building. It looked just about big enough for the family Diana had told him so much about. There was a second house, built in line with the main hotel, in a similar style. That would be the four-bedroomed annexe that he'd heard about, where Andy's family stayed when they came to visit.

The front door of the cottage opened straight into the living room: a dark, badly lit room, thickly curtained and littered with small lamps, rugs and tiny tables. A cardboard box had been filled with framed photographs, face down. It looked like someone had started work on emptying the place. Anthony's eyes adjusted quickly, and he moved gracefully past the obstacles, towards the kitchen. It was basic and functional, just like the one he'd had in the woods back in France. He was, however, in a different position now; he could buy new appliances without worrying about transport. He was planning changes as he walked upstairs. The bathroom was atrociously pink and peach, and he gave it one appalled glance before ducking quickly out again and going to inspect the large bedroom, which had windows on two sides and was empty of furniture, save for a pine wardrobe and chest of drawers.

'No bed?' he asked.

'Diana's mother died in the bed. Diana got rid of it. I've ordered another – it'll be here later today,' Mark explained.

Anthony nodded. 'Ah, so your mother-in-law was your last tenant?' He attempted a smile.

Mark shook his head, humourless. 'We didn't have that relationship. She died before Diana and I married. She disapproved of me completely,' he said sourly, before adding, 'She probably had good reason to, thinking back. Still, what do you think of the cottage?'

Anthony surveyed his new kingdom. 'May I redecorate?' he asked.

'Please do. Your own stuff will arrive tomorrow – I've been told that Ransome Industries people have gained access to your place and are packing it up. Do you want me to hire someone to change this bathroom and kitchen? I hadn't realised quite how bad they were … I never came in here,' Mark said.

'No, I'm pretty handy. I'll need web access to order what I need. Um, I'm not without resources – I own land – but I have no ready cash.'

'It's not a problem. Put everything you need on my account. We have a good agent. He'll make sure you get a good price if you want to sell your land. Otherwise, you can simply rent it out. Anyway, that's getting away from the subject… Use our money, for now – I'll give you my codes. All the buildings are linked, wireless and wired. You can sit in the garden or the cottage and log on if you want to. You're welcome to make any improvements.'

Mark was growing distant again. Anthony longed to hug him, hold him, make up for almost fifty years apart. He could still recognise his cautiously intelligent toddler in the man who stood in front of him. He swallowed painfully, realising it would take time to rebuild any sort of bond. Mark was looking out of the window. He turned back. Surprisingly he was smiling and it transformed his face. 'Have you ever seen *The Sound of Music*?' he asked.

'Many times,' answered Anthony.

'Well, we've got it in duplicate down there. Come and meet the kids. I'm afraid our other mate isn't here – he's gone home with his wife and their daughters, along with poor little Chloe and her kids. But he'll doubtless pop in sometime over the next week. He always does.'

The two men left the cottage, and walked side by side towards the house. The whole pack was lined up, waiting to meet the new arrival. Anthony was overwhelmed by the sheer number of children. 'How many?' he asked.

'Thirty-five, I think,' said Mark, momentarily awed himself by the sight of all the family lined up. He frowned playfully at his youngest daughters, who were blatantly in the wrong place. 'These little ginger nuts are Faith and Joy. They're Diana's youngest, nearly two now. They should be waiting to meet you down near the bottom of the line, but they're obviously very bad little girls.' The twins were being carried by their eldest brothers. Mark reached out and took his firstborn's hand. 'This is Seth, my eldest son, and Noah, his twin. They plan to be architects.' The young men winced at the terrible pun; their father moved on, oblivious. 'Miranda. My eldest daughter.' Both men had to look up at her. She gave her hand to the older man. 'I'm pleased to meet you.'

Anthony took her hand and kissed it. 'The ice maiden,' he acknowledged, bowing to her. 'You are as beautiful as I had heard.' He glanced up at her, admiring her refusal to blush or stammer. She gave him a brilliant smile.

'And you're as gallant as I've been told.'

Mark rolled his eyes. Xan's flair for the dramatic had been passed down to his daughter, and even Diana's unrelenting common sense and bluntness hadn't drummed it out of her completely. 'Moving swiftly on,' he muttered, winking at Frankie and Bill, who were standing restlessly between Miranda and Darlene. 'These two young toughs are—'

'Francis and William, yes, handsome boys. I'm pleased to meet you.' He bowed to Darlene and Sara, who grinned back at him. 'You girls have such energy. You must be a formidable force together.'

'Indeed,' his son said drily. 'Our eldest seven made it back home two days ago by outsmarting those blond bastards. I was worried, but, on reflection, I just hadn't noticed that they're tougher than I was at their age. We're still playing it safe, though, no college or uni while we regroup and assess the threat.'

Anthony glanced across. 'Your girls fight?' he asked. 'Good. I was afraid that you would let them be soft.'

His gaze slid down six inches to meet the deep brown eyes of a small, dark and serious fifteen-year-old girl.

'I'm Bridget. This is Beatrice,' she told him. 'Everyone calls us the Bees,' she added.

Anthony smiled again, taking and kissing both their hands. They blushed, he noted. 'What would you like *me* to call you?' he asked quietly. Bridget blushed even more deeply. 'We prefer Bridget and Trixie, actually,' she replied. Her twin nodded furiously, too shy to speak.

Mark spoke up. 'These two are wonderful daughters and sisters. They've been helping to run the pack since they were about six years old, and I don't think they realise how proud I am of them.' The girls were startled, momentarily pleased, but he hadn't finished. 'But they are a little too gentle. I worry they might be a liability if we ever have real trouble again. I'm too close to them to train them to fight, too scared of hurting them. Diana refuses to accept that they're too soft. Anthony, will you train them to protect themselves and the rest of the pack?'

Anthony winced at Mark's unwitting public humiliation of his daughters; the girls were shrinking away. 'I am certain I can put their gentleness and love of their family to good use. They are your own daughters with Diana, are they not?'

Mark tried to smile. He was puzzled by the hurt in Bridget's eyes, wondering what had happened to suddenly change her mood. 'Yes, my eldest daughters of my own blood,' he confirmed, moving on.

Anthony took the hands of both girls, lingering for a while. 'He didn't mean to hurt you,' he whispered.

'No, he never does,' Bridget confided. 'It's OK, we know what he's like.'

Their grandfather moved on, and for a moment was transfixed, the skinny fourteen-year-old boys in front of him were so obviously Mark's sons. He stared at them, reaching out to trace the shape of their cheekbones, the curve of their lips. 'Forgive me,' he whispered. 'Your grandmother wasn't much older than you when I met her. You remind me so much of her. You must be Caleb and Samuel?'

The boys nodded, nervous.

Mark started to speak. 'Caleb is—'

Anthony nodded, cutting him off. 'Caleb has been hurt – I can see it in his eyes. What happened?'

Caleb spoke glibly, as if he was reciting something. 'I killed someone, one of the men who attacked us. I've talked to my parents about it, and my brothers and sisters, but I still have nightmares. I can't Change.'

Anthony nodded. 'I've never heard of this before, such a total block, but with your parents' permission, perhaps we can work on this together? I once Changed and couldn't go back to human for many months. Perhaps I could use that experience to help you?'

Caleb nodded, a spark of hope in his eyes. Samuel winked at his twin. 'He's too brainy. He overanalyses things, that's his problem.'

Mark burst into surprised laughter. 'My son, the psychiatrist!' he blurted out, hugging both his dark-haired boys close. 'Caleb will manage the Change one day,' he said confidently.

After the fourteen-year-old boys, there was a noticeable height gap to the next children. Mark introduced Janie and Alice. 'Our ten-year-olds.'

'Nearly eleven!' exclaimed Alice.

'Our ten-year-olds, who can't wait to grow up,' Mark added. 'This is Jane … Janie, we call her. The loudmouth is Alice. The two little ones next to them are Susie and Nancy. They're nine.'

'And I'm called *Annie, not Nancy*,' piped up the second little girl insistently.

Mark kneeled down, totally serious. 'I'm sorry, sweetie, I didn't get the memo. You know I have to be told whenever you decide on a new name.'

Anthony took in the dark wavy hair, bound with red ribbons, the laughter in the little girl's eyes, her air of complete self-confidence. These twins believed they held a special place in the pack. He glanced at Diana, who was watching closely, a smile on her face. John's hand had gone to her waist, and he was grinning broadly. John's children again, then.

Mark was still talking seriously to Nancy – Annie. 'Now, this is your granddad. He's a big scary wolf man, and eats naughty little girls for breakfast. We've brought him to live with us to try to get you to be a good girl.'

Annie exchanged a look with Anthony. It said, clearly, *I'm nine, not five. Who does he think he's dealing with?* He winked at her. His fears of being unable to tell his grandchildren apart were disappearing rapidly. He kneeled too. 'Now, Susie, Annie, I promise not to eat you up if you'll help me. I'm an old man, and I might forget names sometimes. If I ask you to remind me, will you promise not to laugh at me?'

Susie winked cheekily. 'Of course. We know who everybody is,' she assured him.

'Moving on,' Mark said, rising to his feet. His mouth twitched. The Quads were standing to attention, totally rigid. He didn't know what their mothers had said to make them stay still for more than two minutes, but it had worked. 'At ease, lads,' he said. They saluted and relaxed.

Anthony was delighted. 'Quads?' he asked.

'Sort of – same age, different parents. This curly-haired pair of cheeky monkeys are Isaac and Ian. Don't let them in your cottage unsupervised – they break things.'

Isaac opened his mouth to argue, but caught Mark's expression and subsided.

'The lanky blonds are Nathan and Joe. Cute, aren't they?' He winked at Anthony, who was enjoying the outraged look on the faces of the two eight-year-old boys.

'Very cute. They'll be tall. And blond.' He was subtly questioning.

'Yeah, Andy and Diana's sons. And Isaac and Ian are Zoe and John's. Diana's are a day older than Zoe's.'

Anthony nodded. Zoe's two had outrageously curly brown hair, hazel eyes and freckles. The four pack brothers were getting impatient.

Mark moved on. 'The, er … Quadettes, I suppose,' he said. 'Meg and Beth?' he said, peering at the little girls. 'Or is it Daisy and Betty today?'

Meg blushed furiously. 'Meg and Beth, like in the book,' she told her father. 'And our sisters, Tara and Louise…' She introduced the other two little girls who were standing with her. 'Are you our granddad? We didn't know we had a granddad.'

'Deny everything. They just want pressies,' whispered Mark.

Anthony grinned broadly. 'Presents? Now I hadn't thought of that! I would *love* to buy presents for you. Just give me a few days to settle in?'

'OK, just a few days,' echoed his granddaughter, turning to stick her tongue out at Nathan, who was muttering about cheeky girls.

'Right, nearly there…' sighed Mark. 'Deborah and Leah, prettiest six-year-olds in the pack.'

Anthony found himself being studied by another pair of Mark clones, female this time, solemn and dark. They stared at him with eyes too old for their faces, and said nothing. 'Reserving judgement, are you? That's good,' he told them, shaking their hands solemnly, and moving on to two solid little boys who were covered in bruises.

'Patrick and Liam, fighters extraordinaire.' Mark was teasing them. 'They show no mercy on the football pitch. Their older brothers and sisters are just beginning to learn to show none back.'

'We're going to play in the Premiership,' Liam told Anthony confidentially.

'I'll buy a season ticket,' he assured them.

'Oh, you might be dead then! You're an old man,' Patrick blurted out.

Mark rolled his eyes again.

'Tactful, aren't they?' his father said. 'Your sons?'

Mark shook his head. 'Zoe and John's,' he said, oblivious to the dig. The line had come to an end, and the rest of the kids were sitting in a rough circle on the grass.

'Harry? Mikey? Is it too much trouble to stand to meet your granddad?' he asked the four-year-olds.

They stood reluctantly and mooched over to the men. 'Hello,' muttered Harry.

'Hello, Granddad,' said Mikey quietly.

'Nice to meet you, lads. Do you like football too?' Anthony asked.

Their faces brightened, and they monopolised him for three minutes, talking about the last Bolton Wanderers match in amazing detail, before winding down with a request that he buy them the latest away strip.

Anthony and Mark were dragged away from them by two insistent little girls who had clearly fully mastered the English language and weren't going to let it go rusty.

Mark finally got a word in edgeways. 'Julie and Leanne!' he managed to tell his father. 'They like to talk,' he explained unnecessarily. 'Now, you've met Faith and Joy … they're Diana's youngest – she can't have any more.' He frowned; it was clearly a sore subject with him.

Anthony silently counted the children he'd met; Diana had given Mark sixteen children, and he still wanted more? Anthony was about to say something, but his son's next words reassured him.

'So they're *my* youngest too. John and Zoe's kids will be the pack babies from now on. And here they are. Amanda and Mia – cute as hell, aren't they? They'll be one in December. Leanne, stop it, please.'

Leanne looked up. She'd been trying to feed her baby sister with grass. Mia, a plump little ten-month-old with an alarmingly green mouth, raised her hands, wanting Mark to pick her up. Amanda stared at Anthony, and her face crumpled.

'Whoops,' said Mark, picking up both girls and calming them down. He was smiling happily now, obviously totally in his element.

'Thirty-five!' Anthony said, awestruck.

'Yeah, and Andy has two daughters with his wife, and I have two sons with my ex-wife. Jacob is the same age as the Bees, and Matthew is a little older than the Quads.' Mark had turned away; Anthony couldn't see his face. After a few moments he turned back. 'And we're taking care of two orphans too, from the murdered pack in Whitby. Forty-one kids to take care of. You know, when I was first a rock-and-roll millionaire, I wasn't planning on spending every penny on food and clothes…'

The kids were starting to drift away in different directions and Anthony gave his full attention to his son. He looked deeply happy, and Anthony felt a weight lift from his heart, a weight he'd never realised was there.

Diana wandered over; she'd been talking to the Bees. She flashed a brilliant smile at her mate and reached to take his hand. Anthony observed them moving closer to each other, infinitely protective of each other.

Anthony began to bow, but was brought up short by Diana's laughter. 'Oh, don't. I'm too old for all that chivalrous stuff, and it just makes me giggle anyway. Save it for Zoe – she loves all that champagne and roses business. You can shake my hand, or give me a hug, it's up to you.'

'Ah, I daren't embrace you, my lady. I will take your hand.' Anthony held out his hand, took Diana's cool fingers into his strong grip, and squeezed gently. Mark glared at him for a second, then was under control again, hiding his sudden jealousy with a strained smile. Diana was chatting already, making small talk about the cottage and what he needed for the next few days. She glanced over her shoulder. Mark had dropped back. She paused, waiting for him to catch up, and then linking arms with him. The kitchen was packed with kids making drinks and grabbing snacks.

Diana raised her voice. 'Oi! We're all eating together tonight. Seth and Noah and the Bees are cooking. Don't spoil your appetites. Seven o'clock, in the big room.' Her eyes rested on Isaac. 'I think that you and your three partners in crime would enjoy setting up the tables and chairs in there. Ask Trixie where everything goes, then get on with it. Anthony will be eating with us tonight.'

She looked around. It seemed like chaos, but everyone was busy with something. Mark and Anthony were already arguing, and she decided to keep out of it. Zoe and John had disappeared. Janie was on the lawn with some toys and the baby girls. Sam had Changed for the sheer fun of it and was lying next to them, soaking up the last bits of sunlight and letting the babies pull his fur and climb over him.

The music-room door was shut, but a light showed. She went to investigate. Slipping inside, she watched happily. Caleb was striking a pretty pose with a guitar, while Bill and Darlene jumped around madly with bass guitars, shouting out an anthem of teenage defiance that was almost forty years old. Miranda was on drums, turning the jaded 'Pretty Vacant' into a raging rock number that stirred something almost lost in her mother's heart.

Bill was the first to look up, and he stopped, grinning bashfully. 'We're just playing about…' he apologised.

'No, you're great. How long have you been hitting those skins, Miranda?'

'A year or so,' she said, carefully putting the sticks to one side and walking over to her mother. 'I kept it quiet, didn't want to upset you.'

'You can't keep being a drummer quiet!' Diana told her. 'But thank you, it was thoughtful of you. I understand why you would have thought that. But you're good, and you could be better, if you want to be. Shall I organise some proper lessons for you? Mark's not a bad drummer, he could teach you.'

'No, s'OK, Mum, it's just a bit of fun. I don't want to be Xan.'

The kids were quiet. Diana shrugged; she'd obviously spoiled the moment.

'I'll go then. Have fun. Dinner's at seven.' She slipped out.

There was silence behind her for a few seconds, then Miranda shouted, "'Ant Music'," ran back to the drums and grabbed her sticks. Darlene swapped bass for guitar, tossed her hair back and pouted in true Adam Ant style, waiting for Miranda to finish the intro. Their brothers backed them up all the way. Within a minute, the interruption was forgotten.

Later that night, the family sat down to eat together. Andy arrived alone at six, and stayed for a couple of hours before heading back to watch over his other family and Chloe.

Mark sat next to his father, and they continued their conversation. Now and again they would fall into furious, baffled silences, before trying again to talk to each other. After coffee, Anthony retired to the cottage, not bothering to assemble the new bed that had been dumped in the dusty living room. He curled up on the plastic-wrapped mattress, trying to find some rest.

Four hours later he was wide awake, stifled by the still air in the cottage. He made his way to the living room and opened the front door wide, letting the cool autumn breeze in to explore nooks and crannies that had been left silent for far too long. He switched the main light on, got himself a glass of water from the kitchen and stood in the doorway. It wasn't long until Mark joined him.

'I wondered how long you'd sleep. How's the bed?'

'I've not put it together yet – I just crashed.' Anthony shrugged. 'Should we do it together?'

'Yeah. Sorry for just leaving you here.' Mark looked up. 'Ah, it's raining. Let's assemble that bed now. There's a toolbox under the stairs – John was always doing little jobs for Diana's mum. Unless you need more sleep?'

'Good for a couple of days now.' Anthony smiled.

Mark headed for the stairs, then paused at the box of photos. 'Diana asked me to bring these back with me. She's been meaning to move them to the big house for ages now.' He turned the top photograph over. It was a school photo of Diana. She was about ten years old, her bright hair wrestled into a complicated braid. Mark picked it up and laughed. 'Her mother must have done that, or her sister. Diana can barely manage a ponytail.'

'Her sister?'

Mark winced. 'Dead. The White Pack got her. Them or some guys who looked just like 'em. It'll be ten years or so ago. They damn nearly got Diana too, but, luckily, Andy was around.'

'Ten years…' Anthony whispered, picking up the next picture. It was a wedding portrait: a thin, solemn man who could only have been Diana's father, and an equally serious-looking attractive woman in a long white dress, wearing a lace veil over her long black hair. He recognised them, but where from? 'Diana's parents?'

'Yes. I never met her dad – he's long gone. Carrier syndrome, Diana calls it. Seth and Noah are the image of him, Diana says.'

Anthony reached into the box and drew out another school photo. A dark-haired ten-year-old girl, unsmiling, with her arm protectively round a much younger Diana. He swallowed. 'What was her name? The sister?'

'Joyce. Joyce Foster. Why?'

'I met her. Ten years ago. I sent her here to find you … to warn you … to warn you about the White Pack.' Anthony stumbled to a chair and sat down, gripping the frame of the photograph. 'I couldn't get into England safely, and I didn't think you'd believe a phone call. I tracked her down and asked her to find you. I thought … I hoped she'd made it. She wasn't going by 'Foster', I'm sure, or I would have made the connection when you all went public.'

Mark didn't sit down. 'She had a media career. She used a pen name for her books, and I think she went by another name for her film work. You sent a woman into that kind of danger?'

Anthony looked up. 'I just came back here with your wife. Remember? And from what I learned of Joyce, she was pretty dangerous herself. But still, this news hurts my heart.' He studied the wedding photograph again, and rummaged through the box until he found another school photograph, this time of a five-year-old Joyce. 'I thought so. That wasn't the only time I met her. A coincidence. It was a long time ago, before you were born, before Diana was born. I was with your mum, on a beach, and this little girl was lost. She came to me for help. Cute little thing … made me yearn even more for a child of my own. I had no idea that she was like us. I got her back to her parents – they were decent folk.' He frowned. 'There was another man, an uncle?'

Mark winced. 'Yeah, he's long gone. Joyce killed him to protect Diana. He was not a pleasant person.'

Anthony studied the image of the five-year-old Joyce. 'She tried to let me know, even at that age. I was a complete stranger and she wouldn't let go of my hand. She was afraid of that man. Now I know why, and I … I let her down twice. She might still be alive if it wasn't for me.'

Mark shoved his hands into his pockets and frowned. 'Look, you're obviously upset. We can sort that bed out another time. Shall I take the photos? Or do you…?'

Anthony looked up, managing a smile. 'This grief, it's ten years old. I will be fine. Take the photos back with you.'

'OK. Breakfast is at seven, but you're welcome to come over to the kitchen and rustle something up, if you want?'

'I'll stay here, if I may?' Anthony stood and went back to his bedroom. He stared out of the window, and let the tears fall.

Chapter 9

'Happy fiftieth birthday, Mark!'

Diana had led him out into the garden. The air was freezing, the day barely light, and nobody else was awake. The cottage door was open, and Anthony was standing there.

'Come in, son, I've got presents for you. I've got you a card, and I'm making breakfast.'

Mark shook his head. 'Diana, why are you colluding with him? This is forty-five years too late. Thanks for trying, Anthony, but I don't need this now.' He stalked back across the lawn.

Diana headed him off. 'You stubborn man. You might not need it, but Anthony does,' she said.

'I know that,' he said curtly. 'We don't always get what we need, though, do we? I know my mother never did – she stayed loyal to him until the day she died.'

'Mark, I'm sure your mum wouldn't want you to be at odds with your dad.'

'How would you know? You never met her,' he drawled.

She flinched. 'That wasn't my choice. She never knew I existed,' she pointed out – Mark's mother had died in the late summer of 1999, of a liver cancer that took hold of her and reduced her to bones within a couple of short months.

Mark stood silent, furious. 'Why are you against me?' he spat.

'Against you?' she said, incredulous. 'How could I *ever* be against you? Look, just be nice to your father, spend half an hour with him.'

'You spend half an hour with him. I'm going in,' he growled, leaving her standing on the frosty grass, at a loss. She turned and looked at Anthony. He shrugged and shut the cottage door.

'Bloody men,' she muttered, heading back to their bedroom. She swore when she found the door locked against her. '*Happy Fucking Birthday, Mark,*' she hissed through the door, before barging into the next bedroom and waking John and Zoe as she used their access to the shared bathroom. She kept up a low monologue about stupid men, stupid pride and stupid, stupid birthdays. The sound of her trying to open the other bathroom door was unnaturally loud, as was the subsequent sound of her throwing the bolt and locking it from her side too.

Zoe stirred. 'John, you're gonna have to calm them down before the kids get up,' she whispered.

Her husband shut his eyes. 'No rest for the wicked, then?'

'It's your fault for being so wicked,' she pointed out.

John listened, until the sounds from the bathroom indicated that Diana was in the bath and calming down. He was just getting out of bed when the door flew open again and Mark stormed into the bedroom. Ignoring John, the Alpha pushed the bathroom door open and strode in. He slammed the door shut behind him.

'Don't mind us...' said John, looking longingly at his warm bed then deciding it was probably time to get up anyway. He listened closely at the bathroom door. Zoe raised an eyebrow. He shrugged.

'She just told him he's a bad dog,' he told her.

'In that case, I'd better use another bathroom,' Zoe said, resigned.

An hour later the bathroom door finally opened. Diana and Mark fell out, all smiles.

Zoe was making the bed. 'All clean now?' she asked sarcastically. She just got two grins in reply.

Chapter 10

For once, the house was quiet. Everyone old enough to understand was taking every chance they got to check the news or log on to the web. There was an air of suppressed excitement. Helen and her daughters, Chloe and her children, and Anthony were all present, drifting in and out of the house, talking about the changes to come if Roni Jerrard's private member's bill got through Parliament. Roni was married to a carrier and was sympathetic to Shapeshifters; she'd worked solidly for months with them, to draft out legislation to protect their rights. There had been many compromises along the way, but the final vote was due, and public sympathy for British Shapeshifters was still strong, images of the Whitby murders still fresh in people's minds.

Just before tea, the vote came. The bill was passed with a comfortable majority, and with almost all the provisions effective immediately. Chloe was in tears when the newsreader announced that the Contract provisions would come into force the following day: any marriage registrar could perform a Contract ceremony, in a place licensed for weddings or in the place of residence of the Contractees. The new legal arrangement applied only to Shapeshifters, and was a group marriage contract that forbade divorce within the pack, or undeclared marriage contracts outside the pack. It made explicit the joint group ownership of all pack possessions, under the ultimate control of the Alphas, and provided for every Contractee in a pack to be recognised as a legal guardian of every pack child, with ultimate custody in the hands of the Alphas.

The older children were paying close attention. 'Will you have a Contract? Will we have a party?' Sam asked his parents.

'No, it would hurt Helen's feelings. We're fine as we are. We've already drawn up similar legal agreements for ownership of pack property and guardianship of you kids anyway. The Contract is for young packs. Shush.'

Diana turned her attention back to the TV. The newsreader was reading the declaration that Shapeshifters were considered to be human, with full human rights and legal protection.

'D'oh,' said Zoe. Diana rolled her eyes. It hadn't been much of a battle, but some religious groups had come out in force, after their revelations several years ago, claiming that the Shapeshifters were the Devil's work; inhuman – that particular battle was still ongoing in the USA. Zoe and John had spent a lot of time on TV and radio dismissing their arguments. John's charisma and celebrity had helped, a lot.

'Controversially, Parliament has voted through the "overpopulation amendment", stripping rights to state benefits from all Shapeshifters except the first four born to a pack. This was a conciliatory measure to anti-Shapeshifters concerned about unrestricted breeding at public expense.' The newsreader paused for breath. 'The Alpha Council has made a statement pointing out that there are *no* packs that are not completely self-sufficient,' he announced.

'That's because we work our arses off,' muttered Andy.

'Yeah, hard work – all that prancing about on stage,' laughed his wife, who was watching with interest.

'Next, the provision that has caused the most concern; the amendment to the Criminal Justice Bill. It provides for a new defence against murder charges, for Shapeshifters only. Any Shapeshifter changing form for the purpose of injuring or attacking anyone, including other Shapeshifters, or trespassing on the property of another pack, will lose the protection of the law.

Changing form to fight to protect themselves or their children is excepted. In other words, the British packs have got what they want – they are free to fight.'

Anthony growled. 'So let's go get the bastards,' he muttered.

John spoke calmly. 'That's not what it says, and these new laws might just scare them out of the country. The Whites haven't been seen anywhere since you arrived, anyway. You must have frightened them.'

Anthony muttered to himself, and then looked at Diana. 'Any more? Is that it?'

'Basically, yes. We've got what we wanted, and sacrificed very little. The Contract is irrelevant to this pack, and wouldn't suit us anyway. The main thing is that it's an option and not compulsory. If anyone wants to marry a normal or a carrier, and be in a pack too, they can, but that marriage and its children will not have greater importance than the Contract, legally. In effect, it's legalising bigamy, but only for us.'

Mark was speechless. 'You witch! Katie will be spitting feathers.'

Helen spoke up. 'Actually, Katie was one of the people Roni consulted. I didn't speak to her myself, but she was the one behind the new question in the marriage ceremony. You have to disclose, now, if you're a Shapeshifter, and also if you're mated. It's a crime to lie.'

Diana nodded. 'I'd agree with that. What about cases like Andy's? You and he were already married when he was infected.'

Helen shrugged. 'You can't deal with every eventuality. At some point there has to be trust – doesn't there?' She poked her husband.

'Oh, definitely,' he said solemnly, looking at her fondly. 'Right, what does that mean for Chloe?'

The young woman had been quiet, but now she spoke up, her voice low. 'It's not retrospective, so it doesn't give me any legal rights over Phil and Mareta. Their grandparents have asked for access, but not custody. I've applied for legal custody of them, and it's progressing, with their grandparents' support, thank goodness. Andy and Helen are kind enough to let Laura's dad and Duncan's parents visit regularly, at their home. As for me, I've had three definite Contract offers already: two of them as a Beta, one as a Third.' She looked down, then at Diana. 'But I'm in no hurry. I'm still in pain, withdrawal, I guess. It'll take a while until I can try to mate again. Duncan had our finances and insurance sorted out, at least. I've managed to sell the land in Whitby to the young Merseyside pack you helped put together last year. They've not moved in yet, but they're putting in better security, knocking down the old farmhouse and building a new one with a pack in mind. I've put half the money in trust for the children, and half of it I'll bring to my new pack. My condition is that I will be the Alpha.'

Diana nodded coldly. 'Then you're still not considering any of the other offers?'

'No. I want Francis and William as my mates,' the young woman said bluntly.

Diana shook her head. 'My sympathy goes only so far. Frankie and Billy are children – I'm not ready to let them go.'

'They're almost eighteen, older than I was when *you* introduced me to Duncan.'

'You were alone then – my boys have a family.'

'They will have a family with me.'

'They have no means of supporting themselves.'

'I have resources, I just explained that. They've started training as builders now, I can support them until they're earning, and we can put their skills to good use in our own home. Diana, I don't want bad blood between us – you saved my life, twice – but this isn't your decision.'

Diana looked around. Most of the younger kids had drifted off, but the young adults had stayed. Mark and John were silent. The two young men under discussion were standing in the background, watching intently.

'Mark? Do you think they're ready?'

'I do. Uni would be pointless for them. They might scrape through their college courses, but only because their sisters did their coursework for them. They have talents, but writing essays isn't one of them. Money isn't a problem, Chloe's made that clear. And we know the girl.'

'She's got two kids.'

'Hon, our boys are used to children.'

'John?' she appealed.

He shook his head. 'Give in, sweetheart. This is one that you can't win. I'm in agreement with Mark and the boys on this.'

Andy spoke up. 'I'm with Diana. They're just kids – it's a dangerous world out there, and I'd be happier with them at home for a couple more years.' Diana smiled her thanks at him.

Zoe cleared her throat, getting Diana's full attention. 'I'm with Chloe on this. Sorry Di. She's the same age now as I was when Andy found me. Her own kids were killed, she's alone, and most of the other packs out there are younger than her anyway, so Diana's argument doesn't hold. Sorry, Diana. Not only that – she's physically weak, with two small kids, and needs protection. I don't understand why Diana is trying to delay this! We've seen the way Frank and Bill watch her when she's here. They want to look after her, and there aren't any other potential mates in the country who could do a better job. Let it happen.'

Diana looked around. Seth and Noah were obviously in agreement with Zoe, and she could find no support from any direction but Andy.

'Fine. I'll back down. Maybe I am wrong on this. Do one thing for me, please? Delay this until after Seth and Noah turn twenty-one? I want all my family together on that day.'

'Next year, then?' Bill said. 'That's fine. It's earlier than we hoped, to be honest. Chloe? Is that OK with you?'

She smiled at him, affection in her eyes. 'After September next year? That's good. It's not something I want to rush into. I was still grieving for Stu when I lost the rest of my pack, and I'm certainly not ready yet. But I know you, and I trust you.'

She looked at the boys. There was no desire for them on her part; they seemed so young. This was a political match for her, and a practical one.

Zoe took charge. 'OK, the press will want a human-interest story tomorrow, to follow up on the legal stuff. I'll get on the web, see what the other packs are planning. If there's no risk of stealing anyone else's thunder, I'll announce this betrothal. They'll love it. "Tragic widow starts new pack with rescuers' sons." We can't fail, and it will stir up more public antagonism to those white bastards. The more we get Chloe and the kids in the press, the more sympathy we get.'

Anthony spoke up. 'And the less of a backlash on us when the time comes to fight back.'

Chloe looked up, her eyes burning. 'I hope it comes soon,' she said, and fell silent. Nobody spoke. Everyone was in silent agreement.

Chapter 11

Diana was curled up on the big sofa with four of her daughters. They'd made a special request to watch *Edward Scissorhands*, and were trying not to go to sleep as the film moved to its conclusion. Zoe had gone out with Mark and John to celebrate her fortieth birthday; Andy and Helen were at their own house. The children were sleeping or busy with homework or their own projects. Diana tried to remember when she'd last been alone with the kids.

She was almost asleep herself; she'd seen the film so many times. Jane commented on how cute Johnny Depp was, and Susie protested. 'Mum, tell her to be quiet, it's a sad bit.'

'Jane, be quiet, it's a sad bit,' she said absently, and drifted off again, wondering if eleven was too young to be thinking that Johnny Depp was cute, then wondering guiltily if forty-eight was too old. She opened her eyes and glanced at the TV, and decided she was definitely too old to be fancying the young Depp. After some consideration she settled on Depp in his Captain Jack Sparrow incarnation, and closed her eyes, drifting off into a fantasy where a romantic hero swept her off her feet.

In her dream, she was dressed in a tightly corseted gown, hair blowing in the wind, bosom heaving. The hero was approaching her, cocky, arrogant, dark curls framing a strong handsome face. His hand was on her waist and he was pulling her towards him; he was far too bold. 'Anthony! You cad!' she cried.

She sat up, bemused, suddenly wide awake. The closing credits were rolling, and her daughters were asleep, warm and happy on the sofa. She looked at them – they were very alike: all four of them pale and dark-haired. Nancy and Susie's hair was waist length, with a natural curl she loved to brush. Jane and Alice had recently had their sleek straight hair cut short, and were constantly reminding her they were nearly twelve and thus nearly teenagers. Asleep, though, they were still her babies. She watched them doze for a few minutes, feeling peaceful and content, then poked them awake. 'Oi! I said you could stay up and watch a film. I didn't say I'd carry you to bed afterwards.'

Jane stretched lazily, and narrowed her eyes. 'Is it very late? Are Daddies and Zoe back yet?'

'No. They're having a nice meal, then going dancing. They won't be back for hours. So get to bed and stop angling for another half-hour because it's not going to happen.'

Jane gave up, and dragged Alice off the sofa behind her. Nancy was rubbing her eyes and scowling; the prospect of the stairs was daunting. 'Mummy, my legs won't wake up,' she complained.

'Ah well, you'll have to sleep down here then. You're far too big to be carried upstairs.'

Nancy exchanged a look with Susie, and struggled off the sofa. They trailed upstairs behind their older sisters, giggling as they overheard Jane say, '…but he has such dreamy eyes…'

'Dreamy eyes, my arse,' muttered their mother, stretching and following them upstairs. The old hotel, impossibly, was almost full, with almost no spare bedrooms left. Zoe's youngest babies had just been moved out of the main bedroom and into the nursery, and Diana's own toddlers had been given a room close by the adults' rooms, which Mark and Anthony had decorated for them. It had been Seth and Noah's room, but they'd happily traded in favour of a room each.

Two large rooms had been knocked together the previous year to form the master bedroom, with space for all the adults. The two rooms to the left of it, at the end of the corridor, were also 'parents' rooms'. That was four rooms. Seventeen sets of twins and a singleton took care of another eighteen, and Noah had taken one of the few remaining spares to leave only two bedrooms free for when squabbling twins needed time out from each other. And Zoe was pregnant. Perhaps it was just as well that Frankie and Bill were moving out soon.

She started the headcount. The Kittens were out, and wouldn't be back until the early hours. Caleb and Samuel were in the music room, pretending to be rock stars; she'd caught them earlier striking poses and practising crashing chords and brooding looks. Ah well, they certainly had the genes for it. Miranda was in her room, chatting with friends worldwide on her computer. She knew that Noah and Seth would be studying hard; they were serious about their work, and the summer holidays weren't being wasted. Everyone else was asleep. She decided to go out and patrol the grounds, although everything seemed safe enough, and the alarms were set. As she passed the nearest landing window, she paused. The cottage's porch light was on, and Anthony was sitting on the step. Her mobile buzzed in her pocket; it was him:

> *Come over and play*
Scrabble and talk to me about my
grandchildren.

> *Ah yes, the old-man act.*
Wasn't it you I saw with an axe,
cutting trees back at the edge of my
woods earlier today?

> *I'm still good for*
something. Are you coming over or
not? I have great coffee.

> *I know, you stole it from*
my kitchen.

> *Old habits die hard.*
Still, it's in my kitchen now. Do
you want some?

> *It's a tempting offer.*
Make it Monopoly and I'll be over
there.

> *No, Monopoly is dull*
with two people. Scrabble or snap?

> *You win, Scrabble it is.*
I'll be there in five minutes. Get the
coffee on.

She paused at the big mirror in the hallway and picked up a hairbrush, pulling it quickly through her sleep-tangled hair.

It was a warm night, and the cottage door was open. She knocked politely.

'Ah, come in, don't stand on ceremony. I'm the guest here,' Anthony said.

She stepped into the cottage, and looked around appreciatively. It had been left alone since her mother died, but Anthony had taken it in hand, disposing of all that 'old-lady stuff' and moving in modern furniture, a music system and entertainment centre, computers and kitchen gadgets. It was tastefully decorated in a masculine style, with lots of low lighting, and not a candle or frill to be seen. She had to admit that he'd been useful over the last six months, taking his sons and Andy well in hand and redecorating the annexe and cottage. They'd made a start on the house too.

'You've done wonders with this place,' she said.

'Diana, I've been without a real home for most of my life. I've dreamed for years of somewhere like this.'

She followed him into the kitchen. The smell of fresh ground coffee and new bread was heady; a loaf was cooling on a spotless wire tray.

'It's like an advert for *Good Housekeeping*,' she laughed. 'I wonder that you ever come into the main house – it's a mess.'

'Yes, it's a terrible mess. You'd think all those children would help you to keep it tidy, wouldn't you?' he teased, putting coffee in the espresso machine.

She followed him into the living room. He glanced over his shoulder. 'Music while we play? I'm in the mood for something loud. Motörhead?'

'I'm still feeling sleepy. Led Zep?'

'You're such a romantic woman. Led Zeppelin it is.'

Diana shook her head, laughing despite herself. Anthony was impossible.

He was setting up the game at a table, placing dining chairs next to it. 'We must be comfortable. I'm too old to lie on the floor playing games.' He winked at her.

'Stop flirting with me, old man, or I'll tell your son and he'll tear your throat out.'

Anthony's eyes clouded over for a moment, and Diana was instantly sorry. He'd had far too hard a life, with too much beloved blood shed, for that comment to be even slightly amusing.

'I apologise, Anthony. That was heartless of me. Forgive me.'

'You are forgiven. You know I would forgive you anything – you're the mother of my grandchildren, you've given me a home, and made my life worth living.' His eyes flashed silver starfire, and she felt dizzy again. Then he broke the contact, and went to the kitchen. He brought back the dark, strong coffee, put on *In Through the Out Door*, and sat opposite Diana.

'I should warn you, I'm as good at this as I am at Monopoly,' she said, her voice firm.

He accepted the change of subject. 'Then, naturally, I shall wipe the floor with you. Prepare to be beaten.'

Diana took the pad and pencil, and divided the page into halves with a preternaturally straight line precisely down the middle. She wrote 'Anthony' on one side, 'Diana' on the other. 'I'll keep score,' she told him.

'You don't trust me?'

'I don't trust you,' she confirmed.

The battle was close-fought, and by the end of it their mutual respect had grown.

'I win, by two points,' declared Anthony, immensely pleased with himself.

'Yes, of course you do. Now put back that 'D' you've been sitting on for the last three goes because you had nowhere to put it. Thank you. I think I win.'

'I take it back: you are a heartless, cruel woman. Can't you allow me a tiny victory?'

'No, because you'll start imagining that you really won, and I won't have that,' she said.

They reached for the board at the same time, and their hands brushed against each other. Anthony hurriedly drew his hand back, and looked away.

Diana bit her lip. 'Anthony, I'd better go.'

'You feel it too?' he asked. 'This attraction?'

'Of course I do. That's why I'm leaving.'

'Diana… I'm sorry, I shouldn't even have asked you here. I was lonely.'

She spun round on him, dangerous and angry. 'I know what you are, and lonely is only the start of it. It wouldn't matter, though, if this feeling wasn't mutual. You're the only other man I've thought about since the day I met my pack. And, look, you're too old for me, too dangerous. You're my Alpha's father and my children's grandfather. I want you, and it's wrong.'

'You want me?' he asked.

'How could I not?' she snarled. 'You make John and Mark look like copies. You're vital, you understand the politics of our world, you sacrificed yourself for years to hide our existence, you've … you were practically *bred* to kill our enemies. You are power, you are the essence of what I need. Of course I want you.'

He reached out.

She pushed him away. 'No. Understand, because we'll only have this conversation once. This is in the open now, but this is when the flirting stops, because we're adults and I love my mates. Not because they're my pack, not because they're good providers for my children and good fathers, good mates, but because they're Mark, and John, and Andy, and enough for me. And I won't hurt them.'

Anthony shook his head. 'Andy has another woman, outside this pack. You're happy to share my son and my nephew with Zoe. Why would it hurt to have this pleasure, for us? You have your Alpha – that will never change. I could be a lesser part of the pack without it injuring my son's position.' He touched her again, lightly running his hand through her hair. She shivered under his touch, his passion, but stepped back.

She spoke clearly. 'No, I will not do this. You can't accept Mark's protection and do this. I'll trust my instincts here.'

Anthony dropped his hand, giving her one last burning look, desire and longing filling the space between them. 'I accept your choice, then. But you can see that I had to try. This is my last chance to be part of a pack, to have true mates.'

'Anthony, he's your *son*. You've spent so long apart from him that you've forgotten that. He's not a rival, he's your bloody son. How can you think of trying to hurt him like this?' Tears flashed for a moment in her eyes, then were gone. He saw them, and relented.

'Twenty years and you've not yet tired of him. It's a wonderful and terrible thing, the Alpha bond.'

She shook her head and this time the tears couldn't be stopped. 'Three years … he's only been mine for three years. We've been married for less than a year.'

Anthony stepped back, shocked by the emotion, understanding her completely now. 'And he's not sure of you? Still not sure you forgive him for that?'

'I think so. I won't give him any other reason to doubt how I feel for him.' She wiped away the tears, furious with herself.

'Then I was wrong to do this, to declare my feelings for you. I misunderstood how things were with the two of you. Do you want me to leave here? I'll go back to France, you only have to ask.'

She looked up, fire in her eyes. 'Oh no, you're not going. That would be too easy for you. We need you. You've got history to teach us – you know where we came from, and how our enemies think. I need you to teach my children to fight. Especially my older children. They don't believe me when I say that things aren't how we thought. They don't understand the danger out there, but they'll believe you. You're staying. But keep away from me, please.' She laughed shakily. 'Find yourself a woman. We'll check her out, make sure she's not been planted by the Whites. You're already the talk of the town – it shouldn't be too hard to find someone for you.'

'Ah, Diana, making plans for me already? Please leave me the dignity of organising my own love life, now I know the reason why *you* won't have me. I'll just have to settle for you being my beloved daughter-in-law.'

She gave him one last hungry look. Her words lied, but she wanted them to be true. 'I'd be proud if you would think of me as your daughter.'

He nodded in acceptance. 'Then go home, daughter. We understand each other now.'

She wanted to touch him, but drew back. The door was still open, the night was still warm.

Outside, Mark was waiting, leaning against the cottage wall, eyes closed. She stopped, shocked.

'How much of that did you hear?' she asked.

'Enough to know that I'm a cheap copy and a sensitive soul. And that at no point did you tell my father … my *father* … that you didn't want him. Go and fuck the old man if you want to so much. I'd hate to think I was getting in the way of your happiness.'

She fought down the anger. She knew him too well for that. Instead, she took hold of his ear and twisted it. 'I hate it when you sulk, Mark. It's very unattractive. Now, do you really want me to spend the night with a dirty old man, or do you want to walk me home and see how much we can cheer each other up?'

'Stop it, Diana, this is serious. You can't brush it under the carpet with a joke and a line. I'm going to bed. Don't try to join me.'

He stalked across to the main house, his shoulders tight: a picture of contained fury. Anthony spoke behind her. 'Can I do anything?'

'No, stay out of his way. He's dangerous like this,' she said absently.

'Of course he is. I would be too, in his place.'

Diana didn't reply, or even turn round. Eventually he closed the door.

John had been watching from the kitchen window. He walked across the lawn, and put his arm around her.

'What's up?'

'Anthony asked to join the pack, in a way. I refused. But not as emphatically as Mark would have liked me to.'

'Anthony? You mean he…? But he's… Oh.' John took her hand, led her to the playground. They sat on the swings. 'Are you saying that Anthony made a pass at you?'

'That's what I'm saying. And before you start, I admit I may have given him reason to think I was interested.'

'And Mark knows about this?'

'John, don't shout at me. I know exactly how Mark is feeling right now – that's what I wanted to avoid. That's why I refused Anthony. But I admitted it wasn't easy, and Mark overheard us.'

'Shit.' John stopped the swing. 'Didn't you know Mark was there? You always know when he's around – you freak him out with it.'

'No, I was…'

'You were too busy with Anthony? Well, that would have made him feel even worse. He'll either think you knew he was there and didn't care, or that Anthony can make you forget about him.'

'I know that. I *know* what the problem is. I just don't know how to fix it.'

John looked at her. 'If Mark wants to kick him out, I'll have to back him up. So will Andy.'

'I know. I don't want Anthony to leave, but it's Mark's decision in the end. How do you feel about this?'

'I think you've screwed up, but I'm not jealous, if that's what you mean.'

'Good. I think Mark has locked me out of the bedroom.'

John looked at her; she was miserable. 'Do you want to spend the night with me and Zoe?' he offered.

'No. Mark wants to punish me. It'll make him feel even worse if I sleep with you two. I need to get in to him without making too much of a din and scaring the kids. Help me?'

'Sure. Come on.'

They went back to the house. Zoe was on the landing, looking nervous. 'Mark's in a foul mood. What happened?'

Diana started to speak, but John shushed her.

'Mark, open the door. We're going to sort this out now,' he called quietly to his Alpha.

'There's nothing to sort out. It's over. I'm leaving. It didn't work out, that's all.' Mark sounded calm and composed.

John laughed nervously. 'You can't stay away, it'll kill you.'

'I'll come back when I need a fix. The bitch won't turn me down, she can't help herself, can she?'

Diana's face was bloodless. Zoe reached out to hold her, but was shrugged away.

'Mark, let me in. We can't discuss this through the door, the kids will hear.' John was concerned, reasonable.

The lock clicked and the door opened a fraction.

'Just you, John. Keep *her* away from me,' Mark growled.

John gave Diana an apologetic glance, and slipped into the room. The lock clicked again.

Zoe tried to touch her again, but Diana smiled and pushed her away. 'Not now, sweetheart. Go to bed, this isn't your problem. I'm sorry it's spoiling your birthday night.'

'Is it Anthony?' asked her mate.

'Yes.'

'I've seen the way he looks at you,' whispered the younger woman. 'He barely knows that I exist.' There was a wistfulness in her voice that made Diana smile, despite herself.

'Zoe, I turned him down. It's not going to happen. And you bloody well stay away from him.'

'You refused him? I didn't think you would.'

'What are you talking about?'

'Well, I wondered if he'd make a pass at you tonight, with you two being alone together and all that. I did wonder if Mark was testing you when he said he'd come out with us tonight.'

'Bastard. I never thought of that.' She paused. 'Look, Zoe, I'm not ready to talk about this, not until I've spoken to Mark.'

In the bedroom, John and Mark were sitting on the big bed.

'I left my wife for that bitch!' Mark was saying. He was motionless.

'That was your choice. Because you're in love with her, remember?'

'Not any more.'

'Bollocks.'

'I'm leaving. I'll find somewhere in town, visit the kids regularly… I need you to keep her out of my hair when I'm here to see them.'

'OK, I'll do that. Just out of interest, is Anthony going too, or is he staying here to console her?'

Mark was pale. 'That bastard. He ruined my mother's life, and now he's after my wife.'

'Ah, she's your wife now? A minute ago she was the bitch you left your wife for.'

'If you can't help, fuck off. I need you on my side.'

'I *am* on your side. That's why I want you to think about this clearly. What did you hear her say?'

Mark composed himself, trying to put his thoughts in order. His eyes blazed. 'She said we … me *and* you … were copies of him, that she wanted him, but wouldn't fuck him because it would hurt my feelings. She said that he was vital, everything she wanted.'

John shrugged. 'That's why he's here. He's pack-bred, he's lived to kill. He's here to teach us. We can't expect the women not to be attracted to him. It's in their blood. And he's so like you…'

Mark looked up, surprised. 'Like me? He's my father, true, but he looks like you.'

John fought down a smile. 'Looks aren't everything. You and he are so alike. I bet he's in a major strop now as well.'

'Fucking good.'

'Now, let me get this straight. She turned him down because it would hurt your feelings, and that's pissing you off?'

'Yes, because she *should* turn him down because he's an old man, and it's ridiculous that she should want him. We should be enough for her! She's got three of us!'

'And that *is* enough for her. We both know that.'

'Yes, but…'

'Did she say she couldn't resist him?'

'No, she obviously could resist him. He kept bloody pushing, though…'

'So what's the problem? Twenty years together, and you're going to leave her because she fancies someone else?'

'Excuse me? She was in bed with Xan within a year, with you after not much longer, and with Andy within two years. She's hardly loyal.'

'That's pack business, you know that. If we hadn't been connected to you, she wouldn't have looked twice at us. Besides, you married Katie right after Seth and Noah were born.'

'Fuck off, John.'

John knew he'd gone too far, and changed tack. 'I'm sorry. But she loves you. Let her in.'

'So she can bewitch me again? I've got no sense when she's around, I can't think straight.'

'Mark, stop this. You've had two decades to sort out how you feel about her, and it's more than just the Alpha bond, you know that. Don't try to put down what we all have together. You love her just as much as I do.'

Mark looked at his Beta. 'She drives me crazy. I've never been so jealous in my life.'

'Good. So let her in, and tell her that.'

The Alpha shrugged. 'I'm not making any decisions tonight. Go to Zoe … leave me in peace.'

John walked towards the door, and then paused. 'Zoe can be very understanding. Would you like…?'

'No! I would not like. Go away.' He lay on the bed, not moving.

John opened the door, and nodded to Diana, who slipped in, closing the door quietly behind her.

'Mark, I'll sleep in the other bed, OK?'

'Suit yourself.'

'You're not a cheap copy.'

'Fuck off.'

'You *are* a sensitive soul, though.'

He heard a slight, mocking edge in her tone. 'Fuck off and shut up.'

'Very sensitive,' she repeated.

He glared at her, incredulous. 'Are you *laughing* at me?'

'Yes, you're an idiot. A sensitive idiot.'

He was silent, fuming.

'Aren't I enough for you?' he asked, his voice tight, angry, contained.

'Most of the time, but then there's always John and Andy.' She refused to be intimidated.

He shrugged off the distinction. It wasn't the point. 'That's what I meant… Aren't *we* enough for you?'

She sighed, wishing he'd just get the point, that he'd understand what had happened. 'Yes, that's *why* I turned him down. Weren't you listening?'

'I wish I hadn't listened. I wish I'd never heard a word of it.' He turned away, his heart heavy.

'Why were you listening anyway?' Her tone had changed – there was a challenge there.

'I saw you talking. I was going to come in and join you, then you started shouting and I waited…'

'And you didn't go out with Zoe and John tonight because you wondered what would happen if Anthony and I spent the evening alone?' she asked quietly.

He was silent for a while, and then whispered, 'What did you do? Dinner? A nice long chat by the fireside?'

'No, I watched a video with four of our girls, then had coffee and played Scrabble with Anthony. Did you enjoy dinner and dancing with Zoe?'

'That is *not* the same.'

'No, it's not. Can I get in bed with you without you tearing my head off?'

'I suppose so, but don't touch me.'

She moved back into their bed, feeling every inch of the separation between them. She lowered her voice so that it just reached him. 'You looked great tonight. Where did you go?'

He accepted the change of subject, but spoke blankly. 'Rock club … Liverpool … it was fun. We were recognised – lots of autographs got signed. John was mobbed by three women who remembered him well. One of them remembered him very well.'

'He's such a tart,' she observed.

'Yeah, he always got all the attention.'

'Not from me, he didn't.'

Mark smiled in the dark, remembering the first time he'd seen her. 'I know, you had a crush on Andy, didn't you? When you first met us?'

'Was it so obvious?' She kept the relief out of her voice, noting the nostalgic pleasure in his.

'Yeah. Sorry, babe, but it was. He didn't do anything for the wolfie side of you, but you always went all fannish around him in the early days. That's why he was so nasty to you at first – he was trying to scare you off..'

'Yeah, well, once I knew you all it was a different story. The shine went off Andy very quickly.'

'I wish you'd met us earlier, before I met Katie.' The anger was gone; he was talking to his Diana again.

'Katie may have saved our lives … I mean, keeping me out of sight, out of public knowledge. She hid the pack.' Diana sounded very matter-of-fact.

'I know. Hard on all of us, though.'

'We're together now,' she whispered. There was a long silence; she listened to him breathing.

His voice fell further. She had to move closer to hear him. 'Ever regret it? Choosing me, instead of John?' He turned on his side, towards her.

'Oh no, I was right. You're the Alpha. You'll always be the one.'

He reached out. 'Why are you dressed?'

'I don't want to be accused of bewitching you,' she said primly.

'No? But what if *I* was thinking of putting some sort of spell on *you*?'

'Again?'

'I was thinking again, and again, and then, maybe, again?'

'Sounds good to me…'

She moved closer, and smiled in the darkness.

Chapter 12

In the morning, he was gone, his place in the bed still warm. She moved to where he'd been lying and, for a moment, enjoyed his scent, his warmth, before getting up and showering. For once they were the first up; the house was quiet. She dressed carefully, choosing casual clothes that flattered her and that she knew he loved to see her wear. She went downstairs and had a quick breakfast of toast and orange juice before quietly starting on the chores. She planned the day as she unloaded the drying rails and tumble dryers in the big hotel laundry room, folding and hanging clothes, bedding and towels and putting them into piles, wondering if she would have time to spend in the lab. Once she'd refilled the dryers and the rails with wet clothes, she reloaded the washing machines with dirty clothes and sheets. This chore had to be done twice a day, or things got out of control. She left the piles of clean dry clothes for her children to sort out and went back to the kitchen, enjoying the silence of the house. The cottage could be seen from the kitchen window, and every so often she glanced out, taking in the drawn curtains, the burning light, the shadows moving backwards and forwards.

Seth was next up. He blinked his way into the kitchen, scratching his head, his robe barely tied. He bent to kiss her on the top of her head. 'Morning, Little Mum. Any coffee yet?'

'No, hon, put some on. What are you up to today?'

He tried to think. 'Oh, maybe go to a beach with Noah – it's still warm enough. We could take a pair of littl'uns with us, if you'd like?'

'You could take the Quads...' she suggested, mischievously.

'Fine, how many of them are we allowed to drown?' he said, deadpan.

'OK, fair enough. Take Patrick and Liam, they've been restless for days. That suit you?'

'Yeah.' He banged a few cupboard doors open and shut aimlessly, then he turned to her. 'I'm glad I've caught you alone. I've got a girlfriend…'

'A girl girl?'

'Normal, yes.' He was quiet, waiting.

'Is it serious?'

'Marriage serious? It's too early to tell. But I'd like you to meet her. She knows about my wolfiness, but she's got some strange ideas about my family.'

Diana felt a lead weight in her stomach.

'I'll talk to your dad. We'll take you both out for a meal. You do know that he'll have a lot to say on the subject?'

'I know, that's why I'm telling you first. Can you see that it's not the same as it was for him? I know there are packs out there, and wolfie girls who might want me, but I'm not sure that's what *I* want from my life. I don't know if they want me for *me*, or because of who I am. Some of the girls on the wolfie forum seem to be more interested in me for my pedigree than my personality. They make me feel weird. But I've known Karen for years, she's not like that. She's really special.'

She hugged him. 'Of course she's special, if you love her. I'll talk to MarkDad.' She paused. 'Sounds of trampling baby elephants overhead… Get that loaf toasted, will you?'

She watched him move. He had more of Mark in him than he suspected; a quiet grace that was only there when he was relaxed.

Bridget and Beatrice were down next, carrying the youngest babies. Amanda and Mia were looking cross until they spotted Diana, then they reached out, shouting. The girls gladly handed them over, and she was cuddling them both when Zoe and John came in quietly, looking at her.

John spoke quietly. 'Where is he?'

'In the cottage.'

'What's happening?'

'I have no idea. They could be killing each other in there, or watching TV. I don't pretend to understand them.'

Zoe looked at her cautiously. 'Are you and Mark OK now?'

'Of course!' Diana smiled reassuringly.

John was still anxious. 'Do you want me to go and check on them?'

'Give them a while longer, eh?'

Diana was distracted by Janie and Alice, who were casually slipping through the back door. 'Oi! You two look very pretty and well dressed for a day around the house.'

'Oh, *Mum*, we're just going into Manchester to shop. We're meeting friends.'

'No, you're not.' Diana's voice was firm.

'*Mum!*' they chorused.

'No, not Manchester. It's ridiculous. You can go into Bolton or Blackburn, if you want, but not by yourselves. Take a big brother or sister with you.'

Janie was pulling a face. Diana was losing patience. She'd had it easy with Bridget and Trixie, and her heart sank at the thought of going through the Kittens' early-teenage stage again with their young sisters.

'Jane. It's not safe out there. Have you forgotten? Even if we weren't Shapeshifters, I wouldn't let a pair of eleven-year-olds go to Manchester alone. But we have enemies.'

Jane rolled her eyes. 'That was *months* ago.'

Diana had a flashback: dead toddlers, bloody against a bedroom wall. She blinked. 'No.'

Jane wasn't happy. 'Mum, I can't spend the rest of my life locked up.'

'I wouldn't dream of locking you up for the rest of your life. But if you're going out, you stay close to home, and you don't go without a protector.'

Half an hour later, the girls were back in the kitchen, a reluctant Sam in tow.

'Will he do? Because nobody else will come with us,' demanded Jane. Alice hung back, chewing her lip a little.

'Will I *do*?' Sam said, disbelief in his voice. 'If you don't want me, I'll get back to my guitar!'

'No you won't. You've got to protect us.'

'Where's Caleb?' asked their mother. She was weighing things up.

'Throwing up. He's been going cross-eyed trying those exercises to change his face.' Sam frowned. 'It makes him ill. I tell him he's trying too hard, but he won't listen.'

Diana made a mental note to speak to Caleb later. 'I'd rather he went with you as well, but if he's ill, he's ill. What about Bill? Frankie? Any of your big sisters?'

Jane looked like she was close to stamping her foot, but wisely reconsidered. 'They're all busy.'

Diana frowned; she'd had other plans for the day. 'OK, I give in. I'll come with you. Ring your friends and tell them there's a change of plan. Sam, I still want you around to watch my back, so don't slope off. Wait for me. I'll be a while – I have to talk to your dad about something.'

Sam nodded, trying to look grown up and responsible. 'Tell me when you're ready and I'll round 'em up.'

Diana watched him walk away. He'd grown over the summer, and was reaching his full height, but he still acted like a kid most of the time. It was fine – he had plenty of time to grow up.

At ten, Mark left the cottage. Diana was sitting under a tree, pretending to read a genetics journal.

'I'm here,' she called. He walked over to her. She watched him cross the grass, wondering if the day would ever come when just looking at him would lose its thrill. He was wearing faded blue jeans and a battered black T-shirt.

He stood for a moment in front of her, enjoying the look she was giving him, before sitting next to her.

'Well, that's sorted then,' he told her.

'Are you going to tell me what's been going on between you and Anthony? Or am I going to have to get it out of him?' she teased.

'You're not getting anything out of him. He's grounded.'

She laughed, then stopped. 'You're serious?'

'Damn right, I'm serious. I had to do something. I can't just ignore him making a pass at my wife, can I? He's my father. I couldn't beat the shit out of him, much as I wanted to. So we've had a long talk, and he's staying. But he's grounded for a month. He only leaves the cottage at night, for fighting practice with me, John or Andy. He doesn't communicate with any other member of the pack, including you and Zoe. That includes letters, waving through the window, emails, webchats, Morse code with the kitchen light, or anything else he might dream up. And he doesn't leave these grounds.'

'Mark, you can't do that, you don't have the right…'

'I think I do, and he agrees. He's on my territory. If you have any objections, I'd be really interested in hearing them.' He tilted his head, waiting.

She shook her head, said nothing.

'No? Good. I apologise for my behaviour last night. I lost my temper, and I was unreasonable with you. I said things I didn't mean. I was hurtful. But I should have put my foot down weeks ago about this – I could see what was going on.'

'Put your *foot* down?' she said. 'I'm not a child!'

'No, you're a grown woman with a stupid crush. Do I need to have this talk with Zoe too?'

Diana lowered her eyes. 'No, I've done that already.'

'Her too? Does John know?'

'It's not like that. She's got a bit of a crush on Anthony, that's all. He's not interested in her.'

'I bet he's not. Make it clear that she's not to go near him.' He smiled – a small, satisfied smile. 'I'm getting the hang of this Alpha thing, I think.'

'I think you are,' she agreed. 'Now that's sorted out, I'm going into town with Jane and Alice. Sam's coming too. Fancy coming along?'

Mark's eyes lit up. 'Hey, we could pretend to be a normal family! Mum and Dad and three kids.'

Diana faltered, shaken. 'Is that what you want? Do you miss that? Being with Katie and the boys?'

Mark was appalled. 'Oh, no, Diana, no. I was joking. I didn't mean that at all.'

She stood, turned her back on him and walked away.

He wondered if they'd ever be sure of each other, and followed her. 'Diana…'

'I've got things to do,' she called back, not looking round.

He followed behind, helpless. She was heading for the lab. The door slammed in his face, and he stood looking at it. He kicked it. 'Fuck.'

It was her territory. He knocked. There was no reply. He went in anyway. She was at the big walk-in fridge, taking out samples. Her face was cold.

'I'm busy. Could you tell the kids I won't be going shopping with them? And please don't let them go alone. Perhaps you could go with them, pretend to be a one-parent family? Does that appeal?'

'Is this a retaliation for last night?' he said.

'No. It's me being pissed off because whatever I do, however hard I try, it always comes back to Katie. You didn't choose *me*. You counted kids and decided you'd rather be here.'

'That isn't true. How can you say that when you know it's not true? So what are you saying? You don't believe that I want you? Diana, I can't make it any plainer how I feel about you.'

She shook her head. 'You talk about wanting me. You talk about how you "feel about me". For once in your life, could you tell me that you love me?'

'I do tell you!'

'In bed. That's different.'

'I'm not like John. I don't go around showing my feelings.'

'I don't want you to be like John. I just want to hear you say it. Here and now. Is it so hard?'

Mark shook his head. 'Katie was never...' He shut up.

Diana was white with fury. 'Katie was never what? Bothered about hearing how you felt about her? Upset that two days after she had your children you waltzed off and married someone prettier? Left her alone for a year until she was almost dead and had to force herself on you?'

'Diana, I'm here now.'

'I'm so *bloody* grateful. Thank you *so* much for that. Now can I get on with this work, please?'

'Diana, you're never like this...'

'I know. I'm tough. I never cry. I'm fucking Wonder Woman. Go now, or I'll have to kick you out.'

'You never cry. You don't.'

She had her back to him.

He spoke with a dawning realisation. 'You never cry in front of me. That's it, isn't it? What sort of love do we have if you can't do that? Why can't you trust me now?'

Her voice was trembling. 'You won't give yourself to me completely. Last night showed that you don't trust me. You said you were going to leave me. Mark, you said that you were going to leave me again. I'd die if you did that, don't you realise? How can you even say that? I need to be sure of you.' She was baffled; everything was falling apart again.

'I've already apologised for that. I knew when I said it I could never do it, and that's another reason why I was so angry. Let's get this straight, then. I'll never, ever leave you again, and I will never threaten to leave you again. Oh, and Katie may have been prettier than you, but that's not why I married her. I was in love with her then – you know how it was.'

'*Mark!* You just aren't helping.'

'What now?'

'Nothing…' She still had her back to him. 'I know – in my head – that you love me. I do.'

'And in your heart?'

'I'm still not sure.'

'Diana, men just don't go around saying "I love you" at the drop of a hat.'

'Like hell they don't. It's just you. Here, I'll ring Andy.' She rang her mate at his home, putting it on speaker so Mark could hear.

'Andy? Hiya hon. I'm in the lab. Can you put Helen on, please? I've lost the permission slips for Eva's bloodwork – she'll know where I put them.'

'OK. You all right?'

'I'm fine. How's Chloe?'

'Better. Putting on weight, dreading the anniversary in October, but looking forward to next year. She'll be fine. Look, Helen's here. I've got to go – Eva's making tea and I promised to help. I love you.'

'I love you too, sweetheart.'

She looked hard at Mark, and then chatted to Helen for a minute before scribbling something down on a pad and putting the phone down.

'OK, shall I ring John?'

'No, you've made your point. I'm an emotionless robot. Please don't ring John. He told *me* that he loved me three times yesterday. I don't need another demonstration.' His expression was dry.

She was looking at him, calmer. 'You still can't say it!'

'Take me to bed and I'll say it a thousand times.'

'I know that, but that's not my point. Come with me… Hang on, I'll put these samples back.'

'Where are we going?'

'The tree.'

He followed her to the old tree in the garden, and she pointed to something carved into the trunk. 'Diana loves Mark' it said, within a heart.

'Do you remember when I said I'd do that?' She was smiling.

'I do. It was the day after we rescued Chloe. Did the kids laugh at you?' he asked.

'Oh yes.'

He looked at the tree, and then looked at her. Sometimes he thought he could look at her forever. How could he not give her what she wanted? Something brittle snapped inside him; it felt like the last shard of their old life.

'Sod it, then. I'm going for a knife – I'll be back in a minute.'

She watched as he cut 'Mark loves Diana' into the tree, below her words, then kissed her forehead.

'You soppy old git,' she said.

'It's cos I love you. Now, do I get laid today or not?'

'You said it! And you already got laid.'

'Doesn't count – I've slept since then. And I've been feeling peculiarly horny since I grounded my dad.'

'I wondered why you were following me around.'

'Ah, that's because I love you.' He felt freed. 'Now tell me – it works both ways, you know.'

'I love you, Mark. See, it's easy.' It was, easier than she could have ever suspected.

'You might get fed up of it!'

'Not gonna happen.' Her smile was getting bigger and bigger.

'Shall we take the kids shopping before or after I fuck your brains out?' he teased.

'Before, I'm enjoying this.'

'I love you.'

'Great. I'll get Sam, you get your credit cards. The girls will appear as soon as they see Dad with his wallet out. It's like magic.'

'I love you,' he repeated.

'Now you're taking the piss.'

'I love you, and I think I'm developing a sense of humour.'

'Now you are definitely taking the mickey.' She was laughing.

'I love you.'

She silenced him with a kiss.

Ten minutes later, three kids piled into the back seat of the Saab, and they were off, Zoe checking them out through the gate, Sam, Diana and Mark all watching for danger as they drove into town, Janie and Alice complaining about not being trusted by themselves yet.

'What are we shopping for?' asked Mark.

'Birthday presents for Meg, Beth, Tara and Louise. They're eight soon.'

'Blimey, doesn't time fly? I thought Janie and Alice were eight,' he teased.

'Dad! We're nearly twelve.'

'You're just eleven,' corrected Sam. He was clearly thinking about something. 'Mum?'

'What, my love?'

'Why is there such a big gap between me and Caleb, and Janie and Alice?'

Mark and Diana exchanged a look. 'Well, we thought eleven children were enough,' said Mark.

Sam dismissed that explanation. 'No, really. Did you fall out or something?'

Diana half turned. 'Really! I remember. We did think that eleven kids were enough.'

'What changed your mind?'

'I think it was because your dad got broody again.'

'*I* got broody?' exclaimed Mark. He was happy and relaxed.

'You got *something*, anyway. And nine months later, we had the girls.'

Janie and Alice were smiling. 'You really wanted us, didn't you?' Alice said.

'Oh yes. I was thinking, if we don't have more babies now, I won't have any eleven-year-olds to mither the life out of me in 2015,' said Diana, deadpan.

'Get down!' Mark said clearly, braking sharply.

His family instinctively obeyed. Gunshots cracked out, and the windscreen shattered. Mark scanned the road; it was empty. There was a muzzle flash from the trees ahead, and Jane screamed as a second bullet grazed the roof. Mark reversed fast to a gap in the barriers and swung the car round to the opposite carriageway. He put his foot down hard and sped away.

'Fuckers. Is everyone OK?' he said clearly.

Diana was crawling on to the back seat. 'Sam's hit. Whites?'

'Probably. How bad?'

'Just get us to the hospital. Janie, ring home. Alice, ring Andy. We've got trouble again.'

Alice was shaking, but called Andy.

'Daddy? It's me, Alice. We've been shot at. Mummy says I've got to call you.'

'Where are you?'

'We're near Chorley. We had to turn round. We're taking Sam to hospital.'

Groping where the blood spurted thickest, Diana had found a wound on Sam's thigh and ripped a length from her skirt to act as a tourniquet. She looked up. 'Just tell Andy that me and Mark are here with you. Everyone else is home except Seth and Noah and…?'

'Patrick and Liam…' rapped out Mark. There were cars ahead, and he was planning a path between them.

Andy was calm. 'OK, we'll be on guard here. Tell Mum and Mark not to worry about us, just look after Sam. I'll ring the police now. Which car are you in?'

'Mum … which car?'

Diana spoke loudly so that Andy could hear her. 'Saab. Andy, we're in John's Saab. Give the details to the police. We need to get Sam to hospital without being stopped for bloody speeding.' She was sweating; Sam was pale, unconscious. Alice ended the call.

'Janie, Andy will ring the police.'

Janie nodded; she was on the phone. 'What? No, we're going to the hospital. It's Sam. He's been shot. I think it was those white-wolf people.' She was almost in tears.

Diana glanced up. 'Janie, be grown up. We need you to be grown up. Remember? Nearly a teenager?'

'I didn't mean it. I just wanted to go shopping. I didn't want Sam to get hurt.'

Diana took her phone. 'Who is it?'

'Caleb. I picked the phone up.' His voice was shaking. 'Sam's been shot?'

'Yes. Be brave, son. I know you can be. Tell John and Zoe. Make sure that someone rings Seth and Noah to tell them what's going on. Tell them I trust them to do what's safest.' She ended the call and concentrated on her injured boy.

Mark had bitten through his lip; blood ran down his chin. 'Get out of my way,' he was whispering.

Diana put her arm around Sam, pulled him close. 'Mark, put the heating up,' she said quietly.

'Done.'.

Janie was looking at her brother. 'I didn't want him to get hurt.'

'Then you shouldn't have shot him, should you?' said her mother.

'But I didn't—'

'Exactly. You didn't. It's not your fault. Now, he's getting cold. Cuddle up to him.'

'How long have we got?' Mark said. He was clear and controlled.

'Minutes…' she said.

Diana's phone rang. It was Zoe. 'I've called for an ambulance. They're on the road now, and they need your exact whereabouts. I've given the paramedics your number.'

'OK, thanks.'

Diana ended the call to Zoe and accepted the strange number that immediately flashed up.

'We're about two miles away, on the other side of the road. We'll cross and wait in the car park of the Red Cat. How bad is he?'

'Very. Can you give him blood on board?'

'We can transfuse if we have a donor.'

'We have four donors. Don't worry about cross-matching, we're all fine with each other.'

Mark was speeding now, having cut through traffic.

'Where?' he barked.

'Red Cat car park. Get a move on.'

A minute later, they pulled into the car park. The ambulance was just pulling up, the back doors opening.

Mark lifted Sam and carried him over to the ambulance, leaving the back seat soaked with blood. Diana ran after him, then glanced back at the car.

'Janie, Alice, get over here *now*,' snapped Diana, and they ran to her.

'Is he still alive?' Mark had lowered Sam on to the trolley.

'He's still got a pulse, but he's just stopped breathing. I'm putting him on a respirator. I'll give him fluids, try to stop the blood loss, then start the transfusion. My name is Mick, just so you know.' He was checking Sam over. 'Are you following us in that?' The paramedic glanced at the abandoned car as he worked on the pale, motionless boy.

'No, we're all staying in here,' Diana said, still utterly calm.

Mark spoke to the driver, loud and fast 'I'm Mark Preston, I'm a shapeshifter. I'm going to Change, I need to know that you're who you say you are. You're in no danger. Please stay calm, and help my boy.' He Changed, and started to check the scents around the ambulance doors, keeping his distance from the medics as they got used to the situation. Satisfied at the lack of White Pack scents, he jumped into the back of the ambulance to join Diana.

'Is the wolf going to stay like that? I'm not sure it's hygienic.'

'He's the boy's father, and he's staying like that to protect us,' she confirmed.

Mark was lying at the foot of the trolley, his daughters sitting at the other side of the ambulance. They were shaking – the reaction kicking in.

The ambulance moved off.

Diana spoke. 'This was a deliberate attack on us. We won't feel safe in a public hospital. What are Sam's chances with private care at home?' She was baring her arm and exposing a vein for the paramedic as she spoke.

'I'm not commenting on Sam's chances yet,' he said quietly. 'I'm gonna cross-match anyway…' he said apologetically, taking a small sample of her blood and testing it quickly against her son's. He looked up. 'Amazing … conflicting blood types, but no coagulation.'

'Freaky, isn't it?' She managed a grin. 'Now hook me up before we lose him.' As she gave her blood to her son, Diana watched Janie and Alice. 'You need a sugary drink each,' she told them, and the paramedic nodded.

'Water and glucose sachets in that hatch.' He motioned, and Janie reached up and started to mix them, giving half to her sister.

The paramedic looked anxiously at Sam: the teenager was grey, his pulse thready.

'I can't take blood from minors,' he said. 'And I can't take any more from you.'

'Take another pint, and put me on a saline drip,' she ordered.

'I shouldn't.'

'But you will,' she told him.

He was lost in those green eyes. He couldn't argue; he continued the transfusion. He checked Sam, and looked up. 'His pulse is weakening.'

'He's a strong boy. Just take whatever he needs from me. Will he live?'

'He's gone…'

Mick stopped the transfusion, and got the defibrillator out. Diana glanced at her daughters, who were holding on to each other, not looking at Sam. His body jerked, then was still again.

Mick turned, got a long needle, and injected adrenalin directly into the boy's heart, then shot it with current again. Again, Sam jerked, then was still. His eyes were glassy.

Diana was pale, watching the man work on her son, shocking him, injecting him, massaging his heart.

Eventually he stopped, and looked at her, shaking his head. 'I'm so sorry.'

She nodded, sitting by her son, taking his cooling hand in hers, brushing his hair back. 'Can you still hear me, baby? Mum and Dad are here. You've been so brave, so very brave, but you're tired. It's time to go to sleep. Sammy, my beautiful boy, my love.' Her voice was calm and reassuring.

Janie and Alice were crying. The wolf stood up and Changed, and lifted his son into his arms. Sammy's hair fell in a soft dark wave over his father's arm.

Mark spoke clearly. 'Can you ask the driver if he'd take us home, please? There's really no point in carrying on to the hospital.'

Mick nodded. The job never got easier, and the dignity of bereaved parents never got easier to bear.

The ambulance turned, sirens off, and made for the house. Diana and Mark cradled Samuel together, silent, lost.

As they got to the gate, Diana's phone rang. It was Zoe.

'Is that you at the gate?'

'Yes. Open it, please.'

'How's Sam?'

'Sam's dead. Open the gate, Zoe.' Diana's voice was tightly controlled.

Mark Changed again, and jumped out of the doors as soon as he heard the click and whine of the gate opening. He sniffed around until he was satisfied there were no strangers around, and jumped back in, licking Diana's hand. The ambulance drove up to the front of the house, where John and Zoe were quietly waiting.

John carried Sam's body up to the room that the boy shared with Caleb. A shocked silence was taking hold all around the house. Diana lifted a half-read science fiction novel and a pack of playing cards from the bed, putting them carefully to one side, then let her mate put their dead son on his bed. Caleb was sitting, silent, on the other bed.

John went back downstairs, struck dumb. Bridget was on the phone, crying, telling Andy the news. The children were drifting around, not knowing what to do, who to turn to. Mick was waiting in the kitchen. John poured two glasses of water, and gave one to the paramedic.

'I suppose there are formalities?'

'Yes. I can certify death, but not the cause. A doctor will visit – there'll be an inquest, as it wasn't a natural death. My partner has informed the police.'

'It was murder,' John said flatly.

'I'll arrange things as quickly as possible,' said Mick. He took a sip from the glass, then his bleeper went off.

'I'm sorry, I have to go.' He left through the back door, and John watched as the ambulance left. He opened and closed the gates, and went back upstairs. The world was quiet; everything seemed to be happening too slowly, and too quickly.

Zoe was holding Caleb, trying to ease his shaking. Diana was sitting on the bed, next to Sam, dry-eyed. John went to her, offering comfort.

She shook her head. 'I want Mark. Where's Mark?'

Mark was halfway through the door as she spoke. 'I'm here.' He was human again, dressed in black. He held his wife as her tears began to fall. He stroked her hair. 'I'm here, I'm with you,' he whispered. He looked up at his cousin, and nodded. 'Let Anthony out. He can go for Noah and the others. Tell him we've lost our son. Get the word out to the other packs that the Whites are back in the country. Remind our friends we can now legally kill in self-defence, but they are not to put themselves at any risk for us – we can fight our own battles. Andy will be here soon – keep an eye on the gate. He'll have the women and children with him. I want someone on the phone to them from now until the minute they get here. Zoe, how are you doing?'

She looked up. 'I'm up to this.'

He stroked her face. 'Zoe, I know it won't be easy, but I want you to put yourself first. Don't tire yourself out looking after everyone. You're pregnant, and I'm not going to lose those babies. I know that you and Diana got into the habit of coping, but John and I are here full-time now, let us deal with things.' He looked at Diana, who had, incredibly, gone to sleep in his arms. 'Shit. She's given Sammy too much blood. She needs to eat and drink.' He kissed his wife's head and carried on talking to Zoe, knowing that Caleb was listening. 'I remember the day that Sam and Caleb were conceived. The Bees were just tiny babies, just a few weeks old. I was hardly ever around then, you know?'

Zoe nodded, glad that he was talking. Caleb had quietened in her arms, listening, his breathing steadier. 'Touring?'

'Yeah, that and being married, and stupid. I was such a bastard, you know? The day after Katie had Jacob, I was round here, wanting my wolfie fix, and Diana was so glad to see me. She was alone a lot then, and it never occurred to me that *she* might want company, or help. She was always so competent and on top of things.'

Zoe looked up. 'Jacob's birthday was yesterday … same day as mine, isn't it?'

'Yeah. Diana and I started these two off sixteen years ago today.' Diana was soundly asleep, but she was crying. He wiped the tears away with a corner of Sam's pillowcase. He smiled wistfully. 'It was a madhouse. Looking back, I wonder how she ever coped. She was alone with nine kids – even Seth and Noah were still under five. And when I turned up, it wasn't with the intention of helping her, or giving her any support. I was there because I wanted my Alpha fix, and because Katie was all wrapped up with Jake. I wanted some attention for myself. The Bees were a month old, and it was the first time I'd seen them since the day they were born, my own eldest daughters. And I just walked in, unannounced, and she must have been busy, must have had so much to do, but as soon as I came in she started making dinner for me, asking how my new baby was… She didn't ask how Katie was – I remember that – but she was genuinely interested in Jake.'

'Did you love her?' Zoe asked.

'No. To be honest, I didn't. I was such a pompous arsehole, you know? I can see the same thing in Noah now, the same arrogance I had. It was always Katie, Katie, Katie, and the band, and making my mother proud of me. Diana and her nine beautiful babies just felt like a dirty secret. Loving her was John's side of things, and I left him to it.'

'But you were her Alpha…'

'Yeah. And every time I saw her in a mad giggling fit over something John had said, I wondered why she'd chosen me – they're so obviously made for each other. Sorry, Zoe … I didn't mean it like that.'

She nodded. 'Oh, I know how close they are. They're practically telepathic with each other these days. It's OK. I love both of them. It doesn't bother me. But you're wrong, you know? It's you and Diana who were made for each other. You were the one she was waiting for – she told me. She knew it when she first saw you.'

Mark looked up, grateful, then continued. 'Anyway. Sixteen years ago… She gave me steak and chips, veg, gravy. I remember thinking it was the first decent meal I'd had for weeks. Yeah, I was a git, wasn't I? I had three new babies, just a month's difference in age between the Bees and Jake, and there I was, complaining about being fed ready meals and sandwiches. Diana seemed worried about something. I might not have loved her, but I did care about her, you know? I asked her what was up, and she asked if I wanted to stop having babies with her now that Katie and I had started a family. She was very reasonable about it, and said that it was OK, she understood, but how would I feel if she had more children with John!'

Zoe nodded. 'She wasn't stupid.'

'No, she played me like a violin. Of those nine kids, only four were biologically mine, although I think, at the time, I was the only one of her mates who instinctively didn't differentiate on those grounds. Alpha thing, I suppose. I've always treated them all the same: yours, Diana's, John's, Andy's. I look at them and see *my* children. Anyway, back to the subject. Every one of them *felt* like mine, but my brain just kept ticking away, and it didn't like the odds, and it certainly didn't want a situation where John's children outnumbered mine.'

Zoe was still holding Caleb, who had stayed silent. She rocked him gently. He was bigger than her, but it didn't matter. 'So you stopped over, that night?'

'No. How could I have explained that to Katie? But I was with Diana all evening. I wanted her to love me, even if I didn't feel the same way. I'm not doing well here – I wanted to tell you about a nice day, about making love with Diana for hours, about how and why Sammy and Caleb were conceived, and I've ended up making it sound like we were both scoring points. It just wasn't like that. It was pretty damn beautiful really, thinking back on it. We both wanted to please each other, and we wanted to make two new lives. And now one of them has been taken away from us.'

Caleb spoke up. 'You love Mum now? Don't you?' He was pale and cold, watching Mark, desperate for him to say the right thing.

'Yeah, I love her. More than I could ever tell. And she loves me too, do you know that?' There was pride in his voice, through the pain.

Caleb stood up. 'Oh, everyone knows that. Can I hold Sammy for a while?'

Mark shook his head. 'He's cold – he's not there any more.'

'I know, Dad. I just want to hold him.'

'Then you do that, for as long as you want to.'

Diana stirred as Caleb climbed on to his twin's bed. She opened her eyes, smiling at Mark, then remembering and looking round. The single bed was cramped, with Caleb lying next to his twin's body, touching his face, straightening his hair.

'He's all bloody,' the boy said softly. 'What's going to happen to him?'

Zoe spoke up; being a writer led her to research all sorts of things. 'It's an unnatural death, so there'll be a post-mortem. The authorities will want his body for a while, but they'll give it back to us…' She was looking at Diana.

'And we'll bury Sammy in the woods. We'll plant an oak tree on his grave.' His mother was calm. 'Caleb, what are you doing?' she asked quietly.

'I'm cutting his hair. Before he's taken away from us. There's enough for everyone to have some, to remember him by.'

'Oh my boys,' she sobbed. Mark held her close.

Someone was knocking on the door. Mark couldn't speak so he nodded at Zoe.

'Come in,' she called.

It was Anthony. His eyes were reddened, his face streaked with tears. He kneeled by the bed and took hold of Mark's hands. 'Whatever you decide to do about this, I'm with you.'

Mark acknowledged his father with a single nod.

'May I speak to Diana and Caleb?' Anthony said.

'Of course. I'm lifting your punishment. It's no longer appropriate.'

'Thank you, Mark. Diana, if there's anything I can do to make this easier for you, tell me.'

She struggled to speak, finally finding her voice. 'Yes, I need some time alone, with Caleb and Mark. Will you help the others to deal with the press, and look after the children? And where are Seth and Noah? I thought you were going for them?'

'The police brought them home. They rang for help, didn't dare go back to their own car. I passed the patrol car on the way up to get them. I spotted the kids and followed them home. Noah wants blood, I should warn you.'

'So do I,' said Caleb clearly, looking up.

'Ah, Caleb. I know what it is to lose a twin. Come to me when you're ready to talk.' Anthony's voice was so quiet, but everyone in the room heard him.

'I feel like I'm dead too,' the teenager said, his voice flat.

Anthony was quiet for the space of five heartbeats, grief taking his voice. Eventually he spoke. 'That will pass. I have to say one thing, Caleb … don't try to be "Caleb and Samuel". We have to accept that he's gone. I don't want to lose you too.' He turned back to his son. 'Mark, our enemies are not giving up. We need to arrange some sort of security for Katie and her boys. Would you like me to deal with it?'

'Yes. Of course. I'll pay for it, whatever it takes. She's not to come here, though, make that clear, although my boys are always welcome.'

Anthony turned to Zoe. 'Your husband needs you downstairs. Everyone else is here safely now. We'll give Mark and Diana some time alone.'

Caleb stood up, and made to follow Anthony and Zoe out of the room.

Mark spoke up. 'Caleb! That doesn't mean you. Come here, son.'

With Zoe out of the room, Diana burrowed into Mark. 'Can I scream the place down now?' she whispered hoarsely. He held her tightly.

'It was so quick, Mark. I couldn't stop it.'

'You couldn't have done anything else. I should have been more careful. I was too relaxed.'

'No, if you hadn't driven out of there so quickly, they'd have got us all. You spotted them even before they started shooting.'

'The Whites? Again?' said Caleb. He was back with them, sitting with his arms around his legs, next to his father.

'Again.' Mark was grim.

'What did Sam ever do to hurt them?'

'Same as all of us – your Granddad explained a few things to me. Sammy was born free of their pack, he has non-Shapeshifting friends. He might even have married a non-Shapeshifter one day. They think of us as rogues, rebels, mongrels, and they won't be happy until we're dead.' Mark managed a small smile. 'The main thing that's kept us safe is your mother's reputation. They think she's the bitch queen from hell. She set up the biggest 'mongrel' pack in living memory, and hid it well enough for us to grow strong. And they hold her responsible for setting up all the new packs in Britain. It's not just her own children who are a threat to them and their beliefs, it's all the Shapeshifting people, all over the country, who are happy in their packs. They're scared of her.'

'But Mum's not *that* scary.'

'She is, to that group of misogynistic religious nutters. She's managed to pass down her way of doing things to all the new packs. Women and men rule the packs jointly in this country, and we tolerate – welcome, sometimes – relationships with non-Shapeshifters outside the pack. It pisses the White Pack off no end. And that's why they attacked today.'

'He's really dead … my twin. What do I do now?'

'You grieve, and you live, and you never, ever forget him. Just like me and his mum and the rest of the pack.' He glanced over at Diana. She was holding Sammy's body and finally letting the tears come freely, rocking him gently to her. And that did it for him. Finally he let his own tears come, and held them both. Caleb laid his head in his father's lap and fell into sleep, wondering why he couldn't cry.

Half an hour later, John came in. Diana was asleep again, wrapped around her son's cold body. John eased her away, lifting her and carrying her into the second parents' room, where Zoe was waiting. He was surprised to hear his own voice; it sounded just the same as it always had even though the world had fallen apart.

'The doctor will be here soon to certify, and the undertaker won't be far behind. They'll be taking Sammy away. It's best if Diana isn't there when he comes. If she wakes up, you have to persuade her to rest. Andy will bring some food and drink for both of you in a minute. Don't forget, she lost a lot of blood, and she's done nothing to replace it yet. If she won't eat and drink, I'm calling for a nurse and she's going on a drip.'

Zoe was stroking Diana's face. 'I'll look after her – don't bring any more strangers into our home. How's Caleb?'

'Asleep. Mark won't let go of him. Andy and I will take Sammy downstairs, show his body to the rest of the family. Anthony has been making sure they all know what happened – it's amazing how many rumours were going round. Helen wanted to call out the doctor to sedate Jane and Alice, but Andy and Anthony wouldn't hear of it. The girls were hysterical, but it's natural, and they've started to calm themselves down now. Miranda is with them, they'll be fine with her. Miranda doesn't want to see Sammy, though, says the new Shapeshifter laws don't cover her, and she's ready to kill as it is.'

'John? Are *you* OK?'

'I'm OK as long as I have to be. Sammy… Hell, I loved that kid. He never once teased Caleb about his problems, not once. Look, Andy's here. He's brought food and drink for both of you. We'll take Sammy downstairs now. Do you want to see him before he's taken away?'

'No, not again. I've seen enough. Go, I'll look after Diana.'

Zoe glanced at Andy; he was standing in the doorway.

He entered the room and put the tray of food down next to the bed. He was dry-eyed, coldly furious, death in his eyes. 'If she's still asleep in half an hour, wake her up and *make* her eat something. And you have to eat too.'

The men left, and went to the next room. A low cry from Mark let Zoe know that they'd taken Sammy. She sat, dry-eyed, holding her sleeping mate, listening to the children's voices downstairs as they said goodbye to their brother. She heard another vehicle arrive, and listened as strangers carried their child away.

'Diana…' she whispered. Her mate stirred. 'Diana, wake up.'

Diana struggled to consciousness. 'Zoe? Oh hell, it's not just a bad dream, is it?'

'No, honey. Will you drink something? Everything is taken care of, and I'm going to look after you, sweetheart. All you have to do today is get strong, because we need you to be strong.'

'They killed my baby,' the Alpha said matter-of-factly. 'I'm going to wipe those bastards out. I should have done it months ago. I'm not sitting here mourning like some old woman. Give me some water, I'm parched. I'm dizzy. What have they done to me? Did you let them drug me?'

'You're confused, love. You gave Sammy a lot of your blood. Nobody has drugged you. Who would dare? Here, drink this.'

Diana drank deeply, and asked for more. Zoe poured another glass of water, and offered her some fruit.

Diana ate slowly and steadily, devouring the chicken sandwiches and the sweets, and drinking another litre of water. 'How's John?' she asked.

'Coping,' Zoe said. 'Anthony and Andy are helping him. Helen is in the annexe with her girls – she's in a state. Chloe is in the woods. She's gone wolf, and her mates-to-be are with her. Can't you hear them howling?'

'Ah, it's Chloe, is it? I wondered. I've never heard her wolf voice before. I thought maybe the stress had pushed Janie or Alice to an early Change.'

'No, it's Britain's very own next Alpha female. Don't worry, Anthony assures me that she won't take our sons on your land – you and Mark have marked it well – she's inhibited so long as she's here.'

'Right now, I don't give a damn. I'm getting used to the idea. Oh, I'm going back to sleep, it seems, whether I like it or not,' she said weakly, and closed her eyes, falling straight into an exhausted slumber.

Zoe laid her down on the bed and covered her gently, noting that her colour was better, her breathing more even and her pulse back to normal. She went downstairs. Andy was talking seriously to the Kittens.

'No! It's not your fault. Look, if you'd agreed to go into town with Janie and Alice, it's entirely likely that all four of you would be dead right now. Yes, you're fast and strong and clever, but Mark and Diana dealt with things perfectly. They saved as many lives as possible – it was just an unlucky bullet that got Sammy. We can't change what happened, and it's absolutely normal for all of us to wonder what we could have done to change things. But it's done, and it's *not* your fault, do you understand me?'

'What if Mum and Dad blame us?'

'What if the sky turns green and the grass turns pink?' Andy asked them.

Zoe managed a smile, and looked up at her tall packmate. 'You tell 'em, Andy. The only people Diana are blaming are the White Pack.'

John was at a computer, exchanging information with other packs. He looked up. 'Another hit. Those young women in London, the ones who are living together but aren't ready to join packs yet, they've reported a wolf attack on them. They fought them off, but they're all wounded. No fatalities, but the Whites tried to kidnap both of the blondes in the house.'

'How many Whites?' Mark was at the door with his father. The Alpha looked exhausted, but was calm.

'Ten, eleven … maybe twelve.'

'How did the women do? Any Whites injured? Killed?'

'The women survived. Those of them with parents have called for help and protection. They'll be fine. The police are swarming around the house. The women think they may have blinded one of the Whites, and there's an ear and half a tail been left behind by the attackers. Mark, come here. Look.'

An email had just come in. It was from a young man who claimed to be from the White Pack:

> *My packmates have gone too far. They are killing women and children. This isn't the war I was brought up to believe in. I don't want to be part of this. How can I surrender to you?*

Anthony nudged John away from the computer and took over. He typed out a reply:

*Bring us the heads of five of your
brothers, and be prepared to be
kept prisoner until this war is over.
Believe us, it has started.*

Anthony met John's gaze. 'That should test his resolve, and his veracity. My bet is that he's just trying to distract us. Ignore him for now, we have things to do. Mark, are you ready for this?'

'Will they be expecting retaliation?'

'No. They'll be expecting us to mourn for days and issue a press release. They think you're soft.'

'Where are they now?' Mark's eyes were black pits of fury.

'A group just tried to attack that small pack in Chester: two women, one man, four babies. Their neighbours ran the Whites off, though. They're a popular family – the women run the local hairdressing salon, the man's a supervisor in a factory.'

'Good, we're getting support from our friends. Where will that group go next? Are they the ones who shot at us?'

'Back north, I'd guess, toward us. They could be – there's been time for that. The Midlands and Welsh packs are pretty strong with good security. The Merseyside pack – Michaela Drummond's lot – is stupidly vulnerable. They have two pregnant women, and haven't got any security in their house. They weren't anticipating trouble yet, and have been putting all their efforts into rebuilding the Whitby site.' Anthony's face betrayed his disgust.

Mark spoke up. 'Right, we'll have to assume they're the next target. We're heading out to help them. Are they urban or rural?'

'Pretty rural, no close neighbours,' said Andy, checking a map.

Mark decided. 'Get Chloe. She can fight with us, she deserves this chance. Her mates-to-be will stay here – home defence if we've got it wrong – or if we don't make it back. That group who hit the women in London could be on our doorstep in three or four hours. Bridget and Trixie stay here too. They'll fight better as defenders on home turf than as an attacking force. Diana and Zoe stay at home – they're in no state to fight.'

Diana was at the door, pale but steady. 'You're going nowhere without me,' she snarled.

'That's my girl.' He didn't even think of arguing. He was shocked but pleased to see her on her feet. 'Go and eat more, though, before we set out.'

'Anthony, you're with me?' he asked his father.

'All the way, son.'

'John, stay here with Zoe. You're in charge at home. Andy? What do you want to do?'

'Kill,' he answered simply.

Mark looked at him; his eyes were shining. 'What did we do to you? You were so gentle,' he whispered.

'You gave me a chance to be part of this. I've no regrets, I promise.'

'OK, wagons roll. Seth and Noah, you're with Anthony and Andy. The Kittens and Chloe travel with Diana and me. We travel as human, but be ready to Change at a moment's notice. Yes, Andy?'

'I just want to warn you, the Kittens and I will be big cats.'

Anthony shuddered. 'Thanks for the warning. I can cope, but it'll put the fear of god into our enemies.'

'That's the general idea.' Andy grinned, his feral smile lighting up the room.

Diana came back from the kitchen, carrying a chicken leg in each hand. She was dry-eyed now, planning ahead.

'Have we got mobile numbers for the Merseyside pack? We need to stay in contact with them.'

Mark nodded. 'Andy has the number. He'll give it to all en route. Everyone fully charged? Anyone need the loo?' They all tried to smile. 'Right, this is for Sammy. Now, will someone get Chloe out of those fucking woods and into a car, her howling is driving me mad.'

Five minutes later they were at the cars. Chloe was dressed minimally in a robe that Diana had brought downstairs for her. Mark hesitated before getting in the driver's seat of the people carrier, looking at Diana.

'I'll drive, if you're nervous,' she offered.

'No. It just seems so long ago – I can't believe it was only this morning we were setting out on a bloody shopping trip.'

'Just hours ago, my love, just hours. Get a move on, I want to get there before dark.'

She slid into the passenger seat next to him, and Chloe and the Kittens got into the back.

Andy got into his own car: a newish Jag with plenty of legroom. Anthony rode in the front with him, Seth and Noah at the back, looking grim. They led the way out, Mark following.

Ten minutes down the road, mobiles rang in both vehicles. It was Zoe, calling both lines. 'They're here,' she said flatly.

'Impossible. They can't get from Chester or London that quickly. It'll be a different lot.'

Anthony had taken the call in Andy's car. 'Do you want us to come back? Will the security system hold?'

'Hopefully, but they've got a minibus and they're ramming the gate with it.'

'Right, you can't allow them to drive up to the house. You need to knock out the vehicle if they get through. I'll say again, do you want us to come back?'

Zoe hesitated. 'You say these aren't the ones you think will go for the Merseyside pack?'

'I doubt it very much. I think the place is infested with the bastards. They're here in force – this is a planned blitzkrieg. Don't forget the ones who attacked the women in London.'

Zoe breathed deeply. 'Then carry on. We'll do what we can. I'll put all the kids in the tunnel under the annexe and lock them away. Thanks, Anthony. Diana, can you hear me?'

Her Alpha spoke up. 'Sure, good work so far. You kill the ones at our place, I'll get rid of a few more when we get to the other pack. Keep us up to date.' She sounded completely sure of herself. There was no trace of emotion in her.

Sara had called Seth, in the other car, and looped him into a call to the Merseyside pack. Simon, the young Alpha, sounded worried.

'We daren't run, we might run straight into them, but this house has very little security. Our women can't fight, they're both too heavily pregnant. What? Hang on…' He was gone. He came back seconds later. 'Great timing – Michaela's gone into labour. Is anyone coming to help us?'

Sara spoke up. 'Simon! It's Sara. Yes, Scatty Sara from the teenagers' forum, you remember? I've missed you since you went all grown-up on us. We'll be there in thirty-five minutes, MarkDad says. Are they there yet?'

'No, not a sign, but we're getting nervous.'

'Don't worry. Mark's with us – he's the best midwife in wolfdom. He delivered me and I was *huge*, and the wrong way round.'

Mark glanced at Diana, hoping to see a smile, but she was lost in a bleak world of her own, her phone on her lap. He sighed and turned on to the motorway, following Andy.

'Sara, you're sharing that call with Seth?'

'Yeah.'

'Tell him that Andy is not to hang around. He's to make the best time he can. This bus can't keep up with his Jag, and a minute or two might make all the difference.' His voice was shaking, and he gratefully took hold of Diana's hand. She was reaching across to him. Her phone rang. Ahead he could see Anthony raise his phone to his ear. Diana followed suit.

'Diana? It's Zoe. They've broken through, but John brought down a tree on top of the bus – it's going nowhere. He's Changed now. So have they – they're getting out of the bus.'

'How many?' Diana became more alert, taking charge.

'Six … nine … eleven … twelve of them. No, ten … eight. Fucking hell, those boys of ours are quick. The Whites are breaking through now. They've got past Frank and Bill, eight of them, big bastards too.'

'Zoe, where are you?'

'Annexe, watching the cameras with Helen. It's shut up tight, don't worry. All the little kids are underground, they're safe. Holy fuck!'

'What? Zoe!'

'I thought it was a ghost … oh hell. It's Caleb … has to be Caleb. He's out there … he's berserking! He's gone wolf, sort of, but he's all teeth and claws. He's got spines coming out of his back! And tusks! It's like something out of your worst nightmare. Bridget and Trixie are flanking him – they've just fended off three Whites who were going for John. Cal just went straight through one of them. I mean it, no figure of speech, straight bloody through – left a hole a mile wide. I've never seen anything like it. He can't be feeling any pain – he must have a cast-iron skull. He broke a-a-a tusk off there. It's caught in the White's ribcage, and Cal gushed a real bleeder for a second, then it just stopped. He's not slowing down. John's gone for the leader – he's just broken his back legs and left him for Frank and Bill to mop up. I'm glad this system hasn't got sound, because the bastard looks like he's screaming on the top note. I can't keep up. Cal and the Bees are like one creature. They won't split up – he's smashing into them and the girls are finishing them off. He can't be feeling any pain at all. The speed at which he's hitting them is incredible – he's not sane! He's like a living bullet. There are only three of them left. Oh, how the *hell* did *she* get out there? Diana, everyone, I'm sorry, I'm going out there. Miranda is out there, somehow. I'm sorry…'

They all held their breath. Helen's voice came through.

'Zoe's going nowhere, don't worry. I just changed the codes on the security system, and she can't get out. We're going to be fine, but I wish someone'd told me that Miranda had changed her name to Buffy. She's out there with an axe, taking heads – trophies, I guess. John and the wolfie kids are keeping the three survivors … sorry, two survivors … away from her. That's one survivor now … and they've got him surrounded. Shit, I've just seen something. Caleb is down, Caleb is down, and the Bees have him. They're dragging him back here. I'm letting Zoe out now.'

'Turn round,' whispered Diana. 'Please turn round.'

Mark shook his head. He'd chewed open the wound on his lip again. The young women in the back of the car were silent.

'Wait and see. Don't imagine the worst,' he told his wife.

'It's Caleb…'

'Caleb has Changed. He's killed. He's avenged Sammy several times over from the sound of things. Wait and see. I can't turn here anyway,' he said, trying to be gentle.

Anthony was speaking to Diana over the phone, his voice low and clear.

'Go back if you want to. The four of us are probably enough to fight off whatever's heading for this other little pack.'

Diana thought for a moment. 'No, we'll go with the original plan. I'm trusting Mark.'

'Good. Helen? Zoe? Anyone there? What's happening?' Anthony was very calm.

'It's Helen. Zoe has got Caleb into the annexe. He's unconscious – still looks like something out of a Hammer Horror – but his pulse is strong and he's breathing just fine. He's going to be OK. She's staying with him. Don't worry about him. The last of the Whites has a broken leg … arm! He Changed back and begged for mercy. It looks like John and the boys aren't letting him go. Hang on, Miranda's getting in there. She's covered in blood. She's speaking to the White. He's just a kid, I can see him now. She's moved him closer to the camera – he's younger than her – she's tying his hands. What the hell? They're all Changing back now. I can't watch this, he's just a kid…'

Diana was silent.

Darlene spoke up. 'Sammy was fifteen. They should reap what they sow. Tell them to kill him.'

Mark licked the blood from his chin. 'John won't. He'll hold them back. He'll let him go. He'll splint his arm, give him some clothes, and let him go. You wait.'

Helen was back. 'John's gone into that minibus they broke in with. He's given the survivor some clothes and put his arm in a sling. He's even given him a phone and some money!'

Diana grinned, her eyes widening and yellowing. 'And he'll contact his packmates and tell them they've been thrashed again, and that the helpless non-Shifting blonde girl took trophies. And I hope to god *that* news gets to those bastards who are heading for Simon. Helen, don't stand down, there may be more of them. If I was in their position, I'd be sending everything I had to wipe us out right now. Eleven dead and one wounded? They'll be howling for our blood. You need to get that gate back up now, at any cost. This time, electrify it. And talk to John about a back way out of the woods. We need another exit from our grounds – one gate is just asking for trouble.'

Sara's phone was ringing. Simon sounded desperate. 'Right, they're here. Six men, armed. I've locked and barricaded the doors and all the windows, but we've nowhere to go. Michaela is hysterical. How long will you be?'

Seth spoke up. 'Andy says less than ten minutes – hold on until then. They might try to smoke you out, so get wet towels ready for the doors. Stay well back from the windows and doors, don't try anything. We're going to stop our car around the corner – you won't know we're there until you hear the Whites screaming.'

Sara was almost bursting out of her seat, listening to her brother. 'Dad, hurry up. AndyDad and the boys will kill them all before we even get there!'

'That'd be good. I know you want revenge, but I'd rather not risk you unless I have to.'

The Kittens were furious, rage building. Diana could sense it and managed to exchange a sneaky smile with her mate.

Chloe spoke up. 'Risk me. I'll die happy if I can get just one of those bastards.'

Simon was speaking again. 'They're at the kitchen window. The barricade won't hold.'

Sara was calm. 'Simon, go upstairs. Try everything you can think of. They might go wolf when they're inside, so scatter glass, nails, anything sharp you can find, on the stairs. It'll slow them down for a few seconds. All of you get into one room, preferably one with running water. Turn the light off and stay quiet. Let them waste time searching for you. If they break through into the room, you'll have to fight. We can't get to you any more quickly.'

The young Alpha sounded more confident. 'OK, we're abandoning downstairs. I've filled the sink with boiling water and broken glass, that'll be nice for whoever's first through the window. I've just shoved a barricade together in front of the kitchen window to slow them down. I'm booby-trapping the door from the kitchen with a bucket of hot water, and we're on our way upstairs. I'll scatter glass as you suggest. I can hear a phone ringing. Are you here now?'

'No, just a few more minutes before Andy's there – he's quicker than us. I think those murdering sods are getting bad news. You stay quiet now…'

'OK, they're through. I'm ending the call.'

Anthony looked at Andy. 'I know,' the younger man said, through gritted teeth. 'Just around this corner… Change… Now!' A few seconds later he stopped in a lay-by, opening the doors and letting out the three wolves.

Anthony was bulky and strong, but slower than his grandsons; lithe and wiry red wolves who shot round the corner, muscles rippling. Andy closed his eyes, praying that Mark would hold back, keep the women out of this fight. Then he undressed and Changed, slipping naturally into the form of a small tiger. He'd filled out a little in the last few years, and the extra bulk was useful. He prowled around the corner, looking out cautiously. As he'd suspected, Seth and Noah had gone in too quickly. They'd been ambushed, and were in the drive of the house, backed up against a white van. Two men had them at gunpoint. Andy coughed, making the sound as wild and catlike as he could. The men hesitated; one of them turning, the other one narrowing his eyes and beginning to squeeze the trigger. Before he could, a black shape took his legs from under him. Anthony twisted around and within seconds the man was lying dead, his head almost off, his throat gone.

The second gunman was shaking, staring at Andy. 'What are you?' he asked.

Andy growled in reply. The three wolves acknowledged that he was in control of things and headed for the house.

As the man raised his gun again, Andy leaped, claws extended, ripping and tearing as he landed. The stink of blood and shit from the downed gunman made it clear it was already over for him, and Andy paused just long enough to bite out his heart before following Seth and Noah to the house.

One white wolf was halfway through the window, but Seth and Noah each had hold of a leg, and were biting and crunching. The wolf was screaming in pain and terror, and Andy wondered why he wasn't falling back and fighting. Then he looked up. Anthony was in the house, on the barricade. He held the White fast by the scruff, in his strong jaws, and was letting his grandsons play. Andy stopped the game mercifully, biting out the white wolf's throat in one sharp movement. Anthony cautiously Changed back to human, pulling a face at the tiger, then opening the door to let the others in. They were silent, padding to the bottom of the stairs. They could hear the breathing of the surviving Whites upstairs – they'd all obviously Changed back to human form.

'Anthony?' one of them called.

'Who's that?'

'Peter. We've spoken before.'

'Ah, yes. You've threatened me before. What are you doing in someone else's home, Peter? Where are your manners? Or have I got you completely wrong, and you're here to pay your respects to the mother-to-be?'

'Stop playing games, Anthony. We're armed, you're not.'

'And yet we've just killed three of your packmates. Fourteen, if you're interested in the combined scoreline from both venues. Have you made your peace with your perverted gods yet?'

The man on the landing replied, his voice dripped with scorn. 'I know I'm doing the right thing, ridding the world of your mongrel family and friends. Did your grandson suffer before he died? Did he suffer like Tomas did?'

Seth growled. Anthony blocked him, laying a calming hand on his back, ignoring the mention of his twin.

'Not a bit. His parents and sisters were with him, he knew he was loved, and he went peacefully. Did you hear what his twin did to your packmates, though? That didn't sound peaceful at all. It just *had* to hurt. But quick. And I understand that Tomas's son let one of your boys go… One of *your* sons, was it? Oh, sorry, I forgot. Old Harald won't let you breed, will he? No sons for you, then.'

'You should have died long ago,' Peter called.

'But I didn't. Now, are you going to come down the stairs alive or dead? We can call the police and have you in a nice comfortable cell for the night. You won't get a better offer.'

Andy was growling, wanting to get up the stairs. Anthony restrained him again, and Andy pricked his ears; he could hear a ladder falling against the wall of the house. He started to growl again, loud enough to drown out the noise and scare the men upstairs.

Anthony was blocking the way to the stairs, keeping Andy and the young red wolves back. 'If you come down now, unarmed, we'll turn you over to the police. This is your last chance.'

'No way. We know there's only two men upstairs with us, and we're pretty sure they're unarmed. We can shoot them, or you, if you come for us. We have plenty of ammunition.'

Anthony heard them whispering, and the floorboards were creaking. His mobile vibrated, and he grinned at the text message from Diana:

> *Make sure they're facing the top of*
> *the stairs. Give me ten seconds to*
> *Change.*

'OK, you've had your chance, you baby-killing bastards,' he said. 'I'm coming up now,' he shouted, and immediately turned and ran back to the kitchen, pushing Andy and his grandsons ahead of him.

The Whites crouched at the top of the stairs, training their guns downwards. They started to fire into the darkness. The bathroom door opened a crack, and Diana peered around, wolfishly grinning as she saw the three backs turned to her. She pushed it open a little bit more with her muzzle then launched herself wholeheartedly at the older man in the middle. He felt the air move and started to turn, screaming as the red wolf bitch who'd haunted his dreams and nightmares fell on him. She was forty pounds lighter, but he stood no chance. Her skinny mate was close behind, and a light tawny bitch behind him, felling the second man. Mark's speed made up for the size difference; he held his prey down firmly while Chloe bit and tore. Mark gave him a merciful death after the young widow had given him a minute of agony. He turned. The Kittens were going for variety, choosing the small but deadly form of panthers. They had targeted the third man. He died quickly and, seemingly, in terror. Mark Changed and knocked on the bedroom door. He stood naked in a spreading pool of blood.

'It's Mark,' he said. There was no reply. He rolled his eyes and signalled to Sara, who Changed back reluctantly.

'Simon, it's Sara. Open the door, and turn round as you do it, Dad's made me Change and I've got no clothes on.'

The door opened alarmingly fast, and Sara slipped through it and grabbed a towel from a pile on a cupboard.

She wrapped herself in it, and grinned at the young pack. A young, very pregnant blonde woman lay on the bed. She was pale and sweating, and was tightly gripping the hand of a black woman who was almost equally pregnant, and looked to be pretty much the same age as her Alpha. Simon, the Alpha male, had moved back to the side of the bed, instinctively protective. Both he and his Beta, Robbie, were mixed race.

'Right, that's seventeen of them dead and one of them frightened silly. I could do this all day, you know?' Sara said to Simon in a conversational tone. The young Alpha was shaking. 'Nice to meet you in the flesh, so to speak.'

Before Simon could respond, Mark came into the room. 'Security is shit here. What have you been playing at?'

'It'll be better in Whitby,' Simon said defensively.

'You're not in Whitby yet. And Chloe is here, so keep quiet about that place. How long has she been in labour?' He glanced at the woman on the bed.

'Only an hour or so – it's our first pregnancy. Whereas Holly's due in about six weeks.'

Diana was at the bedside, examining Michaela. 'About another half-hour, I guess. She's not messing about,' she told her mate.

Mark nodded, and took charge of his own pack. 'Right. Sara, tell the others to take turns to guard the house. I don't want any nasty surprises. Seth, pick up those guns. Don't get your prints on them. Put them in a plastic bag. We'll hand them in to the police – one of them might match the bullet that killed Sam. Simon, you can stay here. Robbie, you Change and defend your home with us.'

'I've never fought!' the young Beta Shapeshifter said. He was in his early twenties, and clearly shaken.

'I can see that, but we can't defend every pack in the country. You have to learn to look after yourselves.'

Michaela was wide-eyed, looking at the roomful of people. Diana was holding her hand. She'd dressed in Michaela's clothes.

'Diana?' she asked.

'Yes, you're safe now. Relax. Just think of those babies – they'll be with us very soon.'

'Diana, I heard about your son. Holly told me.'

'She shouldn't have. This should be a happy day for you.'

'Happy day? I was about ten minutes from being murdered in my bed! But that's not the point. Your son was killed earlier today, and you're here?'

'Michaela, I might cry every day for the rest of my life for my Sammy, but this was a chance for vengeance. I'm getting quite keen on it as a concept. Besides, what was I going to do? Sit there wailing and waiting for updates on how many more women and children had been killed? That's not me.' Diana was white-faced, but determined to reassure the first-time mother.

'Am I having these babies just to see them killed?' Michaela asked her.

'That's up to you, and how willing you are to fight for them. But I hope not. There have been over a hundred Shapeshifter children born into British packs in the last twenty years, and only seven of them are dead, all seven murdered. And then there are all the ones we don't know about, born to carriers. It won't be long before we have more teenagers and young adults who can fight the White Pack, and start their own packs. Within another generation we'll outnumber those puritanical inbreds. You know that we're a strong community, even if we don't often meet up. For obvious reasons.' The last line was delivered drily. Simon and Mark were arguing tensely in a corner of the room. She went over to them.

'Ah, Diana. Tell this kid how many children I've delivered. He wants me out of the room!' Her husband was affronted.

'This Alpha wants another Alpha male out of his bedroom and away from his mate during the delivery of his firstborn? Now that's odd, isn't it? Simon, why don't Mark and I wait outside. You talk to Michaela, and ask her what she wants.'

Five minutes later, Simon put his head round the door.

'She wants Diana. Mother figure, I guess. She certainly doesn't want Mark.' He glared at the other man.

Mark was dumbstruck, but recovered quickly, and started to go round the rooms, dismantling barricades at the upper windows just enough to keep an eye on the outside world. Night had come. The first night to get through without Sammy. The sky was clear and the stars were coming out. There was someone behind him, and he looked round. Seth joined him at the window.

'We've saved four friends here tonight, and hopefully two babies,' his eldest son said. 'That's more important to me than the body count out there. I hate this killing. I hate that I need to do it, that I need this kind of vengeance for Sam. I didn't like it years ago, and I don't like it now.'

'That's one of the reasons I love you so much, Seth,' his father said.

Seth was silent. He didn't know what to say.

'I've not told you that since you were about four years old, have I? It's the day for it, it seems. I delivered you into this world, and I loved you with all my heart as soon as I saw your red hair. That love was so painful, unexpected. I took my wedding vows two days later, and all I could hear was the memory of your first cry. I named you in my heart the moment you were born, although I took my time telling your mother. I could tell you apart from Noah straight away, bless him. He's too much like me. He enjoyed tonight, didn't he, even though Sammy's dead? Noah got real pleasure out of avenging him. I know, he's my son, and I love him, but I can't help liking you more.'

He put his arm around his firstborn's shoulder, and continued. 'Diana said something today. I couldn't take it in… It was when we were alone with Sammy and Caleb. She was just going to sleep, and she said, "Seth's got a girlfriend".'

'Yeah, but now's not the time to talk about it,' his eldest said. There was a catch in his voice. 'Dad, can I have a hug? I miss Sammy already.'

Mark hugged him close, holding him while he wept, feeling his shirt soak through quickly with silent tears. Eventually Seth drew back, wiping his eyes.

'Thanks, Dad.'

'No need to thank me, just doing my job,' Mark said bleakly. 'Tell me about this girl. Are you serious?'

'Dad, she's not like us.'

'Most people aren't. It's OK. You didn't expect me to say that, did you?'

Seth shook his head, watching his father cautiously.

'I think I've changed my views on a few things today. Just don't hurt her, and be honest with her. And don't go looking for trouble, because I can promise you it isn't hard to find.'

Seth wiped his eyes. 'Mum was trouble, was she?' He was smiling a little.

'Your mother's been trouble since I first set eyes on her. Still is, come to think of it.'

Seth decided that was a conversational path he didn't want to go down, and quickly changed the subject. 'Do you want to meet her? Karen?'

'Of course. We'll take you out for a meal somewhere. No need to scare her with the whole family at once.' Mark was getting distracted again, thinking of Sammy, of how there could be no 'whole family' ever again.

'Dad, while we're alone, can I ask…'

'What?'

'Will you ever invite my brothers to meet us? Jacob and Matthew? We know Andy's girls, it seems a shame that we don't know your boys.'

Mark fell silent. Seth drew back; he'd touched a raw nerve. His father rubbed his lip anxiously, the scab from his self-inflicted bites that day was itching.

'I have done. I've invited them to spend every weekend with me since the day I left them. Their mother blocks everything. I don't even know if my letters and presents and cards get through. She speaks to me, but doesn't tell me anything.'

'Has Katie been in touch? About Sammy?' Seth was curious.

'Not yet, there's hardly been time. She may have phoned the house. Seth, why are you so interested?'

'Well, they're my brothers, aren't they? I want to meet them, properly, not just on a screen or the phone.'

'I'll do everything I can. Now, speaking of meals, this has been the longest day of my life, and I've not eaten since breakfast. Let's get to the kitchen and see what we can rustle up.'

As they passed the bedroom, they heard a baby cry. They waited. A few minutes later, another strong pair of lungs added to the din. Simon came out of the room, pale and sweating.

'Boys,' he said. He looked at Mark. 'Would you mind if we called the older one Samuel?'

'No, I wouldn't mind. What does Diana think?'

'She says she's happy about it if you are.'

'Samuel it is, then. Look after him better than I looked after my Sammy.'

He went downstairs. Noah and Anthony were on the lawn. The police had finally arrived, and were taking statements. Five bodies were being loaded into ambulances. The paramedics were puzzling over what to do with the bloodied wolf corpse that was hanging out of the window.

The policeman was confused. 'So you're admitting that your family killed six men, but you're saying we can't charge you with anything?'

Noah was firm. 'You can arrest us, if you want, but we've done nothing illegal. One of them was in wolf form, the other five were trespassing on the land of another pack, with intent to murder. With intent to murder a pregnant woman and a woman in labour, together with their mates. Andy killed two of the attackers – he's my sisters' dad. My mother and father killed one each, my grandfather killed one and my eighteen-year-old sisters took out the last one. Earlier today one of *their* packmates illegally killed my younger brother, Sammy. Sammy was fifteen years old, and on a shopping trip with his mum and dad and little sisters. But go on, arrest us.'

The young policeman frowned. 'Look, I'll phone back to base.'

Five minutes later, he came back.

'OK, I'm to get your details, and we'll have full statements from everyone over the next two days,' he sighed. 'And I'm not to arrest you. There'll be an inquest, and if the coroner decides that any of these deaths were unlawful, then you'll be arrested.'

Mark backed into the kitchen again. Holly was squeezing around, trying to cope with the bits of barricade and the broken windows. She gave up. 'I can't think straight,' she said quietly, looking at the floor.

Mark picked up some glass. 'No wonder. Go upstairs. See the babies and your Alpha, she's sure to want you around. Get some sleep too. I'll order some food.'

Mark found menus pinned to a corkboard in the kitchen. He ordered enough to feed two dozen hungry people: large quantities of curries, rice, naan bread and soft drinks arrived in a van forty minutes later. Both packs tucked in hungrily.

Diana drank an entire bottle of orangeade, and then went to the tap for more water. She looked weary. Mark hugged her. 'Home for you. Chloe, Kittens, come with us.' The women followed him out.

Anthony followed too, and stopped him outside the house. 'If it's all right with you, I'll stay here tonight – sleep downstairs. This young pack are going to a hotel tomorrow. I've given a statement to say they weren't involved in any of the killings here tonight, so they'll get police protection until the new house at Whitby is finished. With your permission, I'm going out to Whitby tomorrow to gee the builders up a little, and help with the security work.'

Mark nodded. 'Good idea. Will you be safe?'

'No, but I'll be staying out of trouble. Can I come back to the cottage, if I want to?'

Mark looked up, puzzled. 'Of course you can. It's your home.'

'Is it? Do you still want me there? After last night?' Anthony was cautious.

'Dad!' Mark said, hurt. 'Of course I want you around. We've got to learn to live together, that's all. It's going to take time. I really don't want to lose you. Come back as soon as you can. Now, it's nearly midnight, and it's not been an easy day. We're going home.'

Three quarters of an hour later, the new gates opened and the people carrier and the Jag were driven through. Diana was fast asleep, Mark was dead on his feet.

Helen and John were waiting. Helen took Chloe's arm and walked with her to the annexe. The Kittens yawned and went to their rooms. Andy signalled to Seth and Noah, and the three of them went to patrol the grounds. John carried Diana to bed, Mark stumbling behind. 'Will you and Zoe sleep with us tonight? I need you,' he said.

'Zoe's already asleep in the big bed,' John said. 'It's hurt us both being away from you.' He kicked the bedroom door open and laid Diana on the smaller bed, undressing her gently, before pulling the covers back on the big bed and settling her down next to Zoe. He climbed in on the other side of Zoe, watching his Alpha pull off his shoes, try to undress and give up, falling exhausted to the bed next to Diana.

Chapter 13

The first real heat of the summer had arrived, on the heels of a storm that had soaked the earth. Mark watched the vapour rise from the woods, the heat haze blurring the lines of the trees. He was sweating in his dark suit, feeling the salt gather in the small of his back, the sun burning on his shaved head. At the edge of the woods, John was waiting, also in black, holding a white-wrapped figure. It was time to bury Sammy, and the pack desperately needed Diana to be there.

Over the last few days she'd spent more and more time with Caleb, as wolf, as mother, as Alpha. He'd refused to Change back to human but had softened, losing the spines – the wicked weapons that had killed so well – softening his skull and changing the shape of his head until he looked like the memory of his twin as a wolf. Diana understood. She'd found the same solace years before – her pack's need for her, and her mates' love for her had brought her humanity back. She was trying to find the key to bring Caleb back – so far nothing had worked. Terrified of losing him too, she'd sworn not to leave him alone while his brother was buried. She was in his room.

'John, give me ten minutes,' Mark called. His cousin nodded, the haze almost hiding the movement. Mark turned back to the house. He climbed the stairs and walked with leaden feet to Caleb's room. His wife was dressed for the funeral: a long black cotton dress. Her head too was shaved, and she'd laid a multicoloured plait of hair before Caleb. 'Caleb, look at this. It's your pack. Dozens of colours, dozens of people who love you and Sammy. They're going to bury him now. Please come back to me.' Caleb didn't even blink, just stared straight ahead, his jaw resting on his forelegs.

Mark scruffed the young wolf, and dragged him to his feet.

'That's enough. Diana, you've tried it your way, now we'll do it my way. Caleb, I'm disgusted with you. You'd make your mother miss Sammy's funeral? After everything that's happened?'

The young wolf whined and tried to hold back. Mark swore and picked him up, carrying him downstairs like a puppy. He strained under the weight, but didn't falter.

Diana was in tears, holding on to the plait. 'Mark, he's traumatised.'

'We're all traumatised. He needs to witness this. I don't care if he witnesses it with yellow eyes or brown eyes, but he's going to watch us put Sammy in the ground. And he's going to see that he's not the only one who is hurting.' At the bottom of the stairs he put Caleb down. 'Do I have to get a collar and lead on you?' he demanded.

The Change shimmered through the young wolf, and Caleb blinked slowly. He spoke, his voice hoarse with disuse. 'OK. I'll get dressed,' he croaked, and walked back up the stairs.

Diana moved towards him, but Mark held her back.

A minute later, Caleb called downstairs, 'Mum, will you cut my hair?' His parents climbed the stairs together, and then together they cut his hair, shaving the stubble away. Diana bound a hank of it around the plait, and carried the rest in her hands. Caleb led the way downstairs, his parents just behind. Diana couldn't stop looking at him. She'd not seen him human since just after his twin was killed, and she was hungry for the sight of him, to see the face of her lost son again. They crossed the lawn, past the cottage and the playground. At the edge of the woods, John stood, unmoving, still holding Sammy. His face was wet with sweat and tears. Mark thanked him and took his son's body, bracing against the dead weight of it. He walked under the trees.

'Caleb, stay with me,' he said quietly.

Caleb turned and took his hair from his mother. He looked guilty, but she kissed him.

'It's OK now,' she reassured him.

Diana took a handkerchief from her sleeve, and wiped John's face. They held each other close and followed Mark into the shade. In a clearing, the pack stood around the grave, waiting. They had all shaved their heads. Standing back, under the trees on the far side, Helen and her daughters, Chloe and her children, and Anthony waited, their heads bowed. Of them, only Anthony had shaved his head; as a blood relative but not a pack member, he had a unique part in the ceremony.

He'd single-handedly dug his grandson's grave, and found a strong young oak sapling in the woods, carefully digging it up and carrying it alone to the graveside, its roots wrapped in a damp sack.

As Sammy's twin and parents reached the graveside, the pack grew silent. Andy and Zoe walked to them, and Mark passed the body to Diana, who passed it to John, to Andy, and to Zoe, who finally gave him back to Mark and Diana. Frank and Bill walked across and laid three ropes across the grave. Seth and Noah stepped forward and anchored one of them. Darlene and Sara took the second, and Miranda and Caleb took the third. Mark and Diana gently laid Sammy on to the ropes, and stood back, watching his brothers and sisters lower him into the deep and narrow grave. The body hit the bottom of the grave gently, and his older brothers and sisters looked nervously at Diana.

She shook her head. 'Don't disturb him again. Let the ropes fall,' she whispered. They gently fed the thin ropes into the grave, carefully avoiding the body.

Diana stepped forward, a smile transforming her face. She looked at her pack. 'I loved my son, Sammy, because he was gentle and beautiful, and I will miss him for the rest of my life. I knew that one day he would play his guitar even more sweetly than his father does. We have lost Sammy and who he could be, but we'll never lose our memories of him. Sammy, your pack will warm you, and protect you.' She threw the plait into the grave, and stood for a moment. Miranda stepped forward, handing a hank of red hair to her mother. Diana let her fingers run through her own hair, then let it fall freely into the grave, watching the strands separate and catch the sun before falling out of reach of the light and spreading over the white-wrapped body, beginning to hide it.

Mark stepped forward. 'Sammy, my love, my sweet son. I loved your laughter. I will miss you because I'll never get the chance to tell you again how much I love you. Sammy, your pack will warm you and protect you.' He took the coiled mass of his own hair from his pocket, and let it fall into the grave, spreading it as he did so.

John was next. He looked at Diana, helpless. She stepped forward and took his hand, holding it tightly. 'Please, John,' she said.

He swallowed. 'I loved Sammy because he was the first of our children to accept Zoe and treat her as a mother, not just another adult. I will miss the sound of him calling the younger kids in for dinner. Sam, my son, your pack will warm and protect you.' He dropped his own hair, dark curls with a hint of grey, watching them fall.

Andy was next. He'd worn his hair short for years now, and had a sparse handful of bright curls to cover his son with. 'Sammy, I loved you because you always called me Dad, even when you'd not seen me for weeks. I will miss your patience with the babies. Sam, son of my heart, your pack will warm you and protect you.' He dropped the bright strands and walked away, joining his mates.

Zoe stepped forward. 'Fake colour,' she said, looking at the bright blonde hair in one hand, brushing her other hand over her brown stubble, 'but this is true. Sammy, I loved you from the moment I saw you, when Diana first said that I could be a mother to her children. I was childless and, from the first, you understood what I needed. You were five years old, Sammy, and you were the first son of my heart. I will miss the joy I felt whenever you turned to me and shared a smile, or ran to me for comfort. Sammy, my love, your pack will warm you and protect you.' She dropped the strands and turned away, standing with her mates, taking the hand that Diana offered and gripping it tightly, holding back the tears.

Diana tried to speak, then tried again. 'Caleb,' she called.

The lone twin stepped forward. 'Sammy, I love you. I miss you. I will keep you and protect you in my heart forever. Your pack will warm you and protect you.' He watched his freshly shorn hair fall – it was long and sleek and dark – and less of the white shroud showed through when at last it had settled. He stepped back, looking round. Bridget took his hand and drew him into the crowd of children. He sighed as he felt their warmth around him.

Seth stepped forward. He was carrying Joy, and together they dropped handfuls of dark red hair and soft ginger baby hair into the grave. 'Goodbye, little brother. I loved you, I miss you. I'll always miss you. Your pack will warm you and protect you.'

Noah stepped forward, cuddling Faith, who was reaching out to catch the mixed colours and textures of her own baby hair and her brother's red hair as the strands fell. 'Goodbye, Sammy. I loved you. I'll miss you. I miss you already.' He hesitated. 'We killed him, Sammy. We know we killed the one who shot you. The police said one of the guns at Simon's was the one that killed you.' He held Faith closer. 'Your pack will warm you and protect you, and we will protect the little ones too.' He nodded to his father, who was watching him closely, and stepped away from the grave.

Miranda was next. 'I loved Sammy. I remember when Sara and Darlene Changed, and I was upset because I knew I couldn't. He told me that I didn't need to Change, I was the best big sister just as I was.' She looked up and shared a smile with her mother. 'Are you sure he's Mark's son?'

Diana wiped at something in the corner of her eye. 'Oh, absolutely,' she said.

Miranda carried on. 'I'll miss him always. Sammy, sweetheart, your pack will warm you and protect you.' She let go of the thick mass of pale straight hair that she'd been cradling. It fell slowly to the bottom of the grave. The body was almost covered now.

Frank and Bill were next, carrying Amanda and Mia. The babies were unshorn but twin locks of their curls fell with the dark mass of curls that the brothers cast together into the grave. 'We love you. We miss you. Your pack will warm you and protect you,' the twins chanted together, turning away and melting back into the pack, finding Caleb and hugging him fiercely

Sara and Darlene waited, watching their brothers. Then they stepped forward, holding hands. 'We loved you, Sammy. For a little brother, you weren't too bad. We already miss you. Your pack will warm you and protect you.' Masses of red hair fell; the body was hidden.

Beatrice and Bridget were next, their faces wet with tears. Trixie tried to speak and couldn't. Bridget looked helplessly around. Caleb didn't hesitate, within seconds he had his arms around his sisters. 'Bridget and Trixie want to say that they loved Sammy. The four of us were together a lot. I guess they'll miss him more than almost anybody. Come on, girls, cover him up, make him warm and safe.' He smiled at them as they dropped their armfuls of hair into the grave.

Janie and Alice followed, white-faced. Diana was watching them, ready to move in to help.

'Sammy, thank you for being a wonderful big brother. We loved you, though we didn't tell you often enough. We're sorry that we teased you. We'll miss you every day, won't we, Janie?' Alice nodded to her sister and continued. 'Sammy, we're sorry we got our hair cut, so there's not much here to warm you, but we want to protect you. Goodbye, Sammy.' The girls let the short dark sheaves of glossy hair fall into the grave. The sun was directly overhead now, lighting the depths of the grave, the mixed hair colours like autumn leaves at the bottom of the hole.

There was a silence, and then Mark cleared his throat. 'Will the little children come forward now?'

Susie and Annie were hand in hand with Julie and Leanne, they showed the four-year-olds where to throw the fistfuls of hair.

'Is Sammy in there?' asked Leanne.

'No, just his body, but we're putting our hair in to show that he'll never be alone,' Annie said clearly. The four of them stepped away.

Nathan and Joe were next, holding on to Harry and Mikey grimly and seriously, obviously convinced the five-year-olds were going to fall into the hole. The four boys each had a small handkerchief full of shaved stubble. None of them wore their hair long, but the four clouds of auburn and gold shavings fell together, catching the light.

Isaac and Ian were supervising Patrick and Liam, following the same ritual. Isaac peered into the hole, and Zoe closed her eyes for a moment, sure he was going to fall in, but he pulled away. 'Bye, Sammy. We'll miss you a lot,' he said.

Finally, the six girls stepped forward together. They stood around the grave: Meg, Tara, Debbie, Beth, Louise and Leah.

Meg spoke for all of them. 'We're all glad we had long hair, because it will keep Sammy warm. We'll miss him, and we promise to look after Caleb so that he doesn't miss him too much.'

The pack stood back, the parents mixing now with the children, hugging them and speaking to them in low voices.

Anthony stepped forward alone. He cast his hair on to the pile, a black and silver sweep making a line along the bottom of the grave. 'Goodbye, Sammy,' he growled, and turned back.

Diana had been expecting eloquence, and was puzzled until she saw the tears in his eyes. She said nothing, and let him go back to the quiet place under the trees where he waited alone.

Helen stepped forward with her daughters. 'Goodbye, Sammy, sweetheart. I'm glad I got the chance to know you, to accept you. We're poorer without you. We'll miss you.'

Finally, Chloe stepped forward with Mareta and Phil. 'We're not pack, we're not even family yet, but we do miss Sammy, and his kindness to us. We can't claim that we loved him – we didn't know him well enough for that – but I am sure we would have grown to love him. Thank you, Diana, for letting us come here to say goodbye.'

Mark took a step forward, his gaze fixed on the edge of the clearing. Standing there was a thin, dark-haired teenage boy, so unexpectedly like Sam and Caleb that it took his breath away. He held the hand of an anxious ten-year-old lad. 'Jacob? Is that really you, Jakie? Matt?' He walked to the edge of the clearing. 'How did you get in?' He looked round, puzzled.

Diana spoke up. 'Mark, I didn't say, in case she changed her mind. Katie rang. I gave her the code for the gate. She promised to wait outside and send the boys into the woods alone. I promised her that they'd be safe.'

Caleb stepped forward. 'You're our brothers? Don't worry, we won't eat you. I'm sorry you couldn't meet Sam, but he looked like me. And like you too, I guess. Do you want to say goodbye?'

Jacob nodded, with the self-confidence of an eldest child, and approached the grave. 'Little brother, I didn't know you, and I'm sorry I'm too late to ever know you. Mum says I'm old enough to make my own mind up. I have, and I'm here.'

Matthew was watching the crowd, hanging back. Anthony was on his knees before him, taking his hand, and Diana could almost hear his 'grandson' speech. She turned her back.

'Diana, thank you for this,' Mark was saying.

'Thank Katie,' she said quietly, making her way to the graveside, and sitting at the side, her legs curled beneath her, careless of the wet earth on her clothes, losing herself in her memories of her lost son.

The pack and their family and friends moved away, until only Mark and Helen and Anthony were left.

Diana finally looked up. 'Mark? I thought you'd be with Jacob and Matthew?'

'Plenty of time for that, my love. Let's bury our son. My dad will help. We need to make sure this tree takes root and thrives.'

Helen spoke up. 'Diana, Katie's waiting outside the gate. I know it'll be bothering you. I won't let her come in, but I'm going to take her out for the rest of the day, go shopping or something so that her boys can stay here with Mark. Do you understand why? I don't want you to get the wrong idea…' Diana realised that Helen was crying.

'You're doing it for me?'

'Yes.'

'Then thank you.' She turned to Mark. 'Do you want to see her? Katie? Before she goes?'

He shook his head. 'We're going to bury Sammy.' He picked up a spade and nodded to his father, who handed a spade to Diana and picked up a third.

Helen walked out of the clearing. Andy stood at the edge of the woods, waiting for her. He wrapped his arms around her and lifted her off the floor. 'Hel, I wish—'

'Wish I was pack?' she said.

'No, I've never been willing to share you!' He was shocked. 'No, I wish you could know how much I love you.'

'I do know,' she reassured him.

'I want to renew our vows,' he said carefully. 'I want you to know that I'm not joining a Contract with the others, but I want to renew my vows to you. I'll give them up, the women, but not the pack.'

'Why?'

'Because I've realised I can. Sometimes time stands still, and you think about what's important. I love them all, but I can be part of the pack without hurting you. I know now that the only time I hurt you is when you know I'm making love with Diana. I can give that up. She'll have to manage with hugs from now on.'

She was nodding. 'Maybe a few kisses too? I can be generous.'

'Marry me?'

'Again?'

'For good. New promises, and this time I'll keep them.'

'This time, so will I,' she said.

'What?' He stood still.

She brushed away another tear. 'Well, I never really gave up Xan, did I?'

'Oh, Xan … that's different… I thought you meant you'd been unfaithful.' They walked together to the gate, sharing memories of Xan, of being young. They opened the gate, and Helen left him there, climbing into Katie's car and closing the door, giving her husband a huge smile as the car moved away.

Andy watched the car disappear into the distance, and thought back over the last twenty years, glad that he'd not lost her, and wondering how he was going to explain his decision to his Alpha. That conversation, he knew, could wait until another day.

Chapter 14

'Happy birthday, dear Faith and Joy ... happy birthday to you!'

John was wincing. Considering they were all the children of musicians, some of the little ones were remarkably tuneless. He decided to blame their mothers, and looked round for them. Diana, of course, was perched on the arm of a big chair, whispering to Mark. The Alpha looked very pleased with himself. He was watching the birthday girls open their presents. Mandy and Mia wanted to open some too, but Mikey and Harry were patiently explaining that it wasn't *their* birthday party. Leanne had stolen a doll from the pile of toys, and was attacking its torso with a plastic knife. Julie had returned to the food table, and was looking round surreptitiously, wondering how much more cake she could eat before a parent stopped her.

John looked for Zoe. He was full, and not enthusiastic about the prospect of parting Julie from food; she had a loud voice. He could only blame himself for that, he knew.

Zoe had disappeared. He stood up, groaning, and picked up his four-year-old. 'That's enough, girlie. Mummy's too tired to be cleaning up your puke.' Julie screamed, as predicted, and he laughed. 'Won't work. I've had kids screaming at me for twenty years now, I'm immune.'

She glared at him, and reached out a hand to scratch him.

'You bloody evil child,' he said, surprised, ducking back before she could reach him. 'Don't you love Daddy?' he asked her mournfully.

Zoe was back in the room. 'She's cranky. She needs to be entertained. She gets bored very easily. Leanne! Don't kill the doll!'

Leanne looked up, offended. 'I'm not killing her, I'm making her better. I'm a doctor.'

Faith looked up. It was her doll under the knife. She ran to her big sister and rescued it, holding it possessively for a full minute before forgetting again and dropping it. Leanne grabbed it back, and started poking speculatively at the eyes. Julie wriggled out of John's arms and joined her, starting a serious discussion about the doll's medical condition.

'Party's fizzling out…' John said, to nobody in particular. Everyone was ignoring him, so he returned to his chair and closed his eyes.

Before he could doze off, the door flew open, and a crashing drum roll made him jump out of the chair. Seth and Noah were standing at either side of the door. Miranda walked in imperiously, carrying a silver marching drum and sticks.

'Ladies and gentlemen, boys and girls, the Werewolf Players present … *Pinocchio!*' She was wearing a white dress, with silver fairy wings strapped to her shoulders.

John grinned and settled back down. Mark was already laughing.

'Presenting! – Caleb Preston as the Wooden Boy,' she said solemnly.

Caleb entered, bowed.

'Seth Preston as Geppetto! Noah Preston as Jiminy Cricket!'

The eldest twins came in, straight-faced.

'Also presenting, for the first time in this role, Sara and Darlene Preston as the Marionettes.'

The Kittens danced into the room, stiff-jointed and blank-faced, and collapsed woodenly into a corner. Diana smothered a laugh. The children were enraptured.

'And last, but never least, Francis and William Preston as the chorus.'

The eighteen-year-olds strode in and bowed, looking around expectantly. John spoke up. 'You get your applause *afterwards*,' he explained. The lads nodded solemnly, and took their places next to the Kittens.

'You will laugh, you will cry,' proclaimed Miranda, 'but you *will* be left begging for more. Let the play commence.'

The kids had gathered around, and were quiet. Their parents settled back and watched, realising that it was more than just a play; it was a demonstration of what their eldest children could do. Miranda narrated as the Players changed their faces and bodies as the play required – Caleb's nose growing and shrinking at will, his skin and hair changing colour, recasting from wood to flesh tones, donkey ears growing suddenly and, seemingly, without any effort. Seth changed his features to those of an old man; Noah grew antennae and insect wings. The Marionettes and chorus changed their features regularly too.

The children stared, open-mouthed. It was magical, and although they were used to seeing their older siblings Change into wolves, this was something quite different.

As the story came to its happy conclusion, the Players took their bows to wild applause.

Diana stood up. 'Fantastic. You've all got a future in showbiz, I think the entire special-effects industry will be quaking in their boots. You lot can do it all so much more cheaply!'

Sara shook her head. 'Oh, Mother, we wouldn't do it *cheaply!*' She laughed. 'But it was fun. We are getting better, aren't we?'

Mark stood up. 'Better every day. You're wonderful, all of you. Where are Bridget and Trixie?'

Caleb shook his head. 'Too shy. They practised, but then they ran away.'

'What a pity. Next time I'll encourage them to join you. Well done, and thank you. Now, party's over, back to reality, or whatever passes for it. Zoe, my love, I think you'd better sit down.'

'I agree,' she said, frowning.

Diana was already by her Beta's side. 'Are they coming?'

'Ready or not,' sighed Zoe. 'My waters broke just before the play. I reckon we've got a couple of hours yet, even so. But I'm feeling very tired.'

John had already run upstairs, and was changing the sheets on the bed in the main bedroom. The room was Zoe's preferred birthing space. Miranda followed him into the room. She waved her wand over the bed playfully.

'Fairy Godmother?' he asked her, laughing. She was having a good day.

'Fairy Queen!' she said haughtily. 'My blessings on this bed, and all who … er…' She faltered; her dad was grinning.

'I'm going downstairs now. I never said anything. You imagined it, clearly.' She flounced out of the room.

Bridget and Beatrice were arm in arm with Zoe, accompanying her as she walked around the house, stopping whenever there was a contraction. Diana was tidying up, taking the party food into the kitchen. All the leftovers would be gone within minutes, she knew. Isaac and Ian were already circling the remnants of the birthday cake like vultures. She picked up the toys and carried them to the birthday girls' room, which looked like it had recently hosted a meeting of Vandals Anonymous. 'Mark? Help me!' she called.

He surveyed the mess. 'How do they do it? They're only three years old! It took Bill and Frank until they were six to manage this level of chaos.' There was a certain note of admiration in his voice.

'Every bloody week! None of the others were ever this bad!' she wailed.

He started to disagree, then looked at the room again and was silent.

Miranda sailed past, stopping to peer into the room. She waved her wand hopefully at the mess, then shrugged and made as if to pass by.

'Miranda, darling daughter…' said Diana.

'Oh no! I keep my room tidy. And I did all the ironing this morning. *All* of it. It took me four hours,' she protested.

'Just strip the beds? Please?'

Miranda gave up and obeyed, carrying the sticky sheets downstairs, then coming back to pick up the small pieces of food that had fallen out of them on the way.

'There's ice cream on the curtains,' said Mark, awestruck. 'Chocolate chip, the evidence says.'

'There's cat hair under the beds, and we don't even have a cat!' replied his wife, her eyes wide open.

'Oh, that's Sara. She lets them brush her sometimes,' Mark explained.

'Mystery solved. Right, let's take everything out of the room, curtains and rugs too, scrub it down, and then put the bare minimum back.' She spotted a lone figure passing the door. 'Caleb!'

'Nope.' he muttered under his breath. 'I'm busy. I've got homework.'

'Your nose is growing. This is easy. Just clean those windows, will you? It'll take ten minutes. Window-cleaning stuff is in the landing cupboard.'

'I know,' he grumbled, and went to get it.

Within an hour, the room was spotless and tidy. A large box outside it held pilfered toys and books ready to be distributed to their rightful owners.

'Right. It'll be fine so long as we make them live in the garden from now on,' sighed Diana.

'Mark!' John was shouting. 'We need you in here.'

The Alphas went into the bedroom. Zoe was delivering a long stream of abuse at her husband, which basically seemed to convey that she was in some pain and he was solely responsible, and that these were positively the last babies that the pack would see.

'They'd better be boys, then,' he said placidly. 'Harry and Mikey think that all babies are born girls.'

Zoe screamed at him, murder in her eyes.

Diana took her hand. 'Zoe, honey. I clearly remember you telling me how much you like babies.'

'Stop winding me up.' Zoe breathed out in slow gasps. She recovered. 'Why did I ever like you?' she asked her Alpha vindictively.

Mark sat down on the side of the bed. He touched Zoe's face gently, getting her attention. 'That's enough drama. We get the picture – you're the star of the show. Now it's time to relax. Can I see how you're getting on?'

Zoe assented, and Mark examined her.

'Oh, very soon, honey. John, stop winding her up. Get behind her, help her. Rub her back.'

'I know,' he said. 'Are they really coming? Push now,' he said encouragingly.

'I know, I've done this before.' Zoe was calm now, holding Diana's hand.

Diana was crying. Mark looked at her. 'Diana, you OK?'

'Just happy, that's all.' She tried to smile.

Zoe gripped her Alpha's hand, almost breaking her fingers. 'You wanna swap places?' she grunted.

'Yes. I do,' said Diana ruefully. 'But we can't turn back time.'

Mark was massaging a pulled muscle in Zoe's thigh, gently encouraging her. 'Good, you're such a good mother. I can see a head now. How do you feel?'

'On top of the fucking world, Mark. How do you feel?' she snarled.

He met her eyes. 'Wonderful. I'm so proud of you. How about a push?'

'I know…' She twisted her head a little to look at John. 'Girls or boys? Guess.'

'Boys,' he said solemnly. 'Girls next time.'

'Bastard,' she said absently, her focus changing.

A little while later, Mark silently handed her son to her. He'd cut the cord and weighed him, but not washed him. That was Diana's job. 'Seven pounds,' he said, awed.

Later, the second: 'Another bloody big one – six pounds ten,' he said. 'John, what are you feeding her?'

John was poking his new sons, seeing how loudly they could scream. Diana was hugging Zoe; they were both laughing. Miranda was knocking on the door. She was still wearing her fairy outfit.

She was given permission to come in, and surveyed her parents calmly before going to look at the babies. 'Beautiful little girls,' she announced.

'Boys,' corrected John.

'I knew that. Beautiful little boys.' She winked at Diana, who hadn't been fooled.

John was watching Diana, remembering the day Seth and Noah had been born.

'Miranda, will you ring Andy, please? Tell all the family that we have two new sons. They can see them later, when their mum has rested.' He looked around. 'Alexander is the elder. Tomas, without an "h", is the younger one, if that's OK by Zoe?'

'Perfect,' she said, not really listening. 'Could someone bring me some food, please?'

'Can't you walk?' asked Diana innocently.

'I could run a marathon if I had to, but I think it's John's turn to do some work,' the new mother said sarcastically.

The babies were settled with their mother and, with a little encouragement, were soon nursing. The room fell silent. Diana and Zoe were looking at each other, not speaking. The men grew increasingly puzzled, until eventually Zoe said, 'Look, will you two go and do something useful? I need some girl talk.'

'That wasn't fun,' she said, after the men had left.

'It's not supposed to be. Are you happy now, though?' her Alpha replied.

'Yes. Of course. Are you? It feels weird – feels like you missed your turn.'

'I know, but we knew when Faith and Joy were born they'd be my last. I'm too old now.'

'Do you think I've got another five years? I'm forty…'

'I'd had nine pregnancies by the time I was your age. One of them was Miranda, and two of them were Andy's babies. I reckon they counted for double, triple even. I was alone for most of them. This is your sixth, all of them smooth Shapeshifter pregnancies, all of them with help. You've had it easy. Maybe you've got another ten years in you. Anthony says his mother was in her fifties when she stopped.'

'Bloody hell. Then why did it take so long for me to get pregnant this time?'

'You were trying? I thought you wanted a break.'

'Did I hell! I just said that so you wouldn't worry.'

'Well, don't lie to me again. Tell me when you want to start trying again, and we'll let you rest a bit more.'

'I want to start trying again next week,' Zoe said. 'Oh, don't give me that look. There's less than nine months between your oldest boys and Miranda!'

'Well, that was hardly planned!'

Zoe looked absolutely serious. 'Look, I know it's cheeky, but I want more kids, and I want them as soon as possible. I know damn well it'll be hard work for everyone else, that's why I'm talking to you.'

'OK, go for it. We'll manage. We always manage, don't we? Anthony has taken over the garden anyway, together with his "gardening class" for the under-elevens. He's a wily old bastard. And he's finally fixed the laundry chute! Do you know how many years I spent carrying dirty clothes downstairs to the laundry room? It took him about three minutes to fix. I could have done it myself, just never got round to it.'

'You're rambling,' Zoe said.

'Sorry. What? Oh, yes. We'll manage. Do you want to try to wean these two early then?'

'No, I want you to adopt them,' Zoe said.

'Of course we will. They're all mine and Mark's, just as much as yours and John's.'

'No, Diana, listen. It should be your turn. You're still strong. You could still be having babies, but something went wrong, you know it did. I want you to take these babies, and nurse them, and look after them.'

Diana stared at her. 'Is this because I lost Sammy? Are you feeling sorry for me?'

'No, I'm feeling sorry for *me*! I'll be around, obviously, but if you nurse them … OK, if we share the nursing, I might get pregnant sooner.'

Diana cuddled up. 'Zoe, I'm a mum. Don't try to fool me. What's the point of going through all that if you're just going to hand them over?'

'You don't want them?'

'You don't want me to have them, not really. I'll tell you what, you guys move into the big bedroom again, with us. We'll all look after them equally. That should give you more energy. And if I can, if it happens, I'll help with the feeds. But they're still *your* babies, OK?'

'Really?' Zoe looked at her new sons. 'They're pretty cute, aren't they? They're huge. What did we call them?'

'Alexander and Tomas,' Diana reminded her, relaxing now. 'Please don't call him Xan, I can deal with it better if we call him Alex.'

Zoe looked at her affectionately. She'd never known Xan, but she did know Diana. She swallowed hard. 'I didn't really want to give them to you.'

'No, you were suffering from some strange temporary insanity. Now, have we got a plan? You lie back and do nothing – we'll run around after you?'

'Sounds like a good plan to me. Are you sure you don't mind?'

'Not at all. What did you expect me to say? I'll tell Mark you didn't mean what you said, about these being our last. He'll be happy about that.'

Zoe sighed, she felt utterly safe. 'Can I go to sleep now?'

'Those boys fed OK?'

'Feels like it. I'm very sleepy.'

'Then go to sleep, my love.'

Diana watched her friend sleep, gently picking up the babies and putting them in their cot. The bigger one screwed up his eyes, but didn't wake. 'Hello, Alex, Tom. Welcome to the world,' she whispered.

Chapter 15

The old wolf prowled the playground, marking the perimeter with a short stream of urine, covering the markings left by the pack children. He sniffed carefully at the marks of the Alphas, and the other three pack adults, considered trying his luck, considered covering the mark of the big grey wolf who spent so little time running with the pack now. He sniffed again, and decided not to. It would earn him nothing worse than a cuff around the head from the grey, but the wiry black Alpha with the eyes that had seen hell would punish him. He growled low, thinking about it, thinking about the last year.

Another slaughter, in South Wales this time. Anthony could smell the blood, hear the screams as imagination drew pictures in his mind. That innocent young pack had been relaxed, enjoying Christmas dinner, unwary. The Whites had changed their tactics a little; the security video showed them arriving on foot, one by one, surrounding the house, not Changing until they were ready, until they outnumbered the four pack adults threefold. The Alpha female had been alerted first – even her human senses had caught the stink of wolf at her door – and she'd taken command, trying to hide the children. The records showed it all. No survivors of the small pack, but they hadn't died without exacting bloody revenge on their killers. The video showed three of the enemy carrying seven of their dead out of view of the cameras. Two more had been injured: walking wounded.

The Alpha had just had time to alert the nearest neighbouring pack seventy miles away. Their Beta had driven there as fast as he could, knowing that nobody else could help. He'd taken the video discs of the slaughter, not wanting them to fall into the hands of non-Shapeshifters. Six hours later, he'd called the police, expressing concern that their friends weren't answering their calls. The video was copied and sent to every pack. Every adult in every pack, every teen wolf capable of fighting, memorised the faces of the killers, human and wolf.

The Alpha Council, for so many years a joke name for a web forum, suddenly became something more serious. Two by two, the pack Alphas of Britain had met, forging bonds of friendship. Anthony had visited packs too, taking with him two or three of his older grandchildren – his son knew he was the Whites' second most wanted target and insisted he be protected. The grandchildren were grimly pleased that their point had been made, that they were now seen as fighters, not children to be cared for. The old wolf's visit to other packs had been a huge talking point; his experience and knowledge of the enemy was invaluable.

Anthony stalked the garden at Silverwood. He growled, remembering. After the first few strikes had been repulsed so thoroughly by Diana's pack, the Whites had disappeared for a few months before reappearing with the attitude of soldiers rather than punishment packs. Always before, they'd arrived with arrogance, expecting fear and terror to do their job for them, fighting lazily and badly. The death count had made them reconsider.

In February, a snarling bloodbath of a fight outside a sixth form college had brought the war back to Diana's pack. Four teenage girls coming out of lessons had seemed like a soft target. The Whites had sent six soldiers armed with knives. By the time the police arrived, summoned by a friend of the girls who'd seen the fight begin, the Preston girls had taken the sole survivor prisoner. The girls had seen the threat the minute they walked out of the college doors, separating from their friends instinctively, drawing trouble towards themselves and pretending they hadn't noticed the six men. Pretending they didn't recognise one of them as a veteran of an attack in South Wales where ten children had been murdered.

They'd walked past their own car, and towards the field at the back of the college, feigning they couldn't remember where they'd left their transport. Bridget had started to tremble.

'I won't leave your side,' Sara promised.

'I'm not scared, I'm furious. I want that baby-killer's guts,' Bridget whispered back. Anthony's lessons had focussed on her protective instincts, and she was ready to fight.

When the men finally fell on them, knives flashing in the moonlight, the girls' training kicked in. They didn't Change, but used every dirty street-fighting trick they'd ever been taught to disarm their attackers, taking advantage of the enemy's surprise at their readiness to inflict as much injury as possible in a short space of time. They threw the knives into the darkness.

'That's evened the odds.' Sara grinned at the man who was circling her; he was wary and bruised, but still confident.

'Six men against four little girls … I don't think so,' he said. He glanced round, the focus of all the men had been on Sara, just for a second, and the other girls had taken advantage of that to melt into the shadows.

'Bye-bye.' Sara laughed, twisting for a second within the trap of her clothes, to emerge as a long-legged cheetah, reaching sprint speed in seconds and racing across the car park towards the road.

'Mongrel heathen bitch,' the leader spat, furious at losing his prey. He Changed, the better to track down Sara and her sisters. Within a minute, the six men were six wolves, suddenly aware of the silence, the smell of four bitches distracting them.

Sara returned, Changing to wolf. Looking as much like her mother as she possibly could, she stood poised just outside the circle of light. The legend of the red wolf bitch was one she fully intended to exploit. The white wolves stood in the lamplight. Hungry growling came from the shadows, threatening them. The younger four were two sets of twins in their mid-twenties. The leader, the oldest of the group, was the baby-killer. His twin had been one of those felled by the Welsh Pack. The sixth man was another singleton. He was quiet and watchful.

In the darkness of her mind, Sara could dimly hear the voice of the savage killer she called Granddad: *We instinctively fight with our twin, protecting them. They'll expect that, so ignore your instincts and confuse the bastards. If you have a choice, take out the leader first — they're heavily into leadership. If you kill one of twins, get the other one as soon as possible, while he's unsteady and shocked, before he goes berserk. Be intelligent. It's our great advantage.*

She could sense Bridget closing in on her, head down so her eyes didn't reflect the lamplight and betray her position. The sisters stood side by side, choosing their target, and then ripped out of the darkness at the leader. He had a choice of where to rip back, where to attack, and lunged for the red wolf on his right. Trixie and Darlene were howling at full volume, distracting the other Whites for vital seconds. Their leader was down, bleeding heavily from the rip in his throat. He was dying. He wore an affronted, disbelieving expression. Sara had a shoulder wound, deep but not long; she'd twisted away in good time. She looked inward, remembering Caleb's lessons and shutting off the bleeding.

Darlene stepped forward, licking her lips then letting her tongue loll out. Trixie was slightly behind her. Two of the Whites ran at them, trying to split them up by sheer momentum. The bitches danced aside, Trixie running underneath one of the twins, low to the ground, her small size suddenly an advantage. Emerging from under his belly, she gathered herself into a sprung ball of black fury and hit his twin in the forelegs, knocking him off his feet. She carried on running to the relative safety of Bridget and Sara. Darlene went for the exposed belly, ripping the White open from balls to chest, and retreated, leaving him dying. His twin didn't even give him time to start screaming but rushed in for the mercy kill, the tear at the throat, the final gushing release of blood. In the same movement, the same run, he made for the wiry red bitch who was still recovering from the attack she'd just made. She couldn't avoid his fury, but lowered her head and took the full force of his rush on her shoulders, her entire body shuddering, twisting, her hips rising into the air as she went tumbling over him, behind him, lying still on the ground, stunned.

He twisted round in mid-air, ready to land on her and tear. But he was hit from both sides by twin black missiles. His back was broken by the double impact, and he landed with an unearthly scream, before dragging himself away. Both of the small black wolves landed, rolling, slightly stunned, behind Darlene. Sara stood before all of them, snarling, daring the three Whites who were still standing to move towards them. The older one was keeping the young twins well back, which gave the girls space to recover. Darlene was groaning, unconscious, beginning to Change back to human form. The Bees were licking her anxiously. Sara glanced back, then without warning ran for the three Whites. She was alone, unprotected. There were ten yards to cover, and in the space of those ten yards she remembered Caleb's berserker strategy and used it, her body rippling as she moved resources from her hips and hind legs to her head, strengthening her skull and growing sharp tusks. The younger wolves yelped and stepped back, leaving the singleton alone. His calculation was momentary. He gathered himself up and moved to meet her, measuring her, taking in that her twin was down, that she was committed to the charge, and that he couldn't avoid her. He watched her eyes: the intelligence, the calculation. He feinted right and then dodged left, jaws shut. But she was there, unfazed, those tusks buried in his side, in his ribs, an inch from his heart. He stopped, unmoving, panting, skewered by her. His eyes met hers, and he Changed quickly to human, still pinned by her. In agony his raised his hands, staring into her eyes. Surrender. She stepped back, careful not to cause further injury, leaving him alive and bleeding.

In a fury of shame at their pack member's cowardice, one of the White twins rushed forward, heading for the girl who was down. Darlene was human, protected only by her younger, gentle sisters. A fraction of a second before he landed on her, she opened her eyes and raised one hand in the air; her fingers were suddenly razor-sharp feline claws. The wolf's guts fell over her in a shower of shit and blood. He didn't yet know he was dead, and landed on her, jaws going for her throat. Bridget was there, finding the right Change, her weirdly long muzzle enveloping his, gripping his jaws in hers, softening the impact on Darlene's vulnerable neck. Sara was watching his twin. He was the last white wolf standing. She was growling, tusks bloody. He howled and charged. Sara finished him quickly and mercifully, tiring of the slaughter.

Darlene stood, coughing, a huge bruise on her neck. She looked round. The broken-backed wolf had dragged himself fifty yards from the battle to die next to her geography teacher's Citroen. She staggered over and checked the body.

Bridget and Trixie had Changed too, and were looking around, picking up clothes, dressing in an assortment of rags. Darlene was coughing, making her way to the bleeding, breathless, wounded man who'd surrendered.

She bent over him. 'She got your lung, from the look of it. We can take you to the hospital, in police custody.' She smiled at him. 'Or we can take you home, as our prisoner.'

There was a certain madness in that smile, and he flinched. 'I will not argue. My life is in your hands,' he told her painfully.

'Damn right,' she said in a more friendly tone.

'I surrendered to your twin,' he gasped.

'We'll take you back with us, then.' She smiled.

Anthony remembered the girls coming home; Sara and Darlene dressed in their hockey kit, the Bees in rags, all of them confident, calm. The prisoner had been moved as soon as he was out of danger. He was unknown to Anthony: a singleton whose twin had died very young. He'd introduced himself as Jan, and offered a complete change of allegiance. He never took his eyes off Sara, and Andy hated him with a passion. Jan was kept under lock and key in the basement. He promised that he'd no intention of even trying to escape. To Anthony's disgust, Diana had said several times that Jan seemed like a nice enough bloke, and perhaps he was telling the truth. After all, you can't help your family. Jan confessed to having no useful modern skills; he was the apprentice tanner back home, and had no other abilities beyond fighting and pack politics.

Jan had begged the pack to tell his family that he was dead. He didn't want to be released. His reasons were simple. In the White Pack, only two or three males got the chance to breed even occasionally: the best fighters, the ones who were closest to the Alpha. Jan was seen as unlucky, his twin already dead. He had no future, no family to look forward to.

In the five months since the fight, Jan had graduated to a couple of hours a day of closely watched freedom in the grounds. He watched the pack hungrily. He was falling in love with them. Three decades of unsatisfied longing for touch, love and intelligent conversation was sharpened to a point by what he saw around him. Anthony almost felt sorry for him. His mother had always said there was nothing sadder in the world than a White with a brain. He was beginning to agree with her.

Anthony emerged from his reminiscence. He'd unconsciously Changed, and was standing naked at the top of the slide, enjoying the late summer sun on his back. The Jag had just pulled into the car park. Andy was getting out, accompanied by his wife and daughters. They were carrying party clothes. Helen glanced at the slide and laughed, dramatically trying to cover her young daughters' eyes. Andy shook his head and herded his family into the annexe. Chloe was close behind, parking next to the Jag in her new Nissan. With her children, she followed her protector into the annexe, pointedly ignoring Anthony. He grinned, and ran down the slide, and walked to the cottage, his beloved home.

He watched through his security cameras as Mark and John went to open the gates for a large van. Men sprang out, looking around with interest at the grounds where strangers were so rarely allowed. They erected a huge marquee, set up tables and chairs, a stage, and left. They were escorted out by the five eldest sons of the pack. Andy, Mark and John carried stuff out of the music room to the marquee, grinning happily. Andy was heard to plead for a roadie, but he was laughed at. Diana, Zoe and Helen, with the older kids, decorated the marquee and set up the lights.

The schoolkids trooped out carrying food, leaving great piles of cooked meat, bread, cakes and fruit on the buffet tables. Another delivery van arrived, bringing beer, soft drinks, wine..

At seven o'clock, a bus drew up: twenty uniformed men. Anthony disapproved; security was the responsibility of the pack, not hired muscle. Mark had overruled him. He knew the industry, knew who he could trust. Paul Dixon had checked out every man and was prepared to personally vouch for them. They scattered around the grounds, armed with tablets linked to the security cameras.

At seven thirty, the pack and their friends emerged from the house. Jacob and Matthew had decided not to come, Jacob citing their mother's distress at the other anniversary two days later. Mark had understood, and, in a last effort to make amends, sent flowers and a long letter of apology to Katie that offered her his undying respect. She'd sent the letter back unopened, and refused to accept the flowers.

Mark had merely shrugged. That marriage was long over in his mind, and he knew now that nothing was left of it but his sons.

Anthony waited until all the guests and family were in the marquee, then went into the house. He let himself into the basement. Jan was loose in his makeshift cell, unchained, playing solitaire on a standalone, unlinked PC. He looked up. 'Here to kill me?' he asked.

'I should. You've got them fooled.'

'No, you've got yourself fooled. I'm for real. I mean it – I want to be part of this.'

'White bastard. If I took you back to your pack, if we left tonight and I took you back to the mountains, what would you do?'

Jan paled. 'I'd do everything I could to escape them. I swear it. They're not my pack any more. They're stupid, small-minded. I never did like them. Take me back if you must, but you are wrong.'

Anthony walked round him, surveying him. The man had the pale straight hair and blue eyes of his pack, but his lips were thinner, his eyes bluer, than most. His eyes seemed haunted by what he'd seen.

Anthony sat down, crossed his legs. He put his head to one side. 'I've seen you watch the redhead. She's too good for you, you know.'

'I know that. She is a young goddess. And she gave me mercy.'

'She's a smart little girl, that's all.'

'I've never met a girl like her.' Jan smiled.

'No, you bastards don't treat your women well, do you? Or anyone else's women, come to that.'

Jan flushed.

'Admit it. You used them – the old ones, the tired old ones, the low-ranking ones, the ones who can't breed any more.

The Alpha throws them to you, doesn't he, throws you the used-up dregs of humanity that he makes of them. Of course, they're bonded to the Alpha. They'll never bond with the cannon fodder, will they? And the slaves too, of course. Do you still do that? Take slaves?'

Jan was white, shaking now. 'Yes, they still do it. I disagreed with it, quietly of course. My own mother was a slave, dark-haired, but she had a blond child with her when she was taken. He wasn't full blood. They killed him. But the child proved that she could bear blonde children They let her be a mother still. Even back then, the birthrate was slowing. And I … I was always gentle with the women.'

'Bastards,' commented Anthony. He looked at Jan for a moment, picking up on his story. 'Who was your mother? Her name?'

'Audrey. Her name was Audrey. I never knew her, though. They took me away from her when I was six – boys aren't allowed to know their mothers, you know that. But it didn't stop her from knowing her sons, watching us grow up. She managed to let us know who she was. They killed her for it. They killed my twin. They killed one of each set of her living twins. They thought I'd been taught enough of a lesson and let me live.'

Anthony stopped dead. 'Not Sylvia? Audrey? You're sure?'

'Why would she be named Sylvia?'

Anthony ignored Jan's question. 'Who is your father?'

'Harald, who else? Are you going to kill me?'

'Fuck, no. Audrey? She was killed? How?'

'Execution. Shot. An honourable death. She had thirty children for Harald – he was prepared to be generous. Of course, half of them were dark-haired. He had them killed as soon as their hair colour changed…' Jan bit down on his lip, and there was a ghost of something in that expression that reminded Anthony of someone. 'Some of them were five, six years old. They were my brothers and sisters! Why can't you believe how alone I felt there? I guess I was lucky, I stayed blond. I learned all of this from gossip, the other women. They talked to me. Like I said, I was gentle with them, they liked me. I'm telling the truth. It's true that I came here to fight you, but I had no choice, I was sent here to fight. Then I found that Harald had sent me to kill girl children. I was disgusted, but my brothers would have killed me if I'd backed out. I would have died rather than hurt the girls, I swear it. You know I nearly did die, doesn't that convince you?'

'Losing a fight to Sara is hardly a sign that you gave in gently. She's a force,' Anthony said quietly.

Jan looked up slightly, smiling. 'You said before she's a little girl.'

Anthony turned his back, unwilling to share the smile. 'Tomorrow, you'll give a blood sample to Diana.'

'Why?' asked Jan.

'Audrey was my sister's name,' Anthony said grimly, opening the door to the basement and leaving Jan standing, shocked.

Anthony stood in the kitchen, sick to his stomach. The Whites must have found Audrey in the place where they'd left Sylvia, and assumed that it was the same woman. Was Sylvia dead too, her body hidden, or had she survived? Was his sister out there somewhere? He mourned for Audrey and her courage, he imagined her racing to warn and save Sylvia, only to be found and taken by the White raiding party. She must have convinced them that she was mother to the dead child. He swore, going back to France to search for a body would be suicide. He closed his eyes and breathed deeply. Tomorrow would be early enough to start the search. For now he had other duties.

He strode through the house and across to the marquee. It looked like any other big family party, except for the surfeit of children of all ages. John and Zoe's youngest babies, Charlotte and Emily, just a few weeks old, were being passed around for cuddles. Seth and Noah were on the top table. Seth was deep in conversation with his girlfriend, Karen. Noah was watching the stage, where his three fathers were busy checking instruments. Diana was at the top table too, speaking intently to Miranda. Mother and daughter were arguing lovingly, Diana kept reaching out, touching Miranda's face. Eventually Miranda nodded. She seemed to be giving in, and moved to the stage. She spoke to Mark, and he hugged her. She sat behind the drums and waved, smiling nervously. Darlene looked up and glared jealously at her. She stalked over to her mother, who laughed and pointed to the keyboard set up. Darlene nodded and settled behind it.

The three men spoke for a few minutes, and then wandered across to their daughters to discuss the set list, finding out what the girls knew, what they could do. Darlene nodded and started to adjust the settings on the keyboard. Miranda looked serious, nervous.

John took centre stage and opened the mike. No squeal of feedback, no nervous coughing. He waited for silence, commanding the stage. The older kids remembered his glory days, and fell quiet. The younger ones followed suit. Diana and Zoe watched him, eyes afire.

'We were the Ransomed Hearts, but we lost Xan and were broken. We're back. We're the Wolfen Hearts. There're two lads here who are twenty-one tonight, and their mother asked us to play at their party. We just didn't have the guts to tell her she couldn't afford us.'

He started to duck as something flew at the stage, then recovered and caught it. A single red rose. 'Thank you, ma'am. Perhaps you can afford us, after all.' The smile he flashed at his Alpha was distinctly wolfish, and Diana felt twenty years younger.

'This is a cover. You all know it.'

The familiar beat, the familiar chords, and a voice even more haunted and haunting than that of its creator. Diana closed her eyes. As her lover, her mate, sang out the opening lyrics of Springsteen's 'Born to Run', she laughed aloud at the sheer corniness of it. Then she glanced to his side. Mark was staring straight at her, mouthing the words silently, making his guitar talk. Suddenly it wasn't corny at all, and a wild thrill spread from her centre, giving her butterflies, weakening her. The look she gave him more than satisfied him, and he looked back down, finding a communion with his guitar, the familiar powerful voice of his cousin next to him taking him back in time. He spun round. The tall blond bass player on the other side of the singer was showing off as usual, at the edge of the stage, flirting with Helen – as usual. The years rolled back, and Mark stepped to the edge of the stage. The teenagers were dancing, the women were watching him with a promise in their eyes, and was it Xan back behind the drums, keeping everyone in perfect order, his hair wild and unbound, the power behind the band? To the side, the gorgeous young redheaded keyboard player was filling out the song, making it richer, more complete. He grinned at her; she was so totally in tune with him. She was laughing at him, it was Darlene, his daughter, and he blinked, turning again. Xan was gone, and Miranda was in his place, lost in the beat, the rhythm. Another blink, and he was back in the present, nodding to his daughters, his children, his mates, and winding down to the end of the song.

John was there again. 'OK, that was fun. Now, this is from our fourth album.'

They played the set that their agent could only dream of, mixing their own stuff with a range of covers, love songs, joke songs, a pomp rock version of 'Happy Birthday' that Queen would have been proud of.

Seth took the mike briefly, to sing a sweetly sad version of Queen's 'You Take My Breath Away'. His girlfriend blushed, and the pair were applauded by the entire party. Noah took over the keyboards from his exhausted sister after forty-five minutes.

After a couple of hours, Mark realised he was the only original band member still on stage. Darlene had climbed back on stage, and it was for her slouching vocals that he was strumming the chords for 'Brass in Pocket'. He looked round. Caleb was watching him hungrily from the side of the stage. Mark hugged him and handed over the guitar. He looked back once; the kids were playing as if born to it. Bridget was playing bass, accurately, though not passionately. He sat down, grabbing food and a large glass of beer. Zoe was utterly absorbed in John, and he had to tap her shoulder several times before she turned round.

'Diana?' he asked. He was suddenly aware of how much he wanted to be with his love.

'Oh, she went to look for Sara,' Zoe said before returning to where she'd left off with her own private rock star. Mark looked round; Andy was missing too. Helen was deep in conversation with Chloe, ignoring her excited eldest daughter who was enthralled by the sight of Caleb wrapped possessively around a guitar.

Mark wondered for a moment about Diana and Andy, and then remembered the way Andy had been with Helen earlier. He wandered to the bar, where he started to chat to Frank.

Diana knocked on Sara and Darlene's door. There was no answer, so she opened it cautiously. The room was empty. She turned and walked the second floor corridors, stopping for a moment outside Seth's door. She heard a slight noise.

'Seth?' she called.

'Mum? What are you doing in here?' She could hear panic in his voice, and smiled.

'I could ask you the same question,' she said.

There was silence.

She took pity on him. 'Happy Birthday, love. Don't stay in there all night, it's your party, after all,' she called, and moved on.

Inside the room, Seth bit his lip and turned back to Karen. 'Sorry, I always feel like a kid when I'm at home,' he said, reaching out to her.

'You don't feel like a kid to me,' she whispered, moving towards him.

For a moment, Diana was tempted to turn back, to ask Seth if he'd seen his sister anywhere, but sense prevailed and she carried on.

Down in the locked basement, Sara stood watching Jan. He was standing against the wall. She put the key on the table. She knew he had no intention of ever escaping.

'Hi, prisoner,' she said.

'Sara… You don't visit often,' he said quietly.

'Ah, I forget that you're down here. How's the lung?'

'Sore. So's the heart,' he said seriously.

'I'm good at that,' she grinned.

They watched each other cautiously. The scar between his ribs itched. He reached to touch it, soothe it, and stopped suddenly as the girl drew next to him, pulling open his shirt, tracing the scar with a long forefinger.

'I did that,' she said, staring at it before stepping back.

He couldn't find the words, just looked at her.

'Why did you try to kill me?' she asked him conversationally.

'I didn't. I tried not to kill you, without getting myself killed. I've explained it a hundred times.'

'In that case, you succeeded. How do you feel about that?' She looked up at him quickly, as if she was trying to catch him out.

'I…'

'What do you want from us? Why did you surrender?'

'I wanted to live,' he managed to say.

'Is that all?' she murmured, her head to one side.

'Sara...' he groaned.

'Yes?' She was almost chirpy, with the same half-mad look he'd seen in Darlene's eyes when he surrendered.

'Sara, you're just a girl, leave me alone,' he managed to say.

'How old are you, Jan?' she said, chewing a long sharp claw that she'd absent-mindedly grown in place of a fingernail.

He sighed. She had his life in her hands; it was getting to be a habit.

'Sara, will you go? Please? If any of your fathers find you in here with me, I'm dead. You know that.'

'Yeah, I'd be pretty much grounded myself,' she said. 'It makes life interesting.'

Once more, he surrendered. 'Sara, what do you want?'

'You, totally,' she said, smiling.

'Fuck,' he said, seeing his life ransomed in her smile.

'Exactly!' she exulted. 'You've got it. You do know how? I mean, life in the White Pack wasn't that boring?'

'I know how, but it is a little different to the situation I'm used to,' he whispered.

'You could tie me up, if that would help...' teased Sara.

'It wouldn't. Sara, you do not know what you're saying. It is not a joke.'

'No, Jan, it's not a joke. I could feel your heart beating, you know? When I had you impaled on me, I could feel it beating, an inch away from me. I could have killed you. But there was something in your eyes that's been puzzling me ever since. You didn't surrender because you were afraid of death...'

'No. I surrendered because it was the only option when I saw you. Sara, you are...' He broke off, helpless in the face of her urgency.

'Are we going to fuck? Because any minute now someone is going to realise I'm not at the party.'

'I'm in no position to take care of you,' he said sadly.

She was looking at him, puzzled, then realised the problem.

'Oh, the Alpha thing. It won't happen, not in this house. The adults have us kids pretty much inhibited.'

'What if you … you know? What if we make a child?'

Sara reached out to him, his nervousness was so appealing.

'Jan, I'm a Shifter, my body is under my control.'

'This isn't your first time?' he said, relaxing a little.

'Hell no, not even my first time in a dungeon. But it *is* my first time with a Shapeshifter,' she said, a small smile on her face.

'Your father will kill me.'

'Only if he finds out,' she assured him, moving closer, reaching for his belt, his zip, purring with satisfaction at what she found waiting for her.

He bit his lip. 'Sara, if you cry rape, I'm dead.'

She laughed, freeing him from his jeans, pushing them down his legs, bending gracefully to slip them off his bare feet.

'Try not to make me scream, then. Take that shirt off the rest of the way, will you? That scar excites me.'

He found out just how much when she pushed him back until he was against the wall.

She took his hand and rubbed it against her heat, her wetness.

He groaned. 'You're too young…' he whispered.

The caress of a draught of cold air made them both stop.

A colder voice spoke. 'Sara. Go back to the party, your father's wondering where you are. Put your knickers back on too, that's a good girl.'

Sara gave her prisoner one last burning look, and backed off. Her mother was perfectly still, watching them. Jan was still leaning against the wall, helpless.

Diana waited until her daughter was out of the door, halfway up the stairs to the kitchen, before she spoke. 'I apologise. This won't happen again.'

Jan was shaking. 'No, it won't… I'm sorry.'

'*You're* sorry? What for? Was it your idea?' Suddenly her attitude was different.

He lowered his eyes. 'No. She came here, she wasn't really giving me much choice,' he admitted.

'I thought so. That's wrong. I'll explain it to her, why it's wrong.' She was watching him carefully. 'Now get dressed.'

Jan obeyed, and was wearing his jeans again when Andy ran down the stairs and stood at the open door, taking in the sight of the younger man half-naked, a prisoner standing in an open room. 'Where's Sara?' he growled, holding himself back with immense effort. He didn't see Diana, who was just inside the room, out of sight.

She walked into her mate's line of sight. 'Sara is fine. She got a bit drunk and went outside for some fresh air. She's probably back at the party by now.'

Andy shook his head. 'And what are you doing here?' he asked.

'That's my business,' she said. She smiled at him. 'Andy, don't worry. It's OK, really.'

He still looked uncertain. She took his hand. 'Come on, hon, let's get back. It's time to start putting littl'uns to bed anyway, and I know you love to help me do that.' She led him away, locking the door behind her.

Back at the party, while rounding up the babies and small children, she cornered Sara.

'What are you playing at?' she asked quietly.

Sara shook her head. 'He's mine. I want him.'

'He's a prisoner, he has no bloody choice about it. Sara, it's wrong, can't you see that? He can't refuse you.'

Sara grinned. 'He doesn't want to.'

Diana gripped her daughter's wrist. 'That's not the point. One day he'll be free, I'm sure of that. You can do what the hell you like then, so far as I'm concerned. But until then, you're barred from seeing him. And I swear to god, if I ever have to lie to Andy again because of you, you'll be sorry you were born.'

She glanced round. Andy was carrying Mia and Joy, who were both dropping asleep on his shoulders. Faith was following him. He made straight for them.

Diana spoke quickly to her daughter. 'You went out for some fresh air because you were drunk, that's what I told him.'

Sara's eyes flashed for a moment, and then she saw the worry in her mother's eyes. 'OK,' she conceded.

Diana smiled, loving her. 'Oh, sweetheart, I just worry about you so much. I'm going to miss you every week while you're at uni.'

'We're really looking forward to it, you know. Don't worry about us, we'll be fine.'

'You'll be alone.' Diana was trying not to fret, but it was difficult. The Kittens were moving to London; Sara to study genetics, Darlene to study Roman history; Darlene had a pet theory about the story of Romulus and Remus.

'We're moving in with the other women there, we won't be alone. They've been in touch with us all summer.'

'Well, be careful. You know you're a real target now.' Diana's eyes were troubled.

Andy joined them with the little girls. He was wearing a black shirt and black denims, his long legs taut and muscular. He greeted Sara.

'Hello, stranger. Where've you been tonight?'

Sara met his gaze; she looked slightly ashamed. 'I had a bit too much wine earlier. I had to go outside.'

'Were you sick?' he asked, feigning concern, not believing her.

Sara kept a straight face. 'No, Dad, not that drunk. I'm fine now, just needed some fresh air.'

Andy glanced at Diana. He could sense a conspiracy between his daughter and her mother, and he knew that Diana was the worse liar, but her face was hidden; she'd grabbed a paper napkin and was kneeling, trying to wipe lemon jelly out of Faith's soft red hair. It was only then that he looked at Faith's twin, belatedly realising she was practically coated with chocolate cake, and that he was going to have to get changed later. When Diana looked up again, she was apologetic. 'Sorry, Andy. They're mucky pups. If my mother was still around, she'd say they took after me.'

He gave up. 'OK, Diana, let's get 'em to bed. How many have you got?'

'Mandy's asleep over there, and Tara and Louise are waiting at the door; they've had enough.'

'That'll do for starters.'

Within an hour, all the younger kids were in bed. The Quads were exultant; they were allowed to stay up 'until the end'. Zoe and John had left already, claiming exhaustion. The band played on, the line-up changing fluidly, covering songs from the last seven decades. Bill was on drums now, Caleb singing and playing guitar, Trixie getting more out of the bass than her twin had done. Alice was jumping up and down with another guitar, managing to have a good time without ruining the efforts of her older brothers and sister. Seth and Karen had reappeared, to some teasing from Noah.

Chloe was sitting alone, watching the pack, the constant interaction between the family members. The band was playing 'Twist and Shout' now, and Bridget and Janie were laughing, trying to teach Susie and Nancy how to dance to it. Diana was sitting with Miranda; they were deep in conversation. Every so often they looked across at Chloe, who sighed. The party was dying down, everyone was sated. It was time. She stood up and stretched, feeling a kink in her neck pop satisfactorily. She knew exactly where Frank and Bill were: Bill was watching her from behind the drums, Frank was still talking to Mark. Mareta and Phil were together, dancing with Eva. Chloe walked across the dance floor towards Diana, refusing to flinch away from the guarded hostility that was gathering in the Alpha's eyes. Miranda reached across and took her mother's hand, squeezing it.

Chloe sat down and took Diana's other hand. She spoke quietly but firmly.

'It's been two years – it's long enough, Diana. They're nineteen now. It's time. I would like your permission, though, and your blessing.'

'Your home is ready, then?' Diana asked.

'We've got the heart of it. We can add to it when we can afford it. Seth and Noah designed it for us, got the seal of approval from one of their lecturers. Bill and Frank built most of it themselves. Andy and Helen have helped to decorate it.' Chloe was watching Diana carefully, determined to be seen as worthy of the boys.

Diana nodded. 'Do you love them?' she asked, almost wistful.

Chloe shook her head. 'Not yet, but I don't doubt that I will. I know I'm ready to love again.'

Miranda was curious. 'How will you choose between them? You can only have one Alpha, and nobody's been able to get a knife between those two since the day they were born.'

Chloe smiled. 'I know who I want. I've been watching them for the last two years, running with them in these grounds, then building our home together. Watch.'

She stood. She was a tiny woman, barely more than five feet. Her long mid-brown hair was tied back in a simple but elegant plait, and she was wearing a plain white knee-length sleeveless dress that showed off the remains of her summer tan. Not beautiful, reflected Miranda, who was studying her, but graceful. Not strong, but watchful and determined. Chloe moved until she was standing exactly halfway between Frank and Bill. She held two empty glasses, and frowned at them. Frank was standing by the bar, and she turned towards him.

'Frank, could you bring me a refill?' she called out.

'Just a sec, sweetheart… I'm just talking to Dad about something.'

She smiled, and waited; the band had just lost its drummer.

Bill waltzed past her, pausing to kiss her cheek affectionately. He brought a champagne bottle back and bowed, flirting. 'Milady?'

'My Alpha,' she replied.

He stood perfectly still, his pupils widening, then bent to kiss her hand.

Diana watched, smiling despite herself. Her children had all learned the art of charm from John and Anthony. Bill recovered and looked around. No one was looking at him except his mother and eldest sister. His hands were shaking as he filled both glasses. Chloe passed one to him.

'A toast, my Alpha. A toast to a strong and happy new pack.'

'A toast to our strong and happy new pack,' said Bill quietly, looking into her eyes.

Diana tore her eyes away, her gaze falling on Mark, who sensed her eyes on him and looked back, smiling.

Miranda was still holding her hand. 'She chose the one who loves her most,' observed the fey blonde, turning to her mother. 'Do you ever wish…?'

Diana shook her head. 'No, I never wished that, not once,' she said. 'Quiet, watch.'

The stillness of the new couple, standing looking at each other in the centre of the room, was beginning to draw some attention. The band had faltered to a halt. Caleb had jumped off the stage and grabbed a bottle of beer. He was moving quickly to the pair. Seth was a step behind him.

Caleb looked at Bill. 'Is this what I think it is?'

Bill nodded gravely.

'Congratulations.' Caleb toasted him.

Seth was next, grinning broadly. 'Fucking fantastic.'

Frankie was turning round, realising what had happened. 'Oh, Bill, you bastard,' he whispered.

Mark shrugged. 'What did you think she was going to do? She had to choose one of you. That'll teach you not to keep her waiting.' He was watching Frank carefully, and was relieved to see him pick up a glass of wine and make his way across the room to his twin and his mate-to-be. By now, everyone was watching.

'What's the toast?' Frankie asked. He was stiff, formal.

Chloe kissed him gently on the cheek. 'To our strong and happy new pack. Frankie, I've made my choice. Bill and I are bound to it. But I won't put you under any pressure. You can join us, or you can make your own pack with someone else. I would like you to join us, though.'

Frank bit his lip, looking at Bill, and then nodded. 'I've just spent over a year building that house. I'm going to live in it too,' he said, trying to joke. Chloe was smiling, watching him. Frankie hesitated, before raising his glass. 'To our strong and happy new pack.'

Mark and Diana joined them, hugging them all. Andy had disappeared. As the drink started to flow again, Mareta and Phil were brought into the circle.

Phil narrowed his eyes at the twins. 'Do I have to call you Dad now?' he asked.

'Damn right you do,' Bill said.

'You're only nine years older than me,' complained Phil.

'It's not age, it's attitude, son,' said Bill gravely, his arm around Chloe, who spluttered champagne out of her nose, choking.

Frankie looked to heaven. 'Bill, she's been yours for five minutes, and she's already half-dead. I think she's made a big mistake.'

Andy walked back in, herding a very sleepy John, who was wearing a pair of jeans and nothing else. Andy apologised. 'Zoe needs her sleep. John wouldn't let me wake her up.'

John rubbed his eyes and went to his sons. 'I'll never leave a party early again. Congratulations, Frank.' He hugged the elder twin.

Frank shook his head. 'She chose Bill,' he said, uncomfortable.

'Yeah, I know. That's why I'm saying congratulations to you. Beta's more fun.' He caught Bill's bemused expression and grinned widely, hugging both of his sons. 'I'd suggest a party, but we've already got one. Will someone get me a drink? And a band… Suddenly I'm feeling awake again.'

He went back to the stage, waiting for Mark and Andy to join him. He looked at the drums vacated by Bill. 'Oi! Miranda!' he shouted. 'Fancy a job?'

As the dancing started again, Diana approached her sons and their new Alpha. She looked grimly determined. 'I'm still sober. I'll take you home when you're ready, if that's what you want? Helen's already offered to look after Mareta and Phil tonight.'

Bill shook his head. 'No. They're coming home with us. We're a pack.' He looked utterly serious. 'And now would be fine – I think we've hijacked this birthday party for long enough.'

The new pack slipped out quietly, stopping, on the way, to receive congratulations. Anthony was sitting on the low car park wall, looking at the stars. They paused as they got to him. He stood up, seeing the situation in one glance, and enveloped Chloe in a bear hug. She could barely return it, so tiny her arms only just met around his broad back. He looked over her shoulder at Diana and smiled at her.

'Daughter, shall I take the new pack to their home? You look exhausted.' He refrained from saying she looked like she was going to burst into tears at any moment.

She nodded, lips pressed close together. 'If they don't mind,' she said quickly, quietly.

Anthony put Chloe down; she was red-faced, slightly breathless. She thanked Anthony. 'No, I don't mind, probably best all round, really. Come and visit us next week, Diana.' She fished in her handbag for the car keys and handed them to Anthony, taking the passenger seat. The twins and her children squeezed into the back.

'Next week?' whispered Diana, watching the car pull away. 'She takes my sons and tells me I can visit next bloody week?'

She turned round. Miranda was behind her; she'd abandoned the drums. 'Aw, Mum. She just wants to make sure they're all hers, before you go stamping your Alpha hormones all over her nice new house.'

Diana nodded. She understood why she and Mark had been barred from the house while it was being built, but it still hurt. She looked up at her daughter. '*You're* not going to get married and leave me anytime soon? Right?'

Miranda took her by the arm, leading her away from the drive. 'I can't see it ever happening, Mother dear. I'll die a virgin fairy queen.'

Diana leaned against her eldest daughter. 'Do you regret it? Trying?' she asked quietly.

'The Summer of Bites?' said Miranda lightly. 'No. I had to try everything. It didn't work, but at least I tried, at least I took things as far as I could.'

'I can't regret you.' Diana's voice was low. 'No matter how strange you find this life, I can't regret you.'

'Mother, you're sad. Shall we go and sing to Sammy?'

'Sammy's gone.' Diana's voice was breaking.

'Then we'll sing to Sammy's tree. Come on, Little Mum. Then we'll go back to the party, eh?'

Together they walked into the woods.

Chapter 16

Anthony parked on the small drive. The house was newly built, the garden still mud. They'd stopped at a supermarket on the way back; although the house had been finished and ready for almost a month, it was still unlived in, and empty of day-to-day necessities. He helped his grandsons' new mate put the shopping away. The twins went upstairs to make beds and settle the kids down.

'Cuppa before you go?' suggested Chloe. Anthony nodded and sat down at the large kitchen table.

Chloe was silent as she brewed up, putting two new mugs on the table. She sat down and sighed. 'Anthony, I'm scared shitless.'

'Of the enemy?'

'Yes, of course. I've felt so protected these last two years, I feel vulnerable now. I want this… I *do* want this responsibility, but it's such a huge risk.'

Anthony nodded. 'It's always the same. And you *will* be a target. Especially when the lads are at work.' His words gave no comfort.

'I won't run away again,' Chloe said, certainty in her voice. 'I'll take one of them with me at least, if they come for me.'

'Look, I'm almost sure there aren't any in the country at the moment. Except Jan, of course. You're safe for tonight, at least.'

'That's a comfort,' she said shakily.

Anthony sighed. 'We can't carry on like this, Chloe, waiting to be hit and trying to hit back before they escape back home.'

'So what do we do?' she asked him.

'We'll figure something out,' he said. Then he changed the subject. 'I'd better get home. I'll bet the pack are still partying.'

'Oh, they will be. Thanks, Anthony.'

'Look, don't be scared – that's what they want, what they've always wanted. You're doing great. You've survived one attack, and saved two kids from it. You fought back when we went to help Michaela's pack. That makes you a winner.'

Chloe looked at the table. 'I still miss them so much. My pack … my first pack.'

'I've never stopped missing any of the ones I've lost. I hope I never do.' He bent and kissed her head. 'Now I'm going. Goodnight, Chloe.'

He walked out of the door, and she stood and locked it, switching on the alarm system. She looked at the wide window and imagined it crashing inwards, a white wolf landing snarling on the clean kitchen floor. For a moment she considered bars across it, protecting her. She shuddered and refused the image.

'I can't live in a prison,' she whispered.

She flinched as the twins came back from upstairs. They looked so young, and her heart sank. It had seemed like such a good idea, but now she doubted her judgement. Bill started to make a pot of tea. He gave her a questioning look, and she shook her head.

'Just had one,' she explained. She looked at his back. His hair was curling at the nape of his neck, growing a little longer than it had for the past year or so. He was wearing a pair of old-fashioned olive combat trousers that looked as though they'd been passed round the family for the last twenty years. Knowing Diana and her thriftiness, they probably had. His shoulders were broad inside his olive T-shirt, his waist slim. His body had changed so much in the two years since he'd first offered to protect her, to care for her. He had that perfect male shape, like his father and great-uncle. And yet she still felt no desire for him. She looked up.

Frankie was watching her. 'I guess I'm in the second bedroom tonight?'

The three of them had planned their home together, making plans with Seth and Noah. Five large bedrooms, two of them interconnected via a shared bathroom, for the use of the adults. One each for Mareta and Phil, and one ready as a nursery. A second bathroom completed the first floor.

Bill sat down close to her, put his mug on the pale wood of the pine table, and passed a second mug to his brother.

'Chloe, would you mind if we waited? If we didn't spend tonight together? If I shared the other room with Frankie tonight?' he said cautiously.

'Well, I suppose not. Why?'

'I don't really feel ready. Only a couple of hours ago I was just another kid. It's just too soon for me to start being a man. You won't understand, your parents were carriers, not full-blown Shapeshifters dripping hormones everywhere.' He was calm, composed, not the slightest bit flustered.

She tried not to smile. 'You mean you can't?'

'Oh, I can. Well, I think I can. Frankie and I sort of gave it up when we made things official, our betrothal to you.' He looked a little more nervous now.

'You did what?'

'Well, it didn't seem fair, going out with girls when we knew nothing would ever come of it.'

Chloe was staggered. She'd spent the last year with these lads, seeing them almost every day as they worked on the house. They'd never mentioned it before.

'Truly? You've been waiting for me?'

'Well, yes, of course, that too.'

'And you want to wait another night?'

'Yes. Chloe, I want it to be perfect.'

'We both do,' said Frankie, looking up from the table.

She had a moment of self-doubt. 'Is it because I'm so much older than you?'

Bill sighed. He looked pointedly at Frankie, who nodded and left the kitchen, making his way upstairs to the second bedroom. Bill waited until he heard water running, then allowed his gaze to meet hers.

'Chloe, I do want you. And I know you were laughing at me, don't think I don't. I'm thick, but I'm not that thick. And I can see in your eyes that you don't want me, not like I want you. I'm nineteen years old, I've not touched a girl for over a year, and I've got you here, and you're mine. This isn't easy.' He stood up and moved away from her, hoisting himself up until he was sitting on one of the kitchen work surfaces. He fidgeted a little. 'And I love you,' he said abruptly, as if confessing to something shameful.

She started to stand, to go to him, to hug him, one of those affectionate sisterly hugs she'd been giving him for two years.

'Oh, Chloe, don't touch me, or I'll fuck you into the ground,' he murmured, looking anywhere but at her.

The sudden thick lust in his voice took her by surprise and sent her memories abruptly back to her first years with Duncan. He hadn't been much younger than Bill when he'd first come to her. She banished the thought; it came with too much pain. It was time for a new start. She could feel a dryness in her throat, a growing heat between her legs. She shifted restlessly.

'And why shouldn't you?' she asked.

'Because of the bonding. I want to make that Alpha bond our first time together. Make it magical. Tonight we could fuck all night, but I don't believe the bond could happen. I've not been away from my pack long enough. It would take the wonder out of it. I *want* there to be wonder. I'm going to spend the rest of my life with you. I'm going to die when you die. Doesn't that deserve some magic?'

She smiled. 'Bill, you're a hopeless romantic. I'll go to bed. I'll see you in the morning.' She stood and walked to the door, stopping suddenly when he cleared his throat. She turned. He was still perched on the work surface, watching her closely, the trace of a smile on his face.

'You want me now, don't you?' he said. 'You didn't before.'

'Bill, all I'll admit is that you'd better sleep with your doors locked.'

'You too,' he said with a sad smile.

She overslept the next morning, waking with a start. The sun was blazing through the thin curtains, the room was bright. There was no clock, and, she realised, no clean clothes to change into. They'd bought just a couple of towels at the shop the night before, and she groaned, realising she was probably the last one up. She wasn't looking forward to the prospect of bathing and drying off with a damp towel rescued from the floor.

She unlocked the door to the bathroom, and blinked. The bathroom was suddenly a familiar place, her towels laid out, cosmetics and toiletries in the cupboards and the shower cubicle. Her robe hung on the back of the door with two others.

The other door opened. Bill peered in. 'Ah, I thought I heard you. Do you always sleep this late?'

She was about to protest when she saw the gleam in his eye. 'Did the fairies visit?' she asked him, waving at the bathroom.

'Yeah, Frankie got a taxi, dropped the kids off at school. Then AndyDad came with a van full of your stuff. I'm sorting it now. I thought I'd do the bathroom first, for you. And JohnDad turned up about half an hour ago with a van full of our stuff. Mum brought your car back too. They didn't want to stay. He said they were stopping by at the DIY place on the way home.

Him and Mum are going to redecorate our room! Faith and Joy are having it! Do you believe it?'

'Oh, your mother's a pragmatist. Don't think it means she doesn't miss you. Where is Frankie anyway?'

'He's gone to work. He's giving my excuses.'

'You're staying here today?'

Bill nodded, trying not to stare at her. She was sleep-rumpled, wearing a long T-shirt and nothing else. He'd never seen anything so beautiful in his life. He swallowed.

'Yes, all day. I'll get on with the unpacking then..' he said, backing out.

She waited until she heard him on the stairs, then stripped off the T-shirt and got into the shower, taking her time.

When she went back into the bedroom, there were a couple of suitcases on the bed, open. She recognised Helen's work in the tidiness of the packing. As she took off her robe and reached into the suitcase for a set of white underwear, a slip of paper tucked into the suitcase lining caught her eye:

> *You lucky bitch, those boys are*
> *gorgeous. Love Helen. PS, destroy*
> *this note, they'd DIE if they read*
> *this.*

Underneath the note, in a scrawl, an addition:

> *Not dead yet. Love Bill.*

She laughed out loud, delighted. She opened the second suitcase, found the pink shift dress that she was looking for and stepped into it, zipping it up. She towel-dried her hair and brushed it out, looking critically at her reflection and deciding against make-up.

She ate breakfast alone, watching with interest as Bill carried box after box into the house. Eventually she offered to make him tea.

He sighed. 'Thought you'd never ask.'

'You shouldn't be shy. If you want something, tell me.' She smiled at him.

He grinned back, wiping his hand through his hair. He was sweating; the day was warm and the work was hard. He smelled clean, though.

Without thinking about it, she leaned across and kissed him. His sweat on her lips tingled. She closed her eyes and licked her lips. When she opened her eyes again, he was watching her.

'I'll lock the doors,' he said. A minute later he was behind her, his lips on her neck. 'You taste so good,' he said dreamily. 'Is it time? What do you think?'

She fought back to sanity. 'Bed, please. Take me to our bed.'

She was lifted into his arms. 'You're like a feather.' He laughed. He bent to kiss her, and then pulled back, wary of what it would lead to. 'We'll just get upstairs first, I think.'

'Control,' she muttered. 'You've got so much self-control.'

'You won't be saying that in a couple of minutes,' he assured her. There was something in his voice that finished it for her; she had no choice or will any more, just a burning desire for the mate she'd been promised for so long. How could she have thought of him as a boy? The expression on his face, the angles of his features, the way the muscles moved under his skin. None of that had anything to do with boyhood.

He carried her upstairs. He pushed the bedroom door open, carrying her through, closing it behind him. He put her on the edge of the bed and locked the door. 'Don't want any interruptions.' he muttered. He wasn't speaking to her, he was thinking aloud. His eyes were losing focus, a yellow gleam coming into them.

'Bill…' she whispered, bringing him back to her. He'd been standing next to the door, almost fainting. He looked at her and licked his lips. She was getting off the bed, moving towards him. He shook his head, pushing, almost forcing her back on to the bed. He sat next to her, leaning towards her, and touched her lips with his own. They felt like cool rain. He kissed her harder. She teased his lips with her tongue, and the magic began, chemical signals rushing between them, starting to make the bond. Her hand was at his belt, pulling at the buckle, working it open.

He was reaching behind her, looking for the zip of her dress. Impatient, he ripped down, pulling the fabric cleanly away. He sat back, looking at her. She was neat, tanned, tiny. He murmured her name. 'Chloe, turn round,' he said. She did, and he unhooked the bra and pushed the straps over her shoulders. He took hold of the waistline of her knickers and pulled them down, then peeled off his socks and T-shirt. He turned her round again and pulled the lacy bra away from her. 'Rest of our lives…' he whispered, looking at her.

She lay down, pulling him down towards her, kissing him again, the communication between them writing a new pathway in her body, her brain. In a sudden moment of clarity, she wondered how things could be different with his twin, but then the thought was gone, and he was licking her body, working downwards from her neck. He was biting her, tiny wounds bringing her blood to the surface. He was licking it, tasting it, dizzied by what it told him about her. He could sense her other men, the men she'd been bound to before. Faded, weaker links than the one they were making now together, but he could taste their signature, written into her body forever. He paused, momentarily jealous.

She was looking at him, raising her knees to her shoulders, open and ready, totally wanton. 'Now,' she demanded.

He couldn't refuse and paused only to dip his head and lick roughly at what she was offering him, tasting her, knowing her. Then he held himself above her with one hand, guiding himself into her slick depths with the other. She screamed and bucked underneath him, and he came, helplessly, unable to stop himself. He looked at her, appalled.

'Oh fuck. Oh, Chloe, my Chloe, I'm so sorry.'

She was lying back, her eyes closed but flickering behind her lids. She had a lazy smile on her face. 'Hard again yet?' she asked him, not opening her eyes.

He nodded then realised she couldn't see him. He gave her his answer without words, and she opened her eyes, a contented smile on her face, as they began to move together slowly, learning each other.

An hour later, temporarily sated and sore, she sat up. He was asleep. She couldn't imagine ever being away from him. She stood to go to the toilet, and he stirred, reaching out.

'Don't go,' he whispered. 'Did we do it? Did we Alpha?' he said, opening his eyes.

She laughed. 'Well, what do you think?'

'Never done it with a Shapeshifter before,' he said. He looked up hopefully. 'Maybe it's always like that?' He gave her a sly look, teasing. He knew bloody well what they'd done.

Chapter 17

Diana and Miranda sat on the shaded porch, cool ivy soothing the madly hot air around them. Diana was sewing new sets of buttons on to two pale blue hooded winter coats. Miranda was sitting next to her, reading a maths textbook. Their silence was companionable, but conscious. They were keeping an eye on the prisoner, who was weeding a flowerbed.

Miranda frowned at her book. 'Mum? Does this make sense to you?' she started.

'If it's maths, don't even ask. You left me standing years ago,' Diana said.

'Well, it's stupid. There's *such* an easier way to prove this.'

Diana looked up, interested, confident of her daughter's abilities. 'If you're right, and nobody's spotted it before, that's great. Bring it up when you go back to uni. That should get you your First, no problems.'

Miranda itched to talk about it. There was nobody else in the family who understood, though; the dancing symbols, the whirling notes, the beat and song of the world in her head. She read on for another couple of chapters and then put the book down. She watched Jan for a while; he was wiping his forehead. He walked over to them.

'May I get some water?' He was careful not to even glance at Miranda; he was taking Andy's warnings very much to heart. Diana reached over lazily, taking a cold bottle of water out of a cool bag. She passed it over, and waited as he drank it down, watching the way he stood, the shape of his hips outlined against the green of the ivy, something indefinable about the way he wiped his mouth. He thanked her and handed the bottle back, then went back to his work.

Miranda glanced at him, then at Diana. 'Well? Do you know yet?'

Her mother nodded. 'Yeah, I know. In the sense that *I'm* convinced. But it'll take me another couple of days to prove it. We're all inbred, to some degree, all related. Except for Andy of course.'

'Jan *is* Anthony's nephew, then?'

'Well, if I didn't know they were Shapeshifters, I'd have to say that they share enough genes to be brothers, or father and son. But we're an inbred lot, and we can't make the same assumptions. I'm looking at the mitochondrial DNA now, the mother's line. That'll be the clincher, really. I wish I had some of Audrey's DNA to look at, then it would be easy.' She was watching the young man again; he was kneeling, absorbed in his work. 'Look at him, Miranda. How many times have you seen that expression? Who needs DNA sequences?'

'Yeah, I can see Anthony's blood there.' Miranda watched the man for a moment, before picking up the book again.

Diana shook out the first coat, smoothing it, putting it aside, and picking up the next one. 'The thing is,' she started, 'no matter how closely related he is to Anthony, we can't automatically trust him. He's just as closely related to the White Pack. He wasn't born here.'

'He was reborn here,' said Miranda, barely raising her eyes from the book.

Diana stopped dead, needle raised. As always, Miranda had found the heart of the matter, dragged it bloody and beating into the open, and left it carelessly exposed for observation. The young woman was again absorbed in her book.

Diana spoke quietly, barely touching her daughter's consciousness. 'Can we trust him?' she whispered.

'Yes, he loves us,' Miranda answered, not looking up.

'What's his strength, Miranda?' her mother asked.

'His patience,' the blonde said absently, turning the page.

'Could he make you happy?' asked Diana cautiously.

A flicker of annoyance, and Miranda looked up, alert. 'What? No. Don't be silly.'

Diana relaxed. The oracle, that weird state of hypersensitivity that Miranda fell into sometimes, was gone. Diana had learned to trust the oracle. Maybe it was time to give Jan his freedom. She finished sewing on the buttons and looked critically at the coats. They'd been new nine years earlier, but she'd learned early on to buy quality, and they were still warm and wearable. Meg and Beth had worn them first and now it was the turn of Faith and Joy, and Diana reflected that this was probably the end of the line. Her last-born seemed to be the end of the line for most things. Mark had nicknamed them the Destroyers only a week ago, with his unconscious casual cruelty, and the whole family had taken it on board without comment.

Diana stood and stretched. She was restless, waiting for Miranda to say what had been on her mind all day.

'What are you doing now, Mum?' asked Miranda tentatively.

'I've got some papers to read. I'll bring them out here – it's nice, being with you.'

'Mum? You know what day it is?' Miranda ventured.

Diana closed her eyes. She'd known this was coming, had been waiting all day for it. But avoiding Miranda on this day would be cruel. 'Yes, I know. Do you want to get the albums out? Look at his pictures?'

Miranda grinned. 'Thanks, Mum. He likes it when we look at his pictures.' She sprang off the bench and ran to her room.

'Fucking barmy,' observed Diana to herself. Miranda had always been a little mad, but the biting, the infections and the fevers of summer 2015 had sent her over the edge. She skated over the world, barely touched by it, at a slightly different angle to reality than everyone else. In an odd way, it had brought her closer than ever to Diana.

Miranda was back within minutes, carrying a thick photo album. She knew much more about Xan than Diana did, and took her mother through the photographs of him as a child, growing up with Helen and Andy, in the band, on holiday. The last photograph was a snap of him taken in Ibiza by a fan. He was smiling distractedly for the camera, obviously in a hurry to get to someone, but pausing to be polite, to please. He looked so young. The second to last photograph was another candid snap, taken by Mark. The young Diana was lying in bed asleep. John was sitting on the edge of the bed, holding two wrinkled newborns in his arms. He wasn't looking at the camera, he was saying something to Andy, who was sprawled on his back on the other side of Diana, frowning at John. Between John and Diana was a long hill in the sheets: Xan, playfully hiding from the camera.

'He was happy,' Miranda said.

'He was then. I think he was happy then. But the next day he was angry with all of us.'

Miranda took up the thread, the story that Diana had given her in place of a father.

'And the day after that, he came to you with flowers so you wouldn't be alone when Mark was getting married. And the day after *that*, you made love, and made me. It's so romantic.'

Diana hid her smile. 'He was a good friend to me when I needed one.'

Miranda was gently stroking the last picture. 'He's glad that you and Helen are friends now.'

Diana shivered. She was a scientist, a materialist. She'd almost single-handedly turned lycanthropy from a legend into a science. She believed in neither ghosts nor visions, but the conviction in Miranda's voice almost made her see Xan, standing behind his daughter.

'He's waiting for you. He won't go on until you all join him.' Miranda was far away, somewhere deep inside herself.

Diana shut the album firmly. 'We still miss him. Tonight we'll drink a toast to him, all of us. But he loved life, not death, and this isn't the way to think about him.'

Miranda blinked out of her reverie and took her mother's hand.

Chapter 18

'We're going to miss Faith and Joy's birthday next week,' Sara said quietly from the back seat.

'And Tom and Alex's first birthday,' added Darlene. She sounded unusually subdued.

Andy was driving. 'I'll come and pick you up if you want? There's nothing stopping you from coming home next weekend.' He was smiling a little.

There was silence for a while, then Sara said, 'No, we'll ring home on their birthdays. What are Frank and Bill doing?'

Diana spoke up. 'They said they'd pop round with presents on both days, but they're not stopping. It's going to be strange, having the four of you gone. Still, at least you two will be back for the Christmas holidays. Do you want me to drive down for you, or are you getting the train?'

The twins looked at each other, wondering just how much of the four-week break they were expected to spend at home. 'We'll let you know, if that's OK?' Sara said.

'Hmm, this it?' asked Andy, slowing down, turning the Jag into a long tree-lined street. It ran parallel to a Tube line, and was dilapidated. A third of the way down the long terrace, a young woman with short light brown curls and an athletic build was standing at the front gate of a three-storey house that looked slightly less run-down than the rest of the buildings. She was waving excitedly. Andy found a parking space two hundred yards further up the road, and parked up. The twins sprang out and ran to the woman. Andy shrugged, and began to unload boxes and suitcases from the boot and the roof rack.

'You *could* help, Diana,' he suggested mildly.

She nodded, picking up a box of books and making her way up the street with it. As she got to the gate, she found herself surrounded by six girls of varied height and colouring, all offering to help. She pointed down the street at Andy and went into the house.

The walls were papered with antique woodchip, but were brightly painted and decorated with posters. A whiteboard in the hall displayed a list of names, with 'Sara' and 'Darlene' added at the bottom. Next to each name someone had written 'home' in red marker.

The fair-haired woman she'd seen at the gate saw her looking. 'Oh, we always let each other know where we are. Common sense, really.'

'And hard experience?' asked Diana, looking at the woman's right hand, which was missing the little finger and ring finger.

'Ah yes, bastards. Well, no sign of them for a while now. Maybe they've given up?'

'I doubt it,' muttered Diana. 'Anyway, you've probably guessed, I'm Diana.'

'And I'm Mary Wilding. I'm in charge, being the eldest and all. I'm a vet, just qualified.'

Diana smiled. 'That's handy.'

'I suppose so. Look, don't worry about your girls. I've been in this house for about seven years now, seen girls come and go. They usually settle down quickly, and we all know about first-night homesickness. We'll be ready with tea and sympathy tonight.'

Diana nodded. Somehow it was harder to deal with the thought of the twins missing her, than with her missing them.

Andy followed the stream of young women into the house. 'Another trip each and we'll have done it,' he said.

Mary looked at him and blushed. 'Oh, sorry. Their rooms are the two attic rooms – we'll have to get everything upstairs.'

With everything safely in the house, Mary led Sara and Darlene upstairs to the attic. 'I'll let you choose who has which.'

The twins looked at each other. 'Well?' said Darlene. 'Do you want the front one or the back?'

Sara shook her head. 'A room each? I hadn't thought of that.'

Mary nodded. 'Make whatever arrangements you want. You could share one as a bedroom, and have the other for studying.'

The twins looked at each other again, and Sara said, 'Maybe we could try having a room each, and if we don't like it, we could change things round?'

Darlene agreed, cautiously, and called down. 'OK, Dad, you can bring everything up now.'

Andy looked at the carload of boxes, and then at the girls' mother. 'Where did she learn to be so bossy?' he asked her wonderingly.

'From being spoiled rotten since the day she was born, probably. And yes, you're responsible.' She raised her voice. 'Your dad and I are going to find somewhere nice and have lunch. The two of you can do your own heavy work.' Andy started to protest, but Diana shook her head. 'No, I hardly ever get to see you these days – alone. Humour me?' She took his hand and led him out of the house.

Mary watched as the tall, still-attractive blond followed obediently behind the little redhead. She reflected that it would take a generous soul to describe the woman as beautiful, or even pretty, but there he went. 'So that's what it's all about. Hmm,' she muttered.

Sara was first downstairs, just in time to see the door close. 'Where've they gone?'

'Lunch, your mum said. From the look on her face, though, she might have had something else in mind.'

Sara shook her head. 'No. They don't do that any more. Dad told her that it pissed his wife off. She probably just wants some attention. She's always been jealous of us,' she said airily. 'I'm Sara, I'm the good-looking one. Darlene will try to tell you the same thing, but ignore her, she's deluded.'

Mary found herself smiling, charmed by the younger woman. 'Well, we all know each other from the web, and you know what we all look like, of course. Take your time settling in. I guess your parents will be back to say goodbye at some point?'

'Oh yes, and I apologise in advance if Mum starts being bossy. Because she will be.'

'Ah, mums always are when they drop their daughters off. I've seen it before.'

'Not like this, you haven't,' said Sara with immense certainty. 'Well, I'll start unpacking. What do we do for meals? Scavenge for ourselves? Or share the cooking and cleaning?'

Mary found herself approving of this straightforward young woman.

'We tend to share everything … cooking, cleaning. We try to eat together when we can.'

'What about fight practice? Every night, or less than that?'

'What?' asked Mary.

'Fight practice. You know?'

Mary looked uncertain. 'Well, we sort of play fight, when we go for a run together. But, if you want to teach us what you know, perhaps we could organise something? We've got a good big back garden to the house.'

'Cool. Oh, and do you mind if we bring boys home?'

Mary laughed. It was usually one of the first questions from new girls in the house.

'Not Shapeshifters, that's the only rule. Oh, hell, that means your brothers can't visit. Everyone else is from carrier families. Will it be a problem?'

'No, we'll just meet them somewhere else. You know them? Do you talk to them online?'

Mary shrugged. 'I used to talk to Seth, but he's not on much any more. I don't really get on with Noah, and Caleb always seems like a kid to me. Bill and Frank still make me laugh, but they've not had time to chat since they moved in with Whatsername, that older woman? I can never remember her name. Mousy sort.'

'Chloe?' interrupted Darlene, who'd been listening in.

'Yeah, her,' said Mary, forcing a smile.

Sara grinned. 'Broke a lot of wolfie hearts, that did. Still, they might be on the lookout for another girl or two, you never know.' She danced back upstairs, leaving Mary reflecting that perhaps the teenagers were a little *too* acute.

An hour later there was a knock on the door. Mary answered it. It was the Kittens' parents back from a short lunch. They didn't stay long, just had a cup of tea in Sara's room, handed a cheque for a year's expenses to Mary, and gave each of their daughters a bank card. As they left, Mary stopped them. She was blushing again.

She held out a battered old CD. 'Mr Ransome, could you sign this for me? It's always been my favourite album.'

Andy's face lit up. 'A young fan? I'm flattered. Do you want me to take it home and get the others to sign it? It's one of the limited edition ones too!'

Mary gained confidence. 'Would you? Honest? I've got some more stuff too, if you wouldn't mind signing it.'

Andy nodded. 'No problem, I'll be here every few weeks to see the girls anyway. There's no rush, is there?'

'No,' she conceded. 'It's great to meet you. And you *have* got lots of young fans, you know?'

He was signing the CD insert. 'To Mary? Right?'

'To Mary,' she confirmed, trying to stay cool.

'Mary. That's a pretty name. Diana, honey, why haven't we got a Mary? Shall I sign it in the blank bit, or over my face?'

'Oh, you choose.' Mary was getting flustered.

Diana kicked him gently. 'You were never this nice to fans in my day,' she said.

'Ah, I didn't appreciate them then,' he told her. 'You don't know what you've got 'til it's gone.' He didn't see the look of longing she gave him when he said that. He walked out, whistling happily.

Diana was about to follow him when Mary stopped her. 'Look, I hope you don't think I'm out of line but … Chloe, is she nice? She's a bit of a mystery to us younger ones.'

'She's a bit wet, but she's nice enough,' said Diana with her usual blunt honesty. 'Why?'

'Ah… Sara said that her brothers might be looking for another woman for the pack. I was wondering…'

Diana blinked. 'Well, that would make sense. They've not said anything to me, but their father was certainly never happy with only one woman, even when he was twice their age. And there's two of them.'

Mary was blushing madly. 'The thing is, I don't want to give up my career. I've spent a lot of time qualifying, I want to work first before I get settled.'

'Hey, I know Chloe's stretching her budget as it is, until the boys start bringing in more than their apprentice wages. She'd be glad to have another earner in the house. Why don't you contact them?'

'Well, I'm a few years older than Bill and Frank. I've always liked them, but I didn't want them to think I was some mad old woman.'

'Yeah, well, you're younger than Chloe. Besides, I don't think that's an issue for them, somehow. Look, keep in touch. It was nice to meet you.'

Mary stepped forward and embraced Diana awkwardly.

Diana hugged her back, suspecting they'd meet again. She left the house and looked down the street. Andy was leaning on the Jag, arms folded, waiting for her. She looked up again at the high windows of the house, seeing her daughters standing at the window of the front attic room. She waved to them, and walked quickly away. She didn't start to cry until she was safely in Andy's car and on the way home.

Chapter 19

The first light of dawn silvered the snow around the stone cottage. Wolf prints circled the building, leading out to the surrounding pine woods and back again. Candlelight burned softly in an upstairs room. In the bed, curled under a pile of blankets, Diana lay encircled in Mark's arms.

'This is very weird,' she told him. 'I feel guilty.'

'It's over twenty-one years since we were alone together,' he said, stroking her hair. 'We deserve this. Just relax. Everything is fine at home, I promise.'

'Why are we here?' she asked him.

He lay back and stretched out, staring at the ceiling. 'Oh you bloody homebody! I know where Caleb gets it from now. It's a holiday – we go away from home, just the two of us, and we have fun, and chat, and get to know each other a bit more. And you let me spoil you until you get fed up. Then I let you spoil me, and we carry on like that until we're ready to go home. And, sweetheart, if you say you're ready to go home now, I'll cry.'

Diana frowned. 'Mark, that's fine. I'm happy, really. There's something unreal about being alone with you, though it's nice, for a change. But stop treating me like an idiot – you're after something, aren't you?'

He gave her a dirty grin, and rolled on top of her. Her expression made him stop and lie down beside her again. 'Fuck,' he muttered.

'Well, we can. But I still want to know what you're really after.'

'OK. I was hoping to have some more fun first, but you won't shut up until you know.'

'Know what?'

Her husband sighed. 'You're not gonna like this.'

'Obviously, hence the week in Scotland alone with you. It's my heart's desire come true, so there has to be a catch.' She put her head on his chest, running her finger down his thin, wiry upper arm and down to his wrist. She found herself distracted by the knotted muscles of his arms and wrists, his long clever fingers, and blinked. 'Stop being beautiful at me – tell me what it is.'

'Well, first of all … oh, god. Can we at least have breakfast first? I'll make pancakes and coffee and bring them up to... No? Shit. Well … Seth's getting married.'

'I know. Karen told me yesterday, just before we left. Is that it?' She'd stopped the play of her fingers over his arm and was looking up, giving him a puzzled look that relaxed him a little.

'Part of it. I didn't think you knew. I'm not supposed to know, but Noah let it slip. Why the fuck didn't you tell me?'

'Oh, I was going to, but it's way off yet. Karen said September. I suppose it slipped my mind.'

'Our firstborn is getting married, and has rejected his heritage, and it slipped your mind?'

This time she laughed. 'Heritage? What heritage? We're mongrels. He's doing exactly what he's been brought up to believe is OK. We're a part of the human race, not apart from it. If he's found love with Karen, that's his right.'

'So you're OK with it?'

'To tell the truth, I think he's making the same mistake you did, but for different reasons. You didn't know I was out there, and he thinks that he can ignore those Shapeshifter women who *are* out there. I just hope they accept he's off limits. I really hope it works out – I like Karen, she's smart and sensible and she's in love with him.'

'So it has your blessing?'

'I wouldn't go that far. Chloe and the boys have my blessing. I think Seth and Karen need more than that. They need a miracle, but miracles can happen.'

'OK, then, we'll talk to him about it when we get back. And tell him that we're happy for him.' He lay back, wondering at her.

'Are *you* happy about it?'

'Not really. I spent most of my life making either you or Katie unhappy, but I was bastard enough to be able to live with it. Seth's too nice a lad to have that sort of life. Noah's another matter entirely. But you're right – Seth's adult, it's his choice. And maybe he will make it work. Maybe he'll settle for a normal life.'

She turned her face to him for a kiss, and for a while they made things work for themselves. Mark fell into a doze, and Diana wandered down to the warm kitchen, making toast and coffee.

She returned and nudged Mark awake. 'Breakfast, hon. Then you tell me the rest of it.'

'The Whites are back,' he said a while later, putting his empty mug on the bedside table.

She stiffened. 'And we've left the pack unguarded?' She was out of bed, looking for her clothes.

'Stop that,' Mark pleaded, and she turned to him. Her colour was high and her eyes were flashing, a yellow glint in them that he loved. 'Stop it, Diana. Trust me on this. Get back in bed, it's easier to talk here.'

She stood poised in the growing light from the window, half-dressed, a thick jumper in her hand. 'Tell me,' she said.

'Join me,' he pleaded, holding his arms out.

'No. Quit stalling or I'm gone.'

He nodded. Sometimes he forgot how dangerous she could be. 'OK, they've not hit anyone. Only a few of us know … Anthony, Andy, the Kittens and me. That Mary woman suspects, but she's not mentioned it to anyone but Sara and Darlene. We've not even spoken to John yet. I thought I should talk to you first.'

'What's happening with the Kittens?' she asked quietly.

'Offerings. Presents,' he said with a shudder.

'Stop fucking around, Mark. Tell me.'

'OK, if I promise you that they're safe, will you come back to bed?'

'Where's my phone?'

'Oh, *Diana*! For once, could you trust me?'

'I want a second opinion,' she said, every word clear.

'Look, Andy agrees with me. He doesn't like it, but he agrees with me. Do you believe me?'

She relaxed, dropped the jumper on a chair. 'Of course I *believe* you. I just doubt your judgement occasionally. That's OK, isn't it?' He sulked. It didn't suit him a bit, and she grinned. 'I've told you before, my love, John can do that and be cute. It's just unattractive when you do it. It looks like you mean it. Anyway, I trust Andy one hundred per cent if the Kittens' safety is at issue. So yes, I'll get back in bed if you stop sulking.'

'Deal.'

A minute later they were settled together again.

'Offerings?' she reminded him.

'Yeah, seems like either Sara or Darlene has a secret admirer. Or maybe more than one. They've had … oh, it's horrible … they've had wolf skins delivered to them. And heads.'

'Really? But why do you think it's an offering and not a threat? Real wolves? Or us?'

'Them. The Whites. Sara took samples from the heads. She's already got the run of the lab at uni, you know?' He sounded proud.

'Course she has. She's just going through the motions. I've already taught her everything I know.'

'Yeah, well. I hope not.' He poked her gently, and she smirked.

He continued, trying to keep his voice even. 'Darlene told Andy. The parcels just come to "Ms Preston". Hand delivered. No fingerprints. Andy told me, and I told Anthony. I didn't know what to make of it. Well, Dad has an idea. He thinks it's some sort of declaration of devotion – an intention to protect them. But the pelts are coming from somewhere, and if they're hand delivered, they're probably being … oh, hell. It's disgusting. What sort of fucking barbarian would…? They're probably being "sourced", shall we say, locally.'

'Jan,' said Diana with absolute conviction. 'I got him a job with Ransome Industries but he quit a month ago, he sent me a message that he was fine, then he went dark.'

'Yes, that's the general consensus. He's hunting down his ex-packmates. And skinning them, preparing their hides and making fur rugs for our little girls.'

Diana was grinning. 'Fucking good,' she said.

Mark looked at her, horrified. 'I'll never get used to this,' he sighed.

'Fucking good,' she repeated. 'They killed Sammy, they killed our friends and their kids, and, personally, I'd be happy to wipe my feet on their fur every morning for the next century. Bastards. Do we know where Jan is? And, by the way, why am I in Scotland being told this? It's not exactly bad news.'

'Jan is a fugitive from his own pack. He hasn't got a penny to his name. And he's courting our daughters with the skins and skulls of his brothers. Don't you find that worrying?'

'Nope. Maybe I'm twisted, but no. It's romantic. Songs will be sung, in future years. In the meantime, though, I'll personally rip his throat out if he tries anything with her before she's ready to form a pack.'

'Her? Not them?'

'Sara. He wants Sara,' she told him confidently.

'You seem sure.'

'He has his reasons,' she assured him. 'Hellfire, this is so romantic.' She cuddled up, smiling happily.

'Think it through,' Mark whispered.

'What?'

'The Whites are still sending men here. Those men are disappearing. That is going to piss them off. Anthony doesn't think they'll give up – killing us is a religion to them. Our pack has been relatively lucky so far, we were already strong when they learned about us. But, Diana, we aren't going to be this strong again for years.'

'What?' She was puzzled.

'Headcount,' was all he said.

Diana nodded, calculating. 'Seth's leaving us. The Kitten's aren't vulnerable – they're Anthony's best pupils – and they're training that house of women into something very scary indeed. But they've left home, I'm beginning to realise that now. Bill and Frank are gone, and the Whites killed our Sammy. That leaves us with Caleb, Trixie and Beatrice, and Noah to fight with us if we're attacked at home again. We'll have Janie and Alice soon – they will be great, I know it – but they've not Changed yet. Noah won't take orders from anyone but you and me these days. The Bees can protect themselves and will fight to the death, but they're not the Kittens. That leaves Caleb as our best fighter among the kids. Give us another few years and we'll have more wolfie fighters. But you're right, we *are* going to be weaker. What are you thinking?'

'It's Anthony's idea, actually.'

'Ah,' was all she said.

'It's time to attack them,' he said. He tried to make himself sound confident, sure. She closed her eyes. He could feel her heart speed up, her breathing quicken.

'Attack? Like we did when we helped Michaela and Simon?'

'No. I mean we should hit them where they live. Leave England, find them. My dad's always known roughly where they live, but one man isn't enough to deal with them. He needs us.'

'It's lunacy.' She laughed. 'We're just a small pack. They've got hundreds of men – Anthony told me. And what about their women and children?'

Mark nodded. 'You remember what Jan told you about their women? They're untrained. We wouldn't hurt them, and I doubt they'd have any urge to fight side by side with the men. So long as we're careful not to hurt any kids, we should be OK.'

'You want to go to the mountains, to the heart of our enemies' territory, and attack them?'

'I'm considering it. Dad says he has a plan.'

'Anthony has wanted Harald's head on a plate for over fifty years. I love your dad, but he's single-minded. He could wait – the White Pack is failing, the world has moved on, the authorities know they exist. Their freedom to kill and steal and be a scary legend has gone. Why can't we just wait for Harald to die? He's the only thing keeping them together. Why risk ourselves?'

'Because he could live for years yet, and during those years we'll be vulnerable again. He's just as single-minded as Anthony. And more to the point, Bill and Frank are alone out there, with two kids and a pregnant woman. They've done well with their home – it has the underground refuge and clear sightlines from all the windows. If they were any other pack, the Whites would go for easier meat, but they're our sons, and I bet they're top of the hit list. And another thing… Karen is safe so long as she's not pregnant – the Whites have some sense, they won't kill a normal woman in this country. But our Seth would be a dead man walking, living alone with her. He wouldn't stand a chance if they found out where he lived. And… I hate to mention it, but Katie's boys are a target too. I *think* they're safe – she's changed her job and her home. I trust her new husband, he's a nice bloke. But they're going to be leaving home soon too, going to uni. They look like me, both of them. They can't stay anonymous forever.'

She thought about it. 'No. It's stupid. You're talking about a suicide mission. We're safer at home. We have nothing to gain by attacking. We couldn't win.'

'What if we could? What if we had a real chance of killing their Alpha?'

'Yeah? He's protected. We'd never get within a mile of him. And even so, what then? They'd have another Alpha waiting in the wings.'

'Trial by combat. That's how they work. They're just one pack – one Alpha pair, no Betas. No breakaways, no friendly packs, no daughter packs. Only a son or brother of the Alpha can Challenge for leadership. Harald killed his father to become Alpha. That's how they work. He survives by being a great politician, keeping his sons and brothers busy fighting among themselves. They all hate each other more than they hate him.' Mark looked excited.

'So?'

'So…'

He whispered to her.

'You devious bastard.'

'It would be hard work.' He agreed.

'You devious, evil, skinny little wretch. I always knew you weren't a nice guy.'

'Aren't you going to scream at me?'

'No.'

'So I didn't need to bring you out here after all?'

'No, doesn't look like it.' She was stunned, looking at the ceiling, trying to improve on his plans. She turned to him. 'So when are we going?'

He shook his head. 'We? You're not coming! It's too dangerous.'

'You die, I die. Whether we're side by side or a thousand miles apart. And you promised me you'd never leave me.'

'But…'

'Fuck you, Mark. This isn't open to negotiation.'

'Diana, I need to be clear-headed. I can't be worrying about you.'

She was looking at him, grinning, feral. 'This is where I lose my temper.'

'Don't. Just for once, do as you're told.'

'I did that. I went on honeymoon with John and Zoe. That's your "once". And look what happened then! Oh no, where you go, I go.'

'Absolutely not. I want you to protect the pack, in case the Whites get wind of things and there's a counter-attack.'

'Zoe can do that,' she said lazily, still sure of herself.

'Zoe has never fought,' he pointed out.

'Not in anger, but she and I practise all the time, wolfie and woman. She can take care of herself. Miranda can too. And even the kids who can't Change can fight. If you want to do this, we're going to have to accept some risk. I'm not leaving your side, Mark.'

'Oh hell. OK. Look, we'll sort the details out when we get home – we need to plan it out properly. Now that everything's in the open, shall we enjoy the rest of our holiday? I had a word with the gamekeeper, and he says there's an injured stag out there that we're welcome to have a go at, so long as we make it quick.'

'Ah, putting me to work again? How much is he paying us?'

'He says we should pay him, but I persuaded him he'd rather be warm and dry today than trudging the moors looking for the animal.'

She kissed him gently. 'Poor thing. The stag, I mean. Now I'm going to feel guilty until we've put it out of its misery. Are you up to it?'

'*Me?*' He was outraged. 'I'll tell you what … if you impress me today, I won't argue any more about you fighting with us.'

She was already up, staring at her reflection in the mirror, thoughtfully tracing the faint silver scars on her belly and breasts, the thickened welt on her ear, the now faded lines across her ribs. Mark stood and joined her, his own fingers joining hers at that last scar.

'If you come with us, I will protect you,' he swore.

'And I you,' she promised, looking at his reflection behind hers. She leaned back into him, and sighed. 'That poor stag, Mark. Let's go get it.'

Chapter 20

'It's always the quiet ones, isn't it?'

'Shut up,' muttered Trixie, trying to regain her concentration, to exert control of the situation on-screen. It was too late; at the level she was playing, any lapse was punishable. 'Game sodding Over,' she said, exasperated, turning around to glare at Caleb. 'What do you want?'

There was no mistaking the fact they were brother and sister. Close enough in age to pass for twins themselves, they shared their mother's pale, almost translucent skin, and their father's dark hair and eyes.

Caleb shrugged. 'Just fancied some company, really. Sorry, I didn't mean to spoil your game. But it is funny: "Little Miss Domestic in Shoot 'Em Up Horror". You should challenge MarkDad. You'd scare the living daylights out of him – he still thinks he's this family's game king.'

Trixie smiled. 'Ah, never mind. It's your birthday weekend, I guess you deserve some attention. What do you want to do?'

The boy shrugged, a little too casually to fool his sister. 'I thought we could get in some fight practice. I'm not really in a celebrating mood.'

Trixie turned away a little too quickly, bending to eject the game cartridge from the old console, using the movement to hide her face – Caleb hated it when she got 'gooey' about his singleton status. She straightened up, poker-faced now. 'Any rules? Or can I thrash you any way I want to?'

Caleb narrowed his eyes dramatically. 'No rules, anything goes.' He smiled. 'You can try to kill me if you want to.'

This time Trixie met his gaze. 'Sure, I will. But don't go crying to Mum if I succeed. Shall we be civilised and take it to the woods, or shall we start here and scare the babies?'

'Woods. Come on then, big sis.'

Trixie trailed behind him. 'Little Miss Domestic, eh?' she muttered under her breath.

Caleb heard and grinned.

As they sauntered through the kitchen, John looked up. 'Going out?' he asked them.

'No, just having a fight,' they replied.

'Good. Play dirty, practise hard, OK?' he said absently, before returning his gaze to the plans for the extended estate. Anthony had finally sold his land in France, having investigated and been surprised by the extent of Joyce's legacy. He'd bought the hundred acres of farmland adjacent to the pack's estate, donating it free and clear to his family. Diana had asked John to work on the financial and ecological implications of securing the entire parcel of land against outside attack, planting more woodland and trying to keep the area stocked with game for the fast-growing wolf pack to hunt. John had a headache.

The teenagers left their clothes in two neat piles at the woodland's edge, and moved into the trees. Trixie watched her brother carefully, waiting for some clue as to his strategy. He walked confidently in front of her, and she sighed, relaxing her mind, thinking herself into the role of predator. Her most natural animal shape locked into her mind, and she let her herself fall into the familiar patterns, enjoying and monitoring the heat of transformation, the pleasant prickling of rapidly growing fur, the feeling of muscles, bones, organs changing position, size. She'd long ago learned not to translate these signals from her body as pain, preferring to interpret them as a muted pleasant glow. Her colour vision was fading and she intervened, changing the inner structure of her wolf eyes to maintain the daylight benefits of human sight. Caleb had disappeared, so she consciously grew vibrissae: long catlike whiskers to pick up and amplify any sound or vibration that would tell her where he was. He was downwind of her; she didn't bother to put energy into improving her powers of scent – normal wolf abilities would be enough. Her head hurt; she'd been maintaining human levels of intelligence in a wolf-sized skull. Brain Changing was the hardest thing to deal with, but she was getting better. Thinking of it as biology rather than her own self helped, and she'd learned by now she could manipulate the meat of it at will, with an acute understanding of where her consciousness dwelled. Good housekeeping starts at home, she thought randomly, and giggled. It emerged as a low growl, and she snapped shut immediately. Caleb wouldn't thank her if he thought he was being underestimated.

As she moved through the trees, avoiding the undergrowth, part of the oak tree she was approaching peeled rapidly and eerily away from the trunk, falling towards her: a branch aimed at her skull. It was moving fast. A primitive fear of the supernatural made her scream out, dodging barely fast enough to avoid a stunning blow. The length of wood connected, hitting her temples hard, sickening her and bringing her to her knees. Then Caleb was on her back, crushing her, his interlaced fingers at her throat.

'Cede,' he said, laughing.

Her confused mind reeled. 'Seed? What does he want? Seed?'

He tightened his grip. 'Surrender,' he snarled.

She struggled, but he had a killing grip, and knew it. She was furious, and tried to turn, to twist, to rake with her claws, but he couldn't be moved. She stopped her struggle and he instantly released her.

He lay down on the mossy floor and started to laugh. She lay there for a while, not Changing, assessing the damage to her body and putting it right, slowly and carefully. It was easier to return to human from a healthy state, less to think about. When at last she returned to her natural state, she was voraciously hungry. Caleb sat up, watching her carefully, trying to guess her mood.

'Did I hurt you? I'm sorry. But it's such a good trick, I had to try it out.'

She smiled. 'It's fantastic. What did you do?'

He was always ready to brag. 'Well, I got the idea from that Pinocchio sketch we did for the Destroyers' third birthday. I realised that changing my skin colour could give us some practical advantages in camouflage. And grabbing a real branch from the tree added to the fun. OK, I admit it, I had to do some preparation. I chose the tree, led you to it, had the branch prepared, and I'd studied the bark patterns all week. But I still fucking did it. I changed my skin colour, my hair colour, closed off my sweat glands as much as possible to hide my smell. I can Chameleon! Have you ever heard of anyone doing that before?'

'No, Caleb. I haven't. You've done it again. Nobody had ever turned themselves into a living battering ram until you went for it, either. Any other bright ideas?'

She'd meant it to be complimentary, but a lingering headache tinged her words with an edge of sarcasm, and brought back to both of them memories of the day Sammy had been murdered, and the two of them, together with Bridget, had worked as one integrated slaying machine, taking bloody vengeance on the White Pack members who'd returned to attack them. Caleb blinked once, and turned away.

'You understand why? Why I'm working on these ideas? You don't think I'm just showing off?'

Trixie smiled. 'Aw, I'll always think you're showing off. It's compulsory, isn't it? I'm your big sister after all.'

He still looked uncertain.

She relented. 'No, I think you're a real asset to the pack. I'm impressed to hell and back. Where do you get these ideas?'

He shook his head. 'I just imagine fights, ways to kill or be killed, and try to work out ways to get out of trouble, or work better against the Whites. Do you think you could manage the same trick?'

Trixie stood up, stretched. Sunlight fell on to her smoothly muscled body, from which all traces of puppy fat had disappeared long ago. 'I'll give it a go. It's prettier than tusks anyway. I might go for the girly version and hide myself in the limbs of a cherry blossom tree.'

Caleb snorted with laughter. 'Yeah, that's you, constantly pretending to be such a girlie girl. I know better.'

Trixie rolled her eyes. 'Not always,' she said, focussing inwards, concentrating hard. She dismissed every pathway that came to her, the familiar changes and the more newly learned ones, looking instead for the slightest alterations. The codes for it were hidden in her DNA, locked away and barely accessible.

Caleb looked up in surprise, seeing his sister become his brother, her body changing slowly and subtly until a young man was grinning at him.

He was appalled. 'You can't *do* that!' he cried out. 'That's just…'

'All wrong?' Trixie said. 'Well, it's bloody hard work. Miranda explained the theory. The heart of our self-image is gender, and that's why we stay the same sex even when we become a different species. But we don't have to. Do you get me? We don't have to stay the same sex. Not if we don't want to, or if we find it convenient to change temporarily.'

Caleb was awed. 'This could change everything,' he murmured. 'It could change our society completely. Are you … um, functional?'

Trixie blushed. 'I can't say I've ever tried to find out. I can write my name in the snow, if that's what you mean? Anything else, I'm not inclined to find out. I'm still learning. I doubt it, in a reproductive sense. I mean, my DNA is still female

– that never changes, does it? It's just the Shapeshifter chromosome letting me move flesh around. Same old trick, different application.'

Caleb stood up. 'Can I touch you?'

Trixie blushed all over. 'No you bloody can't. Sorry, Cal, this is just too weird. I still feel just the same person. Let's go back to the house.' She shimmered again, flesh crawling and shifting until she found her natural state again. She relaxed, smiling to herself at the look of concentration on Caleb's face. She knew he wouldn't be happy now until he'd made a girl of himself. Since he'd overcome his block against Changing, his main interest had been the Change, the process of metamorphosis. This, the ultimate Change, fascinated him. Now that he knew it was possible, he wouldn't rest until he'd found the key that unlocked that potential.

Dressed again, they walked back into the kitchen, both of them subdued and quiet.

John looked up, alarmed. 'What's up? Did someone get hurt?'

Caleb shrugged. He wasn't up to explaining all this to John. He could wait to relate his story, his own discovery. He gave his parent a weak smile as he passed him, and made his way to his own room, needing some quiet time.

Trixie sat down, looking a little nervous. 'Dad, I've discovered something. Well, me and Miranda and Bridget have discovered something. It was Miranda's idea, but she couldn't do it, obviously.'

'What is it, sweetheart?' John put down his paperwork, and ran his hands through his hair. He leaned back and smiled encouragingly.

Trixie stalled him. 'Well, it would be easier if I told all of you at the same time, really. But it *is* kind of important.'

John stood up and put the kettle on. 'OK. Go and round 'em up. I'll ring Andy and ask him to come over. Zoe is watching the babies and writing something wildly bodice-ripping, probably. Find someone to watch the babies, and ask her to join us. Diana's in the lab with the Quads and Quadettes. Mark said he'd be in the garden getting some exercise with Anthony's gardening party.'

Trixie didn't have to be asked twice, and disappeared. John picked up the phone and rang Andy.

'Hiya mate. Look, can you come over? Little Trixie's all excited about something and wants to show off. You know what a quiet little thing she is, it'll do her good to be the centre of attention for once.' He listened for a moment, then grinned. 'I'm not *saying* that you ignore her, you touchy bastard. Are you coming over or not? If you are, you can give me some money for Caleb's birthday present. Me and you and Mark bought him a motorbike.' John smirked; Andy sounded worried. 'No, Diana and Zoe don't know. If they ask, it was your idea, OK?' He listened again, and pulled a face at the phone. 'Well, you don't have to live with them, that's why!' He put the phone down and started to shove teabags into mugs.

Zoe walked into the kitchen and stood behind him, hugging him. 'What's going on?'

John closed his eyes, enjoying the physical contact. 'Trixie's got a trick. She's going to tell us all about it.'

'Oh? And it needs a full meeting of all the parents, does it?' Zoe teased. 'Are you sure you're not just making an excuse to leave that planning document alone for a while?'

He smiled. She couldn't see his face, so he adopted a hurt tone. 'I would *never* use our children like that! How could you say that?'

'Cos it's true. Oh, here's the boss. Don't you think he's getting really sexy these days?'

'He's still a skinny geek, and you can't make me jealous. Have we got any biscuits?' John felt relaxed and happy, watching his Alpha pulling off his wellies before he came into the kitchen.

Mark poured hot water into the mugs and opened the fridge door, pausing to make eye contact with John. 'Emergency? Or excuse for a break?' He added milk to the waiting mugs and removed the teabags.

John rolled his eyes. 'What have I done to get this reputation? Our daughter wants to talk to us, OK?'

Zoe tried to share a mischievous glance with Mark, but he was looking out of the window.

Diana was leading eight kids through the garden. She paused when she reached Anthony, who was patiently teaching the little kids how to plant seedlings out. She spoke to him for a moment, then left the Quads and Quadettes with him, breaking into a run and skipping into the kitchen with a huge grin on her face.

'Tea break? Me and my favourite people? We should do this every day.' She grabbed a steaming mug and sat down. 'Where's the girl of the hour, then?' she enquired.

Trixie popped her head round the door. 'When will Andy be here?' she asked.

'About twenty minutes, give or take. Do you want to wait for him?' John treated her to his lazy grin, and she beamed back at him.

'Yes, I'll come back when he's here. Ooh, biscuits.' She grabbed a handful from the plate that Zoe had put out, and danced out of the kitchen.

'Don't you feed her?' John asked Diana.

'Nope. Free-range kids, ours. I don't understand how they've survived this long.' Diana reached hungrily for the biscuits with one hand and the security plans with the other. She frowned at them. 'John, what does this squiggle mean?'

'Er, it means my pen stopped working and I was trying to get it started again,' he admitted.

'Oh well, while we're all waiting for Andy, we might as well work on this. Zoe, did you ring the conservation people to ask them what sort of mix of trees we should plant?'

Zoe nodded. 'Yes. The bloke on the phone was quite keen to help until he realised who I was. Then he got cagey. I don't think he approves of hunting.'

Mark looked offended. 'Well, I don't either, in that sense. But it's not the same when we're wolves!'

'Not everyone sees it that way, honey,' Diana pointed out. Her attention returning to Zoe: 'Did you get anything useful out of him?'

'Enough to find out that he basically agrees with Anthony. In other words, we've got our own wildlife and woodlands expert on tap, and we should just listen to Old Wolf.'

The four of them looked at the plans, pointing out existing features and potential security issues, and planning their new, extended estate. When Andy arrived, Diana was busy doodling plans for several lodges for visiting adult children and friends.

Andy went to the kettle and started to make more drinks for everyone. John called Trixie on her phone, and asked her to come downstairs.

When she arrived, she was accompanied by Miranda and Bridget. She looked nervously at her parents. 'You won't shout at me?' she asked.

'Depends what you've done,' joked Diana, and then regretted it instantly as her quiet daughter shrank back. 'Sorry, hon. Of course I won't shout at you. Tell us all about it.'

Miranda stepped forward. 'It was my idea. If anyone's getting shouted at, it should be me.'

Her mother frowned. 'Look, nobody's getting shouted at. Stop being dramatic, and spill the beans.'

Caleb edged into the room. Mark glanced at Trixie, who didn't object.

'It's just a little thing really. I'm still exactly the same person. It's not even as much of a change as switching my hair colour – it's just releasing what's absolutely natural to me.' She sounded nervous, rushed.

Her parents looked at her, puzzled.

'What have you done, sweetheart?' asked Zoe cautiously.

'We've worked out how to look…' Trixie's nerve failed her.

'Oh, bloody hell,' interrupted Miranda. 'I was wondering why none of you expert Shapeshifters changed sex. Then I figured out it was all this body image stuff that you bang on about. And I worked with Bridget and Trixie – I figured the girls would be happier about changing than the boys, especially if it was my idea.'

Diana's mouth twitched. 'And what was the result?' she asked.

Trixie managed a smile. 'I can look like a boy,' she said, addressing her mother directly.

Caleb burst in. 'She can, I've seen her. It's like seeing another brother.'

John's mouth was hanging open. 'What?' he asked weakly.

Mark looked up, raised an eyebrow. 'Show us,' he said to the twin girls.

Bridget shook her head. 'I can't, not yet. But Trixie can.'

Trixie blushed. 'Can I do it in my clothes?'

'Of course,' her mother reassured her.

This time the transformation took less than a minute. Trixie was getting more sure of the pathways involved, and her boy-self was becoming part of her self-image. There was no doubt that her face was that of a young man.

'Do you want to see more?' She was obviously painfully shy. 'I'll undress if you want me to?'

Zoe shook her head. 'No need for that, honey. Are you happy for your mum to examine you?'

Trixie nodded, and Diana led her out of the room.

Mark was staring at Miranda. 'You bugger,' he said.

'Are you mad at me?' she asked coolly.

'No, not a bit. Great idea. But don't try to convince me that Trixie has turned into a boy. That's all just on the surface, isn't it?'

Miranda nodded, smiling. 'Yeah, no change to the basic genetics. She's still female, it's just cosmetic. But it could be useful.'

'Or fun,' added Andy thoughtfully.

John glared at him. He was struggling to speak.

Diana and Trixie returned. 'It's a boy!' Diana grinned. 'Well, it was – she's lapsed back. Bloody hell, these kids never cease to amaze me.' She wore an expression of intense pride. Zoe was congratulating Miranda and Bridget on the theoretical work, and Andy was deep in conversation with Caleb and Trixie. Mark was smiling broadly.

John stood up. 'Excuse me? Does nobody else think this is going just a bit too far?'

They all turned to look at him.

'I mean, I know we're Shapeshifters, but I think of myself as an old-fashioned werewolf. I've not said anything about the face-changing, although I think it's weird, and you all know that I get spooked when anyone Changes to anything but a wolf, but I've put up with all of that, because I love you all. But this is just wrong. It's wrong. Can't you see that?'

Trixie was watching him, chewing her lip. The group had fallen silent, with everyone looking at him. He hit the table with his fist. The girl jumped, and turned, fleeing the room. Miranda flashed a filthy look at John and followed her out, closely tailed by Bridget. Caleb stayed, flushing.

'Look, Dad, you can't say—'

'I can't say what? That I don't like my girls pretending to be boys? That I don't like the idea of my pack, my family, playing around with who they are? What next? Am I going to go to sleep with Zoe and wake up with Joey? I can say whatever I bloody well like, because this is my home. At least, I thought it was, until I turned round and you'd all turned into sex-change aliens!'

Caleb shook his head. 'You've hurt Trixie, and you've offended Bridget and Miranda. And I'm not an alien. And I thought it was my home too! You should apologise.'

John turned round angrily; Diana was laughing. 'What's so *fucking* funny?' he bellowed, outraged.

'You, my love. You're funny. Oh, sorry, it was just the image of Zoe as Joe. It doesn't work for me, sorry!' She let out a peal of laughter.

John spun around, glaring at Zoe. 'What about you? Am I amusing you?'

She shook her head, upset. 'No, I don't think it's funny. I think it's sad. I think you should be proud of Trixie. You know she thinks the world of you, and you've let her down.' She walked out, heading for Bridget and Trixie's room.

John appealed to Mark. 'Mark? Help me out here.'

Mark looked at Diana. 'Shut up, Diana. Laughing at him isn't doing anything useful.' He turned his attention to John. 'I understand how you feel. It hurts, in your balls. You're the man, you always have been, and suddenly our little girl can do the talk, do the walk, and you're wondering what's left for you, if it's so damned easy.' He turned to glare at Diana. 'And she's not helping.'

Diana was still snorting with laughter but making an effort to restrain herself. John gave her one last furious glance and then looked back at Mark, sitting across from him at the table.

'Ignore her,' Mark said. 'She'll regret it later.'

Diana stood up and walked past them, putting her arm around Caleb. 'I'm sorry already,' she said to John in her sweetest voice. 'But I've never seen you get this angry before, and over such a little thing too.' She guided her son out of the room. 'Come on, baby, we'll go and talk to Trixie and the girls. Let Mark talk John down.'

When she'd gone, Mark stood up and went to look out of the window. 'Andy?' he said.

Andy glanced at John. 'Well, I'm intrigued. And I'm amazed that it never occurred to me. And I'm bloody sorry that it's come now that I've given up being part of the pack sexually, because, to be honest, there's something very appealing about some of the possibilities. John, I'm sorry. I know you'll find that hard to deal with.'

'Do you think *you* could do it?' asked Mark, genuinely interested.

Andy nodded. 'Of course. I just have to believe that it's possible. I've been working on face-changing – it's no different, really. I won't scare Helen with it, but I think that next time I Shapeshift, I'll try being a female animal, to see how it works.'

'Oh, now I've heard it all!' shouted John. 'My best mate wants to be a woman and shag me!'

Andy shook his head. 'Not at all. I was thinking about the possibilities with Zoe and Diana. I've never fancied you, you big ape.'

Mark fought down a smile. 'John, I understand why you feel threatened. And Diana was way out of line, although I know we'll *all* forgive her, won't we?'

John shook his head. 'She hurt me,' he wailed.

'And you hurt Trixie. So you're going to apologise to her, and praise her to high heaven, and ask her to forgive her caveman dad. OK? Then I'll speak to her. I guess she needs to know that she has my support.' He sighed. His eldest blood daughters seemed to be getting more clingy with him as they got older. He guessed it was understandable; he'd barely played any part in their upbringing when they were small, and it was hard for them to deal with the way he spent so much time with the younger children.

'Diana will never let this go,' John said despairingly 'She'll be teasing me with it for the rest of my life.'

'No, she won't. It'll be forgotten in an hour. She's got better things to do than wind people up or bear grudges. And as soon as she realises that she's really upset you, she won't be able to live with herself. She doesn't seem to care too much about upsetting me, perhaps because I'm always treading on *her* toes over something or other, but for some reason she'd rather cut off her arm than hurt you. She'll be dragging you off into the woods before the night is over, I'll bet my hide on it.'

John looked up. 'Do you really think this is acceptable? Are you happy with it?'

'Honestly? It makes me nervous, but that's because it's strange. Andy likes strange, he likes to experiment, so he's comfortable. You and me are a little more traditional, aren't we? But I think it's good for the pack to have more tricks like this. And Trixie is no more a boy than I'd be a woman if I dressed in Diana's underwear.'

Andy gave him a very interested look, and Mark glared at him. 'Quit it. I don't. OK?'

Andy shrugged, and turned away.

Mark put his arm around John's shoulders. 'Our daughter is still crying up there. Can't you hear her?'

John blinked, uncomfortable.

'You're the only one who can put things right with her. You know that.'

'Oh shit! Even if I apologise, she'll know I don't like it.' John looked miserable.

'That doesn't matter. What does matter is that you care enough about her to apologise for hurting her. She can live with you disagreeing with her, what's upsetting her is the fact that you're angry with her. It's not fair. It's not how we treat our kids.'

John nodded, a suspiciously wet gleam in his eye, and he stood and made his way out of the kitchen. Mark listened to the heavy, reluctant sound of his feet on the stairs, and sighed.

Andy sat down next to Mark. 'I didn't think you had it in you,' he said admiringly. 'I couldn't have dealt with that better myself.'

Mark looked up. 'Thank you. Can I just ask you something?'

'Sure.' Andy smiled.

'Well, did you promise Helen that you'd give up having sex with the pack, or specifically Diana and Zoe? Because I've always wondered what it would be like with a really tall lass.'

Andy glared at him, momentarily dumbstruck, then started to laugh. 'You bloody idiot. You had me going there. I preferred it when you didn't pretend to have a sense of humour.'

'Fair enough,' sighed Mark, picking up the used mugs and carrying them to the sink. 'Thanks for coming. You hanging around?'

'Yeah, I think I'll stay tonight, if you don't mind? I want to be with Caleb on his birthday, especially. I miss the kids. And I need to run with you all – I'm starting to feel isolated out there with the normals. Helen won't mind, just for one night – she's been wanting to go to Chloe's anyway. Will you do me a favour?'

'Anything,' Mark said.

'Just tell Diana and Zoe that it's not easy. Will you? If I tell Diana myself I … well, it's difficult … but I do want her to know that I still miss her. And I know she misses me, so I'm not expecting a reply.'

Mark nodded. 'I can imagine. But love wins out, eh?'

'Yeah, I guess it does.' Andy swallowed, and walked out into the garden, approaching Anthony and the kids and dropping to his hands and knees as he Changed his shape to that of a small polar bear, plump and definitely female, offering his back to the delighted children and giving the small ones rides around the garden. After a few minutes, Anthony glanced over at him, and walked quickly to the house. He stood for a moment in the porch, until Mark invited him into the house.

'Do you know what Andy's doing out there?' the old werewolf asked bluntly.

Mark looked up, glancing out of the window at the scene of unconventional domestic happiness. 'At a guess, making some kids happy and ruining the flower beds. What's up?'

'That's a female bear out there. How long has he been pulling that particular trick? And are you happy to let him do it around the kids?'

The Alpha sighed. 'Not you too? It's too late for the kids, Dad. It was Miranda's idea, and the Bees took it up. Caleb is fascinated by the idea. This is the new idea that Trixie wanted to tell us about. It's out of the bag now. And to be honest, I don't see the problem. Am I missing something?'

Anthony stared at him. 'You're OK with this?'

Mark confirmed it with a tight-lipped smile. 'I'm fine with it. Diana's fine with it too. We both think it's good for the pack – anything that expands our capabilities is good for the pack. It's just cosmetic, though.' He squeezed the top of his nose between his thumb and index finger. 'Are you going to rant? Because if you are, I'm going to take a painkiller.'

His father looked at him, shook his head. 'Fine. I will trust you. Were you planning on telling me?'

Mark frowned. 'Of course I was. It's only just happened. Are we going to be OK about this, or are you spoiling for a fight?' He could feel a headache coming on.

'No, I apologise. Of course you were going to tell me. I'll be in the cottage for a while, I need to think about this, get used to the idea. I'll be suitably congratulatory to Miranda and the Bees when I see them.'

Mark looked up, smiling. 'That would be perfect.' He watched as Anthony retreated to his cottage, and went outside to help Andy with the kids.

Chapter 21

Diana waited in the warm morning sunshine, enjoying the heat of it on her fur, the teasing threat of sunburn at the pink tips of her ears. The world was such a simple place when she was a wolf. She was busy supervising as the delivery driver unloaded the groceries just inside the security gate. It was the same man almost every time, and he was used to her, and she to him. In wolf form, she was better able to check out the van for alien, threatening scents.

Everything was OK, as usual, and she gave the pile of supplies one last interested sniff before watching the man get back into his van and reverse back through the gates. As the gates started to close, a screech of brakes made her jump in surprise. She twisted as she turned, landing on all fours about six feet away from the Mini that had replaced Seth and Noah's old Punto.

Noah leaned out of the window. She growled at him, recognising that he was apologising, but still angry at the shock he'd given her. Miranda opened the passenger side door and got out, walking to her mother and kneeling to hug her.

'Sorry, Little Mum,' she said. 'Look after Seth, he's sad.'

Even in her wolf form, Diana understood enough to lick her daughter fondly. As she loped back to the house she passed Anthony, who was striding down the drive with a large hand truck for the groceries.

Mark was still in bed. He'd been up until late with John and Anthony, jamming in the music room and drinking. He peered out warily from under the duvet as Diana leaped on to the bed, licking his face enthusiastically before Changing back to human and grinning at him.

'What time is it?' He wiped at his face. 'Can I have a proper kiss now?'

'Eight thirty. Time you were up. And no, that's as good as it gets until you're out of bed. By the way, Seth's not gone to uni, and Miranda said he was sad. I want to see what's up. Are you going to lie there all day?'

'Can I?' Mark said hopefully.

'Yeah, sure. I'll send the kids up here so you can entertain them from your sick bed. Don't say you don't get any sympathy.'

Mark swore and retreated under the duvet.

Diana grinned and dressed, then made her way to the other side of the room, where Zoe was still asleep. She was pregnant again, six months or so, but four pregnancies so closely spaced were inevitably taking their toll. Diana had already taken the new babies downstairs so Zoe could sleep. She looked at the shadows under her mate's eyes, and whispered, 'Last ones for a while, babe. We don't want to hurt you,' before kissing her gently on the forehead and moving quietly out of the room.

John was outside it, trying to balance a tray of juice, toast and fruit as he reached for the handle. He looked into the room. 'She still asleep?' he asked.

'Yeah, let her lie in today. And don't you dare give any of that to Mark, he's trying it on.'

John grinned. 'No fear, this is all for me and Zoe.'

She glanced back into the room. Mark had emphatically pulled the duvet over his head. She shook her head and went downstairs, where the kids seemed to be fending for themselves fairly well.

Trixie and Bridget were driving now, and had been happy to take on the job of taking their younger sisters to high school, before carrying on to their sixth form college with Caleb. They'd just left, Trixie carefully manoeuvring one of the family's minivans out of the car park and down the drive. With the older children gone, Diana had found herself fascinated by the new social dynamics. Always before, the children at home had been organised and supervised by girls; even Seth and Noah had accepted being organised by Miranda as children. Diana had been interested to see what would happen when Susie and Nancy started high school.

There was almost exactly a year in age between the eldest sons still at home and the eldest daughters. Seven months into the Quads' 'rule of terror', Diana had to admit they were doing a difficult job well. The Quadettes had figured out they could manage their older brothers well enough by making helpful suggestions, and the eight of them functioned as a miniature pack within the family, with a complex web of alliances and friendships between them. Together they took responsibility for getting the fourteen younger children dressed and fed in the mornings, leaving only the new baby girls needing parental care. With the eight of them at a responsible age and, furthermore, making themselves useful, their parents were relaxing a little from the childcare frenzy that had started when the Quads were born.

Diana went into the large dining room to check things out. Half-gallon jugs of milk stood on a side table, together with several assorted boxes of cereal and half a dozen cartons of fruit juice. A plateful of crumbs, an empty butter dish and two scoured-out jam jars stood testament to the demolition of vast quantities of toast. All the kids were finishing their breakfasts, having learned that it disappeared at 9 am prompt and that no amount of cajoling would persuade the Quads to take sympathy on a latecomer. Nathan looked up when Diana walked into the room, and a look of sheer relief appeared on his face. She could understand; it was rare for the adults to leave them completely unsupervised, and Nathan was taking his responsibility as eldest very seriously.

She went to him and gave his shoulders a friendly squeeze. Unlike his older brothers, he didn't like being hugged in public. However, he thrived on praise, and his mother let him know she was pleased by smiling broadly at the sight of two dozen children almost ready for the day.

'Mum, I didn't know what to do with the babies – I think they're getting hungry,' Nat said with a frown.

'I know, hon. That's why I came down. I'll take them and nurse them, then I need some free time. Can you keep an eye on things for another hour or so? No lessons today until we tell you otherwise, so let them play or study quietly. John will be around if you need him, and if there's a real disaster, you can ring for your granddad. Is that OK?'

'Sure.' Nat was pleased to be trusted. 'Where are ZoeMum and MarkDad?'

'Zoe is sleeping, and I don't want her to be disturbed. She needs her rest. Mark has a hangover, and while I officially have no sympathy, I don't want you to disturb him either. OK?'

Nat was almost bursting with pride. Diana was speaking to him as an equal. He was more used to her regarding him and the other three Quads as human versions of unexploded bombs. She seemed to be constantly waiting for them to do something dangerous, expensive or both. To be fair, they often lived up to her expectations, but trouble seemed to find them quite naturally. It wasn't their fault.

He waved to his twin, who walked over with the List. Diana was impressed by the List. Even the Bees hadn't managed to develop their managerial genius into the wonder that was the List. She accepted it solemnly and looked at it.

> *1) We need more milk. Can you order an extra gallon per day?*
>
> *2) Nobody likes chocolate cereal. Will you stop buying it because it's filling the cupboards up.*
>
> *3) Somebody needs to buy some clothes for Patrick and Liam because there are only three sets of stuff that fit them, and they're growing out of them fast. And we wore all our stuff out when we were their age so there's nothing for them to grow into.*
>
> *4) The dishwasher isn't working.*

Diana nodded. There was nothing on the list that the boys could deal with themselves. She glanced round the room, automatically head-counting. Ian had clearly finished his own breakfast and was sitting between Tomas and Alex, who were still undressed. The Quads reasoned that it was pointless to dress toddlers until they'd eaten breakfast, as it was easier to wipe them down than to change their clothes. The little boys were pleasantly plump still. They were placid children with a sunny disposition, reminding her strongly of her own youngest sons, Harry and Michael. They charmed everyone. Isaac was sitting with Faith and Joy. The Destroyers were four and a half now, and Diana momentarily shuddered to see them conferring with Isaac with the air of conspirators. She couldn't think of a more deadly threat to world peace than the three of them together, and shot an anxious glance at Nat.

He understood and laughed. 'Don't worry, Mum. Isaac's way ahead of them. It's OK—' He was interrupted by a crash as a cereal bowl fell to the ground, accidentally pushed out of the way by Faith's elbow.

There was a short silence, then she jumped down and started to pick up the pieces. Diana moved towards her, envisioning a bloody floor and severed fingers. But Isaac was there first, setting Faith back on her seat and heading to the cupboard for a dustpan and brush. Diana approved. Nathan may not have been familiar with the phrase 'poacher turned gamekeeper', but he clearly understood the concept.

The Quadettes were sitting together at a long table, supervising Mandy and Mia and keeping a watchful eye on the other sets of twins. Patrick and Liam had finished their breakfasts and were clearly ready to leave. Meg favoured them with an annoyed glance, and directed their attention to Diana, who raised her eyebrow. Outmatched, the boys started to pick up used crockery and carry it to the kitchen.

Satisfied that everything was under control, Diana scooped up the babies and went back upstairs. She peered into the main bedroom. Zoe had obviously eaten and gone back to sleep, and John was sitting next to the bed, watching her sleep. He stood up when he saw Diana.

'Feeding time again?' he asked.

Diana hid her disquiet at the dark circles under his eyes; he'd seldom looked so worried. 'It's OK, don't wake her up. I can nurse Em and Lottie – my body knew that Zoe was getting ill before she knew it herself.'

'What is it? What's wrong?' John asked.

'She's just exhausted. She can't help thinking she's responsible for looking after the littlest half-dozen of our children, and it's driving her mad. She's had enough. It's time to stop. She's not written a word for weeks.'

John reached out and took Charlotte from his mate. The baby girl reached out and touched his mouth, and he smiled. 'I don't want to stop,' he whispered. 'I know it's selfish, but I love having babies around. Remember Nancy and Susie at this age?'

Diana didn't reply, focussing instead on Emily's hand wrapped around her finger. The baby was looking at her, eyes wide.

She changed the subject. 'I need to relax, I've not done this for a while. Zoe managed to feed Tom and Alex without any help from me. And Mandy and Mia weren't a problem for her at all.'

John reached out, stroking her hair. 'Hon, can I hold you? While you feed them?'

Diana smiled at him. 'Of course you can. Let's go into the other bedroom, it'll be quieter.' She frowned in the direction of her own bed, where Mark was snoring happily.

Sitting on the bed, wrapped in John's arms as he sat behind her, she fed his children, listening to him ramble on about his plans to build a real recording studio on the new land, about his latest visit to see Chloe's pack, how he felt about becoming a grandfather and about his hopes and fears for the future of the pack.

'What do you think?' he said.

She'd been daydreaming.

He spoke again. 'What do you think we should do? Is there anything you want? An extension to the lab?'

She sighed. 'I want a new bed. These are knackered. I wonder why?' She twisted around to give him an evil grin. 'And I want you to eat all that chocolate cereal that you sneaked on to the grocery list and then forgot about. There are sixteen boxes in the big kitchen.'

John laughed. 'Oh, I can manage that. And Zoe will help me, I'm sure.'

Diana sighed. 'These two are happy now. Will you put them to bed? And here's the List. Will you ask Anthony to fix the dishwasher? You can change the grocery list online. I'll sit down and order new clothes for the kids, and bankrupt us. But first, I'm going to see Seth.'

She handed the babies to John, and stood, stretching luxuriously. 'I was really enjoying being wolfie this morning. Do you fancy a run tonight?'

John smiled. 'And maybe an hour in our favourite clearing?'

'Mmm. OK. It's a date.' She glanced in the mirror. 'Hey, you and your babies got me all rumpled.'

Her lover blinked lazily. 'You're always rumpled. Get over it.'

She stuck her tongue out at him, reaching for a hairbrush and spending all of five seconds smoothing her hair. She tucked her shirt back into her jeans and rubbed her cheeks, bringing some colour into them.

'Right, baby girls mothered, now it's Seth's turn. I wonder what's wrong?'

John shrugged, his attention on his youngest children who were struggling to stay awake; fascinated by him, but nevertheless dropping off to sleep. Diana took the hint and left him.

The door to Seth's room was open a fraction of an inch, the signal that he and his twin had used since childhood to indicate they were open to visitors. She knocked, nevertheless.

'Who is it?' Seth called out. He sounded chirpy enough.

'Your mother. Can I come in?'

'Sure.'

She pushed the door open and stepped into the room. It was preternaturally neat, the shelves and cupboards ordered, the bin empty and clean, the desk pristine. Seth lay exactly in the middle of his double bed, which was freshly made up. A CD was playing: an old Marilyn Manson album. Seth gestured with a remote control and the music stopped. He sat up, looking at Diana, hesitating.

Diana decided to start things off. 'Is something wrong? Why aren't you at uni? Miranda said you were sad.'

'Karen finished with me last night.' Seth spoke the words simply and directly, meeting Diana's gaze. The shock and disbelief he saw there made him smile a little.

'*She* finished with *you*?' Diana said. Then she realised how that sounded. 'Oh, baby, I'm sorry. I didn't mean it like that. What happened?'

He shrugged, opening his hand, holding out a silver ring with a prettily cut sapphire in a setting of smaller sapphires. 'She gave me our ring back. Why did she do that? What am I supposed to do with it?' He was genuinely bewildered, and lay back on the bed, staring at the now empty symbol of a promise. 'She chose it – she liked the idea of a werewolf giving her a silver engagement ring. I told her a hundred times that all that "allergic to silver" stuff is crap.'

'But why?' Diana repeated, ignoring his rambling. 'What's all this about?' She sat on the bed next to her firstborn, stroking his smooth red hair, so much darker and thicker than her own.

He frowned, his narrow pale features suddenly expressing a pain that made her heart clench. He closed his eyes. 'She doesn't want to be married to a Shapeshifter.' He pressed his lips together, and closed his eyes tightly.

'And she's only just realised this? After all this time?' Diana tried to hide her anger.

'Mum, please don't be angry with her.' Seth's eyes opened, and a look close to fear shadowed them for a moment. 'Don't be angry at Karen. She's only just realised the implications, that's all.'

Diana stood up. 'That's not good enough. In fact, it's bullshit. I've been telling her for nearly two years what the implications are.'

Seth looked up, miserable. 'I know. And she's always insisted that none of it mattered. She was convinced that I'd never find a Shapeshifting woman I'd love as much as I love her. And she was fine about me going running. She was even happy about living here, on the estate, in our own house. She said she could handle the risks from the White Pack, because she was convinced that one day they wouldn't be a threat.'

'So what did it?' Diana was grim.

'Matthew,' Seth said.

Diana frowned. 'Mark's Matthew?'

Her eldest nodded. 'Yeah, Katie's youngest. He's had flu. He's been off school for two months, and Jacob was worried about him.'

Diana nodded. It was no secret that Jake had been spending time with Seth, Noah and Caleb. Diana was pleased; it made Mark happy, and she had to admit that the boy was ferociously intelligent.

She shook her head. 'I don't see what that has to do with Karen.'

Seth threw his arm over his eyes. He spoke patiently. 'Twelve-year-old boys shouldn't be ill for two months with the flu. It's the carrier syndrome. We've seen it with Miranda, how ill she became from the bites. Eva and Naomi catch every bug that's going. Jacob carries antiseptic wipes with him because every time he grazes himself he gets an infection. And where are our grandparents? Dead before they got to sixty, for the most part.'

'Karen knows this. I explained it to her. I told her what the implications would be for her children.' Diana spoke stiffly, angrily. She was, as always, reluctant to think about Miranda's future.

Seth shook his head. 'Theoretical children. They were always theoretical children. Then she started talking to Jake, and realised that in a few years' time she would be the mother dealing with sickly kids. And, in another generation, she'd be the one explaining to her daughters exactly why they were having such trouble having children of their own. And she didn't want that. She didn't want to outlive her children, and possibly her grandchildren. So she didn't want me.'

Diana's mind was racing. 'Seth, if she loves you, it shouldn't make a difference. You don't *have* to have kids.'

Seth smiled weakly. 'Mum, you know me. Can you imagine me living the rest of my life without kids? Hell, I can live without a pack, without a dozen sets of twins tripping me up, but I've always wanted four or five little redheads wrecking the place.'

'You could adopt…' Diana ventured.

Seth waved his hand. 'Mum, I said all this to her. But in the end, we both want children of our own. And what it comes down to is: my children won't be good enough for her.'

'Bitch,' said Diana. 'Who does she think she is? How the hell does she know that the next man to come along won't have something unwanted in *his* gene pool?'

Seth breathed slowly and carefully. 'Mother, please don't talk about her like that. I love her. I've not stopped loving her yet. If you know of any quick ways to help me with that, I'd really appreciate it.' He paused. 'I thought not. You'd have used them long ago and got Dad out from under your skin, wouldn't you?'

His mother smiled, she couldn't resist him. 'Hey, it worked out OK in the end. And no, I never wanted to stop loving Mark. How could I want that, when he was your father?'

Seth screwed his eyes up. 'What am I going to do?'

Diana didn't have an answer. She watched as Seth pushed his hair back, unconsciously copying John's mannerism. He looked at her. 'Sorry, Mum, I'm being a pain in the arse. I'm sure you have better things to do. Aren't there littl'uns that need some attention?'

'Not at all. I find the older my children get, the more interesting they are. I'd rather spend time with you than with the babies.'

'Really?' Seth said, genuinely surprised. 'I thought, with Bill and Frankie and the Kittens gone, that you couldn't wait to be rid of me and Noah and Miranda.'

Diana threw a cushion at him. 'Miranda isn't going anywhere, she's promised me. And you can stay as long as you want. You can live here if you marry a normal girl, even. You'll only get asked to leave if you join another pack. As for your bloody twin, he's going to find himself chased out of the place unless he starts showing some respect to John and Zoe.'

Seth looked alarmed. 'Hey, it's not that bad. He's pushing it a bit, but he doesn't mean any harm.' He took in his mother's grim expression. 'Have you told him this?'

'Of course I've told him.' She frowned. 'He doesn't cross me, but he makes it quite clear he's only obeying them because Mark and I have told him to. That's not acceptable. He's not a pack elder, and he won't be until he leaves this pack and starts his own.'

Seth shook his head. 'He really doesn't realise how you feel about this. Honestly. He thinks you and Dad are proud that he's not taking notice of the Betas.'

Diana licked her lips. 'He doesn't understand me? Then you need to make him understand. They're *my* Betas, not his. They're his parents, his elders. And they're only holding back from giving him as good as they're getting because we're living in dangerous times, and we don't need shit from within the pack. Tell him that, because I'm losing patience with him. Now, what are we going to do about you?'

Seth smiled weakly. 'I could lie here all day, moping. I could play *Dark Side of the Moon* and *The Holy Bible* and *Affrika*. I could even write some bad poetry.'

Diana took his hand. 'You could come for a walk with me? Check out the new land, tell me what you think of the potential? You'll be starting your work experience year soon, so perhaps we can give some planning work to your employer?'

Seth slid off the bed, and dragged himself to his feet. 'I'm at your command, but fresh air never healed a broken heart.' He was trying to joke, but Diana had to bite down her fury at Karen, who'd promised so much and taken it all away. At least she'd never see the girl again. Karen wouldn't dare to cross her path.

Mother and son left the house, waving to Anthony as they passed his cottage. He came out, leaning against the door, smiling at his daughter-in-law, his expression a mix of appreciation and self-mockery that Diana had learned to recognise, and ignore. 'Going anywhere special?'

'Just for a walk. Through the woods, out through the back gate and over the new land.'

Anthony nodded. 'Any problems?' he asked.

'We'll be fine, Anthony,' Diana told him affectionately, before linking arms with her son and walking away from the cottage and into the shadow of the trees.

They headed for the new, hidden back exit from the grounds. The gate looked no different from the rest of the fence; the keypad controlling it was ten feet away, hidden and camouflaged behind a tree. It was a way out, not designed to be used as an entrance to the property. Seth tapped in the code, and they stepped out quickly, the gate shutting behind them. Both of them glanced around, looking for signs of recent activity around the gate, but it was clear; no damage to the vegetation, or trampled areas. They moved away from the fence, jumping a small ditch easily to arrive at the first overgrown field.

Seth looked at the land. 'What are the plans?'

'The farm buildings are going to be razed and replaced with a new centre for us. Except for the barn – Anthony wants to keep it standing for the wildlife. We're building a recording studio with production facilities. Zoe likes the idea of a business centre with press conference facilities too. The idea is that it'll be secure. We can have guests, invite people to visit us, without compromising the security of our main home. It will be a secure area, but not integrated with the old place.'

The young man looked round. 'We're rich. Sometimes I forget that.'

Diana nodded; the pack elders were careful to hide the full extent of their wealth from the children. 'Rich enough. This was a gift from your grandfather, we wouldn't have thought of buying it ourselves. But once we had it, we looked at our finances and realised we could afford to develop it, use it.' She hesitated. 'When we're gone, all of us –' she looked at her firstborn – 'when all your parents are dead, our will says that all this land and the buildings on it go intact to the largest daughter pack. That's defined as the pack with the largest number of our grandchildren. Other than personal bequests, the rest of our assets are to go into a charitable fund.'

Her firstborn put his arm around her shoulder, and hugged her. 'I can understand that. It's only fair.'

Diana looked up at him gratefully. 'I'm glad you see it like that. Not that we're trying to encourage you all to have huge packs, of course,' she said hurriedly.

'No, of course not, Mother,' Seth said, turning quickly to hide his smile. 'What are you getting at?' he asked innocently.

'Nothing. It just reminded me, that's all – you said we were rich, and I remembered about our wills. Anyway, do you want to talk about Karen, or do you just want to walk?'

'Hmm. Can you stop it hurting if I do talk about her?'

'Perhaps…'

'Well. OK. Can I rant?'

'Sure.' She pulled him slightly closer. The breeze across the fields was cold, and despite her thick jumper, she felt chilled.

'This time yesterday everything was OK. You know? She was a bit quiet, but nothing major. We were in the library together, revising all morning, and then we met Jake for lunch.'

He glanced at Diana, but her expression didn't change. She knew that Jake had started to get the bus into Manchester to meet his older half-brothers occasionally.

Seth continued. 'Well, we went to a veggie place on Oxford Road. Karen and Jake thought it would be funny to take me there. Anyway, we were eating our curries and Jake mentioned that Matthew was out of bed and thinking of going back to school. Karen said it hadn't been five minutes since he was ill with the flu, and Jake said that Mattie was still sick with the same flu as before. Then to top it all, Jake dropped his fork, bent over to pick it up and banged his head on the table. He dragged out a packet of antiseptic wipes to clean himself up, and Karen just went white. I think that's when it hit her.'

'D'ya think so?' drawled Diana.

Seth shot her a dark look. 'It just pisses me off. Who the fuck does she think she is? What's she planning to do, check the DNA of every bloke who fancies her in case he fathers a sick child on her? Honestly, Mum, you basically knew the score with Xan, you knew about the carrier thing. And it didn't bother you?'

She had to be honest. 'I didn't think I'd get pregnant. I was young, I didn't have enough experience to know how quickly it could happen. But once I knew I was carrying Miranda, I knew I wanted her.'

'So are you saying that you wouldn't do it again? That you'd avoid conceiving a carrier child?' He stopped and looked at her intently.

She scowled. 'That's not a fair question, Seth. What happened with Xan and me had so many consequences. But I can promise you that since the day I first knew about Miranda, I have never regretted her.'

He carried on pushing. 'But would you reject a man because he wasn't a Shapeshifter?'

'Seth. I spent most of my teenage years and my early adulthood doing *exactly* that. I wasn't a great beauty, but I'm pretty sure I was still a virgin at twenty-eight because *I* was picky, not because the guys were.'

'So you think it's OK? What she did?'

Diana stopped dead. She moved directly into Seth's line of sight and looked up into his dark eyes. She could see trouble in them, a rare enough sight that she stepped back a little and faltered before saying, 'No, it was not OK. It was not OK at all. If she'd turned round and said no to you on the first day you asked her out, it would have been OK. But she's been your girl for two years. We've accepted her into our home, treated her as a daughter. She's given you every reason to expect that your future would be with her. I can understand that she's only just realised what it means to be the mother of a carrier, but she's over-reacting. I'm the daughter of two carriers. They were both head teachers, strong, well-respected people. Mark's mother was a successful businesswoman. John's mother enjoyed her life, we all know that. Carriers aren't wasted lives. Karen's being completely unreasonable, and more to the point, she's proved that she's not worth your time and effort.'

'How do you make that out?' muttered Seth. He still didn't want to hear anything said against Karen.

'She didn't give you a chance. She's supposed to be in love with you? If she was, she would have contacted you already today. She would want to talk to you, to work it out.'

She was still making direct eye contact with him when over his shoulder she saw a glimmer of movement, something clumsy moving behind the hedge.

'Shh,' she said, dropping to her knees, her eyes widening. Seth instantly followed suit. She put her finger to her lips solemnly, her eyes wide open. They crouched in the long grass for several minutes, not moving. Then she held up her phone, showing him that it was switched off. *Turn yours off,*' she mouthed. Less than thirty feet away, they could hear voices, several voices.

He reached for his own phone and switched it off. *Whites?* he asked silently.

Diana nodded. *Lots.* Again, she put her finger to her lips.

He was absurdly reminded of his French teacher at high school, who'd used the gesture when he wanted silence in class. Seth found himself fighting down the ridiculous urge to giggle.

His mother was looking at him, thoughtful. *Can you change your face?* she mouthed, making the movements of her lips as clear as possible. She gestured to her hair and eyes.

He blinked. It hadn't even occurred to him. His face shimmered instantly, his hair dulling to a mid-brown, thinning, taking on a slight wave. His eyes widened, faded, becoming a puddled hazel colour. His nose flattened, looking a little battered. His mouth widened and his lips became thicker and bloodier. Diana stared. *Who?* she asked.

Her eldest shrugged; it didn't matter. He didn't move, just looked at Diana expectantly.

I can't, she mouthed.

He closed his eyes. He'd never been so frustrated by the hang-ups of the older generation. *Try..*

She looked desperate. *Go,* she told him, making the shape of each word clear. *Stand up. Walk away. Get to safety. Go,* she begged him with her eyes.

He shook his head. *No. Not without you,* he told her, expectantly waiting for her to find another way.

She took a sneaky glance above the grass, then ducked down again. *Shit. They're closer.*

She thought for a moment, then reached into her son's jeans pocket, drawing out a clean white handkerchief. She'd known it would be there. He'd carried one since his second birthday. She scraped her hair back into a tighter ponytail than usual, clubbing it into a bun, tying the cloth around it. At least it hid most of her red hair. *Thump me,* she told Seth. His eyes widened. *Thump me. On the nose. Hard.*

He was appalled. She glared at him. He closed his eyes and took a wild swing, missing completely. When he opened his eyes again she was staring at him. He couldn't take the disappointment in her eyes, and bit his lip, punching at her with all his young strength.

She grunted a little, then started to scream and shout, jumping up and running away from the dozen men who had been standing dangerously close to her.

Seth understood. He paused to unbuckle his belt and unzip his trousers, then jumped up. 'Come back, you cow,' he yelled after her.

The men were already turning. They got a glimpse of a woman with a bloody face running screaming from a partially undressed man, and started to laugh.

Seth held his hands up, almost comically, in a *What can you do?* gesture, fastened his trousers, then started to run after Diana.

They'd made perhaps five hundred yards before one of the dozen blond men wandered over to where they had been sitting, noting that the grass was flattened in two distinct, compact areas, rather than one sprawling one. His attention was caught by a shining scarlet gleam in the grass. He bent and picked up Diana's phone, taking it to his packmates, handing it to the leader.

'Do you think they were watching us?' he asked a little nervously. 'If the red bitch hears that we've been on her land, we'll have bad trouble.'

The leader was turning the phone over, trying to work out how to switch it on. It was a new model; he'd not seen anything like it before. Finally he hit the right spot, and it opened, automatically displaying a list of favourite numbers. He stared at it in disbelief, it was a roll call of infamy. A pure list of Diana's mates and older children. His head snapped upwards, taking in the fast-retreating figures.

'The dirty bitch, she's rutting with the sheep now.' He smiled. 'She's alone – it's a mile to the gate. We can bring her down. I really think we can do it. The stupid, stupid bitch. OK, no howling, just Change and run quietly.'

The one who'd found the phone spoke up. 'And the man?'

The leader smirked. 'Knock him out, tie him up, leave him on top of her outside their gate. Her Alpha will get the message. Let him know his bitch was a slut.'

'Are we going to attack the pack?' his underling asked, trying to keep the nervousness out of his voice.

The leader shook his head. 'Too risky. We'll leave the bodies, then watch and wait. Let's do it!' He grinned toothily, and started to undress.

Seth had caught up with Diana. She was running steadily. 'Keep back,' she said. 'We're still in sight – if you catch up they'll wonder why you're not stopping me.'

He dropped back a little. 'There's no noise, I think they've fallen for it.'

'Just keep running, baby. Don't look back. Once we're over this rise we'll be almost at the road. We'll call home, tell them to be ready for us, and Change – we can make better time as wolves.' She was speaking evenly, not betraying the fury she felt at her own stupidity. All her energy had been focussed on Seth; she'd failed to monitor her surroundings, thinking of her new land as home, as somewhere safe.

As she topped the rise, she risked a glance behind her. The dozen men were nowhere, but she could make out movement in the grass, running in three directions. One group were heading straight for them, one was running at forty-five degrees away from them but towards the road, cutting off any possible retreat towards the town. The third group was heading at a similar angle towards the road in the direction of the pack's home. Her ruse had bought them some time, but had failed for some reason. She reached for her phone; it was time to call for help. She groaned as she realised that she'd dropped it, that the game was up. She let Seth catch up.

'Give me your phone, honey,' she said calmly, not betraying the panic that was welling up inside her. He raised an eyebrow but said nothing, drawing alongside her and handing over his phone, switching it on as he did so.

She glanced at the contact list – Karen's name at the top – and scrolled down to find Mark's name. They carried on running as the phone rang, and rang.

At last, a sleepy voice said, 'Lo? Seth?'

'It's Diana. I'm in trouble. Seth too. We're outnumbered, and we can't get home.'

Mark was instantly awake. 'Where?'

'At the road, about half a mile from the main entrance, if you were heading for town. Mark, there are at least a dozen of them.'

'I'm on my way. I'll bring John and Anthony.'

'No. You can't leave Zoe alone. And only the little kids are at home. Come alone, in transport, armed … knives, whatever. I might be dead already, so we can risk you, but not John and Anthony. Understand?'

Seth glanced at her, but stayed calm and carried on running. It was her place to plan their tactics; he wouldn't interfere. They'd both increased their pace, running as fast as they could and still speak, making no pretence now of who was being chased.

Mark was speaking. 'Diana, I'm on my way. I'll tell the others as I drive down for you. Stay on the road.'

The phone went dead; there wasn't time for anything except the vitally necessary. She turned to her son. 'OK, Change. Run.'

Both of them aimed their consciousness at a different state of being, instinctively going for their second most natural state: long-legged wolves, natural runners. Diana felt one overwhelming moment of intense pride as she saw the ease with which her son slipped from one state to the other, then concentrated her energies on escape.

Seth stumbled, hampered by his jeans. His mother turned and used her sharp teeth to rip them away. He returned the favour, and they were free of all but a few trailing rags. They reached the road and turned for home.

Close behind them, four white wolves breasted the hill and saw them, raising a howl of ecstatic triumph that was echoed excitedly by the other two groups. Diana's heart sank; she could hear that one group was almost at the road, between her and safety. Still, she ran, knowing that she ran towards danger as much as home.

Mark ran for the car park, still naked, ignoring everyone. Zoe was up, drinking juice and half-heartedly organising some of the younger children into a reading group. As he passed her, he snarled, 'Get them all underground, now.'

She didn't pause or question, but started to usher the children to the basement.

Mark chose Anthony's Land Rover, a tough vehicle that his father loved. The keys were inside and he gunned it into life, heading for the gate. Zoe had her eye on the ball and opened the gate just enough. It shut firmly behind him, and Mark put his foot right down. Hopefully he could be with his wife in a minute or two.

Seth and Diana were running flat out, using the road surface for extra speed, Seth listening warily for traffic. Diana knew there was an ambush ahead, and had all her senses trained on the undergrowth at the side of the road. When the attack came, she had time to warn Seth. They stood in the middle of the road, back to back, as the four Whites circled them. From behind, another four were catching up. Diana suddenly twisted, exposing her back to three of the wolves, and standing side by side with Seth. The pack had practised this move a thousand times, and Seth understood: moving side by side with his mother they mounted a savage double attack on a single white wolf. It took seconds, and the White was down, dying, almost evening the odds with little risk to Diana and her son. The remaining Whites flung themselves on to Diana and Seth; a raging ball of flying blood and fur and outraged screams.

Back at the house, Anthony and John stood at the gate. They could hear the fight and were shaking with fury. They could do nothing but wait; Mark's orders had been clear: they were to stay and protect the pack.

Mark's eyes widened as he reached the fight scene. Two Whites lay dead in the road, and two others were engaging his wife and son in single combat. From up the road, four Whites were within a hundred yards of the fight, with four more in sight behind them. His lips drew back and he drove straight for the closest bunched pack of four white wolves. They tried to dodge, but fell over each other, and he heard screams and crunching bones beneath his wheels.

He reversed and drove forwards several times, before spinning the car round and checking the damage. Three bodies, crushed and lifeless. But one of the Whites had escaped and was on Diana, joining in the savage attack. She was down, jaw clamped closed stubbornly, refusing to cry out. Seth was shaking his own attacker by the throat. He had several deep gashes in his side, but they weren't bleeding. Mark noted grimly that neither of the red wolves was bleeding badly, but they were obviously wounded and weakening fast.

Seth brought death to his attacker and stumbled to his mother, falling on to the surviving white wolf that had arrived in the second wave, scruffing him awkwardly with his jaws and trying to drag him away from Diana. Her original attacker was still savaging her.

The third wave of Whites advanced rapidly. Mark picked up Anthony's hunting knife, jumped out of the cab and ran towards the fight. Diana was unconscious, a white wolf tearing meat from her foreleg. The wolf turned and prepared to leap at Mark, who took a step back, aimed and threw the knife with the grace and skill of a natural killer. The wolf went down and Mark moved quickly to retrieve his weapon.

The four new attackers were nearly on him. Seth was keeping Diana's other attacker busy and Mark kneeled, taking the small bloody body of his mate in his arms, and placing her gently on the front seat of the car.

'Seth. Now,' he called, and his son twisted and disengaged from his enemy, scrabbling weakly into the cab.

Mark didn't have time to move to the other side of the vehicle, so he scrambled in behind his son, pushing past the two badly wounded red wolves and dragging the door shut behind him. The driver's door was still open when he got to his seat, and he flinched as a white wolf launched itself into the cab, falling on to him, biting into his right arm. He concentrated hard, ignoring the pain and reaching for the knife he'd dropped in his scramble to get in. He found it and twisted round, driving it deep between the ears of his attacker. The wolf fell away, taking a chunk of flesh from his right forearm.

His fingers went numb. He reached across with his left hand to slam the door shut against the remaining three wolves. He'd left the engine running, and now he pushed the car into gear and slammed it into action. His right arm was bleeding heavily, and he had to steer and change gear with his left hand.

He took a quick look at Diana and Seth. Seth had collapsed, but was breathing. He wasn't too sure about Diana. He bit through his bottom lip and glanced in the rear mirror. Three blond men stood in the middle of the road, unhurt. Another was injured, hobbling towards his packmates. The bodies of eight white wolves were scattered across the road. The survivors were dragging them towards the verges.

As he reached the gates, they rolled open, and he drove the car right up to the house. John ran up to him.

'Keep Zoe and the kids underground,' he gasped. 'Warn everyone else not to come home until I say so.'

John looked into the cab, disbelief on his face. 'She's dead?' he asked.

'I don't know.' Mark let himself out of the cab, slowly and carefully. Anthony caught him, and Mark stood for a moment, bleeding heavily. He could hear his father, next to him and a million miles away.

'Mark, remember Caleb's lessons. You don't have to bleed. Shut it down.'

Mark shook his head, cursing his stupidity, and used his control to find the bleeding vessels and slow the bleed down to a manageable seepage. He sat back against the car, sliding to the ground. He could hear his mate and his father.

'He'll be fine, if she lives,' Anthony was saying to Zoe.

John was lifting Seth out of the car. He put him gently on the ground next to Mark.

Mark reached out and put his left arm around the shoulders of the unconscious young red wolf. 'Good lad,' he heard himself saying, reassuring his son. 'Diana?' he whispered.

John was holding the limp bundle of bloody red fur gently. 'Mark, she's alive, I can feel her heart beating. I'm taking her into the house.' The joy in his voice was unmistakeable; he'd been convinced he'd lost her.

Mark struggled to stand, but Anthony restrained him. 'Nathan and Joe are watching the gate from the annexe. The other kids are underground and Andy's been informed. I'll stay with you and phone the others.'

Comforted by Seth's regular breathing, Mark opened his eyes briefly, but a red veil fell over them as he fainted.

In the house, John carried Diana up to the bedroom, gently laying her on a clean sheet, and investigating her wounds carefully. They were filthy, clotted, open wounds, unwashed by blood. She'd obviously shut off the blood supply to her injured limbs and flanks.

John ran his hand down her left foreleg, finding it broken and crushed. The right foreleg had lost most of the muscle; it had been ripped away. He shuddered.

Zoe had joined him. She was grim-faced. 'I'll wash all this out. We need to get her conscious, get some strength into her. She can deal with all this herself well enough, given food and water, but in the state she's in at the moment, an infection would just rip through her.'

John nodded. He never understood where Zoe had picked up her many and varied skills, not asking, assuming she'd researched it for some book or other. He only knew that she was too pale and tired to be dealing with this.

'Tell me what you need. I'll watch and learn, then I'll take over. You tell me what to do, OK?'

Zoe didn't argue, or even reply. She was soon busy with a bowl of hot water, clippers, forceps and gauze cloths, cleaning her Alpha's raw flesh, pausing to trim away fur, all the time keeping up a running commentary to Diana about what she was doing. There was no sign of awareness from Diana, but her heart was beating strongly.

Satisfied there were no injuries to Diana's internal organs, Zoe concentrated on cleaning more of the wounds, aware that the job was a futile one unless Diana could take charge of her body's defences again.

John was watching carefully, and she taught him to trim the fur around each wound, pick out the dirt and wash the flesh. She watched him for a while. He too was talking to Diana, but instead of reporting progress, he was chatting inanely about some new acoustic-covers album that he and Anthony were going to bring out.

Zoe was satisfied with how he was working, and went to look for Mark. He was with Anthony. Mark had come out of his faint and was sitting on the running board of the Land Rover. Seth was sleeping now, still wounded, but beginning to heal, an almost miraculous process that had become as natural to the older pack children as the scabbing over of a childhood scrape. Mark was rubbing his son's head, fascinated by the speed of the healing. His own massive wound was bandaged over, and he started to concentrate, to try to close it. It was his first major injury.

Anthony was animated, speaking fast, determined to keep Mark's attention.

Mark tried to wave him away. 'Dad, I just want to go to Diana. I've not got time for your plots.'

'Fine, you're in charge, but we won't get a better chance. She'll understand that. There were twelve of them. You can ignore my advice, and I understand that you're distracted, but this *is* an opportunity.'

Mark looked at Seth, then at Anthony. 'OK, set it up. But nothing goes down without my final say-so. OK?' He turned to Zoe. 'Diana all right?' He could see in her eyes that she wasn't and pulled himself to his feet. His Beta offered her arm to him, and he accepted it gratefully, for comfort rather than support. Together they went into the house and towards the main bedroom.

John was bending over Diana, wetting her muzzle with cold water. Her wounds were clean, but her limbs were cooling dangerously. Mark went to her. Sitting next to her, he sighed.

He summoned some authority into his voice and spoke to her. 'Diana. You're safe now. If you want to save your limbs, you have to give them some blood. Then you have to wake up and eat. Don't worry about the blood, John and Anthony and I are going to transfuse into you.' He caught Zoe's look of alarm; she didn't believe Mark had blood to spare. 'If you don't wake up and eat, I'm going to get the kids up here and let them give you blood. We'll start with the Quads and work downwards. Do you hear me?' There was no response. 'Set it up,' he said to Zoe.

Zoe left, coming back minutes later with the transfusion kit. The pack was equipped for emergencies. Diana had suggested a pack blood bank before, but it was one of those things they'd never got round to.

'OK, my love. I'm going to give you my blood. That means you can increase your blood flow to your legs and tail and ears. Diana. It's Mark. You're going to live. You're safe.'

She didn't move, not a flicker of understanding.

Mark cursed, and Zoe stepped back. The Alpha stood up and moved to Diana's head. He kneeled down.

'Don't you dare leave me. We're going on the attack, and we need you. And I want to live. I can't live without you, can I?

Diana. It's me.' He waited for a moment, then smiled, lost in time and memory. 'Diana, I promise I'll be gentle.'

The red wolf stirred, the eyelids twitched.

Mark smiled. 'My love. I'll always be gentle with you. Now live, for me. I need you.' He moved back; Zoe had found a vein in Diana's chest and was preparing the equipment. 'Two pints. I'll set you up, then call for John and Anthony. If she needs more, Nathan and Joe are big enough. Then Isaac and Ian.' She looked troubled.

Mark was cleaning his uninjured arm. His own wound was already healing, new flesh growing. The blood loss had stopped. He didn't see the irony in starting it again from the other arm. 'No, Zoe, I'll give blood then I'll eat and drink, and if she needs more after Nathan and Joe, it's my turn again. Isaac and Ian are too small.'

'They'll want to,' she pointed out.

'Then a cupful each, symbolic only. And just half a pint each from Nat and Joe.' He reached out with his injured arm, function returning to his hand. He was relieved. For a few minutes he'd thought he'd lost his hand, his music. He reflected that right now it didn't seem that important. He silently thanked Caleb for the knowledge and skills and ideas he was bringing to the pack. Zoe was linking him up to Diana, and he watched his wife carefully.

Her eyes were moving under the lids. As Diana felt her mate's hot blood surge into her veins, she only had time to relax her grim hold on the supply of blood outside her core, before the ultimate Alpha moment hit her, waking her and stunning her at the same time. She could taste the depth of the bond between them, dizzying her as their blood met and mixed. She could feel his bond with Zoe, stronger than ever, stronger than he suspected, and her body stored the information away, adding to her own knowledge of Zoe. Mark's awareness of his pack was different to hers, his response to the children different. She felt

Miranda, deep in there, the scent of her embedded in Mark's soul, information gathered from sticky toddler kisses and affectionate embraces. Almost every signal was known to her. Three were alien, and she drew away instinctively from Mark's bonds with Katie and her sons. That wasn't her territory. All this was happening in seconds, and then her body started to jerk, her heart stopped, then convulsed and restarted.

'*Fuck, fuck, fuck!*' shouted Zoe. 'We can't do it this way. She's a wolf. We can't give her human blood.'

Mark went white as he realised the immensity of their mistake. They'd looked at her and seen Diana, her shape irrelevant. His bowels clenched coldly. He tried to rise, then realised that Diana was Changing, finding the human form that could accept his lifeblood.

Her eyes flickered open. 'Idiot,' she whispered from between dry lips, before fainting again.

'She's dealing with it. It must be because it's you. I bet there's not another pair on earth you could do that with,' Zoe marvelled.

Mark was thinking furiously. Blood was seeping from Diana's wounds, washing them clean. He could almost see the flesh knitting together. Childbirth had made Diana skilled in self-healing, even in the early days when she wasn't aware of what she was doing. She'd gone to sleep again, letting her body heal itself.

He reached out to Zoe and spoke wonderingly. 'That's my blood, doing that. Get John and Anthony in here. Transfuse them to me, and keep taking from me to heal Diana. It's my blood healing her. Can you see that?'

He was in tears, watching, not believing the depth of the bond between them.

Zoe was also crying. 'I can give too.'

'No, honey, you're giving enough for the pack. We know you would, if you could.'

She shook her head. 'I'm fed up of being so helpless. I *can* fight, you know? I want to.'

Mark hugged her to him. 'Hey, we all know that.' She was trembling next to him, the reaction finally setting in. He distracted her. 'Where are the kids?'

'I left them underground with instructions not to move. Nat and Joe are in the annexe, watching the screens. They'll yell if there's trouble. Isaac and Ian are in charge below ground.'

Mark hugged her again. 'You've done well. You always do. I love you, you know that?'

She stilled in his arms. 'I guess I do. But thanks for saying it. You know I love you?'

He kissed her, and then was distracted by a movement from Diana. Her eyes were open; she was watching them carefully. Then she closed her eyes and was gone again.

Zoe left and returned quickly with John. John listened to Mark's explanation, and gladly gave his blood to Mark as the Alpha bled freely into Diana's veins.

When Anthony came up to replace John, he reported that Seth was awake, and ravenous, and human. 'I took the Land Rover up to the fields whilst the Whites were moving their dead into the undergrowth. I've got their clothes, phones, ID. They saw me from a distance, they looked very pissed off. I reckon they'll head for the old farm buildings, they're naked so they'll stay away from the road. Someone needs to deal with 'em fast before they get to spare clothes and their vehicles. Andy's been in touch with Chloe, she's fine, she's in the panic room with her kids. Helen and the girls are shopping, they'll stay in town where it's busy. We need to bring the dead onto Silverwood property quickly, before they're spotted.'

John looked at him, puzzled. Mark explained. 'We're going with the plan. We'll never get a better chance. My dad will spread the word.' He grinned as Diana opened her eyes.

'Seth?' she asked.

'Is eating and drinking,' Mark told her. 'We're going to do it. We've got time for you to rest for a day and get your strength back.'

'I don't need a day,' she whispered. 'Stop giving me blood.'

'Nope. I'll get some from Dad. You get more from me, then you're sleeping.'

She looked at him; he was too glib. 'Is Seth really all right?'

He leaned closer to her. 'He's fine. It's you I'm worried about. You nearly died. If I'd been a minute later you'd have been torn apart. I'm not happy about that.' He changed the subject. 'Can you drink yet?'

She shook her head. 'Stomach's still shut down. Blood's nice, but can I have some of that saline drip too? And some lip balm?'

John went to the bedside cabinet and found some of the honey lip balm he knew she loved. He spread it gently on her lips. Then he kissed her. 'Ready for war?' he asked.

'I've been ready for years,' she whispered, and took Mark's hand and slept again.

Mark looked up as he set up a saline drip. 'I'm staying with her for a while. We've talked about this enough. You don't need me at the moment, she does. John, Dad, make sure the annexe and the underground refuge are bombproof, secure and well stocked – entertainment, as well as food and drink. While we're away, the kids should be using the whole inner estate, but I want to know they've got a retreat if they need it. Anthony, stay with the kids for now, reassure them, make sure they eat. I don't want them above ground or visible until I know we're safe today. Zoe, hon, lie down.'

She protested she didn't want to leave Diana.

Her Alpha smiled. 'Give me a minute, then.' He lifted Diana from John and Zoe's bed to the biggest bed, balling up the now filthy sheet she'd been lying on. 'Right, it's a nice big bed, you can curl up together. Is that OK? And can you deal with the babies tonight? If not, we'll go out for some formula milk, no probs.'

Zoe nodded. 'I think I'll be OK.' They shared a smile, then Zoe's head hit the pillow, and she was asleep.

Mark buried his head in his hands for a moment and lay down next to Diana, holding her close to him. He stayed there for a long time.

Chapter 22

John glanced at the security screen as he carried supplies into the annexe. A large green hatchback was at the gate. He recognised it as Chloe's, and hurriedly opened the gate, dumping the supplies and walking down the drive.

Bill jumped out to meet him, frowning. 'You took your time. We've got four dead men in that car, we can't wait all day. How's Mum? And why weren't you with her?'

John shook his head. 'You're getting the hang of this Alpha business faster than Mark ever did, I have to say. But less of the lip, OK? Diana will live, but it was a close thing. She was with Seth, by the way, and they screwed up big time. They weren't watching their backs.' He leaned into the car. 'Hiya, Frankie, you're looking good. When are you kids gonna sign a Contract?'

Frankie leaned back. 'When Mary makes her mind up that she's happy to settle for Beta. She will, don't worry. She wants to be with us. She's already got a job offer from the local vet's surgery, so it's in her hands. Chloe likes her, Phil and Mareta like her. Bill and I like her – we've always liked her. I'm looking forward to properly meeting her. And the Kittens approve, which officially settles it, of course. We'll all Contract together, then maybe look for extras later.'

Bill was almost hopping with impatience as the two Betas swapped gossip.

'Dad, I'm sorry I was rude, but I need answers. What am I going to do with these bodies? How long will I be away from Chloe? And who's going to look after her?'

John put his hand on his son's shoulder. 'Hold on. It's all in the plan. Chloe and Helen and the kids are coming here. We were hoping to have Janie and Alice as home defence, but they've still not had their first Change. Andy will collect Chloe and the kids later – they're safe underground at your place for now. We'll have a few more guests later. And the bodies … put them next to the lab for now, but cover them with a tarp or something. There are more outside – we'll get them inside the fence when the rush hour traffic dies down.'

Anthony emerged from the annexe. He caught sight of the young men and waved, walking towards them. 'Did you find them?'

'About a mile away from your guess, but they were easy to track; one of them was wounded.'

'Yes, Seth did that. There were eight others, Mark, Diana and Seth accounted for them. Right, get those bodies hidden, and clean the car up. If you have time, clean my car too – it's a little gory underneath. Well done on getting them as human too, it's exactly what Mark wanted.'

Bill flushed with pride. He turned to help his twin carry the heavy weight of their prey from the car towards his mother's laboratory. As he struggled, he remembered the call that had made him slide down the scaffolding at work and run for his car, pausing only to grab his twin and pull him along with him. It had been Anthony, telling him that Diana and Seth had been attacked, almost killed, and the Whites who'd done it were escaping via the new lands and were probably close to the back gate to the main territory. Anthony hadn't specified why Bill had to deal with it, but Bill didn't need any more information; he'd find out everything else once he'd killed the men who had dared to hurt Diana.

The twins had driven as close as possible to where Anthony guessed the men would be, then hidden the car keys and Changed, tracking around for the scent. The blood of the injured White had been easy to find, and within minutes Bill and Frank had risen out of the grass ahead of the men, who were still trying to find their missing clothes. The killing had been quick and efficient, and Bill and Frank were uninjured when it was finished. They'd bled out the bodies at the scene, into the welcoming earth, to save on mess as they dragged them to the car.

Frankie called out to his brother. 'Wake up! Daydreaming again?'

Bill looked up. 'Yeah, sorry. Let's get these four dumped, clean up a bit, and go to see Mum.'

'Seconded,' said Frankie, making no attempt to hide his feelings.

They walked into the strangely silent house, looking round nervously. The ground floor was eerily empty: no children eating, working or playing. Toys lay on the floor, drinks sat on window ledges, books were left on tables and snacks half eaten next to terminals. Knowing the kids were safe didn't make the young men any less uncomfortable. They made their way upstairs and silently washed their arms and hands in one of the family bathrooms, habit taking them to the one closest to their old bedroom. It was the first time they'd been upstairs since they left home with Chloe, and everything felt familiar and yet different. The scent of soap was now strange; Chloe favoured a different brand, and they'd got used to that. Frankie reached for his comb, but it wasn't there. He looked blankly at the shelf, then reached into his back pocket and took it out, nervously laughing at himself.

They made their way to the main bedroom, and stood outside, looking at each other. Even as kids, they'd rarely ventured inside; it was a place for parents and small babies, and the rest of the pack kept out. Bill knocked on the door.

Mark's voice was surprised as he answered, 'Who's there?'

'Bill, Frankie. Can we see Mum?'

The door opened. Mark looked sleep-rumpled and puzzled. He looked at the boys for a moment as if they were intruders, then relaxed.

'Of course. Come in. She's asleep.'

Mark walked quickly to the bed, adjusting the duvet to cover the sleeping women. He stood protectively next to the bed, between it and the young men.

'Dad, she's my mum…' said Bill, almost pleading. 'Let me get closer.'

Frankie spoke up. 'It's just us.' He moved closer, cautiously moving into Mark's space, staying there. 'Hey, Dad, it's been a bad day. Can I have a hug?'

Mark shook his head, sighing. He drew the twins into his arms. 'Sorry, lads. I'm sorry. I just want to look after her, and you don't smell like pack any more. I'll get used to it. This is new – we'll all have to get used to it. You're still our sons, don't worry. Go and sit with her. Try not to wake Zoe up. I'm sure you understand I want her to rest.'

Bill spoke up. 'Do you think Chloe will be OK? Without me?'

Mark was surprised. He honestly hadn't thought about it. 'For how long it will take, yes, she'll be fine. Just leave her some dirty clothes to cuddle up to.' He caught Bill's look, and laughed. 'No, I mean it, seriously. Sleep with her tonight, in the bed she'll be staying in. Get Frankie in with you too. Tell her not to change the sheets.' He glanced over at Diana. 'Look, I want to check on things, to talk to Andy and make sure nothing's been missed. I'll leave you with your mum.'

He took one look back as he left the room. Bill and Frank were sitting on the edge of the bed, watching Diana sleep.

Andy was in the kitchen, making bacon and tomato sandwiches and watching, almost awed, as Seth ate them as fast as they were served. Mark grabbed the latest as Seth reached for it, laughing as he sank his teeth into it.

'Mmm, compliments to the chef. Can we have a plateful of these sent up for the women? And some milk, and juice. And Zoe will want some of that godawful instant coffee.'

Seth stood up, stretched. 'OK, I get the message. I'll get cooking, eh? We're going to be busy later. Who's sorting out the littl'uns?'

'Anthony,' said Mark from around a large bit of sandwich. 'And the blond half of the Quads. They've been bloody brilliant today.'

'Who? Nat and Joe?' Andy was surprised.

'The very same. Making a bit of a bid for fame from under the shadow of Isaac and Ian.'

Andy threw a tea towel at his friend, laughing. 'I'll nip down and see them later,' he promised, before getting back to the serious issue of making bacon butties. Seth started to root through the cupboards, plotting that evening's menu.

Mark sat back. 'Anyone heard from the others yet?'

Andy looked up from slathering butter on thick brown bread. 'John's on the forums, spreading trouble. Everyone knows that Diana got hit. The word we're getting out is that she and Seth are seriously ill, and that we're drawing in our horns and don't want help. Only those involved in the plan know different. The Kittens want to speak to Diana before they go another step, but that shouldn't be a problem. They're with us, they know the score, but they just want to make absolutely sure that she's OK with it.'

'Wise move,' mumbled Mark.

Andy picked up the next sandwich, and continued. 'All the older kids are on their way back from school or college. The younger girls don't know what's going on. We need to let them know as soon as they get home, it's not fair on them otherwise. They're panicking a bit. The Bees won't tell them any part of the plan in case something happens before they all get safely home.'

Mark frowned. 'Send John out to shadow them home.'

Andy nodded, getting on the phone.

Seth returned. 'Curry OK for everyone for tea? I can make four or five varieties. Oh, and Noah's back, with Miranda. She's having a major strop, he says.'

'Miranda?' Mark was puzzled.

'"Three big strapping men about the place, yet Mum nearly gets killed by a bunch of ignorant medieval arsewipes" is about the gist of it. And I'm not her favourite brother.'

Mark looked up, suddenly guilty. 'Karen! I'm sorry, Seth, I forgot Karen. We need to bring her in.'

Seth stopped dead. 'No, you don't. It's over. That's what Mum and I were out there talking about.'

His father scowled. 'Whose decision, Seth? You can't just put people at risk and drop them.'

'Karen broke up with me, Dad. She doesn't want to be part of us any more.'

Mark nodded, satisfied. 'That explains what happened out there, then. We'll say no more about it. I understand now why you were both off your guard.' He reached for a phone, called his agent on speed dial, and settled back, reaching for another sandwich just as Andy finished making it.

'Paul? It's Mark. We've got trouble again. It's serious, but all I want from you is for it to be made very, very public that Karen Massey has broken off her engagement with my son. I don't care how bad it looks, I want her publicly dissociated from my family immediately. For her own safety. She'll be fine if she turns her back on us. If she contacts you and starts complaining, spell it out to her and tell her it's for her own good.'

He listened for a while.

'Yeah, it is true, actually, no spin. I only just found out myself. OK, I'll pass on your sympathies to Seth. She is a nice girl – well, I thought so until just now.'

He put the phone down, looked at his firstborn. 'Paul sends his sympathies. Says he's been dumped so often he has reserved parking at the tip.'

Seth looked up. 'I'm not getting mixed up with any more normal women. Next time I get involved with a woman, she'll be my mate.'

Mark sighed with relief. 'Good. How are you feeling?'

Seth sounded puzzled. 'Karen's a bit of a distant memory. Mum and I nearly died this morning, so suddenly Karen doesn't seem so important.' He glanced at his dad. 'Well, I'll go and get shouted at by Miranda – I suppose I deserve it. Then I'll get back to the kitchen. See you all later.'

Back in the bedroom, Diana was stirring. She opened her eyes and blinked. 'Bill, what are you doing here?'

Her son laughed. 'Frankie's here too. We've come to see you.'

She scowled. 'I'm not an invalid. But I am thirsty. And I'm so bloody tired.'

Bill turned round. 'Frank? She's ready for some food.'

'On it,' his twin said, and left the room.

Diana struggled to sit up without disturbing Zoe. She peered at Bill. 'Is Chloe here yet?'

'Andy's going for her and the kids. Dad says that nobody leaves once they're in here. He wants to keep things secure.'

'Yeah, that's the plan. Everyone else?'

'On their way. When you're up to it, you need to phone the Kittens.'

'Yes, son.'

Bill looked worried. 'Mum, what if we don't make it back? What happens to Chloe?'

'Oh, Bill, you know what happens. She won't survive it. That's the risk we take by being the Alpha, though I didn't know it at the time. But you two do know it. And Chloe's very aware of it, because she lost her first pack. Don't ask me for reassurance, it's too late for that.'

Bill looked at her. Suddenly his childhood was very far away. 'We'd better win, then.'

'Yes. It's not going to be easy. You know that?'

'I'm getting the picture.' He looked sombre.

Frank came in with a tray of food. He put it down carefully and sat on the bed, embracing Diana in a tight, wordless hug that left her breathless. He sat back down, looking at her.

Bill blushed. 'Can I?'

'Oh, Bill, you don't have to ask.' She reached out and hugged him.

'Mark doesn't want me around,' he said dolefully.

'*He* does. His instincts don't. He'll get over it. Besides, *I* want you around, you should visit more often. And bring Chloe too. So what if we argue? It's normal to fight with your daughter-in-law, isn't it?' She took a moment to look at him. 'Hell, it's good to see you. Are you OK?'

'We're fine. We just brought down the last four of that group that nearly killed you. And they stayed human when we killed them.'

'Good lad. They're all dead?'

'Yeah. Seth said that you accounted for one of them yourself. Mark got five. Seth got two. And Frank and I got the other four.'

Diana had reached for the food, and waved at him with the fork. She finished her mouthful and washed it down with milk. 'Good. Tell me about what else is happening.'

She listened as she ate. Bill was enthusiastic about his forthcoming meeting with Mary.

Diana glanced up when he spoke about the young vet. 'You've not met her yet?'

'No. I've known her for years, though, on the forums. And Darlene and Sara say she's OK, just a bit nervous of Chloe.' He sighed. 'I guess I'll have to be careful there.'

'You just be yourself. It'll be fine,' said Diana. 'I like Mary, she's got a lot of common sense. She's coming tonight, you know?'

Bill looked troubled. 'I know. Chloe's been wondering what to wear all day.'

Diana rolled her eyes but said nothing. Next to her, Zoe stirred.

'Go on, disappear. You're waking her up,' Diana said, handing the tray back to him.

Frank and Bill retreated as Diana slid under the duvet again, cuddling up to Zoe and settling back to sleep.

'Nearly dead, Anthony said,' muttered Frank.

'She probably was. Every time she gets hurt, she bounces back faster. She's beginning to scare me.'

Bill gave an almost superstitious look back at his parents' bedroom door, and then put his arm round his twin. 'Let's make ourselves useful and go and see the little kids, eh?'

Frank agreed, and they made their way to the annexe.

At three in the afternoon, Diana got up and had a long bath, scrubbing at her skin, admiring the scar-less new tissue of her arms and legs. She looked for a moment at the old scars from her first fight with the Whites, remembering her dead sister. She considered making them go away, now that she understood how. She dismissed the idea; some scars were meant to be worn forever. She dressed carefully, pinning her hair up, using cosmetics sparingly, as Zoe had finally taught her. She picked up a phone and rang Sara.

'Mother! Are you OK?'

'Back from the dead, hon. Are you ready?'

'It's really going to happen, then?'

'Yes, but you're crucial to the plan. Can you bring Jan in? Any idea what sort of state he's in?'

'Mum, I've not seen him. You do believe me?'

'Of course. All I need to know is your opinion.'

'Well, he's still killing. He's a bit of a psycho, really. He's getting … what's the word? … whimsical.'

'Whimsical?'

'He made me some soft toys. White wolf puppies. With real fur.'

Diana couldn't help it, she howled with laughter. 'That man is sick.'

'I know,' Sara said.

Her mother thought she could detect a note of pride in her voice. 'So, do you still want him? I need to know how we're playing this.'

'I don't know. But I know I can bring him in. He's never far away. I can smell him when I go out running, but he won't approach.'

'Fear of Andy? Or you?'

'Dad, I think. He leaves his mark all over the place whenever he visits. Everyone knows that our house is under his protection.'

'He's a good dad, but he's a show-off too. You girls don't need protection.'

Sara giggled. 'We know that, but don't tell Dad. Please? It's kinda cute.'

Diana thought so too, but didn't say it. 'He'll be here by now. He was going for Helen and the girls, and Chloe and her kids. We'll make sure he's fed and happy, and then he can come for you and Darlene. Mary is coming back with you. If you can't get Jan, we'll wait another night, and you try again. Don't come home without him.'

Sara questioned her mother. 'Do you feel bad? About using Jan?'

'No way, there's a lot in this for him too, the fight and everything. And he loves us. And I really do like him.'

Sara, hundreds of miles away, thoughtfully twirled a long strand of red hair around her fingers. 'You'd do this yourself, wouldn't you? If you'd met him ten years ago? Mark and John's younger cousin?'

'I'd be tempted.' Her mother smiled as she admitted it. 'But that's not the issue now. I'm past all that. Bring him in, Sara. Carefully.'

Diana put the phone down and went to the top of the stairs, she stood there, watching and listening.

Mark looked up and smiled. 'Hey, someone's dressed up.'

John stood and met her at the bottom of the stairs, taking her hand and leading her to the armchair he'd just vacated. He brought her a glass of wine. He couldn't take his eyes off her. She shone.

Miranda was watching her carefully, as if it was some sort of trick. At last, satisfied, she gave Diana a brief, cautious hug, and returned to her book.

Helen was fussing over Chloe, who showed every sign of appreciating the motherly attention.

Mark and Anthony told Diana that they had searched the perimeter, spoken to all the other packs, and brought in the rest of the bodies from outside the fence. They were satisfied that no other attacks were imminent, and had brought the children in from the annexe. The house was back to usual.

Bill was sitting very close to his mate, holding her hand as he chatted happily to his family. The kids were all thrilled to have their brothers back, even it was temporary. The news that the Kittens might be home later had everyone excited, and even the toddlers knew that something was in the air.

For a couple of hours, the family simply sat together chatting, the children seeking out Diana in turn, needing reassurance that she was fine. Seth took the opportunity to get some sleep, while his twin took over preparing the evening meal.

Zoe came downstairs, looking refreshed and happy. She found her babies screaming indignantly at Tom and Alex, who were helpfully taking toys to them and then taking them way again. The little boys reached out happily when they saw their mother, and she spent some time cuddling them before picking up Charlotte and Emily. She crossed over to the big armchair where Diana was sitting.

'Scrunch up?' Zoe suggested, and the two women settled together, taking a baby each to nurse. Chloe looked at them almost jealously.

'Mum lost a child too, you know?' Bill said, understanding.

'Sammy wasn't a baby. And Diana was with him,' Chloe said, the hurt still raw. She was wearing a deep blue cotton suit, with a crisp white blouse. It was tailored to emphasise her pregnancy, not to hide it. Her hairstyle was youthful and fashionable. She'd been agonising all day about meeting Mary for the first time.

Bill had told her a dozen times, 'If you don't like her, it doesn't happen. We're looking for a friend for you, not a rival.' But she was still nervous.

At six, Noah announced that dinner was served, and the family all found their places in the big dining room. They rarely all ate together, but wanted to tonight. They mixed together. Helen found herself separated from her daughters and brought into the heart of the family. Chloe turned to speak to Bill only to realise he'd moved a seat further away, and that Mark was sitting next to her, picking up on an earlier comment about a book that she loved, and asking her if she could recommend any others. On her other side, Mia had a small bowl of mild chicken curry and a naan bread, and was thoughtfully working her way through it.

Eva had seen Caleb settle himself comfortably between two of his younger sisters, and she frowned before realising the seat opposite him was empty. She took the seat, smiling at him. He smiled back, and to her delight spoke to her.

'Eva! My dear. Could I tempt you with a plate of this fine korma? It's very mild. I'm sure you'd enjoy some of this rice too? And some chutney? Perhaps not. Beautiful ladies always seem to be watching their figures.' Caleb was teasing her, as always. She was his cute 'sister' who never failed to blush when he teased her, something his real sisters had become immune to long ago.

She looked at him, reddening furiously, and then whispered something incomprehensible.

He stared at her, then gallantly stood and walked around the table, kneeling beside her so she didn't have to raise her voice. 'Sorry, Eva, it's very noisy in here. What did you say?'

She was in an agony of embarrassment. 'Nothing.' She glanced around. Her mother and sister were busy; nobody was looking at her except Caleb, who was giving her his full attention. 'I said, do you really think I'm pretty?' she whispered.

Caleb smiled. He was used to reassuring younger sisters. 'Of course I do. Who wouldn't? Did someone say you weren't? At school? Tell me who it was and I'll sort 'em out.' She was blushing, and he smiled. She was just a few months older than Jane and Alice, and he knew the symptoms. 'Is it a boy? Is there a boy you like?' He showed a keen intellectual interest in romance, but the topic was a theoretical one for him, and for his sisters Beatrice and Bridget. That trait had been shared by their parents, as teenagers.

Eva was now bright red and convinced that soon the whole room would be looking at her.

'Yes, there's a boy I like,' she whispered, looking desperately at Caleb.

He looked at her, his eyes widening as he understood. Then he blushed. 'Eva, you're my little sister,' he said.

'I'm *not*,' she muttered, furious with him. 'I didn't even grow up with you. I'm not!' She stood up and ran out of the room.

Isaac had just strolled in, taking the seat next to Eva's and looking at Caleb with interest. 'You making the girls cry?' he asked.

'Fuck off, squirt,' said Caleb absently to his younger brother, watching Eva disappear. Isaac stared at Caleb for a moment, surprised, and then started to load a plate with a generous portion of everything on the table.

Caleb looked round. He felt absurdly guilty. He was sure that everyone was looking at him. He looked at Mark, who was pouring wine for Chloe, assuring her that one glass wouldn't do the babies any harm. John was mixing a lethal lime pickle into his lamb vindaloo, and was talking to Trixie; she was laughing. Zoe was sitting with Tom and Alex on either side of her, persuading them to try the milder dishes, her babies behind her, sleeping in a cot. Diana was sitting at the top of one of the tables. She had a sketch pad and was drawing something, deep in discussion with Noah. Probably plans for the new buildings, Caleb thought. At the foot of the same table, Anthony was sitting silently, looking at Caleb. Caleb looked back, trying not to seem guilty. Anthony beckoned to him and he walked over.

'Little girls get crushes. Don't take it to heart,' the old man said.

'I didn't encourage her,' Caleb protested.

'No, but I've been watching that one, and she's been watching you for a long time. Be kind, but don't encourage her. She's just a child.'

'I know that,' Caleb said stiffly. 'I wouldn't…'

'No, you wouldn't. Of course you wouldn't. Let her be, don't follow her. Perhaps you'd like me to suggest to one of your sisters that Eva might be upset? If you're worried about her?'

'Yes, please. That's a good idea. Thank you, Granddad.'

'It will be my pleasure.'

Anthony waited until Caleb had gone back to his seat. He finished a bowl of the rich game curry that Seth had prepared with his grandfather in mind, and stood up. When he reached Miranda, he leaned over and spoke to her.

Miranda looked up and nodded, and went to speak to Eva. The two blondes returned shortly afterwards. Eva's face was very clean and shiny, but she returned to her seat and started to eat again, refusing to look at Caleb.

The pack finished the food, and leaned back, looking expectantly at Noah and Seth.

Seth laughed. 'You greedy bunch. I've got some ice cream. Is that OK? And you can make your own coffee.'

The four parents cleared the table, quietly retiring into the big kitchen with a large tub of ice cream and four spoons.

Diana spoke up. 'We can't leave all those kids without a real fighter to look after them while we're away. It's mad. John stays here with Zoe.'

'Oh no!' Zoe said. 'We agreed. The more fighters, the more we stand a chance of succeeding. If John goes, there's a better chance of all of you coming back than if he stays. I want you *all* back. And I've thought about it. I'd be happier if Bridget and Beatrice go with you. Same principle, really, the more, the safer. I can cope without them.'

They looked at each other. 'OK, it's settled. No last-minute changes,' said Mark.

They moved around the kitchen, enjoying sharing the domestic work, chatting and joking. When they were ready, they went back to the main dining room, where the older children were cleaning up and putting the tables away. Diana noticed that Janie and Alice were helping, including themselves now in the older group. When had that first happened?

Caleb came over. 'We'll get the kids to bed. Jane and Ali want to stay up, is that OK?'

His mother shrugged. 'Yeah, sure. If they think they're ready. Why do they want to grow up so quickly?'

Her seventeen-year-old son pulled a face. 'I wish they wouldn't.'

Diana realised he was talking about more than Jane and Alice, but didn't push it.

She made her way to a room at the back of the house that they'd managed to keep as a refuge from the children. It was a warmly furnished room with sofas and armchairs arranged around a large fireplace. A music centre was hidden behind dark-wood cupboards. Photographs of the children filled the walls.

Anthony was already there, thoughtfully keying in a music selection for the next few hours. Helen had dozed off in an armchair. Her face was relaxed, and Diana realised uncomfortably that Helen was no longer young. Diana was looking at a middle-aged woman who'd taken very good care of herself, but the old-woman-to-be was clearly visible. Diana looked away, almost ashamed, and realised that Chloe was watching her, clearly knowing what she'd been thinking.

'Good old W chromosome eh?' Chloe said quietly. 'No, I know what you're thinking, and you don't look anything like that.'

Shamefully reassured, Diana blushed and sat next to her daughter-in-law. 'Are you nervous?'

'Terrified. You were the one who brought Zoe into your pack, weren't you?'

Diana was taken aback for a moment – she'd been talking about the fight to come – but smoothly changed gears.

'Yes. Well, Andy found her, but didn't quite know what to do about her. At first, Mark didn't even want her in the pack.' Diana smiled, watching as Zoe came into the room, shadowed by John and Mark. 'He bloody does now.'

'Are you jealous?'

'Never. It's not like that. Didn't you love Laura?'

'Yes, of course I did, but we were friends before Andy told us where to find Duncan. It was different. Dunc chose between us, but we were always together.'

Diana hesitated. 'But Laura was always a little bit cruel to you after that, wasn't she? I don't want to speak ill of her, but I got the feeling she put you down a little.'

Chloe turned away. 'She was good to me.'

'Not as good as she could have been, clearly. What's bothering you? That you'll be cruel to Mary? Or that she'll take over?'

The young woman raised her hands. 'Can't they wait until I've at least had my babies before they go looking for someone else?'

Diana swallowed. 'Chloe, they worship you. Do you really think that's how it is? Why don't you tell them how you feel?'

'Because it won't make any difference.'

'It will. Bill will wait if you ask him to.' She smiled. 'Bill will jump off a cliff if you ask him to. And speaking of…'

Chloe blinked, and looked up, smiling at her Alpha who was walking into the room looking for her.

Frankie mooched in behind him, carrying two dozen cans of lager. He opened the patio doors and dropped the cans outside to keep cool, picking a couple out and handing one to his twin. Bill looked pointedly at his mother, who apologised, wide-eyed, and moved away from Chloe, leaving the sofa free for the two young men to sit on either side of their mate. Their body language made it suddenly clear to her that the spare bedroom in Chloe's house got very little use, and Diana hurriedly turned round.

Mark had made himself comfortable by the fireplace and she went to the patio and got two cans of lager, opening one for herself and one for him, and sitting on the arm of his chair, silent.

'How are you feeling?' he asked her.

'Very alive. I'll show you something interesting later,' she promised him.

He raised an eyebrow, and smiled, relaxing, listening to the music.

John and Zoe grabbed another sofa. John sat down, and his wife lay with her head in his lap, dozing off as he stroked her hair.

Anthony poured a large glass of wine for himself and stood at the back of the room, watching as the older children came in and found places to sit, talking quietly. Seth automatically headed for a two-seater sofa, settling down, moving a cushion out of the way, then slowly moving it back, an empty look on his face. Noah caught the moment, and went to sit next to his twin. 'Monogamy is over-rated, kid. You should play the field – like me.'

Seth shrugged. 'Why haven't I got a beer?' he said pointedly. Caleb threw a can to him and the redhead caught it, settling back and suddenly thanking the Fates that he was alive to drink it.

Chapter 23

Mary stood in her room, stripped to her underwear, clothes all over the bed.

'Sara. What the hell am I going to wear?'

'Go like that and you'll wow 'em,' said the redhead.

'Fuck off. If you can't help, go away.' Mary looked into the mirror, seeing a strong, athletic body with wide swimmer's shoulders, mid-brown madly curling hair cut in a simple line just below her ears, rich blue eyes, darker than most. She frowned, unsatisfied.

Sara glanced at the clothes, then looked out of the window again. 'Well, my dad is always impressed when women dress up. That pale green suit will bring out your eyes and flatter your figure. But you've not got a single pair of shoes to match it.'

Mary stared at her. 'That's my graduation suit. And the green shoes match it.'

Sara laughed. 'They bloody don't. Who told you they did?'

Mary hung the suit up. 'Well, I'm not trying to impress your dad. I want Chloe and your brothers to think well of me.'

Sara licked her lips. 'Liar. You want Bill to put you over his shoulder and carry you off to the woods.'

'I repeat. Fuck off,' said Mary casually, refusing to be baited. 'Anyway, what are you wearing for your jaunt tonight, Ms Honeypot?'

'Jeans, shirt, trainers. It's never failed before.' Sara had the infuriating air of those who take their attractiveness for granted.

Mary looked in the mirror. Her eyes were her best feature, and she decided to work on them. She reached for her cosmetics and started to put make-up on.

'Too early,' commented Sara. 'It'll be worn off by the time we get to the house.'

'I can reapply it. Stupid girl,' Mary muttered.

Darlene came in. 'Oh, clothes party.' She went to the wardrobe.

Mary shot her a resigned look. 'Don't waste your time. Everything decent is on the bed. Fucking hell. Why didn't I think about this? Why don't I have any clothes suitable for meeting guys?'

Darlene took out a long silk dress. It had a full skirt, and buttoned from top to bottom at the front. Basically white, it was shot through with tones of blue and green. 'This is pretty. Chloe would wear something like this.' Mary shot her an annoyed look, but Darlene smiled patiently. 'You're dressing for Chloe. The boys are in the bag. You're female, you're young, you're wolfie. That's good enough. It's the wifey you need to impress.'

Mary stood up and examined the dress critically. 'You're right. Why didn't Sara point that out?'

'Sara's got her mind on other things. Right, Sar?'

'Right, Dar,' her twin said, licking her lips, sitting on the window ledge and swinging her legs.

Darlene looked at her. 'Are you even packed yet?'

'We might not be going tonight,' Sara protested.

'If we are, we go straight away. Are you packed?'

'I'll do it now,' Sara grumbled, leaving the room.

'Silly mad bint. Mary? Are you packed? I mean, seriously.'

Mary looked up. 'Do you mean have I remembered that there's more to this trip than romance? I've got a comfortable, warm set of clothes and shoes all packed. That's all I'll need, right?'

'Yeah, I guess. Are you OK with this?'

'Yes. I want to be part of it. I might not come back, but I'm going with you. Do you think the rest of the girls will be OK?'

'They'll be fine without us. Scary kids, the lot of them.' Darlene was speaking about young women who were all older than her, but Mary didn't correct her. They'd all learned more about Shapeshifting and fighting in the few months since the twins arrived in the house than they'd picked up in their entire lives before.

Mary reached into the wardrobe and pulled out a denim jacket. She was starting to put it on when Darlene shook her head. 'No. No, no, no, no, no.'

'No?' Mary said, now totally puzzled.

'The boys like denim, but Chloe thinks it's unfeminine. Wear that green jacket, the shiny one.'

'It's vile.'

'OK, then, give it away. Why do you keep it if it's vile? I've got a pale blue raw silk blazer that'll look great with that dress. It's new – nobody will know it's not yours. In fact, it *is* yours: I'm giving it to you.'

Mary flashed a smile of thanks. The Kittens' clothes budget was legendary. Somehow they'd managed to persuade all three of their dads to give them an allowance. Each of their benefactors blissfully thought he was the only one sending extra money their way.

When the doorbell rang an hour later, Mary looked out of her window, surprised. No car had drawn up.

She went downstairs and looked through the spyhole before opening the door.

'Mr Ransome? Where's the car?'

'I parked a couple of miles away and walked. I'll go for it later. I don't want Jan to know I'm here. And it's Andy to you. So let me in, eh?'

Mary blushed. 'Sorry.' She stood aside.

Andy reached out and hugged her. 'I'm sorry. I shouldn't be snappy with you, kid. I hate walking, that's all.'

Mary knew there was more to it than that, but stayed quiet.

'Where're my girls?' Andy said.

'Ready. We're all packed. Sara's freaking out a little, so I asked the others to distract her. She's in the living room.'

Andy went to the big room at the front of the house that served as a shared living room for the young Shapeshifters. They were all sitting in front of the telly, watching a film and drinking coffee. They turned when he came in and waved, and then all but his daughters went back to watching the film.

Sara stood up. 'Is it time?' she asked him.

'Yes, it's getting late. Do you think he'll be around? No, don't hug me – he'll smell me on you.'

Sara dropped back, abashed. 'Sorry, stupid of me. Yes, he'll be around. I heard him howling about ten minutes ago.'

Andy scowled. 'Does he do that a lot?'

'Once or twice a night. He can't help it, Dad.'

'Sara, just say the word, anytime. Just shout and I'll be there, if you change your mind about this.'

'I'm bringing him in, Dad, that's all anyone's asked me to do. Right?'

'Right,' he growled. 'Go on, then.'

Sara looked around, then pulled on her trainers and went to the door. It felt odd to be leaving the house at night alone, and she shivered as she stepped outside. She reminded herself that she was one of the most dangerous people in London, and smiled at the thought. She walked towards the minimarket – it was about half a mile away, down well-lit streets. She knew very well that it would already be shut, but when she reached it, she mimed frustration and continued onwards. The next shops were a fair distance away; the area she lived in was mostly deserted at night. The route would take her forty minutes, but by nipping through alleys and side streets she could make it in twenty. She whistled casually and walked down the nearest side street. Half of the houses were boarded up, and the street lights were intermittent. She heard a noise behind her. She knew it wasn't a rat. The area had no rats: a benefit of werewolf life.

As she left the street and walked into an unlit ginnel, she heard raspy breathing behind her.

'Sara…' The voice was hoarse with disuse, the speaker about fifty yards behind her.

She turned. 'Who is it?' She suddenly felt ashamed of the lie; she knew perfectly well who it was.

'Sara, it's Jan. Please don't go out alone at night – it's not safe.'

'Come a little closer,' she said. 'I need to see you, be sure it's you.'

'I can't come any closer, Sara. Your father will kill me. He told me.' There was silence.

The girl smiled into the darkness. 'Jan, what if I told you that Dad won't touch you? Come back with me, come home – come back to the pack. I've told them about your gifts, that I trust you. Mum's on your side. And we need you.'

She took a step closer, and heard him step back. 'Diana told you to keep away from me,' he said.

'Only because you were a prisoner at the time,' Sara pointed out. Her breathing was speeding up. She could see him now, pale against the darkness of the alley wall. He was gaunt, perhaps thirty pounds thinner than the man she'd known. He was shirtless, his jeans not much more than rags. She could feel her stomach clench in involuntary empathy.

'Have you been looking after yourself, Jan?' she called out gently.

'I've been looking after you,' he said. There was pride in his voice. Then he blurted out. 'I know you don't need it, but it's all I can do.' He fell silent. 'Can I really come home?' He sounded childlike, lost.

'Yes,' she said.

'And you? Will you be there?'

'We can talk about it, Jan. I promise we can talk about it. But I'm here because we need you to fight for us. It won't be easy. Will you fight for us?'

'Yes.' His reply came before she'd finished asking the question. 'Yes, of course. I'd die for you.'

She moved closer, her eyes filling with tears as she saw the scars that puckered his flesh. 'I don't want you to die.' She raised a hand to his chest, smiling through the tears as she touched a deep, dead white scar above his heart. She traced it as he stood, shuddering, before her. 'Will you come home with me?' She looked at him; they were the same height. She reached out to push his long dirty hair behind his ears in a possessive gesture that told him all he needed to know.

'Sara?'

She moved a step closer until their bodies were touching and kissed him gently. It felt like he'd been wired up to the mains as his starved body recognised her, as the commands buried within him awoke to the presence of an unclaimed, willing female.

He broke away. 'Oh god. Sara. Not here, not here in this stinking alley.' He closed his eyes and pushed her away. 'I'll follow you home.' He Changed, crying out a little as he did so. He made a gaunt wolf, hollow-eyed and rangy.

Sara swore under her breath at the jokes she'd made about him to her housemates, her sister. 'You're a fucking bitch, Sara Preston. That's it. No more. Grow up.' she told herself.

She turned around and left the alley, walking back quickly, the wolf trotting at her heels. She tried to stop crying, but the moonlight was blurred, the street lights making pools in the sky. She wiped her eyes angrily. 'Oh, you bitch. You bloody stupid bitch,' she muttered as she made her way home.

The door opened as she got to the house and Andy pulled her indoors. 'Are you OK, baby?' He watched warily as the skinny white wolf slunk past him into the hall and sat waiting. 'Did he hurt you?'

Sara shook her head. 'No, I hurt him. I'm going to make it better, though. We'll take him home tonight, Dad.' She looked at Andy, and for the first time ever, Andy saw her as a woman, not his daughter. She shrugged. 'Look, give me an hour.'

Andy looked thoroughly miserable. 'We're not asking you for this. Are you sure?'

'Yeah. I'm sure. Did you bring clothes for Jan?'

Andy realised that he couldn't speak. He gestured to a canvas bag at the foot of the stairs. He swallowed, and found his voice. 'He looks like he's lost some weight. They're probably too big for him.'

'Yeah. Probably.' She picked up the bag and started up the stairs to her attic room, the student bedroom that was the last place she'd expected to start her own pack. The white wolf padded up the stairs behind her, stumbling once or twice. He was exhausted, she knew. She started to cry again.

In her room, she drew the curtains, turned off the light and switched on a bedside lamp. Jan Changed, shuddering. He stood, shivering and tired, disbelief showing in every line of his body.

Sara undressed and slipped into bed.

Jan still stood at the side of the bed, shaking his head. 'I'm not fit to be your Alpha,' he muttered.

'Don't ever say that again. It's me, I'm the idiot. I'm not fit to be yours. But if you want me, I will be.'

He swallowed painfully, his throat dry and sore. 'You want *me*? You said it was about the war. I'll fight for you without this, I swear it.'

'Taking you home is about the war, that's true. But this is about you and me. Jan?'

He joined her in her bed, closing his eyes and lying back, trembling. Her touch on his body terrified him. He opened his eyes for a moment, and shuddered; those witchy eyes were watching him. He could feel his body respond, and sighed as she kissed him. She groaned as it started, as the ancient chemicals recognised each other and drew them together at last.

An hour later, Andy brought the car back to the house. Mary and Darlene threw the luggage into the boot and Mary silently got into the front passenger seat. Darlene climbed into the back, and they waited,

Sara came downstairs, holding Jan's hand tightly. They both looked drugged. Sara sat in the middle seat, trying to sit down without letting go of Jan's hand.

Darlene was in shock. 'You bloody well did it,' she whispered to her twin, who ignored her.

Jan was having problems with the heavy door, and Andy swore in frustration, getting out of his seat and going round to shut it. Sara was reaching round Jan, looking for the seat belt, treating him as tenderly as a mother does a baby. Andy watched her struggle for a moment, then helped her to find the belt.

He sighed. 'The guy looks hungry. We'll stop somewhere, get some food and something to drink.' The look of gratitude on his daughter's face made his anger fall away. He managed to smile at her. 'Happy?'

'No. Not until he's better,' she said grimly.

Her father nodded and shut the door. He paused for a moment, and then went back to the house, knocking on the door. He was satisfied when a girl checked at the spyhole before opening up.

'Shelley?' he said.

'No, I'm Lucy. Shelley is—'

'Never mind. I just wanted to remind you what happened tonight.'

Lucy's eyes widened. 'No problems, Mr Ransome. We understand. The girls went out, they didn't come back. We've not reported it to the police because Mary was planning to meet the twins' brothers. We assumed that's where they'd all gone. We'll ring you tomorrow when we don't hear from them.'

'Good. Are you girls OK for supplies? You know not to go out alone?'

'Yeah, we know. And we're fine. Look, I know you're up to something big. I won't say anything, obviously, to anyone else, but good luck.'

'Thanks, sweetheart.' Andy turned reluctantly, and left the house. He got into the car and started it, absent-mindedly enjoying the power of it. 'Keep your eyes open for a drive-in,' he said to Darlene as he set out. He glanced in the mirror: Jan and Sara were dozing, holding on to each other as if they'd found all they'd ever needed.

Diana's phone was ringing. She carefully put her beer down before answering. Helen opened one eye and looked at her questioningly. Diana nodded, answering the call.

'Andy? All OK?'

He sounded dulled, remote. 'We're safe and heading home. Jan's with us.'

Diana bit her lip. 'Is he OK? Is Sara OK?'

'They're fine. Though I guess you'll have to find a room for them tonight.'

'Oh,' said Diana.

'Yeah. I hate this. You know?'

'Andy, I understand, but I can't be sorry. Jan's perfect for her.'

'He's a raging nutcase, Diana. Homeless, and destitute. You should see him… God knows where he's been living.'

Diana felt helpless. 'Where are you?'

'Birmingham, service station. He's eating. Again. I just watched him drink three litres of water and eat six cheeseburgers. Diana, he's a mess! And my Sara is—'

Diana handed the phone to Helen. 'You calm him down. I've forgotten how to.'

Helen took the phone off her and retreated to a quiet corner, talking quietly to her husband.

Diana poked at Mark. 'We're all set. Call the others.' Seth was awake. She looked at him. 'Do you remember their voices? How's your German?'

'I remember four or five of the voices, I could probably imitate one or two. And my German is fine, and my French.'

'OK, go through their stuff. Use their phone to report in. OK?'

'Sure. We're really doing it, eh?'

'Really,' Diana said.

Seth went to the table where Anthony had placed the ID, cash and phones that the Whites had left behind. He sorted through it, then took a phone, checking the contacts list. He looked at a few other phones, then smiled, satisfied.

He took the phone outside, away from the quiet conversation of his pack. At the edge of the woods, he rang a number, and spoke in German, mimicking the voice and accent of one of the dead Whites.

'Hans? It's me, George. It went well.'

He listened while George was berated for being out of touch for so long.

'Hey, we went to celebrate. Is that so bad? We deserve time off. We half killed the bitch and her ugly eldest son. And we have a plan for tomorrow.'

He listened again.

'No, I am in charge of this operation, and I am here, in England. I know what to do. I will bring them back to Harald. Then we will see who is the favoured son, eh?' He killed the connection, and switched off the phone for good measure, laughing at the memory of the outraged spluttering on the other end of the line. He went back to the house, and returned the phone to the pile, saying goodnight to his family. It had been a very long day, and he needed sleep.

He undressed, and went to brush his teeth in the small bathroom he shared with Noah and Caleb. He looked critically at his thin, wiry body, his freckled shoulders and gingery body hair. His face was pale and narrow, his hair a dark red colour that absorbed light without having the life that he saw in his mother's hair or his sisters'. He looked into his eyes. He knew they were attractive but, in his face, they looked out of place. His thick lashes were ridiculous, and he frowned at his reflection.

'Karen obviously wasn't bothered about looks,' he said sadly. 'Ah well, she's free now.' He looked sadly at himself, then tried to smile, turning guiltily as a noise behind alerted him to his twin entering the bathroom.

Noah went to the toilet and stood, pissing, looking curiously at Seth. 'Mourning her?' he asked.

'No. I guess not. Just glad to be alive, really. Noah? Can I ask you a question? On a scale of one to ten, how bloody ugly are we?'

Noah stared at him. 'Well, we didn't get the best of the gene shuffle, did we? But who cares? Just tell the girls that you're Mark Preston's eldest lad, heir to rock-and-roll millions, and it doesn't bloody matter. Even if it's not strictly true, eh? Stop making puppy eyes at the mirror, your face will stick. Are you going to bed?'

'Yeah, I guess. Goodnight, Noah.'

Noah made his way back to the party. He had a vague feeling that he'd miss Karen being around, but he'd never really paid much attention to her anyway. If Seth wanted to get serious with the normals, that was up to him, but Noah saw girls as nothing more than a pleasant occasional diversion from his studies. Once he was set up in practice, and the money was rolling in, then he could look round and see what potential mates were available for his own pack.

Back with the other adults, he checked that his parents were happy. They both had drinks, and were absorbed in each other, as usual. It was as it should be. He adored Diana. John looked up, a friendly smile on his face, and Noah pushed aside a vague resentment and smiled back. John had practically brought him up. Even if the man had no idea of discipline, for years he'd been a better father than Mark had even dreamed of being. Noah was still fond of the old man. His eyes settled on Chloe. She wasn't his type at all, but his eyes were drawn to her. She was flirting with Frank: another of those pointless arguments that the two of them excelled at. This time they were discussing the relative merits of Al Pacino and Robert De Niro. They were circling the subject warily, each of them waiting for one to make a definitive choice so the other could grab the opposing view. Bill was standing drinking in a corner with Anthony and Caleb. Every minute or so, he glanced at his mate.

Noah tried to understand. He was sure that when he had his pack, he wouldn't leave his women alone to flirt with the Beta, even if it was his own brother. It had never occurred to Noah that he would be anything but a pack Alpha. He took a seat next to Miranda and settled back, drinking straight from the can, watching Chloe. She was a tiny little thing, and at the moment seemed to be all tits and belly. He closed his eyes, imagining his future: his own pack, four or five women wanting him. He saw himself running in the woods, leading a howling pack of wives and strong sons. He inwardly laughed at the corniness of it while still enjoying the fantasy. A poke in the ribs brought him back to reality.

'Oh, brother, where art thou?' hissed Miranda.

'What?'

'Whatever or whoever you're thinking about, you'd better hide that hard-on before Bill realises you're watching Chloe.' She widened her eyes dramatically and threw her shawl on to his lap.

'Thanks,' he said. 'I was dreaming of my ideal woman.'

'I gathered that,' Miranda drawled.

'Tall, blonde, mad and lethal,' he teased. 'Name begins with "M" and ends with "A".'

'That's just so wrong,' she told him solemnly.

He gave in; she couldn't be provoked. However, he understood himself well enough to know his preference for blondes was rooted firmly in his fondness for his crazy sister. He positioned the cold can on his groin. It helped matters a little.

'I wish I was coming with you,' Miranda said.

'So do I. Bastards wouldn't know what had hit them.' Noah relished the sudden mental image of Miranda let loose among their enemies.

'MarkDad says it's too dangerous. He wants me at home, childminding.'

Noah shrugged. It was as it was.

'If you don't come back, I'm going to kill myself,' she said simply.

He looked up, shocked. 'What?'

'If you lose, I won't stand a chance alone, none of us will. We'll have to lock ourselves in and live under siege. If they catch me, they'll kill me, eventually. I want to be in control at the end.'

He shook his head. 'Then we won't lose.'

'Will you hold me?' she asked him. 'Everyone else has their twin, or their mate.'

'I'm practically your twin,' he pointed out.

'Yeah, true.' She snuggled up, closing her eyes and starting to nap. Noah kissed her forehead, and looked up to see Caleb watching them. The boy suddenly seemed so vulnerable, so alone, and Noah raised a hand in a lazy, brotherly salute. Caleb waved back, and turned again to Bill. Noah's heart surged with protective pride in Caleb. He suddenly realised that fantasies about his own future pack were all well and good, but he was ready to fight and die for each and every member of his family. The knowledge made him feel unusually peaceful and he closed his eyes, falling asleep on the sofa, still embracing Miranda.

Diana saw them sleeping, and covered them with a throw. Only Seth was missing from a tableau of sleepy companionship that had started over two decades ago.

An hour passed. Chloe became nervous and started to pace the floor. Bill moved away from Anthony. He spoke to Frankie, then to Helen, and went over to his mate.

'Chloe, love. Helen says we can stay in the annexe tonight, the three of us. There's a double bedroom that will be fine for us. Are you OK sleeping in there? I'm sure Phil and Mareta will be fine where they are.' Duncan's children were bunking in with Isaac and Ian, and Meg and Beth.

Chloe nodded. 'They're already asleep. I don't want to disturb them. I thought we were having the cottage tonight?'

'Change of plan. Sara and Jan need privacy and someone to look after them. Anthony is giving them his cottage for the night, but he's going to stay downstairs and make sure that they get fed – Jan's half-dead.' He smiled, remembering. 'Honey, you left *me* half-dead after our first time together, and I was in top shape beforehand. Poor bloody Jan.'

Chloe kissed him impulsively.

'So, we'll take the annexe. And Frankie and I think it's probably best if you meet Mary tonight without the two of us around. So we're going over there before she arrives. Do you agree?'

'Completely. Thank you. And if I don't think she'll fit in?'

'Tell her. And tell us too. We'll be spending a lot of time with her next week, and we need to know the score before we leave.'

Chloe fought down a flash of pure panic, hiding it well. She hugged Bill tightly, and then watched as he grabbed a couple of beers before leaving the room with Frank. She looked around the room; everyone else seemed to be asleep. Standing there, in the middle of another woman's pack, she felt lost and bewildered. She'd thought she was safe, that she'd found two mates to protect her, but they were leaving her behind, going to war. She understood why, and agreed with the decision, but she felt vulnerable.

Diana's phone was beeping and the Alpha answered it without opening her eyes. She groaned and sat up. 'Chloe, hon, they're here. Open the gates, will you?'

Chloe stared at her blankly. 'I don't have the codes.'

Diana shook her head. 'Of course not. I'm sorry. Come with me – I'll show you how to do it.' The older woman stood and stretched, and led Chloe to a panel next to the door.

'There's one of these in most of the family rooms, and in the main bedroom. There's two or three in the annexe, but I don't go in there so you'll have to ask Andy where they are. And there's two in the cottage, one in the kitchen, one in the bedroom.'

She told Chloe the first code, and the young Alpha pressed the keys. A screen lit up showing the areas around both front and back gates. Andy's car was waiting, lights on. He got out and waved when he saw the red light above the gate blink on. Diana told Chloe the second code, and watched as it was punched in. The gates slid open.

'OK, he rang us. He didn't give us the "I'm a fucking liar and I've got ten of the enemy making me do this" code, so we let him in. Anthony and the pack get automatic access. Karen could only come in with Seth. If she turns up, incidentally, don't let her in. Helen and her daughters get let in, but they can't bring anyone with them. OK?'

'What about me?'

'Same rules as Helen, I guess. Phil and Mareta too. Oh, by the way, the code for 'I'm under coercion' is "Don't bother coming out to meet me". Or, if you can't speak, lift your left foot for five seconds. Now. We watch until he's safely inside the gates, and we close them. No code needed. Just hit that yellow button. Cool.' She turned round. 'Hey, Old Wolf, they're here.'

Anthony roused himself. 'Shall we?' He offered an arm to each of the women.

Chapter 24

Mary stood up and looked round, taking in her first view of the pack's home. The car park was surrounded by a low stone wall that was speckled with alpine plants tucked into the crevices. The tiny flowers were ghostlike in the moonlight. The house and outbuildings were clustered at one edge of the property, with the main entrance gate and the drive in one corner. The woods spread all around the buildings, although just a thin line of trees stood between them and the nearest fence line.

The main house itself, an old hotel, looked boxy and basic. There were no trellises or window boxes on the main building or the annexe. Mary understood why: Sara's first action on moving into the London house had been to make the outer walls as unclimbable as possible, as a safety measure. The cottage was charming, though. It was brick built, with a tiled roof, and had its own garden.

She turned and looked at the approaching trio. For a moment she wondered who the man was; he was too old to be John. She realised he must be Anthony, the old guy who lived with the pack – Mark's father. He was supporting a tiny, very pregnant woman who was looking directly at her. She took a deep breath and started to walk towards them.

Diana broke into a run when she saw Jan climbing out of the car. She stood next to the door, reaching in to help him. He clung to her desperately, leaning against her, as Sara climbed out behind him. Sara glared at Diana. 'I can look after him.'

Diana didn't argue. 'You're staying in Anthony's cottage. OK? If you can manage, I'll go.'

Sara wrapped Jan's arm around her shoulder. 'Food?' she demanded.

'Your granddad will be with you. He'll look after you both.'

Sara was about to protest but drew back, her face becoming calmer.

'Thank him for us. I'm taking Jan straight upstairs.'

Diana stopped her for a moment. 'I'm happy for you. I really am. Whatever happens, whatever anyone says, I believe you've got a good man there.'

Sara looked like she'd been hit. 'I know I don't deserve him…'

'I didn't say that. Go.'

She stood and watched as Sara tried to support Jan, half carrying him to the cottage. When they were still fifty yards away, Diana clearly heard her daughter say, 'Oh, fuck this,' and watched her lift Jan in her arms. She easily carried him into the cottage.

'Well, she's not shy, is she?' Diana turned. Darlene was standing next to her, looking mournful.

Diana felt a huge wash of pity for her daughter, who looked bereft. 'How do you feel?'

'Gobsmacked. She's been saying all day that she was just going to bring him here, that she liked him but it was going to be years before she committed to anything. I'm absolutely gobsmacked.'

'Come on, hon, get a drink and go to bed. It's been a hell of a long day.'

Darlene looked appalled. 'Mum! I'm sorry. I completely forgot. Are you OK?'

Diana smiled. 'Never better. Honestly. I've not felt this good in ten, maybe twenty years. Anyway, how's our other guest?'

'Mary? Well, she seems to be introducing herself.' Diana saw Chloe and Mary making their way to the main house. Diana soon caught them up. Chloe and Mary were silent, not looking at each other.

'Mary! I'm sorry. I've not had chance to welcome you. Zoe and I have a little sitting room where we like to hide out sometimes. It's got two comfy chairs, and it's wonderfully quiet. I'll install the two of you in there, eh? Or are you both ready to give up for the night? You can do this tomorrow, if you want?'

Chloe flashed her a grateful look. 'No, tonight is best. Thanks. We'll just have a chat now, I think.'

Diana led them to the small, cramped room. There was an old computer and printer on the desk, reams of paper stacked underneath. On the other side of the room were two very comfortable armchairs, a small fridge and a kettle. There was a box of tissues on the table, and an old, knitted blanket across the back of one of the chairs.

'Make yourselves at home,' said Diana. 'Help yourself to anything in the fridge. I think I put some fresh milk in there yesterday, so it should be OK.'

She left, and Chloe slowly eased herself into one of the armchairs. She rested her head against the blanket and smiled.

'I guess they come in here with the babies sometimes,' she said.

Mary seized the opening gratefully. 'It's a nice room. Cosy. When are your babies due, Chloe?'

'June. They might be earlier, actually. I was early with Tori and Debbi.'

Mary's eyes widened a little. She wasn't expecting to have to talk about this. 'Were they premature? Did you have problems?'

Chloe relaxed a little. 'Do you think you could make us a drink? It's just a little hard to stand up again once I'm down.'

Mary got up gracefully and went to the fridge. 'They've hidden some coffee in here, and some nice tea. What's with that?'

'Anthony is a coffee thief. It'll be Diana's secret stash. Zoe likes the cheap stuff. What about you?'

'Oh, I'll have anything.'

'Me too.' Chloe lapsed into silence as Mary made a pot of tea, and brought it over.

'Hungry?' Mary asked, pouring the tea.

'No,' Chloe said. 'Don't tell me, they've got the EU sweet mountain stashed in there?'

'Half a chocolate cake,' said Mary. Their eyes met, and they smiled.

'Maybe I could handle a small slice,' conceded Chloe.

Settled in the chairs, armed with tea and cake, they gazed at each other again.

Chloe took a moment to take her first real look at the young woman. Mary was about five foot five, with brown hair that curled extravagantly. She had wide-spaced blue eyes that made an otherwise ordinary face captivating. She'd taken off the blue jacket, and the Alpha found herself coveting it and the long silk dress that Mary was wearing but not quite filling. Chloe noted the woman had an almost boyish figure. She was wearing a pair of green court shoes that surely could never have matched anything.

Mary sat calmly, good-humouredly taking the inspection. As the silence grew too long, she spoke up. 'Did you have problems with your first babies?' She leaned forward a little.

'They were early, and tiny, but they were fine. Their father was Stuart, the Beta in my old pack. He died ... before the attack, in a stupid car accident. He was on his way to a football match with his dad. They were Stuart's only children. And now he's dead, and they're dead, and I have nothing but photographs to remember them by.' She smiled thinly. 'I don't know why I'm telling you this. I don't often talk about him. He joined our pack late. Dunc had been with me and Laura for three or four years when Andy rang, said there was a young guy who was alone, and did we want to meet him. Well, we did. He was painfully shy, couldn't believe there were other people like him in the world. He understood me, and I understood him. We fell in love. After he joined us, our pack was complete, working together. When he died, I went numb. I wasn't a great mother to my babies. I was in shock, really, looking back on it. Duncan couldn't deal with losing Stuart like that, he felt responsible, although what he could have done about it I don't know. When the Whites attacked, we were very weak, still reeling from losing Stuart.'

Mary reached across, taking her hand. 'Tell me,' was all she said.

'Nobody wants to talk about them. Phil and Mareta pretend that life started less than three years ago. Bill walks on eggshells with me. If he got any more sensitive, he'd shrivel in sunlight. Frankie pretends I'm nineteen years old – I think he forgets I had a life before them. The only person I think I could even start to talk to is Diana, and she's bloody superwoman.' She looked up, blinking. 'That was a rant. I'm sorry. And it's not fair. Helen practically begs me to talk about them, but what does she know?' She breathed out when she looked up, she seemed lighter. 'Thank you for listening. I needed to say that. I need to remember Stuart.'

Mary stood and poured more tea.

Chloe glanced at her, and then looked again. 'What happened to your hand?'

Mary pulled it to herself unconsciously, instinctively. 'Lost a couple of fingers in a fight with the Whites. Sara says I should be able to heal it, but I think it'll take me a while to get my head round that sort of idea.' She offered a thin smile. 'Don't you find the whole lot of them intimidating?'

'I did, but it's getting easier. I should apologise – here we are in *their* home. I wish you could have met me first in my own place. It's a lovely house.' She smiled, happily bragging. 'We built it ourselves. I helped, you know? Before we were a pack, when

Bill and Frank were promised to me but before we were together. We built the house then. Everything is how I wanted it.'

Mary's eyes lit up. 'That's so cool. Sara and Darlene never tell me about your place. I'd love to see it.'

'Ah, they've never visited. Well, it's not big now, but we have enough land and planning permission to expand for a few years. It's big enough for us and the kids, and these two when they arrive. Bill's already ordering stuff for the foundations for the next stage – another three or four bedrooms, another bathroom, and a playroom. And I'd like a study, I think.'

Mary looked up. 'What do you study?' She was interested, but Chloe blushed.

'Nothing. I'm not clever. I just want somewhere quiet, you know, do the accounts, plan things. I loved doing all that with the old pack. I got a qualification through Andy's dad's company.'

'I loathe all that admin stuff,' said Mary. 'When I have a partnership, or maybe my own surgery, I'll have to deal with it.'

'Oh, I could do that for you,' said Chloe eagerly. 'It would be nice to have a job.'

Mary blinked. 'That would be perfect. Are you saying that you want me around?'

Chloe sat back. 'I'm not sure. This is difficult.'

Mary leaned back too, deliberately relaxing. 'Maybe if you tell me what the problem is?'

Chloe settled back again, her hands protective on her belly. 'If I knew that, I'd be a lot happier. I don't do psychology.' She paused. 'I guess the first problem is that I lost so much, and then I got a second chance. I'm possessive of my men. Could you deal with that?'

Mary brushed her hand through her hair, rumpling it even more crazily. 'Before we go any further, we need to spell things out, don't we?'

'I guess so.' There was a wariness about Chloe that didn't suit an Alpha.

Mary leaned forward. 'OK. I want a home. I'm getting older, and I'm not spending the rest of my life nurse-maiding students. I don't need kids yet, but some would be nice eventually. Not just a token pair either – a sop to me. I want to be able to choose, within the pack, who the father is. Or fathers. Is that fair enough? I want an Alpha who'll treat me fairly.' She paused, taking a breath. 'I'm happy for you to choose any other new pack members. I'm happy to look after your children when you need me to, when I'm at home. I can live with you making the decisions about absolutely anything else except my job and my professional life – that's off limits. And I need some privacy.'

Chloe leaned back, an odd look on her face. 'Who do you want to fuck the most? Frank or Bill?'

'Both of them,' Mary said instantly, then blushed. 'You bitch.'

They looked at each other, and then Chloe giggled. She closed her eyes. 'I sleep with both of them. At the same time. Sometimes I wake up, and one of them is touching me and the other one's asleep. I wake the other up, and it's the middle of the night, and they take turns to fuck me, and it doesn't matter who is who.'

Mary was wide-eyed. Chloe continued. 'There's something about the Prestons – they're so sure of themselves. Duncan and Stuart were never quite like that. These guys just see that something needs doing, and they do it.'

Mary licked her lips nervously. 'Chloe? Are you on something?'

The young Alpha opened her eyes. 'Oh my god. I'm sorry. I've spent the day wrapped up in fear. And you're nice. You're so normal. You must think I'm some sort of freak.' She looked at the younger woman. 'Do you know how to deliver babies?'

'I've delivered cows, horses, sheep, dogs, cats and llamas. It can't be that much different.'

'OK, you're in. We've not signed any Contract yet, you know? We'll do it together, the four of us. They want more women, eventually, I should warn you. Can you deal with that?'

'So long as you back me up as your Beta,' Mary said simply.

'Deal. I think you're sharing a room with Darlene tonight. As for tomorrow, we'll see how it works out. Now, help me out of this chair, will you? I'm going to find Frank and Bill. I'll tell them what we've decided. Welcome to my pack.'

Chapter 25

Diana leaned against the door of Zoe's little writing room, listening to the silence of the two young women within. She reflected on how Shapeshifter society was developing its own rules and formalities. She was sure that no normal woman would have been kept away from newly married sons as long as she'd been away from Frank and Bill. It was a huge relief to be back in contact with them, but they were different now, no longer her own pack. Chloe had claimed them. They all sensed it.

And now it was happening again with Sara. Out there, by the car, Diana had felt a force, an instinct, keeping her away from her eldest Shapeshifting daughter. That hadn't been there before, whenever she'd visited her red-haired twins in London. The old easy pack familiarity had still existed, and she'd been confident the girls would still be her Kittens for years yet. They'd assured her that they wanted to get their degrees and start their research before they even considered looking for a pack.

Diana inwardly mocked herself. The bonding between the new Alphas, out there in the cottage, was hardly a surprise to her. She'd cold-bloodedly considered the possibility, and accepted the risk, when she'd helped Mark to draw up the plans for this attack.

The saddest part about it was that Darlene would be separated from her twin at far too young an age. Diana knew that Darlene found the attraction between Jan and Sara incomprehensible, and would never consider joining their new pack.

She was jolted from her thoughts by voices on the other side of the door. She heard her name mentioned, and guiltily walked away, realising that she had no right to listen to that conversation. She walked up the corridor to the room that her mates and older children were in. As she reached the door, it opened, and Helen came out, looking tired, closely escorted by Andy. He stared again at Diana, surprised still by her vitality. She noticed his glance and winked.

'You're a witch,' he observed. 'It's the only explanation.'

Helen took his hand. 'Well, we're not hanging around waiting for her to cast any more spells. Come on, handsome, I need my sleep.'

Diana stood aside, watching them fondly. She slipped through the door as it closed, and rolled her eyes at the sight of pack members dozing on the sofas and chairs. Anthony's choice of music was still playing softly. For a moment she stood, looking at the scene. Mark was dozing in a big armchair close to the fire. Jane was on his lap, fast asleep, her head against her father's. Alice was on the floor in front of them, leaning against the chair, her head resting against Mark's legs. None of them looked like they could possibly be comfortable, but the three of them looked content. Miranda and Noah were still napping on a sofa. Miranda had always enjoyed her naps as a toddler, and Diana smiled nostalgically, remembering her early efforts to train Seth and Noah to nap with her, rather than wake her up. She'd finally got the three of them well-conditioned, and it still seemed, sometimes, that it only took one of them to yawn to send the other two straight to sleep. Darlene wasn't there; she must have gone straight to bed. John was sitting up straight on a sofa, his eyes closed. Zoe had her head on his lap, and was still sleeping. His hand was on her hair. Diana couldn't see the Bees or Caleb, and frowned, until she spotted a tanned arm sticking out from the biggest sofa, which had been turned towards the patio doors. The three of them must have fallen asleep watching the night sky. The teenagers were curled together like puppies, Caleb holding Trixie's hand.

'Ah. Domestic bliss!' she whispered, before walking quietly to the music player and switching off Anthony's selection. She glanced behind her, then hit her favourite pre-programmed button, and turned, grinning, as every speaker in the room leaped to life, and Blur's 'Song 2' filled the room at a volume guaranteed to wake everyone up.

It had the electrifying effect on the suddenly awake pack that she'd hoped for. John was the only one not to move. He opened his eyes and laughed at her. He'd been shamming sleep then. She stuck her tongue out at him. Her children were getting up and scowling at her, making their way to their own bedrooms. Zoe looked extremely disgruntled at first, then saw Diana's smile and shook her head.

'If you've woken up any of the little ones, you're sorting them out,' she muttered, swinging her legs off the sofa and standing up gracefully. John winked once more at Diana, and led Zoe off to bed.

Mark was rubbing his shoulder when she landed on his lap. 'Ooh, dead arm?' she asked, mock concerned.

'Hmm, baby Jane weighs about seven stone. Whatever happened to her?' he enquired.

'Thirteen years, didn't you notice? Kiss me.'

He obliged.

'Now come to bed. We'll take John and Zoe's bedroom. We need some privacy, and they're in the big room.'

Mark laughed. 'They've never minded before.'

'This is different,' she promised him. 'I said I had something to show you.'

They opened the door to the smaller bedroom, and Mark closed it behind him. He saw the excitement on his wife's face, and decided to lock it. 'There? Private enough?'

She was smiling a secret, gloating smile. 'I wish I could have shown you this straight away, but we wouldn't have got anything else done all day.'

She was glowing, and Mark watched her warily. It was only hours since he'd thought she was dead, since he'd been wondering how long he'd survive without her, and how long he wanted to survive without her.

'Tell me, then,' he said.

'I'll show you. But first, let's get naked. It will be better.'

'I bet you say that to all the boys,' he murmured, realising he could let go of the conviction of her fragility that he'd carried all day.

He undressed quickly and joined her on the bed. She'd already stripped, and was lying back, her arms behind her head. He sat beside her, giving an experimental bounce on the bed.

'We've never used this bed. Me and you, I mean,' he said, surprised at the realisation.

'No, we've not.' She smiled. 'Me and John, yeah. You and Zoe too, but never me and you. But that's not the point. What do you see?' She stretched out fully, looking at him.

'My beautiful wife?' he said, puzzled.

'*Look*,' she insisted.

'What am I supposed to be looking at? I don't get it. You're gorgeous, is that enough?'

She sighed, touching her belly. 'Look.'

He bent down, inspecting the smooth skin, then ran his finger down her ribs. He returned his attention to her arms and legs, smooth and free of scars. She was looking at him eagerly.

'Do you see?'

'Your scars are gone?' he asked.

'Yes and no. I've learned something. Wait.'

He watched as ghostly scars on her body reappeared then faded away.

'We don't have to be scarred, honey. The kids have always done it, automatically deleted scars when they Change, but I've got the hang of it now. I just needed some extra strength, some more information. Your blood gave me both things. It was amazing, Mark. It was Alpha to the max. I've never felt anything like that before. I found out almost everything about how *your* body works, and it gave me an insight into my own. I'd never seen before how easily I've slipped into accepting things – ageing, injuries, pain. I'm not saying I want to be young forever, that wouldn't be right. But I don't have to live with the scars that those bastard Whites gave me.'

'And the others? The other scars?'

'What scars?' she frowned.

He was ahead of her. 'Ah, I was thinking more about the scars that the Destroyers gave you. What about those scars?'

She laid her head on his chest. 'I wanted to talk about that too. It's not escaped me.'

'So are you healed? Can we try again? You have to know how much I'd love to make babies with you again, make love and make life with you. Love-children.'

'They're all love-children,' she said firmly.

'I mean, with *me* loving *you* too.'

'I know, honey, but it doesn't matter now. I watched you tonight with Jane and Alice, and it's clear that all that is in the past.'

'Are you refusing me this?'

'I guess I am. I really don't want more babies. You're fifty-two, I'm fifty. I really don't want more. Let's let this pack grow up – we'll be grandparents very soon.'

'Zoe—'

'Zoe is still young. She has time for more, if she still wants to. I wouldn't get in her way.' She looked at him carefully. 'Do you hear me?'

He looked at her mournfully. 'No. I love her, but no. Never. I don't care what you say, I won't hurt you like that again. She's got John.'

Satisfied, she smiled. 'Can't you see the problem? We could say one more pregnancy, because we love each other now. And where does that leave the other kids? They're not stupid. How would it make them feel? And then, in five years' time, when we love each other even more than we do now? Do we have another set? We have to stop at some time, and I've already got used to the idea that I won't have any more babies. Let's end it here.'

She smiled at him, inviting him to lie beside her. He relaxed slowly, trying to disguise his disappointment.

She was looking at him. 'There's something else.'

'What?'

'Today, the blood you gave me… I can't describe how it made me feel, so I'll have to show you.'

'How? You want to give me your blood?'

She was grinning at him. She sat up. 'Exactly. Look what I can do.'

She held her arm up, that smooth forearm that he still couldn't quite believe in. He'd seen her flesh *eaten* earlier that day. He cried out a little in horror as the skin smoothly parted, and blood began to seep out, rich and dark against her white skin.

'Diana!'

'Shh. Watch.'

The skin closed again, the blood already starting to scab. 'Give it a few minutes, and it will be good as new. Neat trick, though. Can you do it?'

'No,' said Mark, repelled. 'But I can heal now, more quickly than ever. Look, this arm is nearly as good as new. It's scarred but it's workable.'

'Very good,' she said, laughing. 'I don't want a guitar god with an unworkable arm.' She stopped laughing and looked at him gravely. 'My love, I want to do this. Please?'

He stood up, reaching for a robe.

'Where are you going?' she asked.

'Getting that transfusion kit,' he said.

'No, I don't think we need that. Come here. Give me your arm.'

Extending a finger that morphed into a claw, she opened a blood vessel in his arm, watched the blood well out, and then opened her own arm. She pressed them together, and Mark cried out, watching her skin grow out, sealing the gap. He felt an intense itching as their bodies physically bonded together, her skin growing into his.

He looked at her. 'Witch!' he said.

'That's twice tonight. All I need now is to get John to say it, and I've got the set.' She watched him carefully, catching his head with her free hand, lowering him gently to the pillow as her blood hit his system and his eyes rolled back. She lay down beside him, holding him. She was feeling a glowing, muted repetition of the afternoon's experience as his blood flowed into her, but there was no new information there.

Mark had been stunned at the sight of his Alpha's skin growing into his, then intellectually impressed by the new skill. He'd been about to say something when her blood hit his system, and his body chemistry opened up completely to the ultimate fix. Their mutual thirst for each other was something he'd almost got used to, but this time it was being completely, totally quenched. Her blood, her life, was in him, and with her blood came the blood of all her children. Mark's cells had given Diana the story of who he'd touched, smelled, tasted, the bonds he'd built with others. Her blood held stray cells from every child she'd borne, together with impressions of everyone she'd been close to. The outside world was gone, and his soul, his understanding, reached into the heart of her, seizing the information and hungrily finding, written there, the absolute love and trust she had for him. Totally satisfied, his senses roamed through the other cells, loving and accepting all the children. He found John there, knowledge of him strong in her, almost as strong as the bond he himself had forged with her. Released from conscious cautiousness, he allowed himself to investigate further, amazed at the depth of the protectiveness Diana felt towards his cousin. He was momentarily jealous, and then encountered Zoe's essence, the memory of the smell and taste of her. He knew this, and was dizzied to find his experience of her almost echoed by Diana's. Further in, further back, and Andy was there. He drew back, surprised. Diana knew things about his bass player that he'd never suspected. Amused, almost dancing in her soul, still laughing at his discovery, he suddenly touched a memory of a spirit so pure, a love so simple, that he stopped. Then he moved carefully, investigating, finding a joy he suspected even Diana consciously remembered nothing of, buried beneath a scarred, guilty grief that he knew well. He looked inside himself, and matched her memory of that sleepy, newly woken smell of Xan with his own memories, and carefully explored the scents that he'd never known, the memories of touch and love, and affection.

There were strangers there too, buried deep. A memory of a complex relationship with her mother. A change in their relationship matched with the time when Diana's father had died. He explored that, and realised how secure she'd felt with her father, how happy a childhood she'd enjoyed. And there, buried so deep, so multi-layered, was Joyce. He shied away, in much the same way that Diana had avoided his bond with Katie. Just knowing that it was there was enough.

He could feel Diana now, her physical body on his, demanding his conscious return to her. The flow had stopped, and he protested greedily, not wanting this joining to ever stop. He was astonished. His body was seizing her blood and feeding on it. It wasn't replacing his own, or joining it, it was being absorbed, rejuvenating him. He cast about, almost despairing, finding her memory of Sammy at last, and holding on to the essence, the very cells, of his lost son as he returned.

She had separated from him and was watching as his wound closed, scar-less.

'You see?'

'I see,' he said faintly. 'Do we tell the others about this?'

'Tomorrow. It can wait. We've got better things to do.'

'Mmm. I agree. Can we do that again sometime?'

'Don't you think you know enough about me now?' She was curious.

'I know that you're a witch. But you're right, it's too intoxicating. I'll settle for something more conventional.'

She pushed the bloodstained duvet off the bed, lying on the clean sheets. Once more she spread herself out for his inspection. 'What do you see?'

'My beautiful wife,' he told her, before lying next to her and drawing her to him.

Chapter 26

Mary made her way to the room she was sharing with Darlene, and knocked on the door before entering. Darlene sat up, hurriedly hiding the traces of tears. 'Take Sara's bed. She won't be needing it any more,' she said, trying to joke. 'How did it go with Chloe?'

'Well enough,' said Mary. 'We have an agreement, and we're going to take things slowly. I'll get ready for bed. Your mum said we should all get lots of sleep tonight.' She reached for her bag and took out her toothbrush. 'Which bathroom do I use?'

Darlene gave her instructions, and Mary left the room. She stood for a moment in the moonlight coming through a window at the end of the corridor. The house was quiet. Somewhere, a child coughed. Mary spotted the small bathroom and took hold of the handle.

'Hey,' a voice said very close by. She spun around, startled. A wiry young man with thick red hair and startlingly huge brown eyes was standing behind her. He was wearing a short robe, loosely fastened. 'You have got to be Mary. It's nice to meet you at last.' He smiled, then frowned. 'No, don't get me wrong, I was just on my way back from the kitchen – I had a snack attack. I'm not lurking around or anything.'

'Seth,' she said with absolute conviction.

He leaned against the wall. 'Correct. Why not Noah?'

'It's not our first two am conversation, is it?' Mary teased. They gazed at each other nostalgically, old internet friends who'd kept each other sane through many a long night. 'I know the way you talk.'

He pulled his robe more tightly closed. 'Well, it's nice to meet you in person. I used to enjoy our chats. Why did we stop? Do you remember?'

'I think her name is Karen?' Mary looked at him.

'Ah well, that's history now,' he said sadly.

'I'm sorry to hear that. I'm surprised nobody told me.'

'Well, it was only last night that it happened. Mum and I have been half killed since then, and little Sara's got herself mated to a tramp. I suppose Karen and me splitting up got left out of conversation.' He hesitated. 'How's it going with Chloe and my brothers? If it's a sensitive subject, forget I asked.'

'No, it's OK,' she said carefully. 'I think it's going to work out, but there's no rush. In fact, it's probably a bad idea to rush things.'

'Yeah. Well, I guess I'll get back to bed. See you in the morning?'

'Sure. Goodnight, Seth.'

'Goodnight, Mary.'

She watched him move away, down the corridor, before going into the bathroom.

He looked back once before he got to the landing and made his way to his own room.

All the adults were up early the next day, almost competing to take on the domestic tasks and childcare that marked a normal day in the pack. Darlene's return was celebrated with enthusiasm by the younger children, who were curious as to Sara's whereabouts and the identity of the young woman who'd shared Darlene's room the night before.

Diana and Zoe explained that Jan had returned, and that he and Sara were going to start a new pack together. Mary, they told the children, might be joining Chloe's pack, but for now she was to be treated as a friend of Darlene and Sara's. They were surprised at how easily the children accepted the news and knew to stay away from the cottage.

Anthony came into the house for breakfast, wearing a bathrobe and a disgruntled expression. 'I had to sleep outside in the end,' he explained. 'I went wolf and slept in the woods – it was the most comfortable option.' After breakfast he raided the freezer for pizza, and the cupboards for sugary drinks, and returned to the cottage. As he crossed the lawn, he managed to convey a sense of dignified martyrdom.

Mark, Helen and Chloe started to ring the schools, explaining that Seth and Diana had been seriously injured, and they thought it best to keep the children at home in case the worst happened.

Seth went outside again, speaking on the dead White soldier's mobile phone, mimicking his accent and idiom perfectly.

He turned it off again and went back in. Diana was waiting, looking worried. 'Any trace of suspicion? We don't know if there are any codes you should be using when you ring in.'

'We'll have to take the risk, but the sooner we move, the better. When do we go?'

'We're expecting reinforcements soon. After that, we have to wait for Jan and Sara. They have to be at least halfway sane before we leave. Once the Alpha process has kicked in, there's nothing but madness until the first pregnancy starts. After that, it's bearable.' She spoke with scientific detachment.

He nodded, not understanding, but willing to believe. He spoke casually. 'What about Mary?'

'They're going to play it safe – no mating until everyone is safely home. They'll be fine. Mark and I will keep Mary inhibited, and she's not daft.' She looked at him. 'Karen rang. She's very upset.'

Seth was unimpressed. 'She'll have to stay upset. We're not risking this plan to make her feel better. Who spoke to her?'

'John. He said Mark wasn't available, that he was with me and you. He told her we were both seriously injured. He also told her that her own life was in danger from whoever attacked us, unless she disassociated herself from us completely. It's harsh, I know.'

'She was harsh with me,' he observed. 'Are you recovered completely? Are you ready for this?'

'Damned right, I am.'

In the woods, Bill, Chloe and Frank had found a clearing and were watching Mary as she Changed from woman to wolf and back again. Bill had decided that diplomacy called for him not to court the new woman in the pack immediately, but he'd suggested that they meet and get to know each other's scents. Mareta and Phil had joined them at first, learning who Mary was and the place she would eventually take in their home. They got bored quickly, and left after twenty minutes to join Silverwood's younger children.

Chloe was sitting against a tree, her head on Frank's shoulder, watching Bill as he sat with Mary a few feet away.

'It's a handicap. It spoils you for battle,' he was telling her. 'It's not that I mind it, but I don't see the point of it.'

Mary looked at her hand again. The lost fingers and the twisted scarring were something she'd borne proudly, relics of the defence of her home years earlier. 'It shows I can fight,' she said.

'I *know* you can fight. You're alive, aren't you? But our enemies did that to you. I don't understand why you want to accept that sort of change to your body. Look, Change again.'

She did, quite smoothly – she'd learned a lot from Sara and Darlene in the last few months.

He kneeled and inspected her forepaw.

'Chloe, come here. Look.'

Chloe stood and joined him.

'See,' he said. 'When she goes wolf, she's fine. No scars, no loss of toes. She's obviously got some sense of wholeness in her body image.'

The young wolf was growling a little, unsettled by the nearness of these people who were still strangers. She'd not yet learned to keep a fully human intelligence in wolf form.

Frankie slid into a Change, strutting over to her, greeting her again. Mary felt safer; the young black wolf was making friendly signals. She calmed down.

Chloe spoke firmly. 'I don't think we should just let her accept it. It's pointless, and it will send the wrong signals to the children.'

Bill nodded absently. 'It's her body, Chloe. All we can do is try.' He bent and spoke to the wolf bitch.

'Mary, can you Change back now?'

It was quick, very soon after the last Change, and he knew he was demanding a lot from her. The wolf shuddered and stretched and became a woman once more. She was tiring. She sat and waited, gently stroking Frankie's head as he lay down beside her, his head on his paws.

Chloe spoke. 'Mary, do you know that you aren't scarred when you're a wolf?'

'Yes, Sara told me. I don't see what difference that makes.'

Bill spoke. 'It means that you still have a body image of yourself as whole. Miranda can explain it to you better than I can. She understands this stuff, even if she can't do it herself. If you want your fingers back, I'm absolutely convinced that it's possible for you to have them. It's in your head. Your genes don't know that you've been injured. But you have to want it. And it has to be your decision.'

'Does it repel you?' she asked cautiously.

'No, it doesn't. I think it's pointless, but I've seen enough injuries not to be bothered by it. We'll leave it for now. I was just curious, really.'

Mary stood up. 'Can we go back? I'm starving.'

At the mention of food, Frankie's ears pricked up, and he looked hopefully at Bill.

His twin scowled. 'Not our woods any more, kid. I suspect that even Dad would hit the roof if we hunted this territory.'

Frankie morphed gently and smoothly back to human, and lay on the ground, gazing nostalgically around. 'Ah well, at least we can get food at the house.'

Bill looked at Chloe. 'Are you OK to take Mary back? You know the way?'

'Yes, I know the woods. What are you doing?'

'I thought Frankie and I would visit Sammy's tree. You know?' She looked suddenly defenceless and hurt. He winced. 'I'm sorry. I didn't think. Come with us. We can remember your pack at the same time.' He hugged her tight. 'I'm really sorry.'

She was clinging on to him, crying. 'I can't do this again,' she choked out.

Mary spoke up, gently determined. 'You won't *have* to do this again. I'll die before I'll let anyone take another mate from you.'

Chloe wiped her face. 'Thank you. We'll *all* go to Sammy's tree.'

Half an hour later, remembrances concluded, the new pack silently emerged from the woods, making for the house and the promise of food. They saw Mark, John and Andy walking down the drive.

The three men walked in step, silent but totally aware of each other, utterly together. Mark led the way to the gate. He signalled to the camera and stood back as the gate opened a little.

He walked outside the perimeter, and up to a people carrier. He stood back, waiting for the occupants to get out.

A man and a woman climbed out of the front seats, leaving the doors open. John and Andy came out of the grounds and inspected the car, checking it thoroughly.

'Just these two,' John confirmed.

Mark relaxed and waved again at the cameras. The gate opened fully and Andy got into the car and drove it inside the perimeter, parking it away from the house and the other cars.

John stood back while Mark held out his hand to the young woman. 'Michaela. It's good to see you again. How is the pack?'

'Growing nicely, thank you.'

'And Simon, thank you for this. I thought you were going to send your Betas?'

The young man looked uncomfortable. 'Yes. Well. I was. Then I remembered what you did when we were attacked. You all came, with no hesitation. Without that, we would all be dead now. Michaela and I are the strongest – we can help you best.'

Mark was satisfied. 'It's good to know that we have friends, anyway. You were the only ones that Diana and I asked for help, you know? Andy asked another pack he trusts. We hope that will be enough.'

Michaela linked arms with her packmate. 'Mark, is Chloe here? We need to thank her too. She's given us a lot of advice about the farm over the last couple of years.'

'Yes, she's here. It's Alpha city here at the moment.'

Simon was looking round enviously. 'This is a great set-up,' he said.

Mark gazed at his kingdom. 'I know. I've got Diana to thank. She and her mother set it up. I've only been here for a few years. How are things going at Whitby? Does Robbie still have that boat?'

'Oh yes. He and farming didn't hit it off. But he's found his niche with the other fishermen. He does tourist trips too – it's more lucrative.' Michaela looked at Mark curiously. 'Why?'

'I'll tell you later,' he said. 'Come in and meet the pack, have a natter with Chloe. We'll go over everything later, when Raj has arrived.'

Just after noon, Andy, Mark and John went back to the gate to let in the last arrivals. Raj and Hannah's pack had been formed some years before. Raj had been sending Contract proposals to Sara and Darlene for the last two years, much to their amusement.

As Mark escorted him into the living room, Raj was expressing disappointment that Sara had chosen someone else. 'Doesn't she know what an easy life I could give her? She deserves to be pampered, that one. Instead, what has she chosen? An unknown derelict!'

'Jan is my cousin,' said Mark evenly, enjoying the young man's discomfort as he said it.

'Your cousin? Then forget everything I said. He's clearly suitable for Sara. Now, about Darlene? Has she still got this silly idea that she can't make a Contract until she's finished her degree? Hannah and I can easily support her while she goes through college.'

Mark stopped suddenly, and rested his hand on the young Alpha's shoulder. Raj jumped as if bitten, but submitted. Mark's voice was low and amused.

'Raj, look over there. I appreciate that you've never actually *met* Darlene before. Look at her.'

Raj turned his attention to where Mark was pointing: Darlene and Miranda were deep in conversation, totally absorbed in some arcane discussion which could have been on any subject from the extinction of the dinosaurs to the relative cuteness of the visiting Alpha males. Darlene was sitting on the arm of

Miranda's chair, her face lit up with intelligence and fun. Her red hair caught the sun and brought fire into the room.

Mark shook his head. '*That* is a potential Alpha. She won't settle for anything less. Give up, Raj. Anyway, what on earth are you still doing mooching for chicks? You've got four women already, shouldn't you be looking for a Beta boy?'

Hannah had overheard, and joined them. 'That's my job, and I am. Raj, you're a naughty boy. Sorry, Mark, I've warned him before, his eyes are bigger than his … belly. We're happy as we are, for now, aren't we, my darling?'

Raj flashed a brilliant smile at his Alpha. She was slightly taller than him, about five seven to his five six, with long dark auburn hair. Her heart-shaped face and full, red lips were matched by an engaging smile. Her smile flashed dimples that caused Mark to want to make her smile again and again. She had an easy confidence that reminded him of his Diana. At the thought of her, he looked round automatically; she was watching him.

She winked and walked over. 'Hannah, Raj. It's good to see you again.' She looked at them; they were so incredibly young. When she was their age, she'd been living with her sister and other older women, hiding her true self from the world, never daring to think that she might one day meet a man like herself. And this pair had known almost from their first Change that they weren't alone, that a network existed, even if it had been a secret one at the time. They'd known what the Alpha bond implied; they'd planned and chosen the mate they wanted. She looked at Mark again, remembering the confusion and agony of their first days together, the incomprehension of what was happening to them, the long years apart. This pair would never need to know what it was like to hide away, and Diana found herself momentarily jealous of their fortune and their innocence.

She swallowed it down – the past was the past. Today she knew she carried Mark's soul inside her, and that he carried hers within him. She was quite sure that a bond such as theirs could not exist anywhere else; their years together, their love, could never be matched. She'd seen him look appreciatively at Hannah, and understood exactly why he found the young Alpha attractive. She was sure of him.

Her older children moved in smoothly to take care of the guests, making sure that they felt welcome while keeping them closely supervised and away from the young children. Diana felt very strongly that she didn't want the visitors near the little ones.

There were two outstanding items of pack business that had to be sorted out. Diana left the room, and the house, strolling across the lawn to the cottage. Anthony was sitting on the step. He rose as she approached.

'Anything?' she asked him.

'I don't know. They're asleep, I'm almost sure of that. They tore themselves away from each other long enough to have a bath this morning, and all the food I've left out for them has gone. Sometimes I'm glad I never did this.'

She sat on the step, patting the warm stone, inviting him to join her. 'Really?'

'Yes. It's a madness. Some people can give up to it – I would have fought it.'

'Like father, like son,' Diana reflected.

'Exactly.' He made a small, self-deprecating sound. 'I wouldn't want another woman anyway – present company excepted.' She looked up and saw the devil in his eyes, and forgave him. He continued. 'I loved Frances with all my heart. It didn't matter to me what she was, she was perfect for me. Fate brought us together.' He gave a long sigh, then smirked. 'Actually, her father brought us together, canny old bugger. We were just as much an arranged marriage as those two upstairs.'

Diana objected. 'I didn't arrange anything. It was obvious from the start that the two of them…'

'Oh, come on! You could have stopped it easily enough. But you managed the whole affair, made sure that Jan saw this place as the home he'd always wanted. Didn't you?'

She rested her head on his shoulder. 'OK, you may have a point, but keep quiet about it. Andy's still furious about the whole thing. You have to admit though, it's perfect. Jan's old enough to be a match for her, once he has his strength back. And she can teach him everything he needs to know to be useful to us. She will bind him to us. And if I hadn't forbidden her to go near him, she'd have lost interest long ago.'

Behind them, through the open door, they heard the stairs creak, and they looked round. Sara stood at the bottom of the stairs. She was wearing an old T-shirt of Mark's that he'd given to Jan, and a pair of Anthony's pyjama bottoms. Both garments were too short for her. She smiled at her mother and Anthony.

'I've just woken up. How long have you been here? What time is it?'

Diana teased. 'What *day* is it?'

The teenager blinked. 'We've not lost a day, I'm sure… Have we? Oh, stop it, Mum. I'm too tired to be teased.'

'It's almost one o'clock. Is Jan still alive?' Diana kept her voice perfectly level.

'You know something, Mum? You're not funny. He's fine. He's just a bit confused still.'

'And you?'

'What?'

'Do you need more time?' Diana was trying to be subtle.

Anthony looked at the two redheads: they were on the verge of winding each other up. He undressed.

'I'll settle this,' he said. Sara stood still as he sniffed at her, licked her hand. Then he Changed back and dressed.

'You're pregnant. We can go,' he said simply.

Sara was open-mouthed. 'You can't be able to tell so soon.' She appealed to Diana. 'He can't possibly be able to tell. It can only be hours.'

Diana shrugged. 'Mark always could. Often he knew before I did. I guess the honeymoon's over, baby. We'll give you and Jan another couple of hours alone, then we'll see you in the living room.'

Chapter 27

Diana walked back to the house, looking for her packmates. She found Zoe first, in a storeroom, her arms full of sweaters and warm socks. She was crying. Diana hugged her, kissed away the tears.

'We wouldn't be going if we didn't think we'd come back,' she said simply.

'I know. I want to come with you,' said Zoe. 'You've never left me before, all of you.'

'You're in charge, while we're gone. Don't let Chloe boss you about – this is your territory. OK?'

'Damn right.' Zoe blew her nose. 'Are you nearly ready?'

'Nearly. Go to our bedroom. Wait for me there.'

She found John and Andy, and asked them to meet Zoe in the bedroom. Andy hesitated, looking at Helen. She shrugged, trusting him.

Mark was in the nursery. He'd taken a guitar in and was strumming it, singing softly to Emily and Charlotte. Diana stood and watched for a while, then beckoned to him. He smiled, putting the guitar down gently, and followed her to their room.

John and Zoe were sitting on the smaller bed, Andy was standing leaning against the wall, arms crossed. He raised an eyebrow as his Alphas came in. 'Well?'

Diana gazed at Mark, waiting for him to speak. He squeezed her hand.

'We have news. We thought we should share it, before we went.' He explained what had happened the day before, their discovery of the blood bonding. He told the rest of the pack that both Alphas were agreed it was something that should be shared with them. 'It seems to give us more strength, as well as a greater bond,' he told them. 'I feel younger, stronger. And you only have to look at Diana to see the potential. It's scary, and I'm absolutely sure it's something that couldn't have happened years ago.'

Diana spoke up. 'It didn't happen years ago. When Joyce was killed, and I was injured, I had blood from John and Mark. I healed, but it wasn't superfast, and I don't remember anything like what I experienced yesterday.'

Mark pointed out that she'd been unconscious and might not have remembered it.

'It doesn't matter, for now. What does matter is finding out if we can share this with the others.' Diana looked at John.

'I'm up for it,' he said without hesitation.

Zoe took his hand. 'Me too. If you think it's OK, that it won't hurt the babies?'

Diana stared at her. 'I hadn't thought of that. Maybe we should wait?'

Zoe thought for a while. 'You might not come home. I want everything I can have, from all of you. How can it hurt them? It's just their parents, isn't it? Isn't it?'

'Are you sure?' said Mark.

'Sure enough,' affirmed Zoe.

'Andy?' Diana looked up, his blue eyes were fixed on her.

'You bloody witch. Yes, and no.'

'What?' She didn't understand. 'Do you need more information?'

'No, I get it. I understand. Our bond can be strengthened by this exchange of blood. We learn more about each other, and it's physically rejuvenating, at least for you two Alphas. More than that, we don't know yet.'

'So?' Diana was watching him.

'So yes, you can take my blood, but it's one way only. That's the deal. The four of you can find out anything you don't already know about me, if you want to. But I don't want a drop from you.'

John stood up. 'That's unfair. Why shouldn't you get the benefit too?'

'I don't want it. Look, I love you all so much it kills me to be away from you, but you must understand by now where my commitment lies. It's with Helen. I want to grow old with her, and it's already out of kilter. The "W" is keeping me young. She knows it, and she's already getting self-conscious about it. We were born just months apart, we grew up together, and now she looks fifteen years older than me. I don't want more longevity. I just want to get old with the woman I love.' He appealed to Mark. 'Can you accept that?'

Mark nodded. 'I can accept anything that you decide. Have we screwed up your life with this?'

Andy denied it. 'We were all young. None of us knew what would happen. But no, I don't regret anything. Take my blood, and you'll understand that.'

'Let's get on with it then,' Diana said.

John came to sit beside her, holding out a strong, tanned forearm. She bent to bite it, her teeth cleanly opening his blood vessels. She concentrated and opened matching vessels in her own arm. She put her forearm to his, as she had with Mark, and looked inwards. Her flesh crawled around his, but he continued to bleed. She opened her eyes, frustrated, angry.

'My love, oh, John. I can't. I can't join with you like that.' The wounded expression in their eyes said everything about them to their three mates.

John used his fingers to draw his wound together, concentrating hard. It sealed, an ugly red gash. 'I'm getting better at this,' he whispered, the hurt strong in his voice.

Diana closed her own wound absent-mindedly. 'We can still do it, but we'll need that damned transfusion kit again,' she said.

Zoe left to get it.

Mark spoke up. 'John, it doesn't mean that she's not bound to you. I can promise you that she is. But what she did with me must be an Alpha thing.'

John looked at him. 'You try it. We're cousins. It might work. Quickly, before Zoe gets back.' Before anyone could object, he slashed open the painful-looking wound again, watching his blood fall. Mark swore, trying to open a matching wound in his own arm in the same way that Diana had, by will alone. He failed, and slashed at himself with a sharp claw. The cousin-brothers put their arms together. Again, Mark's flesh crawled eagerly around that of his Beta, but no connection was made. They pulled their arms apart. Their mixed blood gleamed in John's still open wound. 'Ouch,' he whispered.

Diana stood up. 'Let me try something,' she murmured, opening a vein in her hand, smoothing her own blood over the mixture of Mark and John's. John's wound knitted closed, echoing her own rapid healing of the day before. 'You need both of us,' she told her Beta.

John nodded his agreement. That was something that had never been in question. Intrigued, both Alphas tried to make a physical connection with John again, this time with the addition of a small amount of the other's blood. Nothing. The reaction was limited to healing.

Zoe came back, and John quickly explained what had happened. Diana and Mark repeated the experiment with Zoe, with exactly the same results they'd seen with John.

Zoe prepared the kit, watching as Diana's rich red blood filled the tubes and started to drip out of the needle, before linking her to John.

He smiled dizzily, reaching out to take Diana in his arms, pulling her to him in a kiss that seemed eternal. He felt a deep, hot pleasure, a dim awareness of the whole pack at one time, and a total, insistent knowledge of how his Alpha loved him, adored him. Warm, comforted, drowsy, feeling a glow of health and youth within him, he protested as the link was broken. He opened his eyes.

Mark was sitting on the other side of him. 'Good?' he asked, casually.

'Fantastic. Let Diana rest for a while – I'll take a hit from you, then Zoe, then Andy.'

Mark laughed abruptly. 'Greedy bastard. You're right, though, it makes sense for the donors to rest. Diana, you OK?'

She was smiling, catlike, almost purring. The expression on John's face as he took her blood had excited her, brought her dominance hormones out in full. The whole pack could sense it. The scent was drifting from the room and through the house. In the downstairs rooms, Chloe, Hannah and Michaela exchanged disgusted looks and fled to the garden, taking their mates with them. The children played more calmly, more peacefully. Anthony, napping on the porch swing, dreamed of his family, his mother.

Diana spoke. 'I'm queen of the world, and you are my king.' She looked at Mark and giggled. 'Hit him.'

Zoe was smiling as she matched the kit up between Mark and John, and again John lay back, sighing as Mark's blood flowed into him. The pack was in there, and also a family recognition that bound the two men more closely. John could sense the bond between Mark and his father, and snatched at it, trying to discover as much about Tomas as possible from the traces of Anthony that he could find. The blood of his Alpha was hot in his veins, hotter than he could ever remember his own being, and his body was seizing it, grasping the information within it. Again, that sudden deprivation, the hungry demand from his body that it continue, then the return to full awareness.

'That was good. Zoe now.'

'Junkie already?' laughed his wife, handing over the kit to Diana and pushing up her sleeve.

'Don't mock until you've tried it.' John hauled himself up on the bed, half sitting. He watched Zoe's blood flow through the tube. 'Just a little,' he cautioned. Diana nodded; she knew what she was doing.

John smiled blissfully as the blood hit him. His addiction to Zoe, his physical need for her, was shaded by his need for Diana, but he loved his wife, and he zoned the world out as he interpreted the pack relationships through her awareness. He wasn't surprised to find that her knowledge of him was closely knit with her knowledge of Diana, a three-way bond that matched in power that of Zoe's addiction to Mark. A vague taste of Andy, associated with a sense of being protected and an unexpected eroticism, was followed by a faint sense of another man. Genuinely surprised, John's mind chased the link and investigated it. The memory of this scent was associated with loneliness. He drank in the sense, the cells, of all Zoe's children, and found an unknown trace. He investigated carefully, then joyously. The hit stopped, the flow was gone, and he opened his eyes.

He took Zoe's hand. 'Hey, gorgeous. Two things. One, your ex-husband was a dickhead. Two, we're having girls again. Come here, we can cuddle. Diana will set Andy up.'

Andy came over and held out his arm. Diana stroked it gently as she set up the transfusion. He sat as the blood started to flow from him.

Diana whispered to him. 'Just John today, OK? We can do it again whenever you're willing.'

'Yes, whatever you think,' he said abruptly.

John closed his eyes, and this time the blood brought back memories of his own. He knew the taste of this blood, the coppery slickness of it in his mouth. He'd bitten into Andy dozens of times, trying to infect him with the strangeness of Shapeshifting. And he could sense the difference in the blood between then and now. He and Mark had created something strong and unique in Andy, a creature who had come to

Shapeshifting as an imaginative, confident, uninhibited adult. John sighed as he tasted Diana again, amused by the difference between his interpretation of her sexuality and Andy's. The strongest signature in Andy's blood was Helen. John recognised her, and gave Andy privacy, avoiding the traces of her and of her daughters. The flow stopped far too soon, and John struggled not to protest.

He hugged Zoe to him, still exhilarated by the fact that he'd been the first one to taste the unborn pack babies. 'You go next,' he urged her.

Diana frowned. 'Next and last, for now. I hate to say this, but we've not got time for everyone. I suggest that we concentrate on Zoe – she'll be the one left alone, after all. And not with Andy. They're not mated, and I suspect that if they share blood, they will be. Andy, you can go back to Helen, if you like? Or stay.'

'I'll stay.' Andy said, his voice low. 'I want to see this.'

Zoe looked up. 'John? Can you be first?'

'Hey, whatever you want. Diana, will you hook us up?'

She did, and watched him carefully. He was pale, but made no move to refuse or draw back as his blood flowed into the Beta, as she relaxed, smiling.

'Look at her...' he whispered.

Zoe sighed as John's blood filled her veins; she was utterly receptive to him. There was nothing secret, nothing held back, and she swam in the essence of him, truly appreciating, for the first time, the depth of his bond with his band mates and the years he had shared with Diana. His awareness of the two women was an order of magnitude bigger than that of the men, and Zoe was amused by that. She felt safe and warm, and was sleepy by the time Diana cut the connection.

'Zoe, is this blood getting to your womb? Those babies are kicking for England.'

'I know that. I'm pretty sure it's not, though. I seem to be absorbing it, rather than circulating it.'

Diana looked at John again. 'I'm not sure about this now.'

Zoe glared at her. 'This is good for me. I feel years younger, and even if it doesn't last for long, I'm going to need energy to run this place while you are away. Diana, please?' Her face was becoming fuller, more youthful, lines of tiredness were disappearing. She reached up and pulled the needle out eventually, looking at John lovingly. 'You should have stopped – you've given me too much.'

'I'd give you everything, you know that,' he whispered.

Andy cleared his throat. 'I'll leave you guys to it.'

Diana looked at him, and followed him downstairs. 'I hate you being left out of things.' she told him.

'Me too, but it's my choice.' They found Darlene in the hallway, looking restless.

Their daughter scowled. 'What are you lot *doing* up there? None of the other Alphas can stay in the house.'

'We're not quite sure. Will you look after Andy while we finish?' Diana said, standing on tiptoe to kiss her Third. He returned the kiss with a rare passion. Diana drew away and ruffled his hair. 'I'll see you later, gorgeous.' She left, returning upstairs to find John setting up the transfusion kit between Zoe and Mark. Zoe was blissful, getting the pack fix of her life from the skinny guy who was her Alpha, who'd tried to deny her entry to the pack, who had avoided her for years, and who was now her lover.

Diana watched, fascinated, as the ravages of continuous pregnancy disappeared, as Zoe's body seized the Alpha blood and feasted on it.

Mark looked up at Diana speculatively. 'It's like you and John. She's clearly getting something out of it, physically, but it's nothing like what you and I felt.'

Diana frowned. Zoe's babies were active, kicking. She stopped the transfusion.

'Zoe, are you sure this won't hurt the babies?'

'How can it?'

'I don't know, but I'm uneasy.'

'How can it hurt them, Diana? The worst that could happen is they'll have some awareness of the rest of you when they're born. How could that hurt? And if you don't come back, and if they survive, at least they'll have known something of their parents.'

John was scratching his head. 'Diana? What do you think?'

The Alpha shrugged. 'I think that Zoe wouldn't hurt her babies.'

Mark sighed. 'Work this out yourselves. You've got half an hour, and then we're saying our goodbyes and leaving. OK?' He left the room.

'Just you left,' said John.

'Hook me up, honey,' Diana said, resigned. 'Just a few minutes, if you still want me to? Then I'll leave the two of you alone for a while.'

They looked at her. 'No, don't,' said Zoe. 'The three of us need to be together. Can you give me your blood slowly? Make it last? I want you both together.'

'Now there's an idea for a send-off,' John said. He locked the door, drew the curtains and stripped to the skin. Diana watched him. He seemed ten years younger: he was moving more quickly, his skin was smoother, warmer. He was undressing Zoe greedily, pausing to kiss her belly as she lay back. Diana let her blood flow through the tube; as it welled out, she fitted the needle into a vein in Zoe's arm, taking her hand and holding it tight.

Let's do this,' she whispered, looking at John.

Zoe moaned as John fastened his lips to hers. His taste of her blood had made him hungry for her; he felt stronger than he'd ever been before. He supported himself above her, aware more than ever of his new daughters growing inside her. She bit his lip, drawing blood, tasting it, exciting both of them. In one oft-practised move, they both moved their hips and he was inside her. They stayed motionless for a long moment as Diana's blood started to burn inside Zoe. The younger woman took time to investigate the way that Diana saw Mark, with curiosity but no envy of that complex, fierce Alpha bond. She wasted no more time. What she wanted, needed to know was how Diana saw her. She could taste herself in Diana's blood, a lesser trace than that of Mark and John. There was a memory, an instinct in Diana's blood of an intriguing new signal, one that Zoe couldn't quite place.

The Beta groaned as John started to move inside her. She opened her eyes. He was powerful and strong above her, deliberately making every thrust, every stroke, a pleasure for her, knowing exactly what pleased her. As her own musky scent rose and mixed with that of his sweat, she made the connection and returned to her investigation of Diana's blood. That new signal meant John and Zoe, and was strong in Diana's bloodstream, associated with lust, tenderness and a fierce, furious protectiveness that shocked Zoe. She gazed at her Alpha, the petite redhead who had rescued her and given her all this. Diana's eyes were burning with lust, her blood flooding with desire for her Betas. The hormones flooded directly into Zoe's body, even overshadowing her own desire for John. She writhed underneath him, wanting more of him inside her, reaching for his free hand, taking it to her mouth and sucking on his clever fingers.

Diana used her free hand to reach between them, toying slowly with Zoe, using two fingers to stroke her gently, matching her movements with John's, slowing the flow of her blood into Zoe's veins to make it last. Her own excitement was building. Watching her two mates and touching Zoe's slick wetness was enough to take her to a plateau of longing. John was thrusting deeper now, faster, judging Zoe's response perfectly. Diana reacted by making her own strokes longer and faster, letting her fingertips rest for a fraction of a second just inside Zoe, before massaging her more quickly, bringing her to an orgasm that spread deep inside her. John felt her spasm, moving his fingers from her mouth and under her bottom, lifting her closer to him. Diana stopped the massage, lifting her finger to her mouth, tasting Zoe, sighing with pleasure as she watched through slitted eyes. Zoe was still coming, a wave of pleasure that rose again and again. After a few seconds, Diana's emotions hit her, and she screamed aloud in ecstasy. John's cries joined her own as he came inside her, a great pulsing release that shocked him with its intensity. The two Betas lay nestled together for a while as Diana slowly removed the needle from Zoe's vein, and closed off her own blood loss.

Zoe turned. She could still sense Diana's hot, hard unreleased desire in her veins, and she reached for the Alpha.

John kneeled on the bed, hard again. His eyes were glowing with pleasure at his restored youth.

'Do you want…?' Diana was asking.

'Oh, I do. I always do,' he assured her, helping her to undress. He and Zoe covered her, kissing her, licking and biting and touching as she surrendered and submitted. They knew time was short, and traded duration for intensity, emerging mere minutes later from the bed, scratched, bitten and sated.

They showered together and dressed in clean clothes. John and Diana chose old comfortable jeans, thick T-shirts and warm long-sleeved knitted sweaters, which they wrapped around their hips. Zoe chose an ankle-length scarlet scoop-neck dress. Together, they went downstairs and waited for the others in the main dining room.

Mark had heard the shower running and went outside to round up his guests. They were all standing in the open air and retreated, nervous, as he left the house. He raised his hands reassuringly.

'We're all done. We were just trying something new, that's all.'

Bill was the first to walk up to him. 'Well, did it work?'

'Hmm, don't know about "work", but it was interesting.' Mark looked at his son. 'It affected you too?'

Raj spoke up. 'Whatever you were trying to do, I think you've established that you and Diana are firmly in charge.' Next to him, wide-eyed, her hand resting lightly on his shoulder, Hannah agreed.

'Good. In that case, follow me to the dining room. All will be explained.'

Seth was waiting just inside as the Alphas of the guest packs came into the room. He contacted his brothers and sisters. They drifted in, in ones and twos. Helen followed Darlene and Miranda. Jan and Sara, the newest Alphas, sidled in through the door, trying to unobtrusively take seats together at the back of the room. Darlene cast an anxious glance at her sister, who responded with a tiny wave.

The Shapeshifters settled down, taking seats around one of the bigger tables, leaving five seats at the top free for Diana's pack.

The five of them stood together at the end of the room, talking quietly. They had their backs to the rest of the Shapeshifters, and Helen, watching them, realised that something about the Alphas and Betas was changing by the minute, their posture was less springy, their muscle tone slackening, their hair dulling a little. Slight changes, but she knew them all so well, and watched, wondering why, when they turned to face her, they all looked so familiar, so unchanged.

John took Zoe's hand. 'We have to look as we usually do. It's nice being rejuvenated, but we'll keep it for ourselves. It's just too dangerous, at the moment, to change things.' She agreed.

Andy took the free seat next to Helen, taking her hand and squeezing it. Zoe sat next to him, sitting down gratefully. John stood for a moment, looking at all the faces, all the strong, confident Shapeshifters, and delighted in the thought of the fight to come. He noticed that Michaela was looking at him appreciatively, and winked at her. He was gratified when she blushed. Satisfied he could still work his magic, he settled down opposite his Zoe, who hadn't missed a thing and kicked him gently.

Diana remained standing, patiently waiting for the chatter to die down. Mark joined her, waiting. Their pack and their children quietened first, then the guests.

'Thank you,' said Mark. 'Thank you for coming, when you don't know why. Thank you for trusting me. This is where we tell you all what we want to do. If you don't want to be involved, then you're free to leave at any time, of course.

'Before we start, I have an announcement to make. We have a new pack in our midst. Our daughter, Sara, has found her match – more than her match, we hope. Some of you may have heard rumours about him. Jan, cousin, would you stand up for a moment, please?'

Mark waited while Jan nervously stood up. He was wearing borrowed clothes and his hair was washed and shining, tied back with a strip of rawhide. He looked at Diana, seeking approval, finding more than he hoped for. He dropped his eyes as he saw Andy glaring at him.

Mark continued. 'Jan was born into the White Pack. His mother was my aunt. She was kidnapped, enslaved and eventually murdered. When we strike, I want you all to remember that his story isn't unusual in that pack, and we may find allies in unexpected places. Be prepared to give mercy, and accept surrender. Jan, relax, sit down, please.'

Simon laughed nervously. 'You're talking as if it's a done deal. It sounds more like a suicide mission to me.'

'If you think it's a suicide mission, why are you here?' Mark was genuinely puzzled.

Simon swallowed hard. 'You saved my pack. If you're going to war against the Whites, I want the chance to go with you.

I want my chance to fight, to kill at least one of the bastards who attacked us when we were at our most vulnerable.'

Mark frowned. 'And you're ready to die to prove your gratitude? That's crazy, but oddly reassuring. Thank you, Simon.' He looked round again. 'When we get there, I don't want any mistakes. Learn Jan's scent over the next few days, wolf and man. Is there anyone here who goes stupid when they're wolf? It's not unusual, and nobody will think the less of you, but we really need to know.'

Raj looked a little sheepish. 'I do tend to get carried away,' he admitted.

Hannah looked at Mark. 'He'll do as I say, whatever shape he's in. I won't let him do anything daft,' she said emphatically.

Diana bit back a grin and spoke up. 'There are still one or two things to organise, but we've been planning this for months.' She outlined the plan, explaining her children's abilities to the strangers, explaining what had happened to her the day before. 'You see, we need to move quickly now, before the Whites get suspicious. Simon, will you speak to Robbie? See if he can help? It would make life much easier.'

'I'll ring him from the car,' said the Whitby Alpha. 'What are we waiting for?'

Mark looked around. A surge of excitement coursed through him. 'We're ready to rock. Let's go.'

The group made their way out of the house.

Diana drew the Bees and Caleb aside. 'This is your last chance to change your minds. Nobody expects this of you, and if you want to stay behind to help Zoe, it's just as useful to us.'

Bridget frowned. 'Mother, I've been in nearly as many battles as you. I'm not missing this one. Besides, I want to be there afterwards. It won't just be a case of killing and leaving, will it? We'll have a responsibility to their children and women.'

Diana hugged her. 'You're right, as usual. I forget what a warrior you are. Beatrice, Caleb?'

'All for one and one for all,' Caleb said simply. 'We fight better together, the three of us.'

In the afternoon heat, the Shapeshifters made their way to three vehicles. Mark and Andy stood next to the one belonging to their pack. Andy was already changing his features and his shape, his blond hair becoming paler and thinner. He stood next to the driver's door. Diana shuddered, recognising the face of the man who'd almost torn her arm off the day before.

'It's just Andy,' she told herself. Glancing behind her, she saw Helen turn away and walk into the house, ushering her daughters before her. Andy's family was staying at Silverwood.

Diana suddenly realised that the group was looking at her, waiting for instructions. She sighed. 'OK. All the face changers, do it now. I know that dead bodies and passport photos don't give us much of a clue, but we'll have to settle for what we have.' She watched critically as her eldest Shapeshifting children morphed their faces and bodies, her daughters taking on male shape. They were limited only, it seemed, by their original body mass. She hoped it wouldn't be too noticeable. She took charge. 'Right. Listen up. We need an even distribution of "Whites" and "prisoners". And we have to be aware that there's no way they'd let Alpha pairs travel together. Car one – Andy and Mark, Darlene, Hannah, Simon, Mary, Frank and Bill. Is that OK? Car two – Raj and Hannah's Toyota – John, Bridget and Trixie, Anthony and our new Alpha pair, Sara and Jan. We can make an exception for them because they'll both look like Whites. Car three – Michaela and Simon's Ford – me, Seth and Noah, Caleb, Raj and Michaela. From the minute we leave these gates, we can't have any kind of activity from a "prisoner". I'm going to go to sleep – I suggest that the rest of you do the same. And no music.

Jan says the Whites aren't into it. Sorry. Chances are we won't be observed, but I don't want to take the risk.'

Zoe was by her side. Diana turned and kissed her lightly. 'You'll be fine,' she assured her.

'I will. I'm going back now. I've pulled the plug on the phones and the web, just in case the littl'uns say something they shouldn't. I'll just have to find some other way of keeping them entertained. And I promise, those gates stay shut until we know what's happened to you. Chloe and I will keep our own phones with us, and switched on. Good luck.'

'Good luck to you too. I'm sure I've got the best of the deal here.' The two women hugged once more, and then Zoe turned and walked back into the house.

Chloe was saying her goodbyes to her mates and Mary. Bill and Frank had already changed their faces and bodies and Chloe was clearly unsettled. Bill reached to hug her, but she drew away. 'I'm sorry, I can't. Good luck, my love, stay safe.'

Bill was upset. 'I'll see you soon. We'll be back as soon as we can.'

'Bill, just get in the car. It's time.' Chloe couldn't bring herself to embrace the man she loved; he looked too much like the killer who'd murdered her children. She settled for putting her fingers to his lips before following Zoe.

Diana took a long look at her home. It was too quiet; all the children were being kept inside. Seth hit the horn of the Ford, and she jumped.

'Get in or we're going without you,' he said. The other two cars were already pulling away.

The people carrier's side door was open, and she found a seat next to a youthful-looking blond stranger. 'Hello, I'm your mother. Who the fuck are you?' she joked.

'It's Caleb, aka Lars. Born 1997 to the White Pack, died furry in 2017 under the wheels of a Land Rover. Our driver is

Seth, aka George. Noah is pretending to be a chap called Johan. Raj and Michaela, you already know.'

'Right. I'm going to sleep. Raj, Michaela, you're supposed to be drugged up to the eyeballs, so you do the same. OK?'

Seth spoke up. 'Right, we're through the gates. I'm in charge from now on. Mother, shut up, sweetheart.'

Diana narrowed her eyes at him and then closed them. Within seconds, she was fast asleep. Raj, sitting behind her, followed suit. Michaela looked around, feeling a little vulnerable away from her own pack, but then told herself she was with three of the people who'd saved her life years ago. She made herself more comfortable, and dozed off.

Chapter 28

When they reached the coast, the fishing fleet was leaving the harbour. They were met by Robbie. Andy barely recognised him as the frightened young Beta he'd met on the day that Sammy was killed. His hair had grown out into loose black curls, and his naturally dark skin was darker, tanned and windburned. The curls were tied back with a twist of red yarn. He was wearing an intricately hand-knitted woollen jersey. His body had hardened, and he looked prepared for anything.

Wolves of the sea, Andy thought, approaching the Whitby Beta and introducing himself. 'We've met before, but I was wearing my own face then. We need two boats. We might not be bringing them back.'

'It's sorted,' said the Beta. 'I'll need money, though.' It had been anticipated, and Andy gave him four envelopes full of cash.

'Two of them are for you and the owners of the second boat, immediately. As we discussed, three times the amount you'd earn from them over the time we plan to use them. The other two you keep in reserve. They're full payment of the cost of new boats, plus fifty per cent, just in case we don't come back.' He understood the anxious expression on Robbie's face. 'Just in case, I said. We fully intend to come back.'

Robbie handed him two sets of keys. 'I bloody hope you know something about boats,' he said. 'This girl is my pride and joy.'

Andy reassured him; he'd been on plenty of boating holidays with Helen in the past, and the second boat would be handled by Simon, Robbie's own Alpha.

Robbie took a last longing look at his boat before walking away, giving a brief and understated wave to his Alphas as he passed the cars they were in. He would go back to the farm and help Holly to care for the stock and the babies.

Seth stood at the wharf. He was speaking fast, in German, into a phone. Jan had advised him on argot and White Pack mannerisms. 'It went well. We have prisoners, lots of them, so we'll have to come home under the radar. We lost two men, though, before we managed to drug all the mongrel bastards. We're practically outnumbered here, and I'm wondering whether we should kill some of them now to avoid trouble. It would make life easier.'

He held his breath, and then smiled wickedly. He spoke again. 'In that case, we'll need reinforcements. And bloody transport. And bring us some food too – it's no joke crossing the North Sea in a fishing boat.'

He listened again before swearing creatively. 'Four? You can do better than that – I want at least ten more men. These bastards are sneaky. If I can't kill them, I need some reassurance I've got enough people to hold them down until we get home.' He paused. 'Fine. I'll contact you when we land.'

He turned to Andy. 'Perfect. Harald wants every single captive alive and available for questioning. That was a tricky bluff, but we got away with it. They're sending more men to meet us when we land. Anthony is a tactical genius – the more we can deal with in small numbers, the better. Are we ready to sail?'

Andy looked round. The cars had gone, and his family and friends were on board two newish, solid-looking fishing boats. He blinked. 'Where the fuck did the cars disappear to?'

Seth held out a hand to him. 'Get aboard, Dad. Robbie's friends drove them away. They're happy – a paid holiday at triple rate! They'll leave the cars on the long-stay tourist car park for us. Come on, if you're coming? Or do you want to hang around for the folk festival?'

Andy shuddered. 'No way.' He took Seth's hand and stepped on to the boat.

Out at sea, away from curious eyes, the pack took the opportunity to slip back to their own shapes.

Mary, alone for the first time with Frankie and Bill, approached them cautiously. 'Do you mind if I sit with you?'

Frankie moved over. 'Nope. Course we don't. What do you think of Chloe?'

Mary looked at him, considering her options. 'I think we can get on. She's clearly smitten with the pair of you.'

Frankie leaned back, stretching his legs out, putting his hands behind his head, posing. 'Who isn't?' he teased.

'You get cuter every year,' she commented absently. He uncomfortably remembered that although he'd never actually met Mary before, she'd been talking to his older brothers and sister on web forums since he was thirteen years old. She sat between Bill and Frank, enjoying their body heat. 'When we get back, we're going to sign a Contract. Until then, she doesn't want anything more than flirtation between us.'

'She's the boss,' sighed Bill. 'Anyway, give us the gossip. What the hell happened with Jan and Sara? I thought she was just going to find him and ask him to join us. Did I miss something?'

Mary told him what she knew, and the three of them settled into an easy discussion, talking about anything but the upcoming fight.

On deck, Diana stood next to Andy, taking in everything he told her about navigating the boat. 'You enjoy this!' she said. 'Always full of surprises, aren't you?'

He put his arm around her affectionately. 'Every year, Helen and I do this. It feels weird without her.' He changed the subject. 'It's all plain sailing now, so do you want to get some sleep?'

'No, I slept in the car. Can I take over, let you rest?'

He considered it for half a second, and laughed. 'No way. I know how you navigate when you're driving. At sea, wandering around the place until you see a road sign doesn't work.'

She laughed low, enjoying a rare moment alone with him. 'How do you feel about Jan, now that it's done?'

He sighed. 'I feel manipulated. And I suspect I know who's done the manipulating.' He gave her a sideways look. 'And I hope she's thought about where the happy couple are going to live, and on what.'

Diana had the grace to look vaguely guilty. Then she shrugged. 'It's done now. Isn't it a beautiful night?'

'Says she, clumsily trying to change the subject. OK, fair enough. But I'm watching Darlene like a hawk from now on.' He leaned back, and she nestled into his shoulder.

'I hope…' they both said at once, then laughed.

'What do you hope?' Andy asked.

'I hope they're happy. I hope she gives him some respect. I hope she really does love him. And you? What do you hope?'

'Me? I hope he doesn't leave her alone and pregnant for weeks at a time until she's almost mad with loneliness. That would be a truly shitty thing to do.'

'Those were the days, eh? And now we're going to be grandparents. It's a bloody miracle we made it this far. I can't believe how innocent we were.'

Andy ruffled her hair. 'Are you happy? At last?'

'Oh, I've always been happy. I just want to be free. You know? I want to know that we can live our lives, send the kids to school, go shopping, meet with friends, without worrying that there's a tribe of murdering religious nutters out there who think I'm the Antichrist.'

'Diana wants, Diana gets,' Andy said, only half joking. 'Eventually. So this isn't just about Sammy?'

'The body count has got way beyond this being for Sammy. We killed his killer, and that was enough for me to find some kind of peace.' She fell silent, and he drew her closer. 'No, this is about wanting a real life, not a siege. I've bloody well had enough. And, by the way, I don't get everything I want, as you know damn well.' She drew away, wiping her face on her sleeve. 'I'm sorry, Andy, that was really unfair. I respect your decision completely. You know that?'

Andy looked out to sea. 'Yes, and it makes it easier. Not to keep to it – that's not an issue – but to feel better about making it. You know it was about Helen, not about you. You did nothing wrong – I wasn't rejecting you.'

'It's about love, and I understand that,' she said a little too brightly.

'So is this,' he said, bending to her, taking her face in his hands, kissing her, closing his eyes and tasting her.

She pulled away, eventually. 'I think I'll try to get some rest. Are you sure you're OK steering us?'

'I'll keep us on the right course, babe, don't worry.'

On the other boat, Simon peered into the darkness, and checked his charts. 'Seth, are you sure you can handle this?'

'Sure, it's just maths. How far to shore?'

'About five miles. It's high tide now. We'll anchor close to shore, and wait for the tide to go out enough for us to walk to the rendezvous. The boat is used to being beached. By the way, Seth, I'll have to start playing prisoner again very soon. And you'll have to get rid of that red hair.'

'Done,' said Seth, slipping alarmingly quickly into another shape, another face. 'It's ever so much easier when you've done it once or twice. Are you sure you can't?'

'I'm like your parents, I grew up with too many inhibitions. I'll keep trying, though. Right, you go over what I've told you about navigating the last few miles, then I'll go gaga on you.'

Seth went through his instructions again. Satisfied, Simon left him, finding a free space on the deck and slumping down, faking a drugged sleep. Around him, the other false prisoners were doing the same thing while the pretend guards adopted their fake personas.

As dawn broke, the tide washed out, leaving the boats beached. The allied packs climbed off the boats, pantomiming a struggle to unload drugged prisoners. They didn't expect the White reinforcements to have arrived so quickly, but took care all the same.

Leaving the beach, they took shelter in a line of stunted trees. They sat in three groups, as they had originally left Silverwood. Jan sat slightly apart from his group. Everyone was silent, as not all of the fake guards spoke German, and it would be suspicious for the White reinforcements to overhear them speaking English.

The day grew warmer, and stomachs had started grumbling for breakfast when an accidentally dislodged branch rolled down a slope, signalling the arrival of a lone White scout.

He strutted into the clearing, grinning at Seth. 'Well, George, you've done it. How the hell did you manage it?'

Seth stood up. 'We overheard the queen bitch talking to her whelp about a meeting, just before we attacked them. We didn't get to kill them because the whole bloody pack came out to rescue them, and we had to retreat. But then the day after, the fools came out again, to the old farmhouse on the land they've just bought. These other Alphas joined them, and this woman here.' He gently kicked Mary, emphasising his point. She moved away slowly, dully.

'Anyway,' he continued. 'We were waiting in the farmhouse for them. They came in twos and threes, and we were able to sedate and capture them. They're very strong, though, the lot of them. Except the queen bitch herself – she's still half-dead.'

He cast a glance at Diana, who lay pale and still on the mossy ground. 'Now, where's our transport?'

'We've brought a coach. There's plenty of room for you to get some rest. We'll take over guard duty.' He glanced around, his eyes stopping at Jan. 'Is that who I think it is?'

Seth forced himself to stay calm. How much did the Whites know about Jan's activities over the last few months?

'Yeah. I guess he was the reason for the meeting. He told me he'd been a prisoner of the Silverwood Pack for months, and that he was being handed over to another pack. It seems that one of their daughters had taken a fancy to him, and he was being moved away to keep them apart. We don't know how much he's told them about us, but he's in a bad way.'

The scout seemed to buy the story, and started to walk towards Jan, but Seth intercepted him, unwilling to take the slightest risk that this man might be able to pick up on Jan's Alpha status, subdued as it was. 'He's freaked out. Don't approach him suddenly, he's had some bad experiences. We think he might have been tortured.' Seth watched cautiously as the White scout paused, then nodded.

'OK, follow me.' He walked out of the woodland and across three fields to a car park where a long white coach was sitting. The doors were open, and eight White Pack men were sitting on the wall, chatting. They looked around, seeing packmates approaching with prisoners, and fell silent, almost awed. An infamous group, it seemed. Anthony, Diana, Mark and John. Then Simon and Michaela, the surviving Alphas of a failed attack that had left six Whites dead. Following them, Hannah and Raj, Alphas of a fast-growing young pack that was beginning to make its mark in British Shapeshifter history. And Mary; a couple of them recognised her, noting the missing fingers, recollecting the young woman who'd repelled an attack on a seemingly vulnerable house of female students. A one-eyed White looked at her with hate. She kept her face down, affecting drowsiness.

Diana stumbled, almost falling. The Whites began to grin, then to cheer and mock. With the information they could extract from these prisoners, they could attack Silverwood and wipe out the whole pack. Every other British pack would be demoralised and vulnerable. The tide had turned.

Mark let his long hair fall over his face, and sneaked a glance through it. Of the eight, one wasn't cheering but watching carefully. He looked about twenty-five and had a broader build than most of his packmates, he was looking at Jan cautiously. He called out, 'Albie. Is that Jan?'

Albie, the scout, nodded. 'It is. He's a bit nervy from all accounts. Leave him alone, Ralph. We can debrief him when we get back home.'

The Whites climbed about the coach, moving to the back, applauding as their 'packmates' led the prisoners on, one at a time. A young blond was in the driver's seat. He was grinning. The last prisoner on to the bus was Anthony, bent over, eyes filmed, his movements tired and resigned. The driver looked at Anthony in disgust.

'Is that the Old Wolf? Look at him! What is there to fear?'

Anthony's head went up, silver fire in his eyes. With preternatural speed he grabbed the driver by the throat and pulled him out of his seat, breaking his neck in one easy motion. It was over in three seconds and, before the Whites at the back of the coach could move, Diana's children and Andy had morphed back to their original shapes. Frankie jumped out of the open door, running to take up guard duty outside the emergency exit at the rear of the coach.

Two of the Whites had fallen to their knees in fear and were praying. Seth caught the words 'possession' and 'witchcraft'. He stood silent, watching as his mother moved to the front of the coach, graceful and wild. She stooped for a moment by the dead driver, checking his pulse.

'Anthony, that was unnecessary,' she reproached him.

'It got their attention,' he said simply.

'What's done is done. And so, we move on,' she said, standing again, waiting for the coach to fall silent.

Her friends and mates moved aside, giving the Whites at the back a clear view of her. Petite, womanly, she glowed with an inner fire. Her hair almost crackled with life. She spoke simply and clearly, a speech she'd prepared for this moment.

'You are my kin, we are one race. This war you have waged against me, and those I love, will soon be over. There has been bloodshed enough, and I do not want to see you dead, any of you. I'm sated on vengeance – I just want peace.' She looked at them, and smiled. 'And, of course, total and utter victory. But that is no longer in question. What is in question is whether the nine of *you* will live or die. I'm willing to accept your surrender.'

Her children were watching the men carefully, studying the way they moved, the way they stood; this was much more promising material for mimicry than dead bodies and passport photographs. Something about their predatory regard sent fear rushing through the blood of the Whites.

The youngest, Ralph, was the first to speak. 'Jan, are you a prisoner?'

Jan smiled. 'Little brother, no, I'm not a prisoner. I'm the mate of Sara, gods be thanked. I have no allegiance to Harald.'

Anthony raised an eyebrow. Jan explained. 'Ralph is Audrey's son also – her youngest. We have three surviving sisters.'

Ralph winced. 'Two – Marguerite is dead.'

Jan closed his eyes. Marguerite was the oldest of his sisters and the source of all his information about his mother and the identities of her children.

The Whites were glaring at Ralph; Jan sensed violence. 'Ralph, come to me,' he said. The two brothers spoke quietly for several moments.

Jan looked at Diana and she joined them. He whispered, 'Diana, my brother wants to join us. Not surrender, join us. Can you trust him?'

Diana agreed. 'He's your responsibility. He fights with you and Sara. If he tries any tricks, it'll be against the two of you.'

Jan was appalled at her willingness to risk her daughter, but understood her logic. 'I am sure he can be trusted,' he promised.

Diana spoke again to the White soldiers. 'There are twenty-one of us now, and only eight of you. Surrender, or choose how you want to die.'

Albie stood up. 'I won't surrender. Do you have the decency to allow me to fight for my life? I want to die as a wolf – I'll fight you all.'

Diana sighed. 'And so it starts. No, you won't fight us all, that would conveniently leave your packmates unguarded. Michaela?'

The young Alpha stepped forward. She was already undressing. She looked inward, and began to Change. Within seconds, she stood quietly in front of Diana. Michaela's wolf form was small and lithe, with long fur the colour of pale honey. Her eyes were a startling blue.

Albie started to object. 'I won't fight a wom—'

'You will, or Anthony will break your worthless neck here and now. You're already a dead man, Albie. You've made your choice. Now fight with dignity.'

Anthony led Albie and Michaela outside. Andy Changed to tiger form, following them, to ensure Albie didn't make a run for it.

Diana spoke conversationally to the Whites. 'Pretty, isn't she? She's got four children, you know. She'd die for any of them. Oddly enough, she almost got killed giving birth to the eldest two. Six of your packmates attacked her home while she was in labour. I won't go into the gruesome details, but they never did get back home, did they? Anyway, she's been carrying a lot of repressed anger since then, poor love. She was pretty annoyed about how defenceless she was, and how appallingly unchivalrous your brothers were. It's time she let some of it out.'

Anthony climbed back aboard. A fine spray of blood stained his face. He wiped at it absently. 'He gets eight out of ten for enthusiasm, but only four for technique. It's over. Michaela's upset – she's never killed anyone before. Simon, I think she needs a hug.'

Simon picked up his Alpha's clothes and jumped off the bus.

Diana regarded the Whites again. 'The odds, not that it really matters, are now three to one. Again, what are your choices?'

Another White stepped forward. 'I surrender. But I won't fight my brothers.'

'Fair enough. Sit there, by Caleb.'

The White looked puzzled.

Diana explained patiently, indicating the seventeen-year-old. 'Caleb, my twin-less son. He'll keep an eye on you.' She looked at the remaining Whites. 'Hurry up, we want to move on.'

A set of twins Jan's age looked at each other, and stood. One spoke for both. 'We will die together. Would you do it? We will not resist, and we trust you to do it quickly.'

Diana closed her eyes. 'Are you sure? This isn't what I want. You're our kin – I'd spare you if I could.'

Jan spoke up. The men had been his friends when he was growing up. 'Paul, Max. Please reconsider. These are good people. You could have a better life than you've ever dreamed of.'

The two men hesitated, looking at each other. Jan walked over and took their hands. For the first time, Diana saw the man that he'd become. 'I've been a destroyer, a killer, for so long, but Diana is right. It's time for it to end.'

The twins shook their heads. 'We want to die. We don't want to live in a world where these godless mongrels rule. The gods would not forgive us,' Paul said for both of them.

'You poor deluded bastards,' said Diana. She sprang with uncanny speed, a razor-sharp claw extended, slashing two jugulars in one movement, almost severing both heads with the strength of the blow. Paul and Max blinked once, and then toppled together. Blood flowed down the aisle of the bus.

She stepped aside, and looked sadly at Jan. 'I'm sorry, honey, but time is short.'

He turned away and went to sit with Sara, who held him close.

Diana looked sadly at the surviving Whites. 'Four of you remaining. Any of you feeling godless enough to live? Or do we finish this now, while I've got my claws out?'

The oldest of them, the one-eyed man who'd glared at Mary, suddenly turned and ran for the emergency door, forcing it open and leaping out. Before he could regain his balance, Frankie stepped up and lazily decked him with a blow to the chin that made everyone who could see wince. Frankie looked up. Diana had walked to the back of the coach and was looking out. Mark and John were standing behind her, arms folded, protecting her back from the last three holdouts.

'Kill him, Frank. He's made his choice. Now, before he wakes up. We'll have no unnecessary cruelty.'

Frankie raised his voice. 'Mary? Do you want to do this yourself?'

She was sitting with Bill. She shuddered. 'No. Just do it. Please.'

Frank kneeled, and broke the one-eyed man's neck cleanly. Then he got to his feet and stared past his mother at the three remaining enemies. 'You – in the green shirt. I know your face. Ever been to South Wales?'

The man looked at him, panic-stricken. He turned, Changing at the same time, running down the aisle, almost slipping in his packmates' blood. Nobody got in his way. He slid out of the open door at the front and the pack waited in silence. Seconds passed. Then there was a terrified wolfish scream and a deep, big-cat cough. Silence resumed.

Diana looked at the two remaining Whites; another set of twins, in their late twenties. 'He forgot Andy is out there too. You've doubtless heard of Andy?'

The men shivered in superstitious dread. 'The Changeling,' one of them whispered. They looked at each other, coming to an agreement without words.

'What are your terms? If we surrender?'

'Stop killing us. It's as simple as that. Any attempt to hurt us, or those under our protection, will make you outlaws in our society, and we will hunt you down. If you agree to these terms, and accept a short imprisonment while we finalise our victory, you can live as free men.'

'Then we surrender.'

'Fine. Four out of ten is fewer than I'd hoped for, but better than none. We'll put you on one of our boats now. When we return, you can go free.' She looked at her allies. 'I need volunteers for guard duty.'

Raj spoke up. 'Hannah and I will do it.'

'Thank you, Raj. Be careful.'

Frank, Bill and Mary jumped off the coach, and helped to escort the three White Pack men to the boat. When they came back, they brought a deck brush, detergent and a water carrier. Bill and Frank swabbed down the coach floor, cleaning away the spilled blood. Diana was supervising the loading of the dead into the luggage space beneath the coach. She spoke quietly to Mark. 'We'll take them to their home for a decent burial. We want to start making friends here.' She looked round, and made her way to Ralph, favouring him with a dazzling smile. 'Ralph, you and

Jan, earlier, you weren't speaking German or English. Sorry, couldn't help but overhear. I mean, I don't speak German myself but several of my kids do, and I know how it sounds.'

Ralph blushed. 'Oh, it's the women's language. We mostly speak German and English, though some of us know French, when we're out in the world. We speak Bavarian at home, but the women, they mostly speak an older Bavarian dialect amongst themselves, with added vocabulary. The women don't go out into the world. Boys tend to forget the language, once they leave their mothers, but Jan and I talk to the women a lot, and we understand it better than most men.'

Diana nodded. 'OK, on the way, could you teach it to me, a little? I want to be able to speak to the women, just a few phrases, you know? Sort of "We come in peace", "Take me to your leader", and "Does anyone know where I can get a decent cup of coffee?" That sort of thing.'

Ralph smiled nervously and followed her on to the coach. They found a seat near the back and began to talk.

John looked at them, and then at Mark, amused. 'She's not keeping him. I don't care how much energy she thinks she has, no male Fourth, cousin or not.'

Mark watched her. 'She's adopting him, not seducing him. I don't think we need worry. Let's get going.' He raised his voice. 'Anthony, you said you could drive this thing?'

His father was just climbing aboard. 'I can drive anything. But we're stopping at the first shop we see – I'm starving.'

'What are you waiting for?' Mark asked, taking the seat across the aisle from Bridget and Beatrice, putting his feet up and going instantly to sleep.

Chapter 29

Anthony stopped the coach; he wasn't sure of the road any more. 'Jan, Ralph, I need help. Give me directions,' he called.

His nephews came to the front of the coach, Sara trailing behind; she didn't want to be separated from Jan any longer than necessary. They were holding hands, and Diana, watching them, smiled.

She was on the back seat with her mates. Andy was sitting by the window, talking with John. She was lying with her head on John's lap, taking advantage of the opportunity to rest. Next to her was Mark, also lying down, almost on top of her. He seemed to be asleep. Every so often he'd open his eyes and look at her. He'd pushed up her shirt, finding exposed skin, and laid his head against it. She felt a tickling sensation and realised what he was doing, concentrating on him for a moment until a tiny connection, only a couple of millimetres wide, had grown between them, their blood passing backwards and forwards – a quiet, secret mating that nobody else could know about.

Simon and Michaela were asleep in each other's arms. Bill was sitting with Mary, enthusiastically telling her about the new building they were planning for the house. Frankie was sitting across the aisle, watching them sleepily.

Darlene was sitting with her oldest brothers. She had been crying, and they'd been comforting her. The Bees were asleep, Caleb behind them also napping.

The coach started up again, and after a few more miles Jan called a halt. Andy went to the front, morphing his features until he was the twin of the dead driver. Anthony moved aside, making sure that Andy was confident about driving the coach.

Andy settled down and looked round. His allies were moving around, all those who could change their faces were doing so, some of them taking the features of the second group of Whites. When they got off the coach, it would look less suspicious if there were members from both groups escorting the prisoners.

Everyone was moving about, the supposed prisoners taking seats next to the windows, slumping against them in an imitation of drugged weakness. Next to each of them, a fake White sat guard.

Ralph sat next to Diana at his own request. He was too nervous to sit with anyone else. She took his hand, feeling how cold and clammy it was; he was terrified. He was about to go to his own home and fight against his father and brothers with a group of invading strangers. He was looking at Jan wonderingly, and then he suddenly twitched. His pulse sped up.

Diana pulled him closer, moving her head slightly so she couldn't be seen from outside. 'I know. You're wondering if it really is Jan, aren't you?'

The young man jumped. 'Is it?' he asked, suddenly even more terrified that he was making a huge mistake.

'It is, I promise. On my children's lives, I promise you. Go and talk to him, if it'll make you feel better.'

Ralph relaxed, his pulse slowing again. 'I know it is, really. Thank you.'

'No problem,' she whispered. 'Thank *you*.' She was glad that he'd thought of the possibility; it showed he wasn't stupid.

They passed through sleepy villages and came to a single-track road. Andy swore several times, manoeuvring the coach around sharp bends, up and down steep hills.

Eventually, by the side of a meadow, at a rare wide part of the road, Jan stopped him. 'We'll walk from here. We'd never bring a vehicle like this any further up, it's too dangerous. Come on.'

Andy pulled the coach over to the side of the road and everyone disembarked. Next to the road, goats watched, chewing happily on buttercups. A teenager sat on some rocks. He waved excitedly and ran over to them.

'I heard you'd done something amazing, but nobody would tell me what. Who are these people?'

'Prisoners, kid. Get back to the goats. You'll learn more later.'

The boy looked abashed, but obeyed. He waved at Ralph, who ignored him.

In silence they walked for five miles, up and down hills. The valleys were cultivated, and women and children worked in the fields, tending goats, cattle, geese and pigs. The allies were silently awed by the extent of the property of the White Pack.

Close to a cliff, a thick, high stone wall was topped by sharpened stakes. A sturdy oak door was shut tightly. Two men had been sitting casually playing cards near the gate. The speed at which they stood betrayed their readiness.

'George. Congratulations. Harald is ready to meet you. Where are the others? Where is Albie?'

Seth had listened carefully to his intonation and accent, and modified his own speech to mimic it more closely. 'We were followed. The Changeling and some of their whelps realised what had happened. Albie stayed behind with the others to deal with them.'

The guard frowned. 'When was that?'

Seth looked worried. 'You've not heard from them? It was half a day ago. If the whelps won the fight, we need to get the prisoners underground now. Open the gate.'

The guard obeyed without question, stepping in front of the column of guards and prisoners. 'Harald is waiting in the main hall.' He looked down the column. 'Jan. Where in the name of the gods have you been?'

'Prisoner,' explained Ralph. 'May we go first?' he asked Seth. 'Harald will be pleased to see Jan again – he thought he was lost.'

Seth grunted. He knew enough about Jan's relationship with the Alpha who'd fathered him to find this amusing, but kept his face straight. 'Jan can offer his respects, yes. Go ahead, the two of you.'

Ralph led the group confidently to the main hall, the fake Whites making an excellent job of pretending they knew the way perfectly well. Men stood in the hallways, watching them pass. There were surprisingly few of them.

Diana reflected for a moment on the size of the pack. Jan had said that five years ago, when her pack had first been attacked, there were a hundred and fifty men of fighting age. Internal politics had accounted for a dozen of them since, but they'd been replaced by youngsters.

In the first attack on Diana's pack, six Whites had been killed. In the second wave of attacks, seventeen had died. Sara and her sisters had accounted for five more in the college car park, and seven had been killed by the Welsh Pack. In the last few days, another eighteen had been accounted for, excluding the three prisoners. Jan had killed and skinned eight in London, alone. And two new recruits for her side: her mate's cousins, Jan and Ralph, another two fighters lost from the White Pack. She added up quickly: over sixty men lost by the White Pack since they'd started their war against her. That left somewhere between eighty and ninety men, plus any boys who'd matured in that time. She was knowingly walking into a situation where she and her allies were still outnumbered by more than four to one, and that was if she could trust that the women wouldn't fight.

Head down, she couldn't see much, but it was clear the walls were no longer lined; they were of barely dressed stone. She was being led through a small door that gave access to only one person at a time. She emerged into a large lamp-lit cave. *Medieval* may be too generous a term, she thought to herself.

On what could only be described as a throne, at the far side of the room, a thickset middle-aged man sat forward, watching eagerly as they came into the room. He was flanked by half a dozen muscular Whites, who occasionally favoured each other with mutually distrustful looks. Jan and Ralph bowed, and moved to one side.

Harald pushed back his long, thinning hair and spoke mockingly. 'Jan, you weakling. You dare to come back a failure? I'll deal with you later.' His eyes crawled over his prizes. 'But not before I've enjoyed this gift that George has brought for me. George, you are my favoured son, and you shall be rewarded.'

Seth moved closer, and bowed. 'It's my pleasure to serve my father,' he said truthfully.

'Well, well, bring her here. Let's see what all the fuss has been about. Then I'd like to have a chat with Anthony. Once the drugs have worn off, of course.'

Noah took his mother's arm and led her towards Harald. Caleb had taken Anthony's arm and pushed him further forward too. Five pack members were now within easy striking distance of the six guards. It would be more than enough.

Harald licked his lips, standing and walking to Diana. 'You're smaller than I imagined, my dear. And uglier. Much uglier.' He looked across to where Mark was standing slumped, half supported by Sara, who was masquerading as a son of Harald. 'And that's your mate, is it? I'm shocked. I expected something a little more physical, a little more impressive from an Alpha. You're a pair of mongrels. Still, perhaps I could fuck you before I kill you, show you what a real Alpha is like.'

He stepped back suddenly as Diana's head snapped up. Her eyes made him think of the hungry depths of the sea, and he was trapped for a moment, unmoving. She drew back her lips in a vicious grin.

'Harald, you filthy, diseased, shitbrained, superstitious old bastard. You're going to die, and I'm going to watch it happen.'

'Drug her,' he whispered, unable to look away. 'She's coming out of it.'

'I was never *in* it, you thick creep. Say your prayers, baby-killer.'

His guards were beginning to stir, realising he might be in danger. He stood and hesitated for a moment, then drew his hand back to slap her.

She ducked and stepped back, laughing. Behind her, her children's faces and bodies shimmered and twisted, finding their own forms. Diana's pack was standing in the Great Hall of the Whites.

Jan yelled and pushed Ralph to the floor, distracting the guards for vital moments whilst Seth, Noah, Caleb and Anthony Changed, ripping out of their clothes and going for the easy kills, the rips to throat and belly that ended things for the six guards within seconds. Diana almost purred with pleasure, looking at the two young red wolves, the sleek black wolf and Old Wolf, streaked with grey, who were all rubbing against her legs, glaring their hate at Harald.

He stared, incredulous. 'You can kill me, but you can't win. There are almost a hundred men out there. I have women, children – there are only twenty of you. You'll never get away with this. You can't masquerade as my sons forever.'

Jan stepped towards him. 'I'm not acting. This is me, Father. And this is the Challenge. Me and you, now. Come on, you bastard, deal with me. Didn't you say that you wanted to?'

Sara stepped forward and kissed him gently. Harald was incredulous. 'You've mated? *You?* He looked down; Anthony was rubbing himself against Jan's legs now, in a show of affection and protectiveness.

Jan looked down and smiled. 'Thanks for the vote of confidence, Uncle.'

'Uncle?'

'My mother's brother. Remember my mother?'

Harald swore. 'That *bitch*! She was never anything but trouble. Fought me every time until she realised that I liked…' He faltered.

Diana looked like she was going to kill him there and then, without regard to the politics of succession. Ralph's pale blue eyes blazed out, his face flushed and angry. Michaela had moved to the young man's side to calm him, releasing Alpha hormones to control his fury.

Jan was standing before Harald now, his friends moving away. He smiled a little; a self-mocking expression that almost broke Diana's heart. 'I'm ready to fight. So you're going to Change and fight me, or you're going to surrender and go into exile. It's your choice.'

Ralph had recovered and gone to the door. He opened it and called out to the four men outside. 'Can you come in? We have a situation here.'

The men came in, cautious. These were ordinary soldiers, ordinary pack members, not Harald's favoured lieutenants. None of them was over twenty years old. They came in one by one, staring at the unexpected sight of Noah and Seth, the Kittens, the Bees, Frank and Bill, Andy and Caleb. Jan and Harald had moved to the middle of the room, facing each other.

Diana smiled brilliantly at the newcomers. 'Welcome. Please, don't be afraid. You're safe with us.'

The men looked at each other blankly. Sara stepped forward, quickly translating her mother's words and adding to them.

'This is a Challenge. You are the witnesses, on behalf of Harald. There will be no intervention, whatever happens.' Sara swallowed as she said that, knowing that Jan's death would kill her too.

The young Whites nodded solemnly, taking in the situation. Ralph stepped forward and spoke to them, reassuring them they wouldn't be hurt. They took up position near the fighters.

Harald looked at Diana with a dull hate. 'Treacherous bitch,' he spat.

Jan started to undress. Harald spun around, hitting him hard, knocking him to the ground as he struggled with his shirt. Harald was Changing fast, so fast his clothes exploded from him. He made a big wolf, powerful and hard. His fur shone silver. His eyes were bright with animal intelligence, and Diana understood how he'd been Alpha for so long. He made a better wolf than a man.

Jan was Changing too, turning to bite at his clothes, rip them away from his legs. Tattered underwear hung from his skinny hips as he faced the threat. He was smaller than his father, thinner, undernourished and still tired from his Alpha ordeal. He put his head down. He was silent in the face of his father's threatening growls.

Harald rushed at him and Jan skipped out of the way lightly, turning instantly to meet the danger as it came from a new direction. Harald continued to rush, and Jan to avoid him. The silver wolf stopped and stared at his son, his tongue out, laughing at him. Jan waited patiently. He knew he didn't have the strength to meet his sire's charges full on. They circled each other. There was no hurry.

Jan glanced over his father's back for a second. Harald caught the movement, and looked, briefly, over his shoulder. Almost unable to believe his luck, Jan darted forward and grabbed the older wolf's ear in his teeth, ripping quickly and dodging back. Harald spun back, furious, and made a lightning dash at Jan, going for the throat. Jan leaped up, yelping in fake terror, and landed on Harald's back, scratching for a couple of seconds with his claws before sliding down and dancing away.

Harald was bleeding from his back and his ear now. None of the wounds was serious, and the blood was already slowing.

He charged at Jan again, but as his son skipped aside, he interpreted the defensive move correctly and followed him, knocking the weaker wolf off his feet and pushing his teeth towards the unprotected belly.

Jan whined in panic, twisting round and jumping into the air, avoiding any injury greater than a long shallow graze. He landed behind his enemy, and grabbed Harald's tail in his jaws. Harald instinctively pulled away, stretching his vertebrae. Jan's teeth found a gap between the tiny bones and bit down, severing the last third of Harald's tail in one clean bite. He spat out the furry flesh, and backed away.

Harald screamed in pain and fury, the raw end of his tail an unbelievable agony. All around, the werewolves winced in involuntary sympathy.

Jan moved around again now, yards away from his wounded opponent. The tail wound was bleeding steadily, fresh blood bright against the stone floor, catching the lamplight. He looked his father in the eye and wagged his own tail, taunting him. Harald screamed and launched himself at Jan. This time Jan took the charge full on, gambling on Harald being weakened. He remembered Darlene's ploy from the car park battle, but improved on it, moving towards the rush. Using Harald's speed and strength against him, he lowered his head, using his shoulders to take the impact, and twisted over Harald's back again in a full somersault, landing on top of him and sinking his teeth into his spine.

Diana and her mates watched, fascinated. Jan bit down hard, just once, tearing flesh away and falling to one side, moving out of reach.

Harald stood panting, injured beyond his own comprehension, his imagined triumph turning to ashes in his throat. He eyed his son, scenting his weakness and exhaustion. He gambled that the younger man was tiring more quickly, and kept his distance. For long minutes the two wolves circled warily. The silver one had stopped bleeding, but couldn't ignore the debilitating pain.

The younger wolf gathered himself together, concentrating, looking for the slightest lapse, the slightest mistake, ruthlessly suppressing his lifelong fear of this big Alpha. He could smell Sara close by, but refused to be distracted from the fight, instead concentrating on his own new Alpha status. Subconsciously, the memory of his time alone with his new mate, the thought of her beneath him, above him and around him, calmed him. A flood of Alpha hormones surged through his system, giving him new strength.

Jan's scent reached Harald, shocking him. He'd not encountered an Alpha male in combat since he'd killed his own father. The older wolf took a step backward, raising his head questioningly as he instinctively sniffed the air.

Jan saw his chance. He put all his new strength into his back legs and launched himself low and deadly at the exposed silver throat.

Harald stepped back, but too late. His blood fell in a bright, vivid stream to the floor. Each and every Shifter in the room stood absolutely still, absolutely silent. Harald took another step back, looking at the fast-spreading pool of his lifeblood. He sat on his haunches and pawed at his throat, looking with disbelief at his reddened foreleg. He sank to the floor, still not believing he'd been beaten.

Jan took a step towards him, and the old Alpha flinched away, but Jan continued to advance, licking at his father's head, his wounded ear, lying close to him, heedless of the blood soaking his own silver fur. He closed his eyes and put his head on his father's neck, giving the comfort of his body heat to the dying creature. Nobody moved. The light went from Harald's eyes, and he was still.

Jan nuzzled at the silver wolf's throat and found no pulse, no sign of life. He struggled to his feet, licking nervously at the blood on his fur and looking round. He cast a backward glance at the carcass and staggered over to Anthony, who licked him thoroughly. Caleb, Seth and Noah joined in, cleaning the blood off him, relishing the taste of it.

Diana broke the silence, speaking to the four young Whites, translated by a dazed Darlene.

'Do you accept this? Or do you Challenge?'

They were stunned. 'We accept.'

'Excellent.' She left the four young men to Ralph, who was enlisting their loyalty on behalf of his brother, and studied Sara, who stood with her hand to her mouth, gazing at Jan.

Jan realised she was looking at him and rolled over in pleasure, his tongue hanging out. She laughed and ran to him, falling to her knees and taking his head into her arms, hugging him. The scent and sight of her gladdened him, and he stood. He threw back his head and howled his triumph.

Michaela went to the door and opened it wide, letting the sound echo through the halls and corridors. The White Pack stopped in its tracks and turned towards the sound. That cry conveyed youth, power and a new, unshakeable self-confidence. Again and again Jan cried out, then sighed, twisting into his human shape, accepting the long sweater that Andy offered him.

Diana's sons and Anthony Changed back, dressing quickly as men came one by one into the room, looking round, their gaze resting on the corpse of their old Alpha. Jan and Sara walked together to the front of the room. Jan kicked the throne over, and stood, watching, as his old pack joined his allies, staring at Diana's pack suspiciously. By the time the flow of Whites stopped, there were fifty or so of them in the room, the rest in the fields or out on other business. There were some hostile stares at first, but as they spoke to each other, they realised the consensus was in favour of a change of regime, an acceptance of the situation. Diana's pack was standing at the edges of the room. She, Mark, Michaela, Simon and Bill were equidistant from each other in a deliberate ploy. They each concentrated on their own Alphadom, their own dominance, and the hormones they released acted to subdue the Whites.

Jan spoke, his voice steady and calm. 'This is the start of a new chapter. We are one kin, one great family. The war is over. I'm here now to accept your allegiance to Sara and to me. Anyone who feels they cannot commit to that is welcome to present themself to me now.'

The threat was implicit, but clear enough. There was no Challenge. One by one, the Whites filed in front of Jan, bowing to him. Sara stifled a giggle, struggling to keep a straight face. Diana saw her and fought back her own grin.

When the procession had ended, Jan spoke again. Darlene translated in a low voice for those who didn't speak German.

'There's a lot of business to be settled, but only five things are important enough to detain you any longer. Firstly, this is Sara. She is my mate, my Alpha. She speaks for herself, but you obey her as you would obey me. Get used to it – she has a temper on her.

'Secondly, send out word to anyone away on a mission that it is cancelled. They are to return here for debriefing. Tell them about the new regime. If they don't like it, they can stay out there, but if they kill a living soul, I'll personally tear their throats out. On the same theme, could someone go and get Raj and Hannah, and my brothers?'

Mary looked at her mates-to-be, and the three of them left together.

'Thirdly, nobody here will be hurt. These people are my friends. They are powerful friends, but they mean us no harm. Harald's children are safe with them.

'Fourthly, we are hungry and thirsty. We've travelled a long way, and it's not been easy. I've seen plenty of meat on the hoof as we've walked in, and if ever there was a time to kill the fatted calf, goose, pig or goat, this is it. Today is a feast day.' He smiled. 'My friends will help. And so will you. The days of leaving it to the women are over, I'm afraid.' He laughed in delight at the thunderstruck expressions on the young men's faces.

'Lastly, where is Harald's Alpha? We need to find her, and tell her the situation.' His expression became more sober.

One of the older men, a small, timid-looking man in his early fifties, volunteered that his name was Ulrich and he knew where she was. Michaela and Diana looked at each other, and left with him. He led them nervously through corridors and up and down stairs, until he came to a locked door that had a small hatch set into it.

'Only Harald knew where the key was. We pass our Lady's food and drink through here.'

Diana stared at him in disbelief. 'She's a *prisoner?* I thought she'd be Queen of the fucking May!' She turned to the door and gave it a hard kick, putting all her strength into it.

Ulrich winced. 'It's strong—' he started to say, then watched as Diana focussed on the lock mechanism, and kicked it again. It gave a little, but didn't break.

'Plan fucking B,' she growled, running at the door and kicking hard at the area below the hatch. It started to give. She repeated the move until a hole two feet in diameter had been punched into the door. Resisting the sudden urge to cry '*Here's Johnny!*' she looked cautiously through the hole. There was nobody to be seen in the room.

She sighed. 'Michaela, do you speak German?'

The younger woman shook her head.

'Ulrich, do you talk to this woman?'

'It's forbidden' he replied.

'Yeah, but do you?' Diana got her answer from the appalled expression on Ulrich's face.

'Ulrich, go get Ralph. We might need someone who has the women's dialect. I bloody hope not, because I bet Harald didn't speak it, which could mean this poor bitch has been locked up for thirty years with nobody to talk to.'

She shouted a phrase through the door. She was pretty sure that it meant she came in peace. There was silence. She repeated herself several times, and eventually caught sight of a small movement by the side of the door. As she had suspected, the woman was hiding directly behind it. The woman moved away and stood nervously in the middle of the room.

Diana judged her to be in her early sixties, realising she could only have been in her early teens when Harald chose her as his Alpha almost fifty years ago. She felt sickened. The woman stood in the middle of the room, trying to look through the gap to see who was trying to get in to her. She was obviously terrified. She wore a long silky robe, slashed deeply at the front and thighs. The room was furnished richly, with tapestries, a huge bed, tables with fruit and sweets laid in dishes, and, incongruously, a large TV and video set-up, with a pile of decades-old videos stacked next to it. There was one window, which Diana could see led to a grand stone balcony, with bars around it.

'The Lady of fucking Shalott with afternoon TV. Now I've seen everything,' muttered Diana. She tried another gambit. '*Sprechen Sie Deutsch?*' she attempted.

The woman stopped her nervous pacing and looked at the door. '*Ja, ich spreche Deutsch,*' she said hopefully.

'Too fucking bad, because that's me all out of conversation,' replied Diana under her breath. She repeated the dialect phrase, and was glad to see that the woman appeared to be marginally less terrified. Diana felt better, at least she knew now the Alpha hadn't been totally incommunicado all this time. She glanced at the TV and realised that she'd been stupid: even the thickest person couldn't help but pick up a language when locked in a room with nothing but TV and videos for company. She shrugged. 'Hey, I don't suppose you speak English, do you?'

The woman turned and frowned. 'Of course I speak English. Do you?'

Diana laughed. 'Just a bit. Look… Well, I come in peace, but I have some shitty news for you. I don't suppose you could let me in? And if you told me your name it would help.'

'You tell me yours – you're the one trying to kick my door in. Which is, I must say, an odd way to come in peace. And I can't let you in. The door doesn't open from the inside without a key. And I don't have one.'

'Diana,' Diana said, pausing.

'Oh. I'm Sabina. I've heard of you.'

'Really?' asked Diana. 'Harald discussed tactics with you? By the way, if I sort of kick this door in a little more, and climb through to join you in a more civilised discussion, will you promise not to hit me with a vase or something when I'm halfway in?'

'I guess so. And I've heard your name, that's all – whenever the greaseball climbed on to me in his monthly rutting visits. He mentioned your name a lot. Are you a rival of mine?'

Diana stood, appalled. 'That's one of the most truly disgusting revelations of my entire life. No, I'm not a rival. Hang on.' She returned to her kicking with renewed enthusiasm. Just as the hole was almost big enough for her to climb through, she was distracted by a sound behind her. Michaela had remembered the route well enough to lead Ralph back to the room; they were walking up the stairs, laughing.

Diana nodded to them. 'It's OK, I don't need a translator any more, but I might need Michaela in a while. Can you both hang around?'

'Sure,' Michaela said absently, and returned to her animated chat with the young blond. 'I can't believe you've never played a computer game. I'd love to teach you.'

'I'd love for you to teach me too,' he said enthusiastically.

'Fuck me stupid,' muttered Diana, focussing on the door's weak spot, 'Michaela's after a Third.' She leaped at the door, leg extended in a perfectly judged blow. 'Whoosh!' she said.

She poked her head through the door. 'Hi!' she said.

'Come in, I've got the kettle on,' said Sabina.

Diana eased through the hole in the door, and looked around for somewhere to sit. There were only two chairs, and she was loath to sit on any that had been used by Harald. She settled for one of the low tables. 'May my friend join us?' she asked.

'Does she kick doors in?' asked Sabina politely.

'No, she just hangs around on corners seducing innocent young men.' Diana raised her voice. 'Michaela, put him down and come in here for a cuppa.'

Blushing furiously, the young blonde Alpha climbed through the wreckage of the door and joined them, sitting on the spare chair before wrinkling her nose in distaste and choosing the second table as a seat.

Between them Diana and Michaela explained the situation to the new widow. They learned that she knew nothing of the war waged by her mate, and that she'd not seen another living being face to face since he locked her in the room.

'This is the first time I've heard of the Alpha bond, I have to say. I must admit, I wondered why I missed him so much before his visits, or felt so relieved after enjoying his attentions. But I put that down to loneliness. And it explains why he kept me locked in here, and why he only ever allowed me to have my first two babies, then no more. I imagined that he had women locked up all over the keep. I guess it was just me. Perhaps he wasn't as mad as I thought he was.' She looked at Diana. 'I'm going to die? Is that what you're saying? That I will die desperate to be with him? That hardly seems fair, considering I despised him.'

Michaela was appalled. 'That stinks. I accepted the consequences of the Alpha bond – I love Simon. But what Harald has done to you is inhuman.'

Diana was calm. 'Have you considered suicide?' she asked Sabina, ignoring Michaela's ranting.

'I've considered it thousands of times. I've attempted it several times, but it's hard to die when you're a Shapeshifter. The worst bit…' she blushed. 'The worst bit is when you become a wolf, you know? I have nowhere to run to. It hurts so much.'

Diana's eyes filled with tears. She reached out and took Sabina's hand, trying not to flinch away from the contact with another Alpha.

Sabina's eyes filled too, and she grasped Diana's hand in turn. 'I've not touched anyone for years. Except him.'

Michaela walked over to her, and the three women held each other, letting their conscious wills override the urge to be as far apart as possible. The redhead broke away first, then Sabina. They were dry-eyed again.

'When did you last get a fix?' Diana asked.

'About a week ago. I'm fine now. It'll be at least a fortnight before I start getting itchy again.'

Diana smiled. 'Then I'm going to give you the time of your life. Do you understand? We'll take turns, me and Mark, and our friends and family. We'll take you around the world, we'll meet beautiful men, or women if you prefer, who'll give you the appreciation you deserve. We'll run in the woods and on the beaches, we'll go to the opera and to rock concerts. We'll do whatever you've always wanted to do. And when you're tired, and it starts to hurt unbearably, whether it takes one month or six, we'll understand. We'll make the end quick, and we'll bring it to you with love.'

Sabina nodded. 'I understand. Can you find my daughters for me? They were taken away when they were babies. If I can have anything, I want them. They'll be all grown up now.'

'Of course.'

'And could I have some clothes, please?' Sabina said. 'Like yours?'

'You can. You can have everything you want, my sweet. Now, you're not the only person who's had a shitty time around here, and we have work to do. Shall we leave this room?'

Sabina hesitated, looking at the ragged hole in the door.

'Shall we leave this cell?' asked Diana, more emphatically.

Sabina nodded. Michaela climbed out first, then Sabina. Diana followed her through.

Michaela winked at Ralph, who was waiting patiently. 'Come on, honey.'

'Where are we going?' he asked.

Diana smiled, reaching to take Sabina's hand. 'To freedom.'

Characters in alphabetical order of first name.

Albie Haraldson. Shapeshifter. White Pack.

Alexander Preston (Alex) Shapeshifter. Sixth son of Zoe and John Preston. Twin of Thomas

Alice Foster. Shapeshifter. Fourth daughter of Diana and Mark Preston. Twin of Jane.

Amanda Preston (Mandy). Shapeshifter. Fifth daughter of Zoe and John Preston.

Andrew Moss (Drew) Shapeshifter. Son of Duncan Moss and Laura Matlock, twin of Phil Moss.

Andrew Daniel Ransome (Andy). Normal, then successfully infected to become Shapeshifter. a.k.a. The Changeling. Bass player with the Ransomed Hearts. Married to his cousin, Helen Townsend. Diana's Third, along with Mark and John Preston. Father of Eva and Naomi Ransome (with Helen Townsend), and of Sara, Darlene, Nathan and Joseph Foster (with Diana Foster).

Anthony Aubin a.k.a Anthony Preston. Shapeshifter. Twin of Tomas. Father of Mark Preston (with Frances Shepherd).

Beatrice Foster / Preston a.k.a Trixie. Shapeshifter. Eldest daughter of Diana Foster and Mark Preston, twin of Bridget Foster. Together Beatrice and Bridget are known as 'The Bees'.

Bridget Foster / Preston a.k.a Bee. Shapeshifter. Second eldest daughter of Diana Foster and Mark Preston, twin of Bridget Foster. Together Beatrice and Bridget are known as 'The Bees'.

Caleb Foster / Preston a.k.a Cal. Shapeshifter. Third son of Diana and Mark Preston. Twin of Samuel.

Charlotte Preston (Lottie) Shapeshifter. Eighth daughter of Zoe and John Preston. Twin of Emily

Chloe Stephenson. Shapeshifter. Mated to Duncan Moss and Laura Matlock.

Darlene Foster / Prestib Shapeshifter. Eldest daughter of Diana Foster and Andy Ransome. Twin of Sara. She and Sara are known within the family as 'The Kittens'.

Deborah Foster / Preston aka Debbie. Shapeshifter. Seventh daughter of Diana Foster and Mark Preston. Twin of Leah.

Diana Foster / Preston. Shapeshifter, daughter of Jane and Gerald Foster. Geneticist. Mated to Mark Preston, John Preston and Andy Ransome, and Zoe Bradwell. Mother of Seth, Noah, Bridget, Beatrice, Caleb, Samuel, Jane, Alice, Margaret, Elizabeth, Deborah, Leah, Henry, Michael, Faith and Joy (with Mark Preston), Miranda (with Xan Kendrick), William, Francis, Susan and Anne (with John Preston) and Darlene, Sara, Nathan and Joseph (with Andy Ransome). Alpha female of the Silverwood Pack.

Duncan Moss. Shapeshifter. Discovered as a teenage werewolf by Diana Foster. Mentored by Andy Ransome. Mated to Laura Matlock and Chloe Stephenson.

Elizabeth Foster / Preston. Shapeshifter. Aka Beth. Sixth daughter of Diana Foster and Mark Preston. Twin of Margaret. Together with Louise, Tara and Meg, the Quadettes.

Emily Preston. Shapeshifter. Seventh daughter of Zoe and John Preston. Twin of Charlotte.

Eva Ransome. Half-blood. Elder daughter of Andy Ransome and Helen Townsend.

Faith Foster / Preston. Shapeshifter. Ninth daughter of Diana Foster and Mark Preston, Twin of Joy.

Frances Shepherd. Half-blood. Daughter of Eddie Shepherd and Dorothy Marsden. Wife of Anthony Preston. Mother of Mark Preston.

Francis Foster / Preston a.k.a. Frankie. Shapeshifter. second son of Diana Foster and John Preston. Twin of William Foster

George Haraldson. Shapeshifter. White Pack

Hannah Byrne / Drake. Shapeshifter. Alpha. Mated to Raj Drake.

Harald Guntherson. Shapeshifter. Alpha of the White Pack.

Helen Townsend. Normal. Married to Andy Ransome. Mother of Eva and Naomi Ransome, with Andy Ransome

Henry Foster / Preston a.k.a Harry. Shapeshifter. Fifth son of Diana Foster and Mark Preston. Twin of Michael.

Holly King / Drummond. Shapeshifter. Beta of the Whitby Drummond Pack. Mated to Michaela Drummond, Simon Singh, Robbie Ainsworth

Ian Preston Shapeshifter. Second son of Zoe and John Preston. Twin of Isaac. Together with Nathan, Joe and Isaac, the Quads.

Isaac Preston aka Zak. Shapeshifter. Eldest son of Zoe and John Preston. Twin of Ian. Together with Nathan, Joe and Ian, the Quads.

Jacob Preston, aka Jake or Jakie. Half-blood. Eldest son of Mark Preston and his wife, Katie.

Jan Haraldson. Shapeshifter. White Pack

Jane Foster / Preston a.k.a Janie. Shapeshifter. Third daughter of Diana and Mark Preston. Twin of Alice.

Johan Haraldson. Shapeshifter. White Pack

John Preston. Shapeshifter. Son of Miriam Hartnell and Tomas Preston. Mated to Diana Foster and Zoe Bradwell, along with Mark Preston and Andy Ransome. Singer with the Ransomed Hearts. Father of William, Francis, Susan and Anne (with Diana) and of Isaac, Ian, Tara, Louise, Patrick, Liam, Julie, Leanne, Amanda, Mia, Thomas, Alexander, Emily and Charlotte. Beta Male of the Silverwood Pack

Joseph Foster / Preston a.k.a. Joe. Shapeshifter. Second son of Diana Foster and Andy Ransome. Twin of Nathan. Together with Nathan, Isaac and Ian, the Quads.

Joy Foster / Preston Shapeshifter. Tenth daughter and youngest child of Diana Foster and Mark Preston. Twin of Faith.

Joyce Bridget Foster. Shapeshifter. Daughter of Jane and Gerald Foster. Sister of Diana Foster.

Julie Bradwell / Preston. Shapeshifter. Third daughter of Zoe Bradwell and John Preston. Twin of Leanne.

Karen Massey. Normal. Girlfriend of Seth Preston

Katie Crawford. Normal. Ex wife of Mark Preston. Mother of Jacob and Matthew Preston (with Mark Preston).

Lars Haraldson. Shapeshifter. White Pack

Laura Matlock. Shapeshifter. Mated to Duncan Moss and Chloe Stephenson.

Leah Foster / Preston Shapeshifter. Twin of Deborah. Eighth daughter of Diana Foster and Mark Preston.

Leanne Bradwell /Preston Shapeshifter. Fourth daughter of Zoe and John Preston. Twin of Julie.

Liam Bradwell / Preston Shapeshifter. Fourth son of Zoe and John Preston. Twin of Patrick.

Lily Moss Shapeshifter. Daughter of Laura Matlock and Duncan Moss. Twin of Rachel.

Louise Preston. Shapeshifter. Second daughter of Zoe and John Preston. Twin of Tara. Together with Tara, Beth and Meg, the Quadettes.

Margaret Foster / Preston Aka Meg. Shapeshifter. Fifth daughter of Diana Foster and Mark Preston. Twin of Elizabeth. Together with Louise, Tara and Beth, the Quadettes.

Mark Drummond. Shapeshifter. Son of Michaela and Simon Drummond. Twin of Sam Drummond.

Mark Preston. Shapeshifter. Son of Frances Shephard and Anthony Preston. Guitarist with the Ransomed Hearts. Married to Katie. Alpha male of the Silverwood Pack with Diana Foster, Zoe Bradwell, John Preston and Andrew Ransome. Father of Seth, Noah, Beatrice, Bridget, Caleb, Samuel, Jane, Alice, Margaret, Elizabeth, Deborah, Leah, Henry, Michael, Faith and Joy (with Diana Foster), Jake and Matthew (with Katie Crawford).

Mary Wilding. Shapeshifter. Friend of Darlene and Sara Preston.

Matthew Preston. a.k.a Mattie or Matt. Half-blood. Younger son of Mark Preston and Katie Crawford

Mia Preston. Shapeshifter. Sixth daughter of Zoe and John Preston . Twin of Amanda

Michael Foster / Preston Aka Mikey. Shapeshifter. Sixth and youngest son of Diana Foster and Mark Preston. Twin of Henry.

Michaela Drummond. Shapeshifter. Alpha of the Drummond Pack. Mated to Simon Singh, Robbie Ainsworth and Holly King.

Miranda Foster / Preston Half-blood. Daughter of Diana Foster and Xan Kendrick.

Nancy Foster / Preston (Anne) Shapeshifter. Second daughter of Diana Foster and John Preston. Twin of Susie.

Naomi Ransome. Half-blood. Second daughter of Andy Ransome and Helen Townsend.

Nathan Foster / Preston a.k.a Nat. Shapeshifter. Eldest son of Diana Foster and Andy Ransome. Twin of Joseph. Together with Joe, Isaac and Ian, the Quads.

Nathaniel Andrew Joseph Ransome. Normal. Father of Andy Ransome, husband of Pippa Ransome.

Noah Foster / Preston Shapeshifter. Second child and Alpha bond twin of Mark Preston and Diana Foster. Twin of Seth Preston.

Patrick Bradwell / Preston Shapeshifter. Third son of Zoe Bradwell and John Preston. Twin of Liam

Paul Dixon. Normal. Agent for John and Mark Preston.

Paul Haraldson. Shapeshifter. White Pack.

Philip Moss. Shapeshifter. Son of Laura Matlock and Duncan Moss. Twin of Andrew.

Phillippa Ransome aka Pippa. Normal. Mother of Andy Ransome.

Rachel Moss. Shapeshifter. Daughter of Laura Matlock and Duncan Moss. Twin of Lily.

Raj Drake. Shapeshifter. Alpha. Mated to Hannah Byrne

Ralph Haraldson. Shapeshifter. White Pack

Robbie Ainsworth. Shapeshifter. Beta of the Drummond pack, mated to Michaela Drummond, Holly King and Simon Singh.

Roni Jerrard. Normal. MP

Sabina Gunterson. Shapeshifter. White Pack

Samuel Foster / Preston Shapeshifter. Fourth son of Diana and Mark Preston. Twin of Caleb

Sadie Birch. Shapeshifter. Friend of Mary, Sara and Darlene.

Sally Moss. Shapeshifter. Daughter of Laura Matlock and Duncan Moss. Twin of Mareta.

Sara Foster / Preston Shapeshifter. Second eldest daughter of Diana Foster and Andy Ransome. Twin of Darlene. She and Darlene are known within the family as 'The Kittens'.

Seth Foster / Preston Shapeshifter. Eldest child and Alpha bond twin of Diana Foster and Mark Preston. Twin of Noah Preston.

Shelley Fisher. Shapeshifter. Friend of Mary, Darlene and Sara.

Simon Singh / Drummond. Shapeshifter. Alpha of the Drummond Pack. Mated to Michaela Drummond, Holly King and Robbie Ainsworth.

Stuart Highfield. Shapeshifter. Deceased. Beta of the Whitby Moss Pack. Mated to Laura Matlock, Chloe Stephenson and Duncan Moss.

Susan Foster / Preston. a.k.a Susie. Shapeshifter. Eldest daughter of Diana Foster and John Preston. Twin of Nancy.

Tara Preston. Shapeshifter. Eldest daughter of Zoe Bradwell and John Preston. Twin of Louise. Together with Louise, Beth and Meg, the Quadettes.

Tomas Preston. Shapeshifter. Fifth son of Zoe and John Preston. Twin of Alexander.

Ulrich Gunterson. Shapeshifter. White Pack.

Victoria Moss. Shapeshifter. Second daughter of Chloe Stephenson and Stuart Highfield. Twin of Deborah.

William Foster / Preston. a.k.a Billy, a.k.a Bill, a.k.a Willum. Shapeshifter. Eldest son of Diana Foster and John Preston. Twin of Frank

Xan Kendrick. Normal. Deceased. Drummer and original lyricist with the Ransomed Hearts. Distant cousin and lover of both Andy Ransome and Helen Townsend. Friend and companion of Diana Preston. Father of Miranda Foster (with Diana Foster).

Zoe Bradwell. Shapeshifter. Beta female in Diana Foster's Pack. Mother of Isaac, Ian, Tara, Louise, Patrick, Liam, Julie and Leanne, all with John Preston.

Children of Silverwood

Seth and Noah (Diana and Mark)
Miranda (Diana and Xan)
Billy and Frankie (Diana and John)
Darlene and Sara (Diana and Andy)
Beatrice and Bridget (Diana and Mark)
Jacob (Katie and Mark)
Caleb and Samuel (Diana and Mark)
Eva (Helen and Andy)
Janie and Alice (Diana and Mark)
Susie and Nancy (Diana and John)
Matthew (Katie and Mark)
Nathan and Joe (Diana and Andy)
Isaac and Ian (Zoe and John)
Naomi (Helen and Andy)
Margaret and Elizabeth (Diana and Mark)
Tara and Louise (Zoe and John)
Deborah and Leah (Diana and Mark)
Patrick and Liam (Zoe and John)
Harry and Michael (Diana and Mark)
Julie and Leanne (Zoe and John)
Faith and Joy (Diana and Mark)
Amanda and Mia (Zoe and John)
Tomas and Alexander (Zoe and John)
Emily and Charlotte (Zoe and John)

Acknowledgements

Thank you to Adrian, this couldn't have happened without his unfailing support.

Thank you to my family and friends who have been my street team and my advocates.

Thank you to everyone who has read the first three books and given me feedback and encouragement. I always wanted the world to meet the Hearts.

Thank you to Fiction Feedback for their editing and critique work.

And thank you to my cover designers, Ravven, who is responsible for the gorgeous covers for the first and fourth books, and who generously worked with Jon Stubbington so that he could follow the theme and produce the beautiful covers for the second and third books.

Also by Jeanette Greaves

Fight for the Future - Ransomed Hearts book 1

The arrival of two young outsiders in Bardale catches the attention of a widowed farmer, who sees in their story an echo of the valley's darkest secret. Werewolves have returned to Lancashire. They may just want a quiet life, but fate has other plans for the brothers, who have escaped their past and must now fight for their future.

Ransomed Hearts - Ransomed Hearts book 2

The story continues in 'Ransomed Hearts' as the next generation of Preston boys make their mark on a world that isn't yet ready for them.

Hearts' Home – Ransomed Hearts book 3

The Hearts are broken, their lives forever changed. Can they pick up the pieces of their shattered hopes in time to face a new and deadly enemy? Diana's darkest secret may be the key to her Pack's salvation, but at what cost?